I ___ ___ you."

That voice! It was her enemy. Alyssa took a step back, bumping the chair. All the horror that had taken place aboard the ship sprang to vivid life in her mind.

Vaughn cursed loudly and moved with lightning-quick reflexes to cover the distance between them. Then, as he watched her flail awkwardly to escape him, he suddenly realized she was blind. A ribbon of satisfaction soared through him. His fingers wrapped cruelly around Alyssa's wrist, and he jerked her toward him. What was this woman doing here, dressed in English finery, looking like the mistress of Shadowhawk?

Vaughn knew without a doubt that this was Tray's doing. Damn him! He was harboring a known traitor!

Alyssa whimpered as the bruising force of her assailant's fingers gripped her wrist. A strangled cry choked from her as she fought to free herself.

"No you don't," Vaughn breathed. "You aren't going to get away from me again. You're going to Newgate, where you'll hang alongside that bastard father of yours."

Dear Reader,

Now that you've had a chance to recover from the holidays, why not take home a book from Harlequin Historicals and treat yourself to an afternoon off?

For starters, we have *Light on the Mountain* by Maura Seger, a compelling story set in nineteenth-century Wales, and the author's first historical for Harlequin. Lindsay McKenna's *Lord of Shadowhawk* features the ancestors of her popular series about the Trayhern family in this tale of an Irish rebel and a titled Englishman. It will be followed by a sequel this coming summer.

Veteran romance readers will be happy to spot *Rambler's Rest* by Penny Richards, writing as Bay Matthews. Her story of a woman forced to pose as a nun and a riverboat gambler turned plantation owner is a prequel to her contemporary title, *Laughter on the Wind*, Silhouette Special Editon #613.

And we are very excited to welcome longtime historical romance author June Lund Shiplett with her book, *Sweet Vengeance*. For her heroine, ex-convict Karalee Summers, justice is long overdue, but revenge is bittersweet.

Four great titles. Four great authors. We hope that you'll find many hours of reading pleasure this month with Harlequin Historicals.

Sincerely,

The Editors

# Lord of Shadowhawk

## Lindsay McKenna

# Harlequin Books

TORONTO • NEW YORK • LONDON
AMSTERDAM • PARIS • SYDNEY • HAMBURG
STOCKHOLM • ATHENS • TOKYO • MILAN

Harlequin Historicals first edition January 1992

ISBN 0-373-28708-9

LORD OF SHADOWHAWK

**Books by Lindsay McKenna**

Harlequin Historicals

*Sun Woman* #71
*Lord of Shadowhawk* #108

---

## *LINDSAY McKENNA*'s

Native American background spurred her interest in history, which she feels is a reflection of what goes on in the present and an indication of what the future will be like. Most interesting to Lindsay are the women of history. She feels their strength of spirit can be an inspiration to the women of today. Her three favorite historical periods are the Old West, medieval times and the Roman era.

Lindsay, an avid rock hound and hiker, lives with her husband of fifteen years in Arizona.

To the BKBBCB
(Burger King Breakfast Booklovers Club Brunch),
who meet three times a week in Huntsville,
Alabama, to discuss their love: romantic fiction.
Thanks Gail Froelich, Shirley Schoening,
Carolyn Purser and Leslie Simmons.
Your care and thoughtfulness will
never be forgotten. Onward!

"Men are cruel but man is kind."
—Rabindranath Tagore

# Chapter One

*March 1, 1798*

Where's that crippled half brother of mine? Vaughn wondered in irritation, his sensual mouth pursed beneath the full, luxuriant growth of his blond mustache. He gave the docked ship he stood on a negligent look, then walked to the gangway, idly watching as some prisoners from Wolfe Tone's rebellion, captured in Ireland, were dragged off in chains. The dead and mortally wounded were being hauled out of the hold and carted away to some unknown destination.

Vaughn hated Colwyn Bay, a wretched port town on the moody Irish Sea. It was too near Shadowhawk, his family's country manor and hub of their agricultural concerns. Theirs? He snorted, raising a polished, booted foot onto a crate, idly resting one elbow on his thigh. Shadowhawk was his half brother's domain. Tray was perfectly suited to being a farming clod alongside his beloved Welsh compatriots and the Irish servants he insisted upon keeping at the estate.

Where in the devil was Tray? He had sent Sergeant Porter on the whip to fetch Tray from Shadowhawk two hours ago, after they had docked. Shadowhawk was a mere hour away.

A slow anger flared within Vaughn, his blue eyes icy as he contemplated his half brother. Tray might be the eldest son of the Trayhern family but he was least liked, least understood and least a man. A smile twitched Vaughn's mouth— a mouth used to giving orders and having people obey immediately or face swift retribution. He didn't wear the red uniform of an officer in His Majesty's cavalry for nothing. Scanning the busy quayside dock, Vaughn pulled his cloak more tightly against the sharp winds. The clouds that churned above the sleepy village reminded him of Tray's eyes, light gray among other shades, depending upon his half brother's many perverse moods. Tray was true Welsh, dark and unfathomable. At least to everyone in the Trayhern family. Except for Paige.

Paige... Vaughn felt his throat tighten at the thought of his deceased older sister. Beautiful, dark-haired, gray-eyed Paige, who had been beloved by all. Even himself. Although she was only his half sister and slated to inherit the vast Trayhern wealth when their father, Harold, died, Vaughn couldn't hold that against Paige. She may have been almost pure Welsh, like Tray, but her sunny disposition and gentleness appealed to everyone.

Vaughn's eyes narrowed upon the raggedly clothed forms of several dead Irishmen being dragged down the wooden gangway to an awaiting cart already littered with bodies. His lips drew away from his teeth in a bloodless snarl. "We've finally avenged you, Paige. I killed five of them myself." To his great surprise he felt hot, blinding tears, and he quickly bowed his head, not wanting anyone to see them. Damn! Tears? Vaughn rubbed his eyes angrily.

It was Tray's fault that Paige was dead. If Paige hadn't stayed at Shadowhawk that summer, she would never have fallen prey to those bastard Irish brigands. Tray knew attacks by the starving and rebellious Irish happened frequently along the coast. He should have protected Paige. Vaughn snorted violently, dropping his booted foot to the deck. Everything Tray touched died.

Slight satisfaction lingered in Vaughn's eyes. At least Tray got some of what was coming to him. Two years ago Tray had married some local Welsh farm girl, and she had died a year later in childbirth. His child was stillborn, and deformed, like him. Pleasure flowed through Vaughn as he savored that low point in Tray's life. Finally! Tray was being punished for all the deaths, the misery and the unhappiness that had been caused by his ill-fated birth. Served the cripple right. Vaughn watched as two sailors carried the body of another dead Irishman by him. Paige had been properly avenged.

Vaughn's eyes narrowed and his blood chilled. There, on a blood bay stallion with black mane and tail, was Tray, making his way toward the ship, the sergeant riding behind him. He glared down at his half brother, familiar feelings of hate stirring in him once again.

Tray wore a simple white peasant's shirt, open at the throat, a black coat and a wool cloak around his broad shoulders, canary yellow breeches and unpolished boots with traces of mud on them. The fool couldn't even dress properly! He wore no white powdered wig, and even his black hair was cut ridiculously short! Tray defied English tradition. He defied everyone, Vaughn thought in fury. He looked like one of those untitled industrialists instead of the eldest son of an earl. The one who would inherit all the Trayhern wealth and privileges someday. Bitterness swept through Vaughn.

"Country bumpkin!" he muttered beneath his breath. Tray should have come in a coach drawn by at least two horses. Instead, the lover of the Welsh and the bloody Irish rode his spirited Arabian stallion through the shouting confusion as if he were accustomed to the rabble that ebbed and flowed around him. No titled Englishman would be seen in hacking clothes on a dock! Vaughn's hatred rose, constricting his throat. The less he saw of Tray, the better. His half brother reined his stallion to a stop and dismounted with enviable grace, always having been an excellent horseman. But that was the limit of his grace.

Vaughn smiled in silent satisfaction as Tray handed the reins to the awaiting sergeant. He watched through slitted eyes as Tray limped through the milling traffic on a clubbed left foot. The wind jerked and pulled at Vaughn's cloak as he measured Tray's progress up the ramp. Their mutual father had rued the day Tray had been born with the deformed foot. Among the titled gentry, the deformity was thought to be the mark of the devil or a curse. In Vaughn's estimation, it was both. Tray looked like the devil—tall, powerfully built and ever watchful. He had black hair and, as often as not, gray eyes dark with brooding anger. And his skin was tanned, proof that he was out in the fields alongside his own people, something an English earl's son would never contemplate doing.

Vaughn felt his gut tighten reflexively as Tray drew closer. He forced himself to relax. Why should he feel fearful around Tray? He was the one sent to Eton. He was the one who had become his father's pride, while Tray remained at Shadowhawk to till the soil and raise the sheep, cattle and horses.

A grimace pulled at one corner of Vaughn's mouth. It was well-known that Tray harbored no bitterness toward the Irish. Vaughn absorbed Tray's anguished expression as a woman in a blood-soaked and shredded dress was carried between two sailors to the awaiting cart, her red hair hanging as lifelessly as her limbs. *Good,* Vaughn thought, *feel the pain, half brother. She's Irish. Dead in the name of the King of England. And there's not a thing you can do about it, Tray. Not one damned thing. You're always standing up for the rights of the Welsh and Irish. Well, swallow your bile, pale brother of mine. Don't retch and shame our name. But you're only half a man, aren't you?*

By the time Tray maneuvered clear of the gangway activities and faced his younger half brother, there was a pallor beneath his taut, bronzed flesh. His gray eyes were almost black with anger as he approached Vaughn. They stood of equal height. Because of his English mother, Vaughn was slender and by far the more conventionally handsome of the two, while Tray personified typical Welsh blood, and was heavily muscled, stocky and full-faced.

Tray swallowed hard, forcing down the gorge that wanted to rise. The smell of death clung like a nauseating perfume aboard the four-masted ship. Blood was being washed from the upper deck with bucket after bucket of seawater. Tray could not shut out the moans and cries coming from below the deck.

"Sergeant Porter said you wanted to see me immediately," Tray said tightly, his mouth pulled into a thin line. God, the carnage and waste that surrounded them! And looking steadily at Vaughn's amused features, Tray felt even sicker. His half brother was actually enjoying the swelling sound of pain that rose around them from the Irish prisoners below.

Vaughn's crooked smile disappeared and he flicked a look of anger toward him. "Speak to me in English, damn it! I won't be caught speaking Welsh."

It was Tray's turn to smile, but it was a bloodless one, matching the pallor of his flesh. "You're still half-Welsh, whether you want to acknowledge it or not."

"Yes, and you revel in the fact you're nearly all Welsh like a pig rolling in the mud!"

Tray drew his black wool cloak more tightly around himself. The winds were icy, like Vaughn's fury. "I'm Welsh, in body and in spirit. The few drops of English blood bred in me have long since been given back to the soil of our land."

"Enough of this. I didn't ask you to come here to discuss our unfortunate mutual lineage."

Tray gazed at his half brother. As usual, their meeting was barbed and double bladed. Hate kept their liaison alive. "Why did you send for me, Vaughn? I'm not interested in this—this—"

"Bloodletting? Call it an eye for an eye." Vaughn raised his arm, pointing to the cart below being filled with bodies. "I evened up the score."

Tray's voice grew deadly quiet. "What are you talking about?"

"Paige. Didn't you know? It was my cavalry unit that broke the back of Tone's rebellion near Wexford. We rode down the Irish throats and gave them exactly what they deserved for revolting against England."

Tray's eyes flashed thunderstorm gray as he stared at Vaughn. "Get to the point, Vaughn. I won't waste my precious time on your tales of carnage."

Vaughn laughed. "That's right. I forgot, you get squeamish around men who are doing a man's job. Can't stand the sight of blood. Can't fight." His lips pulled away from his teeth. "You couldn't even defend Paige when she needed a man to protect her!"

Tray stiffened. "Swords and pistols don't change things, Vaughn. They only create more hate and thirst for vengeance. No, I don't condone your soldiering. I don't condone war."

"That's why you let Paige wander down to that beach alone!"

"Paige has been dead thirteen years, for God's sake! Let it rest!"

Vaughn turned away, resisting the urge to strike Tray's stubbornly set features. He took a few deep breaths, trying to wrestle with his explosive temper. When he turned back around, his blue eyes were midnight colored as they scorched Tray.

"Father wrote and told me that you need another hand to work on that farm of yours. There's an Irish brat of nine or so years in cell two. Go get him and take him home, and tell Father it was the best I could do. He doesn't like the Irish any more than I. If you don't want him, Father can arrange to send him to one of our coal mines."

Tray's mouth tightened. "Are you using nine-year-old boys to win Father's favor now, Vaughn?"

Vaughn's features whitened and he stalked back toward Tray, his hand clenched into a fist. Tray tensed, and the movement halted Vaughn. There was a dangerous quality to his Welsh half brother, and the look in his colorless gray eyes warned Vaughn that for all the peaceful tenets of Tray's life, he would be a formidable adversary if provoked. Tray outweighed him by a good two stone. Although he would be hampered by that club foot, which was encased in a specially made boot, he had seen Tray move with startling agility.

"Just take the boy and be gone!" Vaughn whipped his cloak around himself, shouldering past Tray. He hesitated a moment at the top of the gangway. "Don't be here when I get back, half brother."

Tray watched Vaughn stride down to the wharf, snarling orders to the sailors. Grimly, Tray turned and tried to prepare himself for what had to be done. Walking across the wet, slippery deck, he ducked into the first hold and down stairs dimly lighted by lamps.

The stench of vomit, blood and excrement assailed his nostrils and he hesitated at the bottom of the stairs. Tray's stomach knotted as he surveyed the hastily erected cells containing the survivors of the Irish rebellion. A sailor standing guard came to attention.

"Sir?"

Tray hated speaking in English but switched to it from his native Welsh. "Show me where cell number two is," he asked, his voice hoarse.

Prisoners clung to the iron bars, crying out as Tray and the sailor passed by them.

"Water, sir! Take pity upon us. Water..."

Tray glared down at the sailor, who stood several inches shorter than himself. "Why haven't these people been given water?"

The sailor flashed him a smile. "Why, sir, these aren't people. These are animals."

"Now look here—"

"Captain Trayhern's orders, sir. The lot of 'em gets water twice daily. A cup in the morning with their bread and a cup in the evening."

A desolate cry shattered the murky atmosphere and Tray snapped up his head. Halfway down the darkened aisle he saw a young, red-haired boy fighting two sailors who were trying to drag an unconscious girl out of a cell.

"No! Don't take her! Don't take her! You can't! You—"

One of the sailors reached around and with a vicious thrust of his foot sent the boy flying off his feet. Tray lunged forward. In four strides he reached the cell and shoved the sailor away from the girl, who had been dropped on the floor between them.

"You dog," Tray snarled, pushing the burly sailor back. He looked up at the other sailor. "Get back, both of you." Tray saw the boy slowly get to his knees, blood trickling from his nose and mouth.

"This is cell two?" he asked one of the sailors.

"Aye, sir, it is."

"Then begone!" Tray turned to tend to the girl.

"But, sir, she's near dead. Captain Trayhern's orders were to take her off the ship. We can't have the dead smelling up the ship for the journey to London."

"No! You can't take her! She's alive! Alive!" The boy launched himself at Tray, his small fists beating on him with unrelenting fury.

"Easy, boy," Tray breathed harshly, gently gripping him and holding him at arm's length. "She's going nowhere." Tray looked up, daring any of the sailors to protest his decision.

The guard shuffled uneasily. "But, sir, Captain—"

"I'm Lord Trayhern. My brother wanted these two for my estate. Now I suggest you stand aside so that I may take them out of this hell!"

The sailors and guard stiffened, their eyes widening. "Lord Trayhern? The Earl of Trayhern's son?"

"That's right." Tray jerked his head toward the dimly lighted opening at the other end of the passageway. "Leave us. Immediately!"

Tray waited until the English sailors had left and then released the boy. Instantly, the child dropped to the girl's side, his young face puffy and swollen from the blows he had received. His blue eyes were mutinous and filled with hate as he dared Tray to come any closer to the girl whom he embraced with his thin arms.

Tray turned and faced the boy, his bulk filling up the small passageway, blocking any attempt at escape. His square face was shadowed as he squatted down beside them. The hardness melted from Tray's features as he broke into Gaelic, the native language of Ireland.

"Rest easy, lad, I won't harm either of you."

The boy's spirit suddenly sprang with hope, although he remained leery. Who was this stranger who looked as if the devil himself had carved his face out of the cliffs of Ireland? Sean tightened his hold on Alyssa's shoulder as he flattened protectively across her. The man spoke Gaelic! Was he Irish? He didn't look it. Hot tears wavered in his large blue eyes as he saw the stranger's face soften.

"You can't take her to that cart! She isn't dead," he cried out, his voice high and off pitch.

"No one's taking her, lad. I promise you that. Is she your sister?"

Sean's lips trembled as he fought back the deluge of emotion that this man's soothing presence was releasing. By the love of the Mother Mary, he mustn't show his fear. Alyssa needed him. She was the only one left. He had to protect her. He'd give his life if any man tried to hurt her or make her cry again. Sean valiantly fought back the tears, the stranger blurring before his eyes.

"My cousin."

"And your name?"

"Sean. Sean Brady."

"And hers?"

"Alyssa—" A huge sob welled up and broke from Sean. He gripped her hard, burying his head against her breast. "They hurt her! I heard her screaming again and again. And they killed Shannon!"

Tray swallowed hard and reached out, gently touching the boy's thin shoulder as sobs racked his small body. He was dressed like so many other Irish peasants: no shoes, loosely hanging black wool trousers and a dirtied white cotton shirt.

Sean's weeping continued as Tray rubbed his shoulder to help ease the pain the boy had witnessed. It was senseless. Women and children were prisoners of a war that should have been fought by men only. And when Tray remembered that Vaughn had been instrumental in all the carnage that surrounded them, he choked down the threatening nausea.

Tray focused on the girl who lay between them and felt his heart wrench in his chest. My God! Flashbacks of discovering Paige on the beach just an hour after her murder swept through him. Only this time, instead of Paige's blond hair, the girl called Alyssa had auburn-colored hair highlighted with burgundy, shot through with gold beneath the lamplight. Her skin, almost translucent, was drawn tautly across her high cheekbones. Tray held his breath as Sean's words struck him with the force of a hammer hitting an anvil.

A bloody lump rose from her left temple and he wondered how she had received the blow. No man's fist could have caused that kind of injury. Anger mixed with repulsion as his gaze moved downward over her limp body. Clearly, she had been abused. The once beautiful, frail Irish girl, dressed in man's clothing, now appeared nothing more than a broken doll. Sean had pulled the ragged ends of her tattered white peasant shirt across her chest. The dark blue wool pants she wore were torn, all the buttons missing. He saw dark blood stains between her thighs and swallowed hard. Images of Paige lying dead on the beach, her arms stretched outward in death, her beautiful silk skirt and petticoats torn off her, her legs parted and bloodied, slammed back into his memory. Tears stung Tray's pain-narrowed eyes. God, no. Sweet God, not again . . . not this innocent girl, too. . . .

He moved dazedly as he gently pulled Sean away from her. "Is she alive?" he demanded hoarsely.

Sean kept a hand on Alyssa's shoulder. "Sh-she was. They beat her and—and—"

"They won't anymore," Tray promised thickly, placing his fingers against the slender white column of her throat. There! Just the faintest pulse throbbed slowly beneath his fingertips. "She's breathing. How long has she been unconscious, Sean?"

The boy leaned back, hope written on his face. "Since yesterday afternoon. A-are you going to help her?"

Tray pulled off his heavy cloak and carefully wrapped the girl within its folds. "I'm here to help both of you."

"B-but, who are you?" His small voice was strained. "Are you Irish?"

"Maybe not by blood, but through the milk I drank when I was a babe," Tray said, sliding his hands beneath the girl. He gently scooped her into his arms. It was as if he were lifting a mere hundred pounds of grain against him instead of a human being. My God, she was nothing but skin and bone! His heart constricted as her head lolled against his shoulder; her bruised and swollen lips were cracked and parted. She was as vulnerable as the newborn lambs that he helped deliver every April. Holding a deluge of emotions in tight check, Tray concentrated on Sean.

"Stay near me, lad. I'm going to take you and your cousin with me to my home. Do you understand? You'll have to ride on the back of my stallion. I don't have a coach and time is of the essence. Your cousin is badly injured and I must get her home and then send for a doctor to help her."

"Y-yes, sir. I can do that." He shyly reached out, his hand wrapping tightly in the folds of the wool coat Tray wore. "Who are you?"

Tray grimly ignored his question. He limped along the passageway and up the stairs, never more glad to reach the fresh salt air of Colwyn Bay than now. *I'm the black sheep of the Trayhern family,* he thought with grim irony. *An unwanted son who will inherit everything and who is hated by almost every family member. Except for Paige.* As they walked down the gangway, Tray mentally answered Sean's earlier question. *I'm Irish because an Irishwoman raised me as her own. Because my father accused me of killing my mother and sent me north so I could be out of his sight.* Sadness enveloped Tray, as it always did when he thought of the mother he had never known.

Her name had been Isolde, a beautiful Welsh name for a lovely black-haired, gray-eyed woman. And in his father's grief over her death, Harold named him Tristan, a Welsh name meaning sorrowful. And sorrow had followed his existence from the day of his birth. Tray would never forget when Sorche, his Irish wet nurse and foster mother, had answered his gravely asked question as to why he was named Tristan. Sorche sadly told him that his father blamed him for Isolde's death and he would forever be called Tristan as a result. That day he had begged Sorche to call him Tray, because in Welsh the name Trayhern meant "strong as iron," and he would be strong, he promised her. He would turn into the boy that his father wanted him to be; he would no longer bring sorrow and unhappiness to everyone.

Tray slowed his pace as he neared the area where Sergeant Porter was holding his blood bay Arabian stallion. So much for a seven-year-old's dreams, he thought wearily. From that day forward, everyone at Shadowhawk called him Tray. But try as he might, Tray learned that his father would never be proud of his crippled son.

"Hold the girl for me until I get mounted, Sergeant," he commanded, placing Alyssa in the stunned soldier's arms.

Porter's eyes widened with shock. "My lord?"

The Englishman gave Tray an angry look but stood there with the girl wrapped securely in the warmth of the black wool cloak. Rasheed, the Arabian stallion, moved mettle-somely beneath Tray as he mounted.

"Stand," Tray ordered the stallion in Welsh. Obediently, the animal became a living statue as the girl was transferred back to Tray's arms.

Tray looked down at Sean, who was shivering, his arms wrapped about his skinny body. He glanced at Porter.

"Sergeant, give the boy your cloak. I'll make sure you get it back."

Porter glared at the young ruffian, but he shoved his cloak into the boy's awaiting hands without a word.

"Now help him up here. Behind me."

This was scandalous! But Porter did as told, flushing red to the roots of his brown hair as he grudgingly obeyed. Didn't Lord Trayhern realize the picture that he presented? No one rode anywhere on a lord's horse, especially two Irish prisoners of war!

Sean's arms wrapped tightly around Tray's waist.

"All right, lad?" he asked, barely turning his head.

"I'm ready, sir."

"Good. We won't be going any faster than a brisk walk, but hold on. Rasheed hasn't been run for a few days and he's feeling his fettle."

Sean's narrow face brightened, his left eye almost swollen shut. "We're good riders, sir! There isn't an Irishman alive who can't ride a horse!"

Tray managed a tight smile and returned his attention to the unconscious cargo in his arms. With just a light pressure of Tray's left calf against Rasheed's barrel, the animal turned around. Soon they were free of the cloying, snarling quayside traffic and headed out of dingy Colwyn Bay for Shadowhawk, which sat on the cliffs above the restless Irish Sea.

The afternoon was dreary and cold, and Tray felt Sean huddling close, seeking his bodily warmth. Tray pulled the girl more tightly to him, concerned. Her translucent skin was bruised and bloodied. He lifted her barely exposed face to his and placed his ruddy cheek against her nostrils, willing her to be breathing still, willing her to be alive. He felt the utter relaxation of her body against him and the pitiful outward bow of her rib cage beneath his fingers. His heart took a sudden, pounding leap. There! He had felt it. A baby's breath of moist heat from her nostrils. *Live, sweet Alyssa,* he begged her silently, *breathe... just a bit longer and you'll be safe and warm.*

As he looked down on her waxen features, Tray wondered if she would live. That same pallor had existed on Paige's face when he had discovered her on the beach. His thoughts sped forward. He would have to get a doctor immediately. As long as she was still breathing, he knew the girl could be saved. For the first time since his wife's death, Tray felt a ribbon of hope thread through him. How could that be? A nine-year-old boy clung to him and a girl who could be no more than eight and ten years lay unconscious in his arms.

"Tell me about yourself, lad. How did you get caught up in this rebellion?"

Sean tried to still his chattering teeth. The wool cloak helped, but his bare legs were exposed, hanging like thin branches across the stallion's broad back. Was this man really the son of an Earl? If so, he was English and not to be trusted. Sean decided it was safer to lie. "M-my family and I were working on a farm outside of Wexford when we were trapped by the soldiers."

"And the English thought you were part of the rebellion?" Tray asked grimly.

"Yes, sir. Me, my cousin Alyssa and—and my sister, Shannon. They thought we were a part of it. But we weren't, sir. I swear it."

"How old is your cousin, Sean?"

"Seven and ten, sir."

She was of marrying age. Tray hesitated for a moment. "Married?"

"No, sir. Alyssa wouldn't stand for just any man to ask for her hand."

Tray's expression eased momentarily as he drank in her pale features. Although her auburn hair hung in dirtied ropes about her square face, he could imagine the fire that lay beneath those proud yet vulnerable features. One look at that stubborn, slightly cleft chin would warn any man that she was not to be taken lightly. Anguish burned through Tray. He knew Alyssa had been raped by one man, if not more than one. And doubtless she had been a virgin before the English soldiers mistook her as part of the rebellion. His black brows drew down into a scowl.

"Was she betrothed?" If she was, the man might not ever want her; she would be soiled, if she even lived. And Tray found himself wanting Alyssa to live. He wanted to hear her speak, to hear the quality of her voice. What color were her eyes? Their long auburn lashes lay thick and curled against her shadowed cheeks. Her femininity was obvious even beneath the specter of bruises and dirt.

"No, sir. She didn't want to marry. Said most men were clods of dirt."

Tray couldn't suppress the chuckle that welled up inside his chest. "She did, did she?"

"Alyssa has never been known to watch her words, sir." Sean shut his eyes. "That's what got her in trouble on board ship."

Tray's hands tightened reflexively against Alyssa's limp form. "What do you mean? What happened?"

"They—they took my sister, Shannon, and killed her," he began in a wobbly voice. "A-and Alyssa started screaming and shouting. She turned the air blue, calling them all kinds of names. She accused the English of being weak and spineless, because they took their anger out on women. She tried to get them to take her instead of Shannon, but they didn't do it."

"Then what happened, lad?" Tray asked softly.

Sean sniffed. "They came back and took Alyssa up on the main deck, and I heard her trying to fight them off. And—" His voice faltered. "One of the prisoners near the entrance of the hold said she fought them. An English officer took her. I—I guess she hit him and tried to escape, then a sailor struck her down with a club. The Irish prisoners below started shouting and screaming. Almost caused a riot, sir."

"You've told me enough," Tray said grimly, staring down at the girl. Sean's small arms tightened around him and he felt the boy's head against his back. Without hearing a sound, he knew the child was crying. How like the Irish to hide their tears in silence. Tray's own eyes watered dangerously as he continued to look down at the girl. She was an innocent victim, as was Sean. His stomach knotted as he sharply recalled a beautiful young girl with the same color of hair as Sean's. Had that been Shannon's battered, lifeless body they had carried off the ship while Vaughn was standing there, smiling cruelly at him when he arrived? His instincts screamed that it was, and he drew in a long, ragged breath.

"We'll be home soon, lad," he soothed.

Sean lifted his head, his face flushed with tears. "Home, sir?"

"Yes, home. No one at Shadowhawk will hurt you, Sean. You'll be given a bath, hot food and a bed. No more pain, lad. I promise you."

"And Alyssa? What will you do with her?"

"I'll take care of her personally. We'll get a doctor to tend her just as soon as we can."

Sean shut his eyes, suddenly weary as never before. This stranger who spoke Gaelic and yet looked neither English nor Irish seemed to be promising him the impossible.

# Chapter Two

"Sorche! Sorche!" The cry for the head housekeeper of Shadowhawk echoed down the halls of the main house.

"I'm coming!" she called, hefting her five and fifty-year-old body out of her gilt wood armchair, placing her stitchery aside. As always, Sorche wore a white mobcap over gray hair that was pulled neatly into a bun at the nape of her neck. Her dark blue cotton dress was nearly hidden by a huge white apron, because she had just come from the kitchen to devote a few free moments to her stitchery. Her face was round with ruddy cheeks, and her blue eyes were small and sharp for her age. The woman hurried down the carpeted hall toward the main entrance, where the noise and activity were coming from.

Sorche rounded the last corner and came to a halt in the marble foyer. Craddock, the butler, whose calm features never looked harried, looked harried now. Like most Welshmen, he was short and stocky. And he wore his dark blue uniform poorly; it always appeared rumpled and in dire need of a pressing.

"Sorche," he gasped, scurrying to her side and gripping her hand. "Quickly! Lord Trayhern needs you in his bed-chamber!"

"Bedchamber?" Sorche rumbled, smoothing her white apron across her ample body. "Whatever for?"

"He's just brought in a very sick young woman and a boy, and he needs your assistance with the girl. I'm on my way to tell Stablemaster Thomas to send his fleetest horse and best rider to fetch Dr. Birch from Colwyn Bay."

Blustering, her mobcap almost toppling off her head, Sorche made her way down the west wing. Goodness! The day had been nonstop excitement since that Sergeant Porter came in earlier, huffily demanding Tray's appearance at Colwyn Bay in his starchy English voice. What was going on? Craddock was in a coil, wringing his hands like an Irish fisherman! The man never came undone like that. Just what had Tray brought home this time?

Then a beatific smile wreathed Sorche's plump face and she picked up her skirts and set off at a running walk, almost giving the appearance of flying down the long, walnut-paneled hall. It was just like Tray to bring home all kinds of lost waifs. As a youngster the boy was forever bringing home stray cats and dogs, claiming them as his own. And a baby robin that had fallen out of its nest and injured its wing. And a baby rabbit, mauled by hounds. And... The list was endless.

Sorche knocked politely on the closed door to Tray's bedchamber.

"Enter!" Tray called.

She opened the door and came to a standstill in the middle of the huge room, her hands moving to her hips.

"Mother Mary and Saint Joseph! What have you done this time, Tray?" she breathed, her gaze moving first to the young ruffian who huddled like a frightened puppy near Tray and then to... A cry of compassion broke from Sorche and she flew around the bed.

Tray stood back, grateful for Sorche's presence. She always knew how to help and how to heal those less fortunate than herself. He pushed several strands of dark hair off his brow and went to his foster mother's side.

"The saints preserve this poor lamb. Oh, Tray..." Sorche gently pulled back the black wool cloak, revealing Alyssa's waxen features. She gasped, momentarily clutching at her breast where her crucifix lay hidden beneath the apron. "May God have mercy. Whatever has happened to her, Tray?"

"Part of Vaughn's war booty," he snarled, leaning over Alyssa. "She's suffered a blow to the head, Sorche. And—" He cast a glance at Sean. Lowering his voice, he said in an almost inaudible tone, "She was raped."

"Oh, no... quickly, we must fetch hot water, towels and—"

That same instant, Craddock appeared at the door to the bedchamber, having been summoned by bell rope. "Yes, my lord?"

"Have someone from the kitchen assist Sorche," Tray ordered darkly. "Oh, and have Briana come and take care of this boy. His name is Sean Brady. He's in need of a bath, new clothes and a hot meal—in that order. Sean, you go with Craddock. He'll see to your welfare, lad."

Sean hesitated, torn between the awful pallor on Alyssa's drawn features and the orders of the stranger who looked at him through kind gray eyes. "But, sir, my cousin..."

Tray came around the bed and placed his arm protectively around Sean's shoulders, coaxing him over to the butler. "Much needs to be done to help her, Sean." In that moment, a foothold of trust was tentatively established between them.

Sean licked his lips. "Yes, sir. A-and, thank you...."

Tray squeezed his shoulder. ''Don't thank us yet. We have yet to save her life, lad.''

Sorche peered sharply at the girl's face as she began to remove the wool cloak.

''They were trying to drag her out of the cell and throw her on a cart of the dead and dying,'' Tray explained quietly, his eyes flat as he drank in Alyssa's unmoving features. ''Under Vaughn's orders,'' he ground out.

Sorche's full mouth puckered into a forgiving line. ''You saved them, that's all that matters. Come, help me remove the cloak. We must get her out of these flea-infested men's clothes and bathe her before the doctor arrives. Dr. Birch won't touch her if she's this filthy.''

''But—''

''I'm too old to lift her by myself, Tray. And what maid do we have that can carry this poor girl? I know it's not proper, but under the circumstances, it can't be helped! Now quickly, come and help me. We must clean her up so that Dr. Birch may examine her once he arrives.''

Tray remained in his study, waiting for Dr. Birch to finish his examination of Alyssa. He paced, hands behind his back, his eyes fixed on the carpet beneath his booted feet. Anger churned with restlessness. Vaughn would remain in Colwyn Bay for a few days while the ship took on water. No doubt he would make a useful sum by selling some of the hapless Irish prisoners to the shipbuilding industry across the bay in Liverpool and, just as quickly, gamble the ill-gotten pounds away at the gaming tables. Tray's mind turned to Alyssa, as it did every unoccupied moment. What was it about her that drew out his heart and touched it? He rubbed his brow.

''Lord Trayhern?'' Dr. Birch's voice was quiet.

Tray turned toward the Englishman. He quickly took in the grim caste to Birch's pinched features. Motioning him to sit down, he poured the doctor a glass of sherry from the sideboard and handed it to him.

"Thank you," Birch said, lifting the glass to his lips. The fiery liquid slid down his throat, warming his stomach. He looked up at the lord of the manor.

"I think this is the worst case you've ever asked me to treat, animal or human," he began with an effort, taking another sip of the sherry. His grizzled brown-and-white brows moved together as he studied the ruby-colored contents of the glass.

"I know," Tray said softly, walking back to the window, folding his hands behind him. The silence grew, broken only by the sudden onslaught of pelting rain and the wind howling furiously around the manor. "Will she live?"

Birch walked stiffly to Tray's side and they both stared out the window together. "The girl is gravely hurt, my lord," he told him in a low tone. "Her skull is not cracked, but the force of the blow has surely addled her brain enough to make her unconscious. Someone must tend her almost hourly until she wakes, if she wakes. Has she urinated yet?"

"Her trousers were wet and smelled of it."

Birch gave a little sigh. "That's good. Her kidneys have not stopped working. If they do, she is as good as dead. Someone must—"

"I'll be that someone, good doctor. Simply tell me what I must do."

Birch gave him a surprised look. "It will be a thankless task, my lord. Surely one of your servants who has more time on his hands—"

"No, I will do it."

"Very well. I'll get Sorche to prepare a special herbal tea that must be carefully given to her every waking hour. That way, her kidneys will continue to function and she will be getting some nourishment.''

''I see,'' Tray said.

''Her head wound must remain open to the air and be allowed to drain. It should be washed thrice daily with another herb I'll have Sorche prepare for you.''

''Anything else?''

Birch's eyes grew dark and angry. ''That girl in there was once a virgin, but she isn't anymore. Whoever raped her like that ought to be hanged. She's still bleeding. I'll give Sorche instructions on how to change the packing on a daily basis.''

Tray's mouth thinned. ''Very well. I'd like you to examine the boy before you leave, good doctor.''

''Of course. If the girl worsens, send one of your servants for me. There's little else to be done for her unless she wakes up.''

''I will,'' Tray promised.


Tray quietly entered his bedchamber nearly an hour later. The rain had stopped momentarily, but it would come back, pummeling against the french doors once again. March in Wales was cold and wet. His gaze moved across the room's expanse and fastened hungrily on Alyssa's unmoving features. Something old and hurting tore loose in Tray's chest as he devoured her with his gaze. She looked frail in his huge bed. How long had it been since Shelby had lain there beside him? Tray shut his eyes for a brief second, the pain almost unbearable as it swept across him. God, how he missed her.

Opening his eyes, Tray went about the task of gathering the items he would need to tend to Alyssa. He tried to ignore the widening ache inside him when he gently lifted her into his arms in order to dribble a few drops of the herbal

medicine between her parted lips. Her damp head lolled
against his chest and the smell of jasmine encircled his nostrils. Tray inhaled the scent, his heart heavy. It was the
scented soap that Sorche had used to clean Alyssa's smooth,
long limbs, limbs that were well shaped but pitifully thin
from lack of food. Tray's mouth drew into a grim line as he
carefully rested her head against his shoulder. Taking a clean
cloth, he dipped it into the vile concoction and placed it to
the corner of her mouth.

"Come, sweet Aly, swallow the brew. I promise you, my
beautiful redheaded colleen, that it will speed your recov-
ery." He continued to talk to her in low, gentle Gaelic tones.
Was he trying to soothe himself or her? Tray wasn't sure.
The slender curve of her throat was exposed to his view and
he watched it closely as he allowed a few more drops into her
mouth. His breath caught and froze when he saw her swallow. It was a miracle! A miracle! Dr. Birch had said that in
the most successful cases, the patient would automatically
swallow instead of letting the liquid flow into the lungs. Tray
pressed a small, feather-light kiss on her drying hair.

"Good, colleen. Stay alive. Sean is waiting for you. He's
safe, well fed and probably sleeping by now. And you, my
sweet Aly, drink just a bit more and then I'll let you rest for
another hour. Now come, let's see you swallow again."

She swallowed, and Tray felt his hopes swell like a rain-
bow after a hard rain. He kept up the soft Gaelic banter
throughout the feeding. Afterward, he changed the cloth
Sorche had placed beneath her. It was wet with urine and
slightly pinkish with blood, but Tray considered these
healthy signs. Alyssa was fighting back. Fighting to live despite the horror she had suffered at the hands of the English.

It was near midnight, as Tray started to retire, that Alyssa
began to tremble. Worried, Tray laid his large, calloused

hand on her brow. He felt no fever. He built the fire higher, increasing the warmth in the room. And yet it didn't stop her trembling. Neither did more blankets.

Grimly, Tray paced the room, alternately glancing at Alyssa and then glaring off into the darkness outside. It began to rain again, the wind lashing and howling outside Shadowhawk. With a growl of impatience, he took off the pile of blankets, allowing them to drop to the floor, then shrugged out of his robe and slid into the bed.

As gently as possible, he moved next to Alyssa, fitting his powerful body next to her shivering form. She was so pitifully small in comparison to his heavily muscled frame. Tray slipped his arm beneath her neck, carefully drawing her head onto his shoulder and fitting her protectively against him. The silk of her floor-length nightgown provided a minuscule barrier between his naked body and her. Alyssa's trembling abated noticeably.

"Sleep, Aly. Just rest. No one is going to harm you, little one. No one. I'm here. I'll protect you...."

She wasn't running a fever. He began to lightly stroke the length of her long, beautifully formed back, willing away the terror she must be experiencing in some dark, distant chamber of her mind.

He lay awake for a long time, absorbing the feel of the woman next to him. He had lived seven and twenty years before he knew the wonder and joy of a woman lying at his side. Those twelve months with Shelby had taught him with what hunger a man could need a woman, to touch her, to feel her pressing herself to his length, telling him silently of her need of him as a man.... And now he held this child-woman, whose vulnerability shouted at him while she rested undemandingly in his arms. Alyssa was soft against the hard planes of his body, her shallow breath against his shoulder like mist on a cold Welsh morning. Tray found himself reaching his hands upward, threading his fingers through her hair. It was still snarled and tangled, and he suddenly felt a need to brush it until it was sleek and shone with its unusual burgundy highlights. *Tomorrow,* Tray promised her, *tomorrow I'll brush your hair, Aly.*

Tray felt the barest movement of her breasts against his chest and he realized with agonizing clarity that she still hovered on the brink of death. He placed his hand gently between her breasts, taking care not to brush them, and felt the slow, weak beat of her heart. If only...if only she would survive. Removing his hand, he drew Alyssa back into his arms, his jaw resting lightly against her hair.

"Listen to me, Aly, you've got to live. According to Sean, you're too headstrong and outspoken to die. I want to hear your voice and your laughter. I've wondered what color your eyes are, little one. Are they blue like Sean's? Or perhaps a sultry brown to match the wine richness of your hair? I want to know about you. After what the English have done to you, I don't imagine you'll ever see fit to trust men again. Or ever learn to love a man."

His voice grew saddened and thick with exhaustion as he continued in a hushed tone. "I'm sorry it happened, little one. It makes me feel ashamed of being a man. It wasn't right. Believe me, I'd do anything in the world to show you that not every man is like that, sweet Aly...."

As Tray slipped into the deep folds of sleep, his arms remained wrapped protectively around Alyssa, and he found a measure of peace he'd never experienced before.

# Chapter Three

Tray welcomed Sorche into the bedchamber with a warm look in his gray eyes as the older woman waddled over to him. It had become a ritual between them; each evening before Sorche retired, she would come and sit with Tray and they would catalog Alyssa's daily progress.

"Her hair needs combing," Sorche noted gruffly. She pulled a brush from her pocket. "Here," she urged, placing it in his hand, "get the snarls out of her hair."

Tray gave Sorche a sheepish glance. "I don't know how to brush a woman's hair, Sorche. Perhaps you should do it again."

"Nonsense! You know how to brush a horse's mane. Go on, sit beside her. Now pick up a few strands and gently pull the brush through them. That's it. Goodness! Hair isn't alive, you know! Go on, a bit more pressure. There... good!" Sorche beamed proudly, watching Tray's hesitant progress. "She has the most beautiful color of hair I've ever seen."

Tray nodded, watching the auburn tresses begin to gleam like rich wine shot with gold as he drew the brush through her thick, clean hair. "Unique. Like she is," he murmured.

Sorche made herself comfortable in a chair beside the bed, watching her foster son. Although the light from the fireplace cast shadows upon Tray's face, Sorche could tell he was happy. Since Alyssa's arrival, there had again been a flicker of hope in his somber gray eyes. She took out her embroidery, occasionally looking up to check his progress.

"It's been seven days now. What did Dr. Birch say today?"

"That she's healing rapidly and there is no sign of infection."

"Thank the Mother Mary for that!" She frowned, her fingers poised above her stitchery. "And when will she awake, Tray? Did he say anything about that?"

"No," he answered, laying the newly brushed strands across her pillow. Sliding his long, large-knuckled fingers beneath another handful of hair, Tray slowly began to draw the brush through it, finding a deep sense of pleasure in the action. How would Alyssa react if she knew that it was he and Sorche who bathed her daily and tended her healing wounds? Would she flee in terror like the wild Welsh cobs that ranged over the mountains? Or would she react like his favorite mare, who loved to be petted and would sidle even closer to take full advantage of his knowing hand?

"Seven days," Tray murmured, almost to himself. "She's lovely, isn't she? The bruising has yellowed and her flesh is no longer swollen. My God, why hasn't someone taken her hand in marriage? I don't understand it."

Sorche chuckled. "Mind you, what Sean said about her, she's a spitfire."

His mouth thinned momentarily. "I wish we could get more information out of Sean."

"He's frightened, Tray."

Tray nodded. "I suppose you're right," he conceded softly, feeling the heavy silk of her hair as he ran it through his calloused fingers. "Sean won't even tell me her last name. Or where her family is from. I keep trying to convince the lad that we aren't out to do them harm, that we mean to help them get back to Ireland.''

"Be patient, Tray. The boy will uncross himself. He's frightened and in awe of you at the same time. You're a natural father.''

Tray glowered.

"Don't put on that iron Trayhern mask with me. You should be contemplating marriage again, Tray. Lord knows, every woman of the gentry has paraded past you and you all but ignore them. You need an heir.''

Bitterness tugged at him. "Let Vaughn continue being the stud in the family, Sorche. I've no interest in the women who want to be courted by my attentions. Tell me which one of them would be happy out here on Welsh soil with a husband who took joy in plowing, delivering lambs or breeding a better Welsh cob? No,'' he growled, "Shelby was the only one who understood my need to be with the land and the people, Sorche.''

"Shelby was Welsh,'' she said softly, seeing the pain come to Tray's face.

Tray's hand trembled as he held the brush just above the last thick strands of Alyssa's hair. "And I killed her,'' he whispered rawly. "Was I right to rescue Alyssa? Will she die, too? Will I awake as I have so many times before in the night, only to see that her heart has stopped beating? I wonder if I will destroy her by just being in her presence. Or if she awakes, will I in some way kill her while she remains at Shadowhawk to mend?''

Sorche moved to Tray's side, laying her hands on his broad shoulders. "Stop torturing yourself, son of my heart,'' she begged gently. "And believe me when I say that you've caused no one's death. You forget, I was Isolde's governess. I raised her and watched her grow into a beautiful young woman. She died giving you birth because her hips were too narrow. It wasn't your fault. No more than it was when Shelby died." Her gnarled, arthritic hand gripped his arm, her voice fervent. "Shelby had taken that bad fall in her eighth month, Tray. I'm sure that's when the baby was killed. And she was narrow-hipped just like your mother was, besides being in frail health."

Tray pulled his gaze from Alyssa's peaceful features and rested his hand over Sorche's bent fingers. "There are days that I know all of that in my heart and accept it."

"And there are many days when you carry guilt as if it were a mantle around your shoulders, my son."

"Yes." Tray managed a weary smile for her benefit. "As you can see, I'm not perfect." And then he glanced down at his twisted foot, his voice lowering. "Neither physically nor in any other way."

"You're kind."

Tray laughed quietly. "Softheaded."

"You're generous."

"I'm known as a pincher of pennies."

"You love children."

His eyes darkened to pewter. "Yes, I do. It doesn't matter to me whether they are Welsh, English or Irish."

"Stay the way you are, Tray. Your servants and tenants and those who deal with Shadowhawk need you. You're fair when many others are unscrupulous."

He looked up, a tender light in his eyes as he regarded his foster mother. "You must be tired. Do you want me to walk you to your room?"

Sorche leaned over, pressing a kiss to his slightly curled hair. "Alyssa needs you more than I. And if old Craddock saw you escorting me to my suite, he'd think you were daft."

Her laughter was a delight to hear. Tray's spirits lifted as he watched her leave, the only woman in the world besides Shelby who had loved him unconditionally. Who thought nothing of his clubfoot. Who made him feel like a whole man and not half of one, as Vaughn often accused him of being.

"Good night, Mother."

"Good night, son of my heart."


Tray allowed himself to simply gaze down at Alyssa. She was so beautiful that it stole the breath from his body. Her face was square and her skin now showed alabaster, with a slight hint of rose across her cheeks. Her lips were sculpted to perfection and slightly full, the corners lifting softly upward. It was a mouth that begged to be touched, kissed, tasted and wooed into trembling need. The winged arch of her brows only accented the possibility that her eyes would be large and clear with intelligence. Her entire face spoke of fine breeding. Whatever her origins, whether landed gentry or common farmer, hers was a face come alive from the old master painters he had studied as a boy.

The times when she would begin trembling unaccountably during the night, Tray would jerk awake, his embrace tightening to draw Alyssa firmly against him. And each time, when he rested her head on his chest, her ear pressed over his heart, Alyssa would still and her breathing would soften, her limbs slowly relaxing beneath the ministration of his hand as he stroked her shoulder and back. She drew out a fierce protectiveness in him he had never been aware of before. Tray found himself plotting to find out who had almost killed Alyssa. For the first time in his life, he wanted to strike back, to injure the party responsible for her needless abuse. Alyssa was bringing out shocking emotions Tray had never known were within him. Not until now....

He stood up and walked to the hearth, listening to the howl of the March wind as it came off the Irish Sea and whipped around the walls of Shadowhawk. Tray rested his hand against the mantel, staring down at the licking orange-and-yellow flames. He shifted from one booted foot to the other. He ought to bathe and go to bed. And hold Alyssa. Tray raised his chin, his gray eyes focusing on the girl, who looked fragile in the expanse of his bed. Alyssa was restless this evening. More so than any other night. He hoped it was a good sign. Or was she reliving the horror aboard that hellish ship?

Alyssa was breathing hard, her eyes wide with terror as she twisted to look up toward her father. Her heart pounded in her breast like a bird thrashing to escape. Mother Mary, she prayed, give him strength. Don't let him tell that English dog anything! Gathering the last of her own strength, Alyssa screamed, *"No! No! Don't tell him anything! No!"*
Everything merged into a nightmare of cartwheeling fragments as Alyssa tried to fight off the British officer as he began to rape her. Perspiration dotted her brow and she thrashed wildly, trying to free herself. And then she heard another voice, that disembodied voice that called her back and gave her a sense of protection, of peace.
"Easy, Aly. Easy. You're coming awake. It's all right. You're safe. No one will hurt you...."
A sob tore from Alyssa's lips and she felt herself growing heavier and heavier, safe in the arms that held her, rocked her. Slowly, her senses came alive. She could smell a man, an earthy male scent. And wind. She heard wind shrieking, and a fire snapping and popping in the background. Another sob rose from her raw, dry throat.
Tray watched her worriedly. Alyssa had suddenly become hysterical. If he hadn't rushed to her side when he did, she would have flung herself out of bed. He pressed small kisses to her hair and rocked her gently, feeling her heart pounding like a wounded doe's against his chest. A film of

perspiration covered her face and dampened her night-gown.

"Alyssa? Can you hear me? You're safe now. No one's going to hurt you, little one. It's Tray. I'll just hold you until you open your eyes. Relax against me. There's no need to breathe so hard. There's no one here to take you away. You're safe . . . safe. . . ."

Nothing could have prepared Tray for the next moment, when she slowly lifted those thick auburn lashes to reveal large eyes the color of sea foam, eyes that reflected the utter horror of her dishonor aboard the ship. His hands tightened unconsciously upon her as he stared down into their incredible gemlike beauty. Tray saw flecks of gold in their depths, the pupils large and black as they studied him. And then they welled up almost instantly with hot, scalding tears. A lump caught in his throat and he watched helplessly as those tears gathered, formed and streaked down her now flushed cheeks. It felt as if someone had slammed a fist into Tray's chest.

"No . . . no . . ." Alyssa babbled, her fingers digging into her skull.

"Don't," Tray whispered harshly, laying her back on the bed, pulling her hands from her face.

Wild terror widened her eyes and Alyssa struggled weakly. "No . . . Mother Mary, no!" she wailed, her voice echoing pitifully throughout the room.

Confused, Tray pinned her arms beside her head, little realizing that by doing that, he had triggered the rape to life in Alyssa's frantic mind. She struggled briefly, finally lying limp beneath him, gasping. He immediately released her wrists, feeling the sting of tears in his own eyes. What was wrong with her? Couldn't she see that she was safe?

"Listen to me," Tray rasped, his voice thick and unsteady. "There's no need to escape, Alyssa. Look around you! You're not on board a ship. You're at Shadowhawk. No one is going to harm you, colleen.''

Alyssa's breathing softened and she turned her head toward him. Her lower lip trembled as she shrieked, ''I can't see! I can't see! My eyes . . . my eyes . . .'' She weakly lifted her hands, trying to understand why she couldn't see anything even though her eyes were wide open.

''God's blood, no!'' With trembling fingers, Tray gently caressed her temple. How? Why? Dr. Birch had said nothing about blindness. ''Listen to me, little one, stop crying. Stop,'' Tray continued in soothing Gaelic, trying to restrain her hysteria, ''Please. You're tearing my heart apart.''

The touch of a man's fingers upon her skin had sent a shot of paralyzing terror coursing through Alyssa, but then the dark, chanting magic of his voice assuaged her fear. Alyssa dropped her head back on the pillows and tried to control her terror. Sweet Mother of Jesus, he was a man, just like the man who had hurt her. Gradually, allowing his soothing words to sway her, she relaxed and felt his grip loosen. The moment he released her, she cringed against the headboard, her arms wrapped around her exhausted body.

''Who are you?'' Alyssa begged, her voice cracking. ''Don't touch me! Don't touch me!''

She felt his weight leave the bed and buried her head more deeply into her arms, fearing a blow. She was breathing hard again, like an animal backed into a corner with nowhere to escape. Alyssa blinked. Why couldn't she see? There was no blindfold upon her. Her attention was torn between the darkness that enveloped her and the movement of what she knew to be a man in close proximity to her. Her ragged gasps punctuated the silence and she swallowed, in dire need of water. When the blow she was expecting did not come, Alyssa cautiously lifted her head. Where was she? And who was the man? And Sean! Alyssa's eyes narrowed as she tried to control her own raging emotions.

"Where are you!" she cried, but the words came out as a broken whisper.

Tray stood frozen in guilt and shame as he watched Alyssa cower in the bed. She was trembling, the covers drawn tightly against her body. What should he do? She hated him, hated his touch. He swallowed painfully, his gray eyes anguished as he stared down at her. Although she could not see his gesture, he lifted his hand in a sign of peace and quietly began speaking to her.

"Alyssa, my name is Tray. I know you can't stand the touch of a man, so let me get my mother, Sorche. You shouldn't be moved yet. You're still injured. Believe me, I won't hurt you. Please, just stay where you are and I'll bring Sorche."

Alyssa's breasts rose and fell quickly and her slender fingers gripped the sheets more tightly. Just the calming tenor of his voice shed layers of the fear that cloaked her. "Wh-where am I?"

"At a friend's home."

"And Sean? Where's Sean?"

"Just down the hall. As soon as I get Sorche and attend to your needs, I'll bring him to you."

She gave a jerky nod of her head, biting hard on her lower lip. "He's alive?" she quavered.

"Alive, well fed and happy. Now all we have to do is make you the same way, little one. Please, lie back down. I won't hurt you. I promise."

Little one... The way the endearment rolled off his tongue caressed the open wounds of her soul and relaxed her. "A-are you Irish?"

Tray managed a sliver of a smile. "Raised on the milk of the Irishwoman who will care for you, Alyssa."

Some of the panic drained from her pale features.

"Now stay quiet and I'll get Sorche," he promised.

Alyssa tensed as she heard the scuff of his booted feet against the carpet. A door quietly opened and closed, and she was left in a room she could not see. Releasing the blanket, she stretched out her left hand, investigating the area around her. She had outlined the shape of the huge bed by the time the man called Tray returned with his mother.

Sorche waddled into the room, the white mobcap askew on her now frizzy gray-haired head. Awakened out of a sound sleep, she was barely sensible as she came around the edge of the bed to where Alyssa sat, tense and wary.

"Child," she whispered, reaching out and putting her hand over Alyssa's, "you are safe here."

The comfort of Sorche's gruff voice tapped the well of conflicting emotion within Alyssa, and she let out a single sob. The woman sat down near her, gently pushing the heavy hair away from her face. "Thank all the saints you've come back to us," she murmured. "We were so worried for you, child. You've been here seven days now and no one held much hope of you recovering except Tray. Our prayers are answered."

Alyssa groped, finding and clutching at Sorche's arthritic hand. "I can't see, Sorche . . . my eyes . . . what happened? Why am I blind?"

"I don't know, child. Tray is going to send for Dr. Birch. He's the one who examined you and brought you back to health. He'll be here before dawn. Is there anything we can get you? Are you hungry?"

"I—I want to see Sean. I need to know he's alive."

Sorche glanced up at Tray, whose features were almost as tortured as Alyssa's. "Tray will get him up. What else? Would you like some good cabbage soup?"

Alyssa shook her head, her fingers moving to her throat. "Water. Just water. I'm so thirsty."

Stiffly, Sorche got to her feet and went to the sideboard, pouring a large glass of water for her from the pitcher. Alyssa was far weaker than she thought; she couldn't hold the glass. Sorche coaxed her to lie back against several pillows and then guided the glass to her lips. Before Tray returned to the chamber with a sleepy-eyed Sean in tow, Alyssa had drunk four glasses in succession.

Before they entered the bedchamber, Tray knelt down in the hall, his hands resting on Sean's small shoulders. The boy's eyes were still puffy with sleep, his red hair mussed. "Listen to me carefully, son. If your cousin asks you where she is, tell her you're at a friend's home. That isn't a lie. Right now she's upset about her blindness and she doesn't need any more shock. She doesn't need to know she's in Wales. It will do nothing but aggravate her, and it might affect her health. You don't want Alyssa hurt any more, do you?"

Sean slowly shook his head, his blue eyes widening. "Blind? But—how?" he blurted.

"I don't know, Sean. Perhaps the blow to her skull caused it." Tray's fingers tightened momentarily on the boy's arms. "We'll know more when Dr. Birch arrives. Come, you were the first person she asked for when she woke up." Tray got to his feet and kept a hand on Sean's shoulder. The Irish boy seemed to sense the seriousness of the moment. Instead of flying to his cousin's arms, he walked up to her with a sober expression.

"Lys?" Sean whispered, holding out his small hand, lightly brushing her arm.

"Sean? Oh, Sean!" Her voice stronger, Alyssa reached out until she found him.

Sorche sniffed, wiping the tears from her cheeks as she watched them hold each other in a long embrace. She felt Tray's arm go around her shoulder, drawing her near, and she leaned gratefully against his powerful, seemingly tireless body. As usual, it was Tray who was keeping everything and everyone together.

Craddock appeared at the doorway in his rumpled nightgown, blear-eyed. "You rang, sir?" he mumbled.

The butler's entrance diverted Tray's attention from the reunion between Alyssa and Sean. The boy had buried his head against her shoulder, sobbing hard. At least there was one male she didn't hate. Perhaps there was hope, after all. "Yes, get Dr. Birch here as swiftly as possible. Have Stablemaster Thomas hitch up the grays and send the coach. With the weather the way it is, I don't want the good doctor falling off his horse or getting thrown. Send two outriders to light the way."

"Yes, Lord Trayhern. Right away."

Tray sat in a chair near the fireplace, his long, muscular legs stretched out before him. It had been three hours since Alyssa had awakened and now the excitement had worn off, leaving everyone exhausted. Tray felt gutted emotionally and he was sure Alyssa felt even worse. Sean had spent the better part of an hour with her, patiently answering her questions and successfully avoiding telling her where Shadowhawk was located and who their "friends" really were. Tray rubbed his brow tiredly and watched Alyssa as she slept fitfully on the bed once again. After Sean left, Sorche had given Alyssa more water and tucked her in, clucking over her like a mother hen. A soft smile touched his lips. Sorche gave endlessly of her love and affection. She was a miracle in his life, and his heart had lightened as he observed Alyssa falling beneath her spell, as well.

Tray's head dropped to his chest, eyes closed, the pleasant crackle of the fire soothing him. He felt shocked and rebuffed by Aly's initial shrinking away from him. Anger and frustration roiled within him. He didn't blame Alyssa for her reactions to him. After all, he was a man.

Tray was almost ready to give in to badly needed sleep when he heard Alyssa stir. Immediately his head snapped up, his eyes narrowing upon her as she threw off the bed covers.

"Don't get out of that bed!" His voice cut like a whip through the quiet of the chamber and Alyssa froze. She had placed her feet on the carpet, her thin ankles and beautifully formed feet visible beneath the folds of the peach-colored nightgown. Tray was up in an instant, limping toward her, his face set.

Alyssa heard him coming and shrank back as he approached. "Wh-where's Sorche?" Her voice was small and quavering.

Tray glared down at her and ran his fingers through his hair. "Asleep."

"Oh..." Alyssa tensed as if he were going to strike out at her any moment. It did nothing but feed the rage he had been feeling since she had awakened.

Swallowing his feelings, Tray asked, "Why? What do you want? Can I get it for you?"

Color swept her cheeks and Alyssa licked her lips. "I—I don't mean to presume upon your graciousness, but...I drank so much water that I have to...I mean—"

Tray's face relaxed. "I see," he said. He squatted down in front of her. "My mother is very old, Alyssa. She couldn't carry you to the water closet. And none of my other maids could do it, either. You're not exactly a sprite of a colleen."

Alyssa's heart was beating hard in her chest as she listened to the humor in his tone. "I—I will walk. If you can just—"

"Listen to me, little one, you're as weak as a lamb. I know it's not customary for a man to take a woman to the water closet, but in this case, neither of us has much choice."

Her shoulders dropped and Alyssa turned toward his voice. "If I can stand, will you direct me with your voice?"

Tray rose, a scowl forming on his brow. "You're too weak to walk."

Her chin jutting out in defiance, Alyssa forced herself to her feet. She wavered badly and threw out her hands to find nothing but air. But the fear of him as a man was greater than her fear of falling, and she prepared herself to hit the floor. As she lost her balance, Alyssa felt strong, masculine arms closing around her body. He lifted her as if she were a mere feather wafting on a summer's breeze. She stiffened, a cry lurching from her throat.

"You don't have to remind me that you want nothing to do with men," Tray growled tightly, carrying her through the bedchamber to an adjoining room, which housed the bath and the water closet. He sat her down, making sure she would not fall again.

"Please," Alyssa begged, "leave me."

Tray hesitated, but he heard the humiliation in her hoarse voice. "Very well. Call me when you want me to carry you back to the bedchamber."

"A-all right."

Afterward, Alyssa rose and pulled the nightgown down around her body. She stood, her hands braced against the cool stone-and-wood enclosure. She tried to fight off the dizziness that washed over her, and her fear of Tray coming back pushed her into action. Hand outstretched, she met the

hard, masculine wall of a man's chest. Jerking her hand
back as if burned, Alyssa would have fallen if Tray hadn't
reached out and brought her into his arms.

A strangled sound of fury left Alyssa's lips and two bright
red spots appeared on her cheeks as she lay stiffly in his embrace. "You—you were there all the time!" she gasped,
trying to push away from him. "You gave your word—"

Tray slipped his arms beneath her, lifting her up against
him. She was pitifully thin; his fingers could feel each clearly
defined rib through the nightgown she wore. "No, I wasn't.
I had just come back in to check on you."

This time, as they made their way back to the bedchamber, Alyssa noticed that the man walked brokenly. Was he
hurt?

Why did she care? He was a man. And men were little
more than monsters. She erected a barricade against Tray as
he carried her back to the safety of the bed. Once deposited, she pulled the covers across her lap and leaned against
the headboard.

The sound of shod horses clattering up the cobblestoned
expanse leading to the main entrance of Shadowhawk tore
Tray's attention away from Alyssa. He recognized the
sounds as a coach approaching. At the thought of Dr. Birch
arriving momentarily, he felt another weight slipping free of
his shoulders. Perhaps now the doctor would be able to tell
them why Alyssa was blind.

# Chapter Four

Alyssa saw the grinning face of the English officer as he leered down at her, his too-handsome features looming before her in sinister distortion. Tossing restlessly, moaning, she tried to escape from the hard male body that straddled her. She watched in horror as he slowly reached down and jerked at her thin shirt to deliberately expose her breasts to all. No, sweet Mother of Mary, no! Alyssa began to sob, knowing she would have to live through the same sequence once again as she hovered between wakefulness and sleep.

Then the bed shifted beneath her and she felt the weight of someone nearby. To her great relief, she heard his voice— that soothing Gaelic breaking through the terror, shattering the grisly scene dancing before her mind's eye. Without hesitation, Alyssa welcomed the safety of his embrace, resting her head on his chest. The soothing sound of his heart allowed her own heart to eventually beat in rhythm with his.

"Rest, sweet Aly," he rasped. "I'll hold you this one last night and make your dreams leave you in peace. Sleep, little one. Sleep the peace of angels, because God knows, you deserve it."

Tray bit back a groan as Alyssa nestled more closely against him. He lightly stroked her head, running the gos-

samer threads of her hair through his fingers as he had done
for seven nights before. This would be the last time he would
sleep with her now that she had regained consciousness. The
doctor had seen her briefly and wanted to examine her more
thoroughly the next day. It was nearly three in the morning, and everyone was exhausted.

Tray's heart wrenched as Aly nuzzled him like a lamb
seeking its mother, her slender hand resting on his chest. In
sleep, she trusted him even though he was a man. He lay
there a long time, aware that dawn was slowly breaking the
hold of night. He desperately needed to rest, yet he also
needed to hold Aly and somehow atone for all the cruelty
that life had thus far dealt her.

He had forgotten the contentment that a woman could
bring to him. Alyssa made him feel whole, complete. Yet he
wouldn't humiliate her further by allowing her to discover
that he had held her during those nights when she had hovered at death's gate. And Alyssa's trampled pride would not
allow her to accept him holding her at night any longer. He
would now have to move to the adjoining bedchamber. A
soft smile tugged at Tray's mouth as he rested his arm on her
back. Sean had been right: Alyssa was a spitfire.

Alyssa jerked awake with a gasp.

"Relax, miss," a voice she recognized as Dr. Birch's
soothed. The man placed his hand on her shoulder. "I need
to examine that head wound of yours a bit more closely."

Alyssa froze.

Tray grimly watched Alyssa wrestle with the terror. She
suddenly ducked away from the doctor's continued ministrations. Damn her! Tray wrestled with his anger as he
stalked around to the other side of the bed, making sure she
would not try to bolt, thereby injuring herself further. He
glanced at Birch and then down at her.

"Alyssa," he growled, "stop this. You can't run every time someone touches you. The doctor needs to examine you."

Alyssa winced beneath Tray's biting tone as if he had physically struck her. He was obviously used to having his own way and ordering others around. One part of her rebelled; and yet, with frightening despair, she knew she could not escape because her blindness prevented it. Hot tears scalded her eyes and she tipped her head back, squeezing her eyelids closed and forcing down the tears.

"Please..." she whispered brokenly, "ask me anything you want, Doctor. But don't—don't touch me. I—I can't stand it. You don't know what happened...."

Birch sat quietly on the edge of the bed. "We know what happened to you, child," he said gruffly. "I'll be very gentle with you. Now, you must sit there and stop agitating yourself. Do you understand?"

Tray limped back to the fireplace, his mouth set in a hard line. Alyssa's pleading cry tore at him as nothing else ever had. God's blood! What was this unexplained power she held over him? Each time agony showed in her lovely jade-colored eyes or Tray heard the trembling fear in her rich voice, he responded to it as if he were a part of her.

That morning, he had gently dislodged himself from Alyssa's sleeping embrace and had stood at the bedside, staring hungrily down upon her peaceful countenance, which, in slumber, lost that mask of fear. The perfectly sculpted features of her healing face had tempted him almost beyond reason.

Tray rubbed his brow in consternation, hating himself for what he had felt earlier as he stood there. He had experienced a stirring of heat in his loins, and his imagination had taken flight. Ruthlessly, he tried to sort and examine his emotions. Shelby had been dead for longer than a year.

There were many Englishwomen from Liverpool who begged him to attend their parties and balls after the official period of mourning, but he had declined. They all vied for the title of Lady Trayhern—and the vast Trayhern wealth he would inherit when his father died. Tray's memory veered sharply to a time in his life he never wanted to dredge up again.

He had been the master of Shadowhawk since he was six and ten, with Stablemaster Thomas as his mentor. There had been little time to hone his appreciation of girls when he was growing up. The only other females were Welsh and Irish servants or tenants, and they all knew who he was: the lord of Shadowhawk, someone to treat with deference but never to become friendly with. Those had been painfully lonely years. And it was only when his neighbor to the south, a wealthy Welsh farmer, had come to visit with his son that Tray truly began to understand the shame of his clubfoot and how that condition affected women.

Evan Deverell was two years older than Tray and would often come riding up on one of his father's handsome thoroughbreds and invite Tray to visit Colwyn Bay with him to enjoy the delights of the young Welshwomen, who, he promised, would welcome them with open arms. After a particularly bountiful fall harvest, Tray was in the mood to celebrate. He bathed, donned his best clothes, mounted his bay Welsh gelding and rode happily into Colwyn Bay with his friend.

The cobbled streets of Colwyn Bay were dreary with recent rain when they entered Evan's world of gambling parlors. They drank until their heads reeled and then found themselves in the arms of women who traded their bodies for a few coins. Drunk for the first time in his life, Tray had staggered up to the room of a pretty girl named Glynis, which was gaudily decorated in reds and golds. She giggled as, in his inebriated state, he tried to unbutton his trousers. Glynis pushed him back on the feather bed and divested him of his black wool coat and white, ruffled shirt. He sat there, blinking at Glynis through blurred eyes as she kept up a giggly chatter, her blue eyes small and sparkling as she yanked and pulled on his right boot until it finally slid free. Tossing it aside, he laughed with her, feeling a rush of fierce sexual hunger as she leaned down between his sprawled legs to caress him through his tight-fitting breeches. A shudder of absolute pleasure had rippled through him like hot iron being poured through his awakening loins.

Glynis must have seen the shock and sudden desire mirrored in his stunned expression because she smiled coyly and continued to caress him with knowing fingers, sending shafts of longing coursing through his virgin body. Tray gasped as she gently shoved him down on the bed, proceeding to free each captive button on his confining trousers. The bulge in his breeches left nothing to guess about, and Glynis seemed absolutely delighted as she deliberately grazed his hard maleness one more time before shifting her attention to ridding him of his other highly polished boot.

The skimpy, translucent lavender gown made Tray achingly aware of Glynis as a woman. He watched in fascination as she straddled his left leg, positioning the boot between her slender thighs. He lay there, eyes wide as he watched her small rear wriggle provocatively as she struggled with the boot. Pouting, she turned and told him to push on her derriere so that the naughty boot would come off. He willingly complied, gently placing his foot squarely on that beautiful, lavender-swathed flesh. With squeals of delight, after a few halfhearted tries, Glynis wrestled the leather free. She did a little dance before tossing the boot aside and turning back to Tray. Her gaze flew to his left leg, thin, misshapen, the atrophied calf.

Tray squeezed his eyes shut, still hearing her gasp; in his mind's eye he again watched the revulsion and horror cross Glynis's face as she stared down at his twisted left foot. She backed against the wall, her eyes large as he looked in confusion at her. And then she started screaming.

"Monster! Monster! You're the devil's own! Help! *Help!*" She fled from the room, shrieking at the top of her lungs, the words *monster* and *devil* ringing throughout the building, bringing patrons and whores tumbling out into the hall to investigate.

Tray opened his eyes and stared out the french windows at the moody gray sky. He flexed his left fist, still remembering the humiliation, the rejection. Slowly, he lifted his chin and his gaze rested on Alyssa. Was that how she felt now? He was ashamed of the anger that he had felt toward her earlier. He mustn't allow his frustration to transform into impatience with Alyssa. Whatever she was feeling was aimed at all men, not just at him. Tray moistened his lips, drawing himself up and wandering back to the other side of the bed.

"Listen to me carefully, child," Birch said in his coaching tone. "It is imperative you remain in bed for at least another week. Your dizziness will probably continue and you must rely on these good people to help you."

Her stomach knotted. "C-can't I even try to walk to the water closet?"

"Not just yet. If you fell, you might strike your head again, and that would be grievous to your health. Right now you must eat and gain back some weight. And rest."

"And my eyes?" There was a quaver in her voice.

"I don't know. The blindness could be temporary or permanent. That's why it's important that you rest and stay quiet, so we can find out."

Alyssa swallowed her tears. Dear Mother Mary! Never to see the lush emerald green of her beloved Ireland? Or the radiance of a golden sunrise and rose pink blush of a sunset? She raised her fingers, briefly touching her head wound. "You think I may see again if—if I follow your advice?"

Birch grimaced. "My child, I can't promise you anything. I have seen men and animals who were similarly struck in the head go blind for weeks, perhaps months, and then either slowly or suddenly regain their sight."

Alyssa's voice rose in hope. "In every case?"

"No. Only in half of them."

Her slender fingers moved to the hollow of her ivory throat, and her eyes darkened with pain. "A-and those who didn't?"

"Blind for life."

Alyssa looked away, fighting against the tears. "If I can't see ... if I can't see, I don't want to live!" She turned her head from the doctor to hide her unhappiness.

Tray fought the impulse to kneel down and take Alyssa into his arms. He watched her helplessly, knowing that if he did try to comfort her, she would lash out at him.

"Nonsense, child. Give yourself time to heal. I'll come once a week to see you. You're young and you've made rapid progress thus far. Trust Lord Trayhern. He's overseen your rescue since he took you off that accursed ship. He is your benefactor, and so is Sorche. You are among friends here, and the sooner you realize that, the more speedily you will heal."

*Lord* Trayhern? Alyssa felt a sharp pang of despair. She didn't even have the strength to remind the doctor that he was English, that they were all English and therefore her sworn enemy. Misery enfolded her like a cloak and Alyssa closed her eyes, unable to think about the problems that now faced her.

"I'll leave now," Birch announced. He got off the bed and picked up his brown leather bag, motioning for Tray to follow him out into the hall.

"I'll be back in a moment, Alyssa," Tray told her. She did not respond. Her auburn hair hung in thick, burnished sheets about her pitifully thin shoulders, hiding whatever impression his words had made upon her. His mouth tightened and he led Birch out into the empty hall, shutting the door quietly behind them.

Alyssa tensed when Tray reentered the room. She was pale, and the lack of color to her skin emphasized the shadows beneath her jade eyes.

"It's just me," Tray announced, walking over to her.

She said nothing, staring straight ahead, her lips trembling.

He shoved his hands in the pockets of his trousers, watching her darkly. "Are you hungry?"

"No!"

"Thirsty, then?"

"Go away!"

"I'm afraid that's impossible, little one. I own Shadowhawk, and you and Sean are my guests."

Alyssa jerked her head toward him, her hair flying about her shoulders. "Don't call me little one! I hate it! I hate you! You're English!"

Tray stiffened, his features growing hard. "That's one point we need to straighten out between us," he said through clenched teeth, approaching her bed. He saw Alyssa shrink back to the safety of the headboard. "I'm Welsh by birth."

"Then you lied to me! You said you were Irish! And you speak Gaelic."

"My mother died giving birth to me, Alyssa. I was given to Sorche, who is Irish. She wet-nursed and raised me.

Welsh blood runs in my veins but I was brought up beneath her loving Irish hand." Seeing Alyssa cringe at his words, Tray realized he was snarling at her like a dog. Cursing mentally, he stalked back to the fireplace. "You are in a Welsh household, Alyssa," he began again, his voice more neutral. "I'm the lord of the estate. I have no more love of the English than you do. Don't forget, they conquered our fair lands first before they put Ireland under their yoke of dominance."

Alyssa raised her chin defiantly, her eyes glittering. "You're a titled lord?"

"Yes," he admitted wearily, "the son of an earl."

"The Welsh hold no titles, just as the Irish can't!" she spat. "You lie to me again. Do you take me for an addle-brained—"

Tray curbed his flaring temper. "Alyssa, I hadn't intended on giving you my life story, but I see I must. Two hundred years ago Culver Trayhern was given an earldom in South Wales by the King of England. But he and every firstborn son after him, including my father, Harold, wed Welshwomen. What few drops of English blood were ever in me have been put back into the soil of Shadowhawk long ago. I'm far more Welsh than English, believe me." He was, but Vaughn wasn't. Vaughn reveled in his half-English breeding through his mother, the Lady Edwina.

Her mutinous look wavered and then she released a sigh. "I'm so tired . . . just leave me alone. I want to sleep."

Tray scowled. At that moment, Alyssa appeared so frail, almost as if she would disappear before his very eyes. He lowered his voice. "Then sleep. I'll be here when you awake. If you need anything, call. I'll be in the adjoining room."

Alyssa slid beneath the covers, her head aching abominably. Sleep was an escape from a man called Tray, whose voice flowed over her like thick golden honey, soothing her ragged nerves.

It was midafternoon when she awoke. Alyssa lay there a long time, listening for noises. She heard the snort of horses in the distance and the faint bleat of sheep, but the wind distorted the sounds as it gusted against the windows and rattled them beneath its power. A fire crackled nearby and she longed to be able to get up and walk over to it. Fire was always comforting to her. Not that she was cold. No, for once in her life, she was warm. Her fingers moved in a caressing gesture over the smooth texture of the sheet around her. Never had she felt material of such fine quality. So this was how the rich lived? Her father had always told her the English were decadent, that they taxed the poor Irish Catholic farmers out of their land, putting the hard-earned money of the laborers into their own pockets. That money bought such finery as this, Alyssa thought hazily.

Her sharpened hearing caught the sound of heavy boots scuffing across a thick carpet. She stiffened, her lashes lifting.

"How are you feeling?"

The care in Tray's deep voice dissolved her acid retort. His voice . . . why did it seem so familiar to her? Her heart gave a little lurch. She tried to speak but found her mouth gummy.

"Water?"

Alyssa nodded and struggled into a sitting position. She heard the water being poured and the familiar sound of his approach. Never had she relied so keenly on her hearing as now.

"Hold out your hands," he commanded her, "and I'll place the glass between them."

She obeyed his instructions. When her fingers brushed his, she froze momentarily. But driven by thirst, Alyssa gripped the glass firmly. He removed his hand and she eagerly drank.

"More?"

She shook her head, holding out the emptied glass. "No, thank you," she whispered.

Tray smiled tentatively. So, Alyssa could be civil when she chose. Or was it that she had just awakened, her defenses not yet in place? It didn't matter. Tray made sure he didn't touch her fingers a second time as he lifted the glass from her hand. After setting it on the sideboard, he moved back to her.

"It's been a while since your last trip to the water closet."

Alyssa felt the heat of blush rapidly sweep from her neck up into her face. The scarlet color graced her cheeks and Tray took pity upon her.

"I don't think Dr. Birch will be angry if I hold your hand and you try a few steps toward the water closet on your own instead of being carried all that way. What do you think?"

Alyssa was so grateful she almost cried. She hadn't expected any enemy of Ireland to show humanity. Swallowing the lump forming in her throat, she nodded and lifted her hand outward. The graceful gesture reminded Tray of the ballerinas he had seen performing in London. His mouth compressed and he gently pulled back the covers and gripped Alyssa's hand firmly in his own.

"Come to the side of the bed and then just rest a moment," he counseled softly.

Alyssa did so, wildly aware of his powerful, calloused hand surrounding her own, swallowing up her cool, damp fingers. The vibrating tenor of Tray's voice thrummed through her like a beautifully played Irish harp, and she couldn't ignore the sudden flutter of her heart in her chest.

"All right, stand, slowly."

She was weak. More weak than she could ever recall being in her life. But with Tray's assistance, she stood, wavering, but standing nevertheless. She felt the heat of his body, so close to her own, and suddenly wished that she could see his face. Faces told her so much about a person. And right now, Alyssa felt one part of herself desperately wanting to reach out and trust this stranger, yet she knew she couldn't.

"How do you know so much about all these things?" she muttered, frowning.

Tray's laughter was deep and free. "I'm treating you as if you were a newborn foal who is trying to get to her feet for the first time. Have you seen foals? First they push upright on their straight little front legs and then promptly fall back down on their noses. Next, they push with their gangly hind legs, getting to their knees in front." His voice lowered intimately, heightening her already aware senses. "And then those tiny front legs come up and there they stand, wobbling and wavering on all four feet for the first time in their life. It's quite a moment." Amusement laced his voice. "And then the mother will urge her newly born foal to nurse. In this case, we'll nudge you toward the water closet. Shall we take your first faltering step, little one?"

His voice was a mesmerizing drug, and without a word, Alyssa took her first faltering step forward. A delicious sense of protection and care surrounded her as he called her little one again. She hadn't the meanness to tell him not to call her by that pet name.

"And another..." Tray urged, and so it went. Alyssa took ten steps before she felt her knees giving way. Her right hand flew out in his direction and he caught her, his arm sliding around her waist, allowing her to fall against him. The shock of her thinly clothed body meeting the masculine hardness of his brought a gasp from Alyssa.

"Easy, Aly, I'm not going to hurt you. Easy..." He slipped his arm beneath her thighs, lifting her up against him.

Alyssa's muscles tensed. He was a man, and her enemy.

"Ten steps isn't bad for a first time," he told her conversationally as he carried her to the marble-tiled bath area, trying without success to ignore her reaction to him. Her once flushed features were now pale and taut, and he could feel Alyssa retreat inside of herself. He gently set her on her feet. Taking her right hand, he verbally laid out the dimensions of the water closet before releasing her.

"Call me when you're done," he told her. "I'll be in the drawing room working at my desk. You may have to raise your voice a bit so that I'll hear you."

Tray tore his gaze from her waxen features and those large, haunted jade eyes that tore his soul apart. She didn't believe a word he had said. Well, what did he expect? Going to his mahogany desk, he took up the quill and forced himself to concentrate on the work before him.

For the first time in almost eight days, the sun broke through the low-hanging gray clouds and its beams cascaded through the french doors, making the blue drawing room come to vibrant life. The warmth felt good and Tray lifted his chin, allowing the sunlight to fall across his face. He preferred being outdoors. Although he did not regret the past week with Alyssa, he missed the fresh salt air and his daily ride on Rasheed along the beach.

His thoughts were interrupted when he caught sight of Alyssa, clutching at the woodwork of the doorway in order to stay upright. His chair tipped over as, too late, he raced to catch her before she fell. Alyssa's auburn hair spilled like a wine waterfall around her face as she crumpled to the carpet.

"You little fool," Tray breathed savagely, gripping her arms and pulling her upright. "What do you think you were doing? Why didn't you call for me?" Tray swallowed the rest of his anger as he saw tears form in Alyssa's luminous eyes as they lifted toward his voice.

"I—I thought you were lying," she choked. "I thought you were watching me all the time. I couldn't stand the thought of—of—"

He groaned and knelt with Alyssa in his arms, burying her head against his chest. "God's blood," he whispered rawly. "I would never do anything to humiliate you, Aly." His voice softened. "So you decided to see if I was secretly watching, knowing I would stop you from walking out of there?" Her logic was faultless. Had he been that devious, Tray would rather have admitted his lie than risk her falling. She knew him better than he cared to admit, which was rather unsettling. He didn't want to be vulnerable ever again. He gave Alyssa's cheek a gentle caress, his voice coaxing. "You have to learn to trust again. Trust me."

Belatedly, as he lightly held her in his embrace while she valiantly refused to cry, he remembered what Sean had said: Alyssa had not been betrothed. She would have been protected from men. She was only seven and ten and, until recently, a virgin. She would have been protected from men all her life. At no time would she have had her maidenly privacy disrupted by a man. And now, he was the one to see her in little more than a nightgown and to carry her to and from the water closet. And she lay in his bed. Tray's mouth quirked in understanding as Alyssa raised her head and pushed away from him. He released her, but only inches separated them.

"Better now?" he asked, his own voice unsteady.

"Y-yes."

"Tears are the language of the heart. There's nothing wrong with crying, little one."

"Men don't cry. Why should I?" she asked defiantly. "I'm ready to go back to bed."

He gave her a patient smile. "Sometimes it's better to cry, to let all your feelings out instead of bottling everything up. You've been through a great deal."

She looked up, a challenging tilt to her chin. "And I suppose you cry?"

"Yes, I have. Several times," he admitted quietly.

Her eyes widened. "Oh . . ."

"Do you want to try to walk or do you want me to carry you?"

Alyssa's lips parted as she considered her answer. Her heart gave a funny twist in her chest. He had given her a choice. Tray could have dragged her back to the bed by her hair, as the sailors had dragged her from the cell, without consulting her on the matter at all. But he had not exerted his male dominance upon her, even though it was in his power to do so at any time. Alyssa tilted her head in confusion, trying to understand this complex man.

"Carry me?" she responded honestly.

Tray rose on one knee, his face thoughtful as he picked Alyssa up. This time she wasn't so stiff and unyielding in his arms, and when he felt her relax ever so slightly against him, his heart soared. Despite the abuse and pain, there was still a core of trust in Alyssa. Trust. He could have exploded with happiness, but he masked it and said nothing as he deposited her on the safety of his bed once again. Tray helped her with the covers and she lay quietly with her hands in her lap, looking almost serene. Her stomach growled, and she immediately placed her hand across her middle.

"Hungry?" he asked, breaking the mellow silence between them.

"Yes."

"I'll have Sorche bring you something to eat."

"Thank you."

Alyssa listening to him leave the room, her stomach still rumbling, telling everyone within earshot that she was indeed starved! She had heard the carefully cloaked amusement in Tray's voice when he had asked her if she was hungry. He could have embarrassed her with a snide comment, but he hadn't. What an odd man he was!

Again, Alyssa found herself wishing mightily to know what he looked like.

# Chapter Five

Alyssa seemed in the best of moods when Tray returned from his long overdue gallop along the cliffs of Shadowhawk. The brisk ride had lifted his spirits, and when he had knocked lightly at Alyssa's door and heard her voice ring out, his heart pounded briefly. He gave her a smile of welcome, even though she could not see him as he entered the bedchamber.

"You look improved," he noted, walking over to the fire and warming his cold hands.

Alyssa shyly lowered her head, her fingers nervously entwined in her lap. "Sorche is responsible for that. She chatted with me while you were gone."

"I imagine she is happy to have someone new to talk to."

Alyssa nodded. Tray's voice was lighter, devoid of...unhappiness, perhaps? She licked her chapped lips and mustered the courage to talk with him directly. "Sorche said you own an Arabian horse. Is that true? I've heard that they're very rare. Did you carry us here on one?"

Tray's eyes lightened and a slight smile hovered around his mouth as he drew up a chair near the hearth and sat down, sprawling his long legs out in front of him. "Ah, I should have expected it," he baited her. Alyssa lifted her chin and he suppressed the rest of his smile in that fleeting instant in favor of drinking in her unparalleled beauty. The blue silk nightgown she wore brought out the emerald highlights in her eyes and the wine darkness of her hair.

"Expected what?" she challenged, her voice stronger.

"That you would have an interest in horses."

"The Irish are famous for their love of horses. We can gentle brutes that can't be tamed by anyone else."

Tray relaxed and enjoyed her spirited exchange. My God, her face was so expressive, so readable. He found himself wanting to burn those images into his memory. "You won't get any argument out of me. Sorche told me the Irish have a secret method of taming a horse."

"We do. And I know that secret."

One dark eyebrow rose as Tray rested his chin against his hand. "Really?"

"Yes."

"That wouldn't be a bit of Irish blarney, would it, Aly?" he teased.

She flushed when he called her Aly. The man was forever giving her pet names! "You don't believe me?"

"No, I didn't say that. It's just that I know there are very few Irish horse tamers who pass on their trade secrets. Especially to a young and beautiful woman such as yourself. Taming a horse is a man's task, not a woman's."

Alyssa's lips parted in consternation. "A man's task? Indeed! I'll have you know that I've gentled horses no man could get near!"

Tray's gray eyes grew light with amusement. "There isn't an Irishman alive who doesn't indulge in a bit of stretching the truth. I'm afraid you'd have to prove that to me, little one."

"I can. I mean I could, if... if I weren't blind," she stumbled lamely.

Tray winced as he heard the excitement drain from her voice. "Well," he soothed, "perhaps when you're better, and when Dr. Birch says that you can ride, I'll let you go with me. Would you like that?"

An instant's hope flickered to life inside Alyssa and then died. He was handing her dreams, only dreams. She bowed her head, muttering, "Sorche said you were an unusual man. But you're a lord and I'm a commoner. No lord rides with someone like me."

Tray roused himself, scowling at the truth in her words. "We'll see," he said.

Alyssa raised her head, her eyes large and sad. "Please," she whispered rawly, "tell me what you're going to do with us. I'm blind and of no use to you. And I've heard tales of small boys who are taken to Wales and sent to coal mines, never to be seen again." She raised her hands in an open gesture toward him. "Are we slaves? Will you send Sean to the mines to die?"

Tray rose, his face ashen as he stared across the room at her. "Did Sorche tell you anything?" he asked tightly.

"Only that you were told to come to the ship and pick up a boy."

Tray expelled a deep breath and drew a chair near her bed. "I owe you some answers. My half brother, Vaughn, demanded my presence aboard that ship to pick up a small boy who had been captured in the rebellion. Vaughn told me I'd find Sean in the ship's hold." His voice softened momentarily. "And I found you there along with him."

Alyssa swallowed, her eyes unnaturally bright. "Sean told me how you saved me from being killed. The sailors were going to throw me on the cart...."

Tray avoided her gaze. "Anyone would have done the same," he muttered. "As for what I'm going to do with you, I'd like to return you to Ireland once you've fully recovered. Both of you.''

A small cry shook Alyssa and she clasped her hands together. ''You mean that?''

''You have my word upon it,'' Tray promised grimly, dreading the moment he would have to let her go.

Confusion laced her voice, ''You're so different . . .''

Tray gave a harsh laugh, crossing his booted feet and staring pensively down at them. ''Different? Now you're being kind. People usually use much different words to describe me, such as devil, or monster.''

''No . . . they couldn't. They're wrong.''

He chanced a brief look at Alyssa and closed his eyes, unable to deal with the compassion he saw flooding her face. ''It's good that you're blind or you'd agree with them. Just ask Sean. Hasn't he told you that I'm like a huge, hulking monster, silently treading the halls of Shadowhawk like a satanic effigy?''

Alyssa heard the bitterness in his quiet voice, unable to understand his sudden sadness. ''Why, no. He's frightened of you, but only because you're English.''

''Welsh,'' Tray corrected. ''Now, what other questions do you need answered?''

Just the gentle teasing in his voice gave her the courage she needed. ''My father, Colin.''

''What about him?''

''He was on board that ship, too.''

''A prisoner?''

Alyssa nodded.

Tray sat up. ''Don't tell me your whole family was caught in the middle of that uprising?'' His tone was incredulous.

Alyssa chewed on her lower lip. If she told Tray the truth, that her father and her brother, Dev, were a part of the rebellion, he might well send Sean to the coal mines to die. She had to continue the lie Sean had invented for them. "Yes."

Tray clenched his fist. "Damn those hotheaded English soldiers," he hissed blackly. He had heard that the English army under General Lake's banner were killing, maiming and torturing thousands of helpless victims who had taken no part in Wolfe Tone's poorly executed rebellion in Ireland. Tray looked up into her innocent features. "That ship doesn't leave until tomorrow morning. They're taking on water at Colwyn Bay. I'll send one of my servants to locate my half brother and we'll see what can be done to free your father, Alyssa."

His words took her aback. Did Tray's power extend that far? Colin Kyle had taken part in the rebellion, and so had she. She clasped her sweaty hands together, fear racing through her. She was a prisoner who had been intended for Newgate Prison in London, to be hanged beside her father. Alyssa blanched with guilt. She had abused Tray's generosity by lying to him. And now she was going to try to use his family connection to free her father. If she protested against his intervention too strongly, Tray would question her closely, and she didn't want to risk Sean's safety by blurting out the truth. Perhaps . . . perhaps Tray's brother would be too busy to come to Shadowhawk. Then Tray would never know the truth, and both she and Sean would be safe. Oh, Mother Mary, why had she lied! Tray didn't deserve her deceit.

"Now it's your turn," Tray said, breaking into her cartwheeling thoughts. "Tell me about yourself, your family. Are you seacoast Irish or inland born?"

Alyssa closed her eyes momentarily, trying to contain all her roiling emotions and fears. "My last name is Kyle," she began, her voice low and unsteady, "and I was born in County Wexford, near the town of Wexford. My family farmed for a living until—until my father was unable to meet the taxes that the English placed upon us because we were Catholic.''

Tray grimaced. How many independent Irish had had their farms stolen from beneath them, their homes burned or destroyed, their families forced into a life of wandering impoverishment? He was familiar with the religious persecution. Catholic farmers were given only a twenty-one-year lease on their land, while Protestant farmers were given three lifetimes to keep and till their farms. Eventually the Catholic farmers had ended up as squatters, barely surviving in windowless, thatched hovels made of mud and straw, built on other people's land. The Kyles were probably no different. ''Brothers? Sisters?''

''Two older brothers. Devlin is four and twenty. Gavin is three and twenty.''

''And you were their spoiled baby sister?'' he baited gently, smiling, thinking how pretty she must have been with her innocent green eyes, beautifully shaped mouth and freckles sprinkled across her nose and cheeks.

Alyssa twisted the sheet between her fingers. ''Loved, but not spoiled,'' she countered.

''And your mother? You haven't mentioned her.''

Alyssa grew still. ''Mama died the first winter we were driven from our home. She had consumption, and Father didn't have enough money to get a doctor to treat her.'' She compressed her full lips and her hands stilled.

''I'm sorry,'' Tray said, breaking the silence between them.

She gave a small, defeated shrug. ''That was a long time ago.''

''How old were you when she died?''

"Six. I don't remember much about it. Gavin took care of me while Father and Dev hunted the countryside for food."

Tray's face mirrored her pain. "But when you were old enough, you took over the duties of caring for all of them?"

She nodded and then gave a small, forced laugh. "Even to this day I'm not a good seamstress. I can't card wool properly...I can't do much very well, if you want the truth."

"That's because your mother died before she could teach you those skills properly," he countered quietly. "How old were you when you took over the household duties?"

"Nine, ten . . . I don't really recall."

Tray stared hard at Alyssa, fighting back the images that her young life brought to mind. Had the Kyle family dug holes in the ground and burrowed in them like animals to stay out of the wet, damp weather of winter, with nothing more than a few thin rags covering their starving, flea-bitten bodies? Had they eaten grubs and insects to stay alive, and chewed on the bark of trees during the cold months to keep from starving? His heart contracted as he stared at her unmarred face. She had gone through so much in her short life. And now, she had been a victim of the rebellion, once again caught, abused and brought to her knees by the damned English. His fists knotted until his knuckles turned white.

"You're getting shadows beneath those lovely eyes of yours, little one. Why not sleep? It's nearly five in the afternoon. You've done much for one day."

"Do you think you'll be able to reach your half brother before he sails?" Alyssa asked, praying that he could not.

Tray rose heavily to his feet. "I don't know. All we can do is try. If that fails, I'll send word to London for Vaughn to come back to Shadowhawk at his first opportunity. He has it within his power to do something for your father, but I can't promise you anything definite right now.''

''By doing this much, my lord, you've helped.''

Tray felt a smile tug at one corner of his mouth. He felt oddly buoyant as he left the bedchamber and walked down the hall toward his study.


The next four days brought a consistency to Alyssa's life that she had not known in years. To her great relief, Tray's half brother was unable to come to Shadowhawk before sailing, but he had promised to ride from London after the ship docked. Sean was safe for a while. Perhaps Lord Trayhern could be convinced to allow the boy to remain at Shadowhawk, despite their lies.

Alyssa moved restlessly in bed, mulling over that last thought. After the truth came out, would Lord Trayhern allow Sean to stay or keep his word and return them both to Ireland? She pushed herself up in bed, resting against the headboard, her face thoughtful. What of Dev and Gavin? Had they escaped the English soldiers and fled into the countryside? She drew her lower lip between her teeth, frowning. How she missed her brothers! And each time she thought of her fiery-tempered father in manacles and chains, she wanted to cry. The English would hang him at Newgate. Why couldn't they just be allowed to live in peace? Why did the English have to tear their farm away from them? Losing their land had killed her mother. She could remember her mother saying that they had lost everything. Everything. That was what had killed her.

Alyssa ran her fingers through her long, heavy hair in an effort to tame it into some semblance of order about her shoulders. Tilting her head slightly, she heard a cock crowing strongly in the distance. It must be morning. Alyssa's thoughts swung back to Lord Trayhern, as they often did in quiet moments. She had never realized that the English could be as kind as he was. She was bewildered by Tray's care of her and Sean. Who would want a blind Irish girl who was useless to his household? And then a cold terror seeped through her sleep-ridden mind: she had heard of the lords taking mistresses. Reflexively, her fingers went to her cheek.

Lords, it was whispered, took only beautiful women as their mistresses. Alyssa's fingers lingered on her rose-hued skin. Except for having occasionally seen her reflection in a quiet pool of water, she knew little of her appearance. No one had ever said she was beautiful. Dev often teased that she had turned down all marriage proposals because she was waiting for a rich Catholic Irishman to come along. That wasn't true. She loathed the idea of being torn from her family; she loved her brothers and father too much to part from them. She would rather live in the embrace of the forests, trying to make a home for them in some burned-out thatched hut or whatever they found along the way, than live with a strange new family.

And then an excruciatingly painful thought came to Alyssa. No man would want her now. She was damaged goods. No self-respecting farmer would consider her for a wife. Alyssa bowed her head, feeling the hotness of tears that matched the burning anguish in her heart. Hadn't her father impressed upon her time and again that a woman's purity was the most valuable asset she could offer a man? A soft sob escaped from her lips. No one would ever want her now; she was blind, and no better than a common whore.

"Little one?"

Alyssa jerked her head to the left, toward Tray's soft voice. Tears splattered across her cheeks and she clutched her hands protectively to her chest.

Tray quietly pulled a chair over and sat down, facing her. He had risen more than two hours earlier, working in the adjacent drawing room, which began to resemble his study more and more with each passing day. His gray gaze lingered on Alyssa's flushed features and he saw anguish in her haunted expression.

"What is it? What's wrong?" he coaxed gently.

"N-nothing, my lord. Didn't you know that all Irish weep easily? Remember, you told me it was all right to cry."

A slight smile pulled at his well-shaped mouth. In the past four days, some of the natural tension between them had dissipated, and upon occasion, when Tray was able to get past her defenses, they could talk almost as if they were friends. He hoped this would be one of those times. At least she was no longer trying to hide her true feelings from him. He pulled a handkerchief from his trousers and leaned forward.

"Here," he offered, placing the linen against her clenched hand.

An understanding silence stretched between them. Tray sat back, watching Alyssa dry her eyes. "People usually cry when they're very happy or very sad," he noted quietly, knowing there was little in her life that she could be happy about. "Are you crying because you miss Ireland?"

Alyssa knotted the handkerchief in her lap, her head bowed and face hidden by the natural barrier of her hair. "I awoke happy this morning, my lord. And then...then I began to think of the future." She compressed her lips and closed her eyes, her voice low with strain. "I'm blind. I'm damaged goods. Of what use am I to anyone? No man will ever look at me as wifely material now." She opened her slender fingers in a gesture of frustration. "What man who must work from dawn to dusk in the fields would want a helpless blind girl? He would need a strong woman at home to care for him."

Tray's mouth grew into a grim line. He had no defense against her, nor, he was discovering, did he want any. Alyssa was simply herself, without the training that society normally placed on women of his class. Her freshness and vitality made him feel more alive than he could ever recall.

"You've been here almost two weeks and I haven't found you to be in the way," he said, forcing a lightness to his voice he didn't feel. It wouldn't do any good to dwell on the negatives of her situation. "And Sorche was telling me that as you grow stronger, she'll teach you how to card wool. She also felt that you could help in her kitchen, since you're insisting upon walking around. So you see, you aren't useless." And then his voice deepened. "If I hadn't already given my word to send you back to Ireland when you recovered, I would ask you and Sean to remain here at Shadowhawk."

Alyssa's lips parted and she turned toward him. Sweet Jesus, if she could only see! Then she could tell if Tray was lying to her or not. She could look into his eyes and know if he spoke the truth. She was getting more adept at listening and judging the quality of the voices around her. And if this method could be trusted, Lord Trayhern meant what he said. Then another thought occurred to her.

"As what?" she asked faintly.

"What do you mean?"

It took all her courage to blurt it out. "I've heard of lords taking a mistress. I—I don't ever want to be touched by another Englishman. I don't want to bring further shame on my family by being known as a mistress to an enemy of Ireland."

Tray tried patiently to take her fervently spoken admission in stride. "Is that what you're afraid of? That I would turn you into an unwilling mistress?"

Alyssa gave a small shrug. "I don't know what to think of your attentions, my lord. In Ireland, the titled English ride into our villages, pointing out the young women they want, who are then dragged off to their manor or castle. When next we see them, if we see them at all, they are always dressed in finery, yet look so sad."

Her voice trailed off and Alyssa crumpled the handkerchief between her hands. "Father always told me that love could exist between a man and his wife, and that there was no need for a mistress. He said my heart would tell me when I found a man I could love. But now it's too late. I'm soiled, like those women who were dragged off, shamed and dishonored. I couldn't bear to stay here at Shadowhawk. For any reason."

Tray had to stop himself from reaching out and caressing her wine-colored hair. Her words cut like a sword through his heart. Did Alyssa realize that she had welcomed his embrace each nightfall when she was unconscious? He had savored those precious hours with Alyssa at his side, soothing away the dreams that plagued her sleeping hours. Regardless of how Alyssa felt, a large part of him wanted her to remain at Shadowhawk. And yet, Tray had to acknowledge her view of the situation. He kept his voice carefully neutral when he spoke.

"When I was married, Alyssa, I never once considered having a mistress. And your father is right, there can be love between a man and his wife. I had that once and I can assure you, it leaves a man no desire to have a mistress."

Alyssa's eyes grew deep jade as she heard the carefully veiled pain in his tone. "You were married?"

"My wife died over a year ago while giving birth to our child." *Who had a deformed foot, like me,* he almost said. Why was he telling her this? He never spoke of his personal life to anyone. Not even to Sorche, who had tried repeatedly and without success to get him to talk about his grief over losing Shelby and his son.

"I'm sorry, my lord. You didn't deserve that kind of misfortune. You have been so kind to Sean and me."

Tray held her compassionate gaze, watching as she effortlessly reached out to comfort him when her own immediate situation was far worse than his. A lump formed in his throat at her unselfishness, and Tray had to swallow hard before he spoke.

"That's behind me now. You can't live in the past. You must live in the present. And speaking of the present," he went on, trying to ignore the pain in his heart, "I thought if you felt up to it, you could accompany me to the stable. One of my favorite Welsh brood mares has just given birth to Rasheed's first foal of the year. It's a beautifully formed little bay that strongly resembles his sire in every way. Since you have a fondness for horseflesh, I see no reason why you can't put some of your knowledge to work with the foals and get them accustomed to a human handling them." Tray was totally unprepared for the blossoming glow that shone in her face. Alyssa's lips parted and he groaned inwardly, wanting to kiss their ripe softness. And when he saw her eyes glisten with tears, he knew that this time they were tears of happiness.

"My lord—"

"Call me Tray," he ordered abruptly. "I don't like being reminded that I carry an English title any more than you like being reminded of the English. Well, will you come with me after morning tea?"

"Yes. Oh, yes, my—I mean...Tray..." She said his name softly, fervently.

He nodded, knowing he had to leave and not wanting to. There was important work that begged for his attention, yet it was the first time Alyssa had smiled for him. He felt his chest swelling with such happiness that he thought he might die from the reward of the sweet, welcoming smile that danced in her eyes and pulled her lovely full lips upward.

Fortunately, Paige had equaled Alyssa in height, so the dress didn't drag or rise above her slender booted ankles, although the burgundy velvet riding habit was a bit out of fashion.

Sorche stood back, admiring her handiwork with Alyssa's costume, a huge smile wreathing her ruddy features. If they didn't make a lovely pair! Tray's dark good looks matched perfectly with Alyssa's alabaster skin and auburn hair, which was tucked into a chignon at the nape of her neck. "Mind you, Tray, don't keep her out long! If Dr. Birch finds out that you're doing this, he'll flay you alive!"

"She's too lovely to tire. I won't keep her long, Mother."

Alyssa reached out, her hand encountering Tray's arm. Shyly, she placed her hand across the wool of his coat sleeve and rose. Her heart was pounding at the base of her throat and she felt a giddiness sweep through her. The resonant tone of Tray's voice sent an ache through her untutored body, leaving her breathless, slightly frightened and deliciously aware of being a woman. As always, from the day that she had begun exercising on her own, Tray would simply offer his arm and she would walk at his side.

"I assure you," Tray said, "I don't intend to get Alyssa chilled."

Swallowing a smile, Alyssa stepped forward. She was grateful as Tray painted a verbal picture of where they were. He seemed to monitor her needs, never taking deep strides that would make her run to keep up. As they sauntered down the long hall paneled in dark walnut, which he said was graced with many portraits of the Trayhern family, Alyssa became acutely aware of Tray's decided limp. She could feel his body shift with each stride. Had he injured himself? Was he in pain? Biting back those questions, Alyssa remained silent, keeping her hand light against his arm. She didn't want to cause any undue distress to his injured leg.

"Did I tell you how lovely you look in that riding habit?" Tray said, looking over at her. God, Alyssa was such a beauty! The tendrils of auburn hair at her temples and hairline softened the angularity of her thin features, making her appear temptingly feminine. He boldly drank in the warmth that rested in her now emerald eyes and the upward curve of her lips. "I'm looking forward to the time when you can sit on a horse. I'll wager you're a fine horsewoman."

Alyssa felt heat rise from her neck and sweep across her face. Bewildered by her reaction to Tray, she touched her flaming cheek in distress. He made her feel like laughing with joy. "Thank you, my—Tray. I didn't know one could ride if blind."

"Why not? I'd accompany you. I have a Welsh cob gelding who's trustworthy. He's quite old, but steady. I think you could handle him."

"At one time, I could handle any horse," she replied longingly, remembering those wonderful days not very long ago.

Tray opened the door that led outdoors. He guided her down the stairs, taking a firm grip on her hand. Alyssa had finally stopped cringing every time Tray touched her, partly because he made a point of touching her elbow, arm, shoulder or hand each time he visited with her. Alyssa daintily took the steps without problem. At the base of the stairs, he again offered her his arm and they resumed their leisurely walk to the stable, which stood on the other side of a huge hedge. The day was cool, with scudding gray clouds moving swiftly across the lush green landscape of the valley and snowcapped peaks in the distance.

"Any horse?" he challenged in a teasing tone. "Even stallions?"

"Yes, even a stallion."

"My lady, pardon me for saying so, but women shouldn't be handling something so fierce and dangerous as a stallion."

Alyssa winced inwardly when he called her "my lady." Because of her birthright and her humiliating dishonor, she could never claim that title. Yet she didn't want to correct Tray. His voice sounded light and ebullient, as if he were truly happy.

She raised her chin, a glint of gold in the depths of her emerald eyes. "Stallions respond even better to a woman's hand than a man's."

"Indeed?"

"Men use a whip and brute strength to force a stallion to respect them. It's only the pain that the horse kneels to, not the man. But if you use firmness, your voice and the whip only upon rare occasion, the stallion becomes your friend."

Tray studied her profile, thinking that she had the most provocative lips he'd ever seen. The slender length of her neck was like a white swan's, and he found himself wanting to place small, moist kisses along its entire length, to feel Alyssa respond to him, woman to man. Ruthlessly, he crushed all those longings, knowing that they were only dreams. And dreams never came true. Tray addressed her impertinence over the topic of stallions instead, with a bit of mockery.

"Firmness? Your voice? With a stallion? Never."

"All right," Alyssa fired back, "how did you tame that Arabian stallion of yours? Did you beat him into submission? Did you draw welts upon his skin, bloody him and force him to kneel to you?"

Tray slid his hand beneath her elbow as they approached the stone stable. "Has anyone ever accused you of being outspoken?"

Alyssa halted at his side as she heard a door opening. The wonderful scent of sweet, dried hay enveloped her like a heady perfume. On its heels was the exquisite fragrance of horses and freshly rubbed leather. She inhaled the odors deeply, relaxing.

"My father taught all of us to speak our minds. I suppose your gently bred Englishwomen are taught to bridle their speech?"

He grinned, guiding her into the freshly swept cobble-stone-floored stable. The horses welcomed them with a chorus of whinnies and neighs. "Sometimes silence is the better part of valor, my lady. For men *and* women."

"Well, I won't be bridled! If you ask me for an opinion, I will state it plain."

Tray's smile widened as he slowly eased Alyssa into a walk, moving toward the stalls, which faced one another in long rows. "And I never want you to change that about yourself, little one. I like your honesty. It's refreshing."

She seemed taken aback. "You do?"

"Of course. You remind me of my stallion, Rasheed. A little while ago you asked me if I beat him into submission." Tray pulled her to a halt, mere inches separating them, his hand resting gently against her arm. "I spent a great deal of time, travel and money to acquire Rasheed. I believe his beauty, intelligence and spirit could enhance our more cold-blooded Welsh stock. Ahmed, my Egyptian groom, came with Rasheed. After I had purchased the horse, we began the long journey back to Wales. Ahmed taught me some Arabic and I taught him some Welsh. The

Egyptians, like the Irish, understand horses. Ahmed told me if I ever raised a whip to the stallion, the horse would never forgive me, nor would I ever gain his trust.'' Tray reached out, lightly brushing her flushed cheek, feeling the velvet pliancy of her skin beneath his fingers. Alyssa stood, her unseeing eyes wide and dark, head slightly tilted, listening to his every word. She blinked once, assimilating his grazing touch, but did not cringe back in fear as she had so many times before.

"I have the trust of all my animals that live here at Shadowhawk. And I have the trust of my servants and the tenants who till the soil around my estate. So you see, little one, I agree that firmness coupled with love breeds respect. And trust.'' He gave her arm a light squeeze. "Come, I want you to meet the stallion who carried you and Sean from the ship to Shadowhawk." He added dryly, "He has a decided weakness for females."

Her heart thundered achingly in her breast in those precious seconds when they stood so close to each other. Alyssa could feel the heat of Tray's powerful body, and his male scent was like a welcoming perfume to her awakening senses. Gathering her scattered wits she replied, "Like his master, no doubt."

Tray's laughter was deep and rich, ringing through the scrupulously clean stable.

# Chapter Six

Alyssa's eyes positively glowed with life as Tray introduced her to his stallion, Rasheed, who immediately thrust his small velvety muzzle into her outstretched hands. Resting his hand lightly on her shoulder, Tray watched Alyssa seduce the horse with a soft, cajoling voice and gentle hands as she lavished him with strokes of praise and affection.

"Oh! He's wonderful. Wonderful!" she breathed, taking time to shed her kidskin gloves. Her long, slender fingers outlined and caressed the stallion's head and tiny ears.

"If I didn't know better, I'd say that you, my lady, have put a spell on this rascal," Tray noted wryly. "He's standing like a lamb beneath your hand." Indeed, Rasheed normally would snort and bugle in his stall when anyone approached. Now he stood like a docile gelding, head and neck extended across his stall door to receive all of Alyssa's loving attention.

"He feels so warm and sleek," she whispered, running her hand down from his jaw and following the proud curve of his neck. "And powerful."

"He's all of that," Tray agreed, idly scratching Rasheed's forelock, his gaze locked upon Alyssa. My God, she was radiant. Tray felt as if the breath had been knocked from his body, his heart beginning to pound like a trip-hammer as he watched her come to life. So, this was the real Alyssa. The child-woman who adored nature and animals as much as he did. Her cheeks bloomed rosy with health, and her softly confident voice revealed an inner joy that blanketed both him and the quiet stallion.

"Look at this!" Alyssa whispered, slowly running her hand the length of Rasheed's head.

"What?" Tray asked, pleasure at her unexpected happiness making him smile.

"His forehead . . . why, it's sunken inward. Why? Has he been hurt? A bone broken, perhaps?"

Tray captured her fingers, now cool and smudged from scratching the horse so vigorously. He had expected Alyssa to suddenly freeze, but she waited calmly, her hand relaxed within his as he guided them down the length of Rasheed's head. "Only the Arabian has this dished type of head. Here, feel how the concave shape of his skull allows his nostrils to drink in larger drafts of air."

Alyssa drew closer, her body nearly touching Tray's as she allowed him to outline Rasheed's flaring nostrils with her fingers. A tingle of unmitigated excitement spiraled dizzily through her. Why hadn't she been aware of how gentle Tray's touch had been before? She felt the rough calluses on his palm chafe pleasantly against her flesh, and her attention shifted unconsciously to Tray—not the very rich lord of an estate, but the man. She allowed him to guide her fingers upward, tracing the outline of Rasheed's nostril passage. If her instincts served her correctly, Tray seemed reluctant to release her hand. As reluctant as she was to have him do so. She had to swallow against the onslaught of new emotions that threatened to engulf her, and her voice was faint when she spoke.

"I have heard that the Arabian's endurance is greater than any other horse's."

Tray savored her nearness. "I've ridden him against local horses, even highly touted and very expensive thoroughbreds, and he's bested them all at any distance." He gave the blood bay a friendly pat, watching the stallion nuzzle Alyssa's neck and shoulder. "It seems you have brought the lord of Shadowhawk to his knees, my lady. I've never seen Rasheed quite as gentlemanly as he is in your presence. I'm impressed."

Alyssa blushed becomingly. "I love horses, Tray."

"I'm jealous. I only wish I were Rasheed, able to stand there and receive such undisguised affection from your hands."

Tray's lowered voice vibrated through Alyssa. She was stunned by the veiled emotion she heard in his carefully modulated admission. Her thoughts skipped like a rock tossed across the surface of a pond in their effort to change the path of their conversation.

"Tell me why you bear calluses on your hands. We always thought English lords had only soft, manicured hands."

Tray smiled, pleased with her alertness. How many people, upon contact with his hand, had noted that? Not one. "Just as you find happiness working with horses, little one, I find joy in working closely with the land. It's the Welsh blood in me. On any given day in late spring, after the lambing season and through late autumn, I'll be with my men out in the fields, hauling rocks out of a field so that it may be plowed, or tilling the soil."

Her lips parted in shock. "You? Tilling the fields?"

"Of course. Where is it written that a lord can't feel the warmth of the earth he owns in his hands?"

"Well . . ." Alyssa lifted her head in the direction of his deep, soothing voice. "You're so different," she admitted lamely, "from the English who try to rule us in Ireland."

Tray placed his fingers beneath her elbow, gently guiding her away from Rasheed and down the aisle toward the brood mare stalls. "I wonder when your selective Irish ears will believe that above all else, I am Welsh. And the Welsh love their land as ardently as the Irish love their horses. We've a special pact with this wild, desolate country of ours. Our heritage traces directly to the Druids. And everyone knows that the Druids held special sway over the land and trees. I'm not different, little one. I'd sooner be with my land and my Welsh countrymen than anywhere else."

Alyssa's voice grew husky with emotion. "I owe you an apology."

"No, just your understanding, Aly. That's all I ask between you and me."

His intimate comment created a gamut of feelings within her. As Tray opened the door to a stall and drew her inside, Alyssa could not shake the feeling of warmth that existed like a living, throbbing force between them. After all her abuse at the hands of her English attackers, Tray was showing her that not all men were to be feared or hated. Suddenly, she was curious about this enigmatic Welshman. She planned to ply him later with more questions of his heritage.

"Ah," Tray murmured, drawing Alyssa near him, his hand coming to rest on her shoulder once again. "Our little charge is up and wobbling around. The mare is gray with large dark dapples on her sides. I call her Jenny."

Alyssa smiled over at him, waiting for him to guide her toward the foal. "You call your horses by human names?"

"Another oddity of mine," he assured her, thinking how beautifully her eyes shone when she smiled. He led her to the dark foal at the Welsh mare's side, guiding Alyssa's outstretched hand forward until she could touch it. "I like matching my animals' names to their own individual character.''

Alyssa smiled as the foal boldly stepped forward, its tiny body warm and fuzzy against her as it began to nip at her fingers. ''That's true,'' she agreed softly, lovingly running her hand over the foal. ''Each animal, like each person, is different.''

Tray stood back, arms crossed against his chest, and watched as she bestowed the same effortless affection on the foal as she had earlier with Rasheed. ''I hope you apply that philosophy to me, as well.''

Lifting her head, Alyssa smiled shyly. ''A lord who works in his fields. A man who never lifts a crop to his stallion. I think I will have to erase all that I know about the English and judge you on your own merits instead.''

Tray's gray eyes glimmered with warmth. ''I think I would like that, little one.''

The morning was magic for Alyssa. The sun warmed her skin as Tray walked her from the stable back toward the manor. She suddenly reached out, gripping his forearm, turning to him. ''This afternoon, after my nap and before tea, I thought that I could join you in the drawing room next door. You could tell me more of your Welsh heritage. I mean—that is, unless you have something else to do. . . .''

Tray stared down at her, disbelief etched in his widening gray eyes. Alyssa wanted more of his company? His heart took a hopeful lurch in his chest and he tried to calm his reaction. Was it a miracle? Was she truly beginning to trust him?

He forced down all those emotions, his voice smoothly neutral when he answered, ''Are you sure you don't want to join me out of boredom? I realize now that your room must be like a prison to you, since you seem to thrive on the out-doors."

Alyssa shook her head. "You've given me so much to-day. I'm loath to be put back into bed for the rest of the day."

A beginning of a smile pulled at his mouth as he slowed her to a stop, opening the door to her bedchamber. "Ah, then it is out of boredom," he taunted gently, leading her inside.

"No." Alyssa gripped his arm as she had done before. "If you have the time, and if I'm not a burden to you, please tell me of Wales. Of yourself. I promise you, it's not out of boredom."

He guided her to a chair near the warmth of the fire-place. After she sat down, he pulled the bell cord, ringing for a servant. "Very well, my lady, join me in the blue drawing room at your convenience and you and I will talk upon my favorite topic—Wales."

She gripped her kidskin gloves between her hands, look-ing up at him. "And about you."

Tray saw Maura enter the chamber. "We'll see," was all he said. "Maura will take care of you now." He lifted his head toward the dark-haired servant. "See that she joins me in the blue drawing room after she's rested, Maura."

Maura curtsied with a bright smile on her thin Irish face, noting Lord Trayhern's relaxed features. For once their dark lord appeared truly happy, which only increased the tooth-iness of her smile. "Yes, my lord."

Alyssa nervously smoothed the silk skirt of what Maura referred to as a "simple country dress." As she ran her fin-gers across the material, Maura told her its pale lavender color set off the beauty of her hair. The girl sat her down, insisting upon brushing her long locks until, she was told, they gleamed with burnished gold and wine highlights. The satin slippers on her feet felt odd, for she was used to going barefoot.

Still, Alyssa could not control her erratic pulse as her fingertips moved lightly across the high lace collar that surrounded her throat. The round buttons down the front turned out to be pearls. Pearls! And the long tube sleeves were gathered with lace around each of her wrists. The agony of wanting her sight back knifed through Alyssa as Maura prattled in great detail about what the dress looked like upon her. Maura reminded her of a flitting bird, fluttering excitedly around Alyssa as she added the last touches to her toilette. The maid held up many bottles of perfume for her to sniff and insisted that she choose one. When Alyssa hesitantly picked the jasmine scent, Maura applied a bit behind each of her ears and to the pulse points of her throat and wrists.

By the time she was led into the adjoining room, Alyssa's nervousness was blatantly broadcast by the embroidered linen handkerchief that she knotted and twisted between her fingers as she was led to where Tray stood.

"Come," he invited, "join me here by the fire. Maura? Have Craddock bring us some warm chocolate."

"Right away, my lord."

Tray gave Alyssa an amused glance as he guided her toward the settee next to the huge, open marble hearth.

"Why are you behaving like a nervous young horse?" he teased, releasing her in front of the settee. Tray watched as Alyssa awkwardly lifted the voluminous folds of the silk skirt and sat down. Her burgundy hair cascaded in soft, curving tresses below her small breasts, making her appear even more intensely feminine. Tray sat down in the chair adjacent to her.

"I'm just not used to all this attention," she admitted in a whisper, lovingly touching the material of her dress. "And these clothes. They were made for a queen, not a commoner such as myself."

"You are a queen," he parried quietly, *"Arhiannon."*

Alyssa tilted her head, mystified by the musical language that she could not identify. "What did you just say?"

Tray smiled. "That was a Welsh endearment. I called you my queen."

Her heart skidded sharply. It was as if Tray had reached over and physically caressed her with that lovely Welsh name. Alyssa tried to parry his cajoling flattery.

"Not many queens are born in a thatched hut, raised with the soil of their homeland beneath their fingernails and the darkness of it forever dyed on the bottom of their feet." She raised one dainty foot outward. "It feels strange to be wearing slippers."

Tray rubbed his jaw, watching her animated features. "What are you used to wearing, Aly?"

She blushed as he used his pet name for her again, and her heart gave a lurch in her breast that made her feel slightly giddy. His voice was like rich honey pouring over her each time he called her Aly, as if it, too, were a loving endearment. Was it? Rattled, Alyssa blurted out, "I'm used to what you found me in. My white shirt, black trousers and barefoot."

A frown formed on his face. "I know women in Ireland wear dresses. What could possibly persuade you to wear men's clothes?"

Alyssa gulped back the true answer. For the last four years of her life she had lived in the embrace of the forests, avoiding attacks by the English. She dressed like her older brothers and father, sitting astride her huge chestnut gelding instead of sidesaddle, as ladies were taught to do. It had been her responsibility to find new places in the forest to hide, set up camp and cook for the many men who followed her father and brothers. Sean and a few younger boys were charged with trapping and finding food for the group.

"I...well...you know, living with a father and two older brothers." She licked her lips. "I wore Gavin's castoffs because he was more my size. We didn't have money enough to buy a dress. Or shoes." That wasn't a lie, thank the saints.

Alyssa cringed inwardly, hating to lie to Tray. He, of all people, didn't deserve her deceit. After all, he had saved her and Sean from sure death. Yet her dishonesty was necessary to their continued survival. If she would only get better soon, then Tray would keep his word and send them back to their beloved emerald isle, where they would be safe from English hatred, melting back into the woods, free once again to live and try to find her brothers.

The scowl on Tray's face deepened as he visualized her running shoeless in the damp cold of winter. When he had washed her limbs before she had regained consciousness, he had been poignantly aware of the thick soles on her feet and the stained darkness of the soil rubbed into their calloused surface. "So being around men dictated your choice of clothing?"

"That and little money." Alyssa tilted her head. "Don't be sad. I love the freedom that trousers give me. I can see why men are more active." She gave him a little smile, picking at the folds of the skirt. "I feel trussed up like a horse in harness in this."

Tray smiled distantly. "Men should respect women for the beauty that comes from their hearts and show that affection by providing for them in the best possible way. While you're here, I hope you find the dresses a pleasing change from your other attire."

"Oh, I do! I mean—" her fingers flew to her throat, caressing the pearls "—Maura said these were real pearls. And the lace, it's so fine..."

"As you are—a priceless pearl," he assured her throatily.

Craddock knocked and entered, mercifully saving Alyssa from further embarrassment. Each time Tray spoke in that low, roughened tone, it aroused feelings in her she never knew existed. It was as if her young body were blooming beneath the unexpected caresses of Tray's touch and voice. The sensation left her mouth dry and pulse beating unevenly. Craddock placed a cup and saucer in her hands, and she was grateful for the diversion. When Alyssa placed the liquid to her lips and tasted it, however, she was taken by surprise.

Tray smiled, seeing bewilderment clearly written in her expression when she sipped and tasted the hot liquid. "What's the matter? Isn't it to your liking?"

Alyssa held the saucer between her hands. "Oh, no...what is it?"

He had to stop himself from chuckling at her conspiratorial tone. "Chocolate. From the West Indies. It's the latest rage, I hear. They grind the nut into a powder form, pour scalding hot milk over it and sweeten it with honey. What do you think of it?"

"Wonderful! It tastes so rich..."

Tray gloried in Alyssa's discoveries. Just to watch the tip of her tongue slide across her full lower lip sent an unbidden shaft of pleasure and hotness through him. She was like a doe, incredibly gentle and graceful in all her movements. "Have it whenever you want," he invited. And then his voice became more serious. "As a matter of fact, I think you ought to eat whenever you feel the least bit hungry, to regain that lost weight."

She smiled tentatively, testing her ribs gingerly with her exploring fingers. "I'm like that poor horse I used to see pulling a cart in Wexford, merely a bag of bones."

"Far more lovely than the horse, I assure you. But too skinny for your health's sake."

Alyssa finished off the chocolate and Craddock reappeared to take the cup and saucer from her. She folded her hands in her lap, enjoying the warmth of the fire and the peace that inhabited the drawing room. When had she ever felt like this? She could recall similar feelings when riding her gelding, allowing the sun to warm her thinly clothed body. Or standing along the strand of beach near Wexford, watching the restless, deep jade Irish Sea.

"Better now?" Tray's voice intruded gently.

"Yes, thank you." Alyssa hesitated, then asked tentatively, "What do you look like?"

Tray stared down at his left foot, which resided in a specially made boot to accommodate its deformity. If Alyssa could see him, she would shrink back in terror. "If you are talking of physical beauty, then my half brother is the handsome one. Vaughn has every eligible woman in London after him for marriage."

"I don't care about your half brother. It is you that I want to know about," she countered gently. "Is your hair dark?"

"Yes."

"Brown?"

"No. Black, like a dark, storm-ridden night."

She laughed delightedly, clapping her hands together. "Are you trying to frighten me with your gruff snarls and growls for answers? Never have I met a man so unwilling to brag upon his looks! Why, my brother Dev would gladly bend your ear to tell you what a rake he is. And Gavin would simply stand there with an arrogant look on his handsome face, expecting you to faint at his feet! Are all Welsh so humble?''

A sour smile touched his mouth. ''No, sweet Aly, just me. For—well, let's just say for reasons. I have black hair, gray eyes and Sorche tells me I'm built like a powerful bull, although my height is greater than most other Welsh.''

''And who do you resemble more? Your mother or father?''

''My mother, God rest her soul,'' he admitted, still feeling a dull pain at her loss even though he had never known her. ''Sorche tells me I have her eyes and color of hair. My father contributed his frame and height to round me out.''

''And are your sensitivity and kindness also gifts from your mother?''

He stirred uncomfortably and yet also found himself hungry to speak with her about his life. ''Sorche was my mother's nurse and often told me that Isolde would cry easily. Mother saw beauty in every living thing.'' Tray's voice lowered and he rubbed his brow. ''She was the light of my father's life. She brought happiness everywhere she went.''

Alyssa compressed her lips. ''It must have been terrible to lose her. I'm sorry you didn't get to know her, Tray.'' Her tone grew soft. ''But I think she would be very pleased with the way you help others. No one suffers under your hand, it would seem.''

He managed a harsh laugh and rose out of the chair, limping slowly back and forth in front of the fireplace. ''You misjudge me, Alyssa. My reputation here is one of a man who would ask for your last ounce of sweat and the last drop of blood from your raw and bleeding hands.''

''I do not think unfairness is in your character,'' she countered.

"No, I try to be just. But God knows, I'm far from perfect." Deformed, as a matter of fact, he added bitterly, glancing over at Alyssa. If she knew he was deformed, would she shrink back in terror? Would repugnance and revulsion be mirrored in every nuance of her face as it had with women in the past? Shelby had barely been able to tolerate his deformity. She would pull away from him if his leg accidentally brushed against hers, and she always avoided looking at *it*.

During the spring planting, he spent endless hours out in the fields with his men; it was then that his left leg would ache with fiery pain. Once, he was in so much agony that he lay writhing on the bed, his distorted muscles gone into spasm. Only massage would gently unknot those angry, taut muscles. In his agony, he had begged Shelby to rub his leg, but she tearfully refused, fleeing from their bedchamber. He lay there, fists clenched among the sheets, biting down hard on his lip for nearly an hour until the spasms finally abated and he could manage to sit up and rub his leg himself. Even Shelby, who loved him as fiercely as he had loved her, could not tolerate his twisted limb.

Alyssa's voice broke into his tortured memories. "Who, of all God's creatures, is perfect? I know my father makes mistakes." She smiled wistfully. "And my hotheaded brother, Dev, makes many of them and then boasts about it afterward. No, I think you have a conscience Tray, and that is what separates you from most other imperfect men."

He managed a grim smile, studying her. It was incredible to him that this mere slip of a child-woman could look beyond the obvious and see the truth. She was blind, yet there was something in her makeup that gave her insight and maturity far beyond her years. Alyssa possessed a far greater intelligence than he had ever encountered, and he was hungry to talk at length with her on a myriad of topics just to probe her instinctive insights and feelings.

"I'm sure God never made any woman imperfect," he teased, a slow smile pulling at his mouth.

"Perhaps He blessed the Englishwomen with perfection," Alyssa tossed back with a lighthearted laugh, "but He created imperfections in the likes of me!"

Tray rejoiced at her pure, silvery laughter. "Never!"

"Oh, yes!"

"How are you imperfect?" he challenged.

"I have a terrible temper when I'm pushed too far. And you've already tasted my frankness. Dev accuses me of being the most bullheaded woman whose path he's ever had the sorry luck to cross. And Gavin groans when I break into tears over the beauty of a sunset or the flight of a gull as it glides against the blue of the sky."

Tray walked over to her. He knelt down on one knee, gently taking both her hands in his. "If that is imperfection," he said in a roughened tone, "then I revel in it." His fingers tightened briefly as he saw the startled quality in her wide, innocent eyes. "From what I've witnessed thus far, my lady, you are a woman who knows her own mind. I respect anyone who has an opinion and will stand firm on it. I don't call that stubbornness. And as for your being hotheaded, I would say that it is the nature of your Irish blood. Can one not admire a hotblooded thoroughbred or, indeed, an even more spirited Arabian stallion, because he is temperamental? No," he whispered hoarsely, "your temper is your spiritedness, not to be confused with the behavior of a woman who throws tantrums like a spoiled child."

He reluctantly released Alyssa's trembling fingers and remained in a kneeling position before her. Huge tears had formed in her eyes and he brushed them away with his hands as they trickled down her rose-hued cheeks. "And as for crying because the beauty of a sunset struck your heart or the grace of a gull freed you for an instant from this prison we call earth, I would have gladly shed tears with you at your side...."

## Chapter Seven

Alyssa was roused from her deep and restful sleep by a bustle of activity in the hall. Was it morning yet? Eyes puffy from sleep, she struggled into a sitting position, her auburn hair tumbling across her white flannel nightgown. She heard the door open and then close.

"Maura?"

"No, Tray."

"Is something wrong?"

He walked over to the bed and sat on the edge of it. "Why would you ask that?" As his gaze caressed her sleepy features he had the wild urge to reach out and tame those rebellious strands of hair away from her face.

"There seems to be more noise than usual out in the hall. Is it morning?"

"Yes. Barely dawn." Tray hungrily drank in her relaxed features. He had barely slept all night, replaying their words and picturing her animated features during their discussion yesterday. "I wanted to come in and say goodbye before I left, Aly."

Surprise widened her eyes. "Goodbye? What? I mean, why?"

Tray automatically reached out, his large, calloused hand covering her small, slender one. "A rider came a few hours ago telling me that several of my brood mares at the other estate, which lies south of Shadowhawk, are about to foal.'' He gently ran his thumb across her palm, noting that her hands had calluses on them, too. Knowing that she worked just as hard as he did made Tray feel even closer to her.

Alyssa closed her eyes. "Oh, I thought it was something dangerous."

He smiled and released her hand. "No. I had bred Rasheed to five mares the same week. And now, they are all coming due." His voice took on a wry quality. "I'm afraid I've neglected some of my farming duties since you and Sean have arrived. Normally, I'm down at our other estate a week before the foaling occurs."

Alyssa's shoulders relaxed and she twined her fingers in the blanket on her lap. "How long will you be gone?"

"Perhaps a week. It depends entirely upon the brood mares and when they decide to foal. I've already talked with Sorche and she has promised to look after you. Sean begged me to allow him to come along, but I told him that you would need his company in my absence."

She felt a lump rise in her throat. "I'll miss your reading to me and our talks in the drawing room," she admitted softly.

"Sorche will read to you in my absence."

"I'll miss our walk in the garden that you promised me."

Tray's features grew gentle and he picked up her hand, pressing a kiss to her jasmine-scented skin. "May I make amends, my lady, upon my return?"

Alyssa's lips parted as she felt his masculine mouth graze her flesh with provocative lightness. Her entire hand tingled pleasantly from his kiss. "Yes," she whispered weakly, aware of her heart pounding in her breast. She felt bereft as Tray released her hand and rose from the bed.

Tray stood there, staring down at her intensely, memorizing her upturned, innocent face. "I'll be back as soon as I can, little one," he promised.

Ten days... Alyssa turned away from the brilliant sunlight, realizing it was late afternoon by the sun that cascaded through the crystal glass of the window. She morosely counted the steps from the window to the chair that sat near the fireplace in her bedchamber. She was restless, like a young horse who had been stall-bound. As she sat, carefully folding her silk skirts round her, Alyssa admitted the truth to herself—she missed Tray.

Sorche worried about her. She had been waking up at night, screaming. Embarrassment had flooded her when Sorche admitted that Tray would often sit at her side, gently stroking her hair and soothing her nightmares away so that she would drift into sleep, free of those haunting memories of the man who had cruelly raped her. And although Maura, who stayed near her while Tray was away, tried to duplicate those methods when the past came to terrorize her, Alyssa could never return to sleep. She pondered Tray's power over her subconscious. Was he a Druid? She recalled with great fondness how her schoolmasters had plied her with the power of the Druids. Was it his touch? His hand upon her brow, soothing her like a frightened child? She did not know.

Ten days had left her listless. At night, after Sean kissed her on the cheek and hugged her good-night, her mind often returned to the fact that she had lied to Tray. He didn't know she was a criminal to England, as was Sean. What would he do if he found out he was harboring fugitives? Would Tray turn them over to the English? Would she find herself at Newgate, waiting to be hanged, and Sean sent to a short life in the Welsh coal mines?

She had rehearsed the words to tell him the truth, to apologize for her lies. He would be angry, no doubt. Alyssa tried to think of a way to focus Tray's anger on herself and not Sean. Tray was not without a heart. Perhaps she could persuade him to free Sean, or at least keep him here at Shadowhawk as a servant.

Alyssa's mind searched relentlessly for the right time and place to admit her deceit to Tray. They couldn't live indefinitely at Shadowhawk and not be discovered. Time. She needed more time in order to know Tray better; in order to know how best to approach him and make her confession. If only Tray would return home—to her.

The sound of horses drawing a coach up the cobbled drive to Shadowhawk awakened her. Although she had no idea of time, Alyssa was vaguely aware of shouts, someone running down the hall toward the foyer and the snort of horses. She had cried herself to sleep and now her head pounded unrelentingly as a result.

"Lord Trayhern's home! Welcome, welcome, my lord. We've missed your presence." The booming voice of Craddock carried throughout the house.

Alyssa sat bolt upright, her hair swirling around her shoulders. Anxiously, she reached toward the bottom of the bed, trembling fingers locating her velvet dressing robe. In a haste born of need, she managed to get it on and the sash tied poorly around her waist. The room was cool, which meant the fire was in need of being replenished. She heard further cries and shouts of welcome from the other servants and then Sorche's voice sounding loudly over all of them. Alyssa forced herself to count the steps from the bed to the fireplace, her left hand outstretched as she crossed the expanse in darkness. Tray was home, Tray was home, her thudding heart said, pounding unevenly in her breast. She felt the smooth, cool marble of the fireplace and leaned down, finding and retrieving a few split logs and throwing them into the coals on the hearth. As the coals hungrily licked at the wood and sparked to new life, they bathed her bedchamber in a warm glow. Alyssa waited.

It was nearly two in the morning and Tray could feel exhaustion pulling at him. What had kept him awake and alert as he sat in the coach speeding toward Shadowhawk was the promise of seeing Alyssa once again. Sweet God, how he had missed her! For the first time, he had taken little joy in helping the foals be born and seeing them stand for the first time. He had often thought of how he would have enjoyed having Alyssa there at his side. It was so easy to share the simple pleasures of life with her.

Tray pulled Sorche aside as they walked toward the west wing, where the main bedchambers were located. "Alyssa? How is she? And Sean?"

Sorche squeezed him affectionately, keeping her hand on his arm. "Sean is wonderful! But Alyssa..."

Tray's gray eyes grew dark as he stared down at his foster mother. "She's not well?"

A knowing smile twinkled in Sorche's eyes. "My son, she has been pining away since the morning you left." And then she scowled. "Hasn't hardly eaten a thing! I kept telling her that she'd be carried away in a gust of wind, but she just lost her appetite."

Tray clenched his fist at his side and said nothing. It wasn't Sorche's fault that Alyssa wasn't eating properly. Damn! Didn't Aly realize how terribly underweight she was? It wasn't healthy! "What else?" he asked tightly.

"The poor lamb has been having those dreams every night. At times, I'd wake up and hear her screaming."

Tray looked down at her sharply. "Didn't you have Maura stay with her?"

"Of course I did. Maura slept in the chair every night. And when Alyssa would begin screaming, Maura would stroke her head like you did, but it had very little, if any, effect. Alyssa would just curl into a knot, hugging a pillow and sobbing."

His eyes narrowed. Hellfire and damnation! He knew his leaving wouldn't do her any good! And God knew, he hadn't slept well himself, missing those dark nights when he would doze lightly in the chair after Alyssa fell asleep.

"Don't blame yourself, Mother. You did all that was possible." He gave her an affectionate smile and leaned down to kiss her brow. "I'll see Alyssa before retiring. Tell Craddock I won't be needing his services tonight."

Sorche nodded and halted. "Don't be angry with her, Tray."

He placed his hand on the brass doorknob that led to Alyssa's bedchamber. "How can you be angry with an Irish fairy?" he posed softly.

Sorche grinned broadly, her eyes twinkling. Irish fairies were revered as magically beautiful creatures who held sway over men with the power of love. "You can't," she returned. "Good night."

Alyssa slowly lifted her chin as a soft knock sounded at the door. She stood frozen beside the mantel, the light from the fire bathing her body. Her lips parted as she breathed out his name like a reverent prayer.

"Tray?"

"Yes," he murmured, closing the door behind him. Suddenly, all his exhaustion lifted as he came inside the room, drinking in her translucent beauty. Ten days had healed all the bruises that had discolored her face. Hungrily, he took in Alyssa's clear, flawless emerald eyes, his body tightening with a hotness that took his breath. My God, she was like a lovely wraith wavering before the fire, the dark green velvet of her robe cascading over her slender body, the curved ripeness of her breasts rising and falling quickly beneath the fabric. His gaze swept from her tightly knit fingers resting in front of her, up across her breasts and exposed, slender throat to her magnificently parted lips. Tray groaned inwardly, wanting to taste her softness, the womanliness that he knew still awaited untouched within her, regardless of her cruel experience. The dark wine of her hair shot through with gold lay like a cloak across her proudly drawn shoulders, and he longed to comb his fingers through those shining tresses, burying his face in the feel and scent of their strands.

He fought to control his roiling emotions and walked over to her. Mere inches separated them as he picked up her hand, pressing a warm and moist kiss upon it, inhaling the scent of her body woven with the faint fragrance of jasmine. "In ten days," he told her in a low, gritty tone, "you've grown more beautiful, if that's possible, Aly."

She trembled beneath his voice, his touch firm upon her damp, cold fingers. There were a hundred things she wanted to blurt out to him, but all of them were inappropriate to say to a man who was little more than a stranger to her. "The sun left my life when you departed, my lord," she whispered softly, lowering her lashes, her voice aching with tears.

Tray released her hand and gently cupped her chin, raising her head so that her eyes, when they opened, would be trained on his. The excruciating temptation to drop a kiss upon her lips was almost unbearable, yet he knew she would recoil if he did so. Fighting the dangerous signals of his male body, he grazed her jaw with this thumb. "It was no less dark without your presence, Aly, believe me," he admitted rawly. He released her from his hold and stepped away to the safety of the other side of the fireplace. He surveyed her flushed features, aware of the darkness lingering beneath her thick lashes.

"Are you going to become like Rasheed and eat poorly each time I leave you behind?" he teased gently.

Aly managed a slight grimace and found the chair, sitting down before her weakened knees gave out beneath her. "I saw you took him along."

"For the very reason I've told you. He goes off his feed, gets moody and kicks his stall to pieces." A slight smile touched the corners of Tray's mouth. "Tell me, have you been temperamental and kicked your bedchamber to bits, too?"

Alyssa laughed delightedly. "I've not eaten much, to be truthful, my lord. As to my temperament, well, you must ask Sorche and the servants about that." She raised her hand, gesturing at the room around them. "And, as you can see, I've not damaged your property."

Tray grinned, caught by her expressive face and glowing eyes. Was he seeing rightly? Had Alyssa missed him as much as he had her? He was too exhausted and too happy right now to doubt his feelings. "I see I'll have to take you along with me next time to keep you out of trouble. We've got lambing season coming upon us in another few weeks. I'll be leaving again soon for the high country to help my shepherds."

Alyssa gasped, clapping her hands together like a child. "You would take me? I can be of help! I've often helped during lambing."

"If Dr. Birch says that you can travel, little one, you may go with me." His voice took on a warning. "But you must show me that you're ready to travel. I have to see you eating heartily and putting back on that weight, Aly. And you have to prove that you can walk and continue to rebuild your strength."

"Oh, I will! I promise I will, Tray! I love working with animals so much. Please, let me accompany you next time. I promise I won't get in the way!"

He smiled, reassured that Alyssa was all right. "Not only that, but you must be able to sit astride a horse for hours at a time." Her face lit up with so much happiness that it brought unexpected tears to his eyes. Clearing his throat, Tray said, "If the sun deigns to shine this afternoon, we shall test your horsemanship abilities. Good night, *Arhiannon.*"

Her lips trembled as she whispered, "Good night, Tray..."

Maura was humming an old Irish lullaby as she deftly wove the thick strands of Alyssa's hair into one huge braid down the middle of her back. Alyssa didn't want her hair piled high upon her head, as was the custom among the English. Instead, feathery bangs brushed her arched eyebrows and delectable tendrils wisped around her temples.

Alyssa could barely sit still, having slept long and deeply after Tray had left her bedchamber. Miraculously, none of the ugly, haunting dreams disturbed her sleep. At noon, after completing her toilette, Maura had brought in a light wool riding habit that she said matched the color of Alyssa's eyes. Alyssa yearned to be in Tray's bantering company once again. How she had missed his deep, thoughtful voice and his gentle, teasing manner.

"You look lovely, Miss Alyssa," Maura sighed, standing back and smiling. "Here's your hat," she said, pinning it at an angle on her head. "Lord Trayhern said the wind was a mite sharp out there and he felt a wool riding habit, boots and a warm hat were in order." Handing her forest green kidskin gloves, Maura proudly led Alyssa toward the back door and to the stables, where Lord Trayhern and Stablemaster Thomas were patiently waiting for them.

Alyssa took a deep breath of air, aware of the tangy salt of the sea mixing with the scent of the land that it bordered. The sun was shining brightly and she lifted her face toward it momentarily, bathing in the warmth of its rays.

That simple gesture made her look exquisite in Tray's dark gray eyes. He slanted a glance toward Thomas, realizing the old man was just as taken with Alyssa's natural beauty as he was. What man wouldn't be? he thought dourly, reaching out to take her gloved hand. Maura made a small curtsy and walked quickly back to the manor.

"My lady, you shame the very beauty of the land surrounding you," Tray murmured.

Alyssa smiled, lifting her chin, giving Tray's hand a small squeeze of welcome. Nothing could ruin this day for them. "Tell me, are Welshmen as tripping with their tongues as Irishmen?"

Tray smiled and gestured for Thomas to bring the small gray Welsh cob gelding to them. "I don't know. You tell me. I'm sure many young men praised your unparalleled beauty. Now, if you'll be patient with me, I'm going to lift you into the sidesaddle."

"Sidesaddle?" Alyssa asked, disappointment in her voice.

"Of course."

"But—I mean, I usually rode bareback . . . like a man," she admitted hesitantly.

Tray threw back his head and laughed deeply. "I might have known! You wear a man's pants and ride like one, too, I'll wager." He tried to swallow his mirth, realizing she was embarrassed. "Have you ever ridden sidesaddle?"

"A few times, my lord. Enough to know I won't make a spectacle of myself by falling off," she charged coolly, a glimmer of feistiness in her eyes.

Tray slid his hands around her narrow waist and her hands instinctively came to rest on his powerful forearms. As he lifted her into the awaiting saddle, Tray caught the faint scent of her sweet fragrance, his senses reeling with the closeness to her. He gently settled her into the saddle, keeping a hand on her hip until he was satisfied she would not fall.

"Very good," he praised, admiring how straight Alyssa sat, her small shoulders proudly squared. She possessed a natural horseman's posture, he thought, placing the leather reins in her hands. Tray mounted the mettlesome Rasheed, who now danced beneath him. He spoke quietly to his Arab, and instantly the blood bay arched his magnificent neck, head perpendicular to the ground, and became still. "I've attached a halter lead to Old Ned, just in case he decides to take charge."

Alyssa leaned down, patting the small gray horse with obvious affection. "Old Ned and I will become the best of friends," she promised. "He won't run away with me."

But I might, Tray thought, feeling that dazzling smile of hers nearly make his heart explode within his chest. "Be patient with me this one time, Aly. Being blind may cause some problems you've not been challenged with as yet. If you're going to get dizzy, I want to be an arm's reach away to stop you from falling."

Alyssa nodded, prepared to begin their ride. "I'm ready, my lord."

He warmed to the way she teasingly called him by his title. "Very well, let's start off at an easy walk, shall we?"

Just the movement of a horse beneath her once again brought a flush of joy to Alyssa's cheeks. As Tray guided the spirited Rasheed toward the snow-dotted upper pastures that gently climbed up toward the rocky mountains in the distance, he saw another new and intoxicating facet to Alyssa. From the moment they had begun the ride, she had opened up to him, spinning story after story of her youthful days in Ireland. He discovered a great deal about the young Alyssa, which only made the woman now riding scant inches from him, occasionally touching his highly polished boot with her own, enthrall him that much more. Her laughter was like the sweet summer wind; her eyes the color of the forests he loved so much. She rode in graceful concert with the horse she was astride. Tray had never laughed so much or so often as he did in that one hour. And, Alyssa shyly admitted on their way back to Shadowhawk, neither had she.

"Please, Tray, can we trot? I yearn to go at more than just a walk! Haven't I proven to be good as my word? No dizzy spells, no loss of balance?" She reached out, her fingers coming in contact with his muscular thigh and brushing the fabric of his buckskin riding breeches. She instantly withdrew her hand, mortified by her blunder.

Her touch had been anything but embarrassing to Tray. The lightness of her fingertips grazing his hard, muscled thigh tightened his entire body into painful longing for her. He savagely quelled his desires, responding to her request as if nothing had happened.

"We're about five minutes away from the stable. Think you can trot that far?"

"Of course!" she cried, nudging Old Ned with her heel.

They arrived at the stable breathless with laughter. Tray dismounted and came around to Alyssa. The laughter died on her lips as he spanned her waist with his large hands and lifted her free of the saddle. As he gently lowered her to the ground, her breasts lightly brushed against his chest. Old Ned sidled toward them unexpectedly when Rasheed turned, and to keep Alyssa out of the melee, Tray set her down between him and the stable wall, briefly pinning her body intimately against his. He saw the smile die in her eyes and her lips suddenly part in silent protest. Tray flushed beneath his tanned features. Unable to see what had occurred, Alyssa clearly thought he had done it on purpose.

"I—I think it's time I go in," she whispered, her hands resting flatly against his broad chest.

Tray cursed silently and stepped away, breaking contact with her. "Of course." His voice was curt and cool. Damn!

Stablemaster Thomas appeared and he glowered at the man. "Take her inside, Thomas."

"Yes, my lord."

Tray stood there, watching Thomas guide Alyssa back toward the steps of Shadowhawk, seething with inner rage. Well? Hadn't he wanted to press her body next to his? Of course he did. A hundred times before. It hurt him to see the sudden terror in Alyssa's eyes as she had brushed against his chest. She was beginning to trust him, but not as a man. Just as some neutered friend who wouldn't harm her. He raked his fingers through his dark hair, throwing the reins of the horses to the awaiting stable boy, and limped away, embroiled within his own fury. He wanted to be more than a friend to her; he wanted to become man to her woman, love her, care for her and cherish her as she so richly deserved.

Alyssa awoke alert and refreshed after her daily nap. Stretching languidly, she rummaged around and found her velvet dressing robe, then slipped it on. The melodic strains of a harp being lovingly played came from the blue drawing room. She sat on the bed, listening to the pleasant alto sounds. She quickly rose, tightening the sash at her waist, and began counting her steps toward the other chamber. As usual, the door was partially open and Alyssa quietly stepped around it.

Tray sensed Aly's presence, his hand freezing on the strings of the medium-sized harp that rested against his shoulder. He gently placed the instrument aside and rose.

"Did I awaken you with my poor playing?"

Alyssa shook her head, a tentative smile on her lips. Her hair was unbound and soft, untamed tendrils framed her face. "No," she whispered softly, "I had just awakened. That was beautiful, Tray. Why didn't you tell me you played the Irish harp?"

He smiled at her, thinking how like a sleepy child she appeared; all her defenses were down and vulnerability showed in her drowsy features. He picked up her hand, placing it on his arm, and guided her to the settee near the fire.

"You never asked," he told her, ringing for a servant.

Alyssa pouted, not realizing how provocative she appeared. "Must I tear all these wonderful talents from you? Why can't you be like other men and brag about your accomplishments?"

Tray rested his arm against the mantel, leisurely exploring her with his eyes. "I may have been raised by an Irishwoman, but I didn't take on all the traits of the Irish. At least not the gift of boasting," he amended, smiling.

Alyssa pulled up her legs and tucked them beneath her, relaxing on the settee. "Humbleness is a Welsh trait?"

"We let our abilities tell others what we are and are not," Tray agreed soberly. He lifted his head as Craddock appeared at the door.

"Are you hungry, Alyssa? It's nearly ten and dinner has already been served. Craddock's here—and he could get you something from the kitchen."

Alyssa remembered her promise to Tray to try to regain her lost weight. "I'll have whatever Tray had," she told Craddock.

Craddock's grizzled features looked stunned for a moment. "Miss Alyssa, he ate enough for a horse!"

"Then give her a cob's portion," Tray said, suppressing a smile.

She clapped her hands, collapsing into a fit of laughter after Craddock bowed and left. "Is that what I am to you? A lowly cob, useful only for working?"

"No. You're small, barely one-third of me. Why do you think I call you little one?" he taunted.

Shrugging shyly, Alyssa folded her hands in her lap. "Is that also Welsh? Pet names for everyone? You name your horses. You give me names."

"Be happy I've given you pleasant names."

Her smile broadened. "I truly missed you, Tray."

The admission caught him off guard and he sobered. Alyssa was so different from cultured Englishwomen, who were taught to coyly hide behind their fans and bat their kohl-lined eyes at men, playing conversational games that were supposed to ensnare them in their elegantly laid traps. In the past, Tray had coolly made the proper replies, the proper gestures, but never encouraged these flirtations. Yet he found Alyssa's frankness dangerously alluring.

"Didn't your father ever teach you never to be blatantly honest with a man?" he baited gently.

Her expression mirrored her bewilderment, artless in feminine wiles as she lifted her chin toward him. "My father taught us that truth and honesty were to be worshiped next to God. If I have offended you—"

"No, sweet Aly, you've not offended me. You've complimented me, and I feel a bit guilty for teasing you because of your forthrightness. Am I forgiven?"

She thought about it for a moment, puckering her lips. Then Alyssa's face blossomed into a forgiving smile. "Only if you promise to take me riding again tomorrow!"

"If the weather remains mild," Tray countered.

"And I have one more request of you, my lord."

He raised one eyebrow. "I'd give you anything you wanted, little one. What is it?"

She was stunned by the sincerity in his voice. Making a small gesture with her hand she asked, "Will you play the harp once more? It brings back so many wonderful memories of Ireland. And of my family...."

## Chapter Eight

Vaughn brooded as the gray stone of Shadowhawk came into view. The coach ride had been long and tiring. He could have stayed in London and taken up an invitation to several parties and a ball that would take place this coming weekend if it hadn't been for Tray's urgent request that he return to Shadowhawk with all possible speed.

He absently stroked his carefully groomed blond mustache between his manicured fingers. Today he was dressed like any well-bred gentleman, in highly polished black boots, fashionably tailored gray trousers and matching coat, with a white silk shirt underneath. It was a relief to get out of the itching, poorly fitting officer's uniform he had to wear all the time. Well, soon his stint in the army would be up and he could return to his favorite pastimes. His brows drew together as Shadowhawk loomed ever closer before him. Let Tray play farmer. He would simply spend the money he made in the London gambling salons on ladies, the opera and his greatest joy, horse racing.

The coach came to a slow halt, the clatter of horses' hooves sounding sharply against the cobblestones. The late morning was cloudless and exceedingly sunny, making Vaughn squint as he stepped lightly from the coach. Pursing his full, sensual lips, he hoped his stay at Shadowhawk would be brief. He couldn't stomach Tray for long.

Craddock opened the door for him. "Welcome, Master Trayhern."

"Where's Tray? I don't have much time and I want to get this over with."

The Welsh butler bowed deeply, keeping his face expressionless. "Lord Trayhern is in the blue drawing room. I can show you—"

Vaughn flipped his gloves and hat to the butler. "That won't be necessary. I'll find my own way."

"As you wish, Master Vaughn."

It had been nearly a year since he had last been to Shadowhawk. Vaughn strode down the wide hallway, magnificent in his carriage, his broad shoulders drawn back in pride. Halfway down the carpeted hall, he slowed, listening. The soft strains of a harp being played brought him to a halt. He turned and gripped the brass doorknob and pushed the door open.

Alyssa looked up from playing the harp. Tray had encouraged her to try her hand at the instrument, giving her a lesson each morning. Thinking that he had returned from being called to the stable, she smiled.

"I don't think my musical ability will ever match yours." She gently set the harp back down.

Vaughn's eyes narrowed. He shut the door, staring across the room at the woman who sat elegantly with the harp. She looked familiar, and yet... He cocked his head. Didn't she see him? God knew, she had the most beautiful green eyes he'd ever encountered. Why did she look so familiar?

"Tray?"

Alyssa heard movement and tilted her head, puzzled. Tray always announced himself whenever he came into a room so he wouldn't startle her, as did the servants. Again, she heard someone walking closer to her. She reached out, fingers clutching the harp for support, and rose. "Tray? Is that you?"

Vaughn halted, disbelief etched in his widening eyes. He stood frozen in the center of the room, staring at her. Staring at Alyssa Kyle, daughter of Colin Kyle, the traitor. His lips drew back from his teeth, his snarl coming out low and filled with hatred.

"You . . . I thought I'd gotten rid of you."

That voice! Alyssa gasped in terror, her clenched hands flying to her breasts. She took a step back, bumping the chair. All the horror that had taken place aboard the ship sprang to vivid life in her mind. This was the same man who had humiliated and raped her on the bloody deck of that wretched vessel. Her mind whirled in confusion. Who was he? How did he get here? Tray hadn't told her they were expecting anyone, and yet she had heard the coach draw up outside. Lips parted, Alyssa took another half step back, knocking over the chair. "No!" she whispered rawly, holding out her hand. "No, stay away from me!"

Vaughn cursed loudly and moved with lightning-quick reflexes to cover the distance between them. Then, as he watched her flail awkwardly to escape him, he suddenly realized she was blind. A ribbon of satisfaction soared through him. Good! The Irish bitch deserved it.

As he reached out to capture her outstretched arm, his anger grew tenfold. What was this woman doing here, dressed in English finery, looking like the mistress of Shadowhawk? His fingers wrapped cruelly around Alyssa's slender wrist and he jerked her toward him. Vaughn knew without a doubt that this was Tray's doing. Damn the bastard! He was harboring a known traitor! A criminal to the Crown! Well, he had gone too far this time. Too far!

Alyssa whimpered as the bruising force of her assailant's fingers gripped her wrist. She remembered his strength, the entire rape, the pain. Her unbound hair flew around her shoulders as he savagely yanked her to him, her breasts colliding against his solid chest. A strangled cry was choked from her as she fought to free herself.

"No, you don't," Vaughn breathed, a grin coming to his mouth. "Struggle all you want, whore, but you aren't going to get away from me again. You're going to Newgate, where you'll hang alongside that bastard father of yours."

The world exploded around her. Alyssa felt herself being wrenched away from her enemy and she lost her balance, falling to the carpeted floor. The growl of Tray's voice broke through her terror.

"Get away from her." Tray positioned himself between Vaughn and Alyssa, breathing hard.

Vaughn glared at him. "Harboring criminals now, brother?" he snarled.

Tray's eyes narrowed dangerously. "The only criminal here is you." He took an ominous step forward. "Touch her, and I'll make sure you won't again."

"You're a traitor, a traitor to England." Vaughn jabbed a finger down at Alyssa. "That's Alyssa Kyle."

"I know."

Vaughn tensed. "Do you also know she's the daughter of Colin Kyle, one of the three men responsible for the Irish rebellion that erupted in Wexford? Or are you conveniently forgetting that she was caught beside her father, firing pistols at our English soldiers! I saw her kill one of my own cavalrymen. She's a hellion!" He straightened up, his blue eyes turning feral. "I gave orders to have her thrown on the death cart. And now I find her here."

"Sit down," Tray growled at Vaughn, his feelings torn between hurt over Alyssa's deceit and hatred for his half brother.

He turned, devoting his attention to Alyssa. She was so pale that Tray thought she might faint, and the blue bruises around her left wrist sent a shudder of fury through him. A hundred thoughts and emotions careened through Tray. He had kept Vaughn's visit a secret, wanting to surprise Alyssa. Vaughn had been the only person he could think of to help free her innocent father.

The instant his hands wrapped about her arms to help her rise, Alyssa cringed, holding her hands up against her face as if to ward off a coming blow.

"It's Tray," he said through clenched teeth.

As Tray brought her to her feet, Alyssa found she could barely stand. Gripping his soft chamois shirt, she fought back a sob.

"I'm sorry, Tray," she whispered. "So sorry..."

Grimly, he led Alyssa back to her bedchamber and then rang for a maid to take care of her. His stomach knotted as he saw the same terror Alyssa had exhibited upon first coming to Shadowhawk. He laid a firm hand on her trembling shoulder.

"Maura will be here shortly," he said, his voice clipped and hard.

Alyssa raised her chin, her cheeks wet with silent tears. "Tray...I tried to tell you so many times...I—I tried to tell you, but I didn't have the heart to make you unhappy after all you had given us." She sobbed, burying her face into her hands. "I didn't mean to hurt you. I'm sorry...sorry...."

Her words tore at his heart. Tray grimly turned on his heel, moving through the partially opened door and going back into the drawing room. All of his anger focused on Vaughn, who stood belligerently before the fireplace, arms across his chest, glaring back at him. He limped to a halt a few feet away from him.

"I think you owe me an explanation," Vaughn ground out. "You called me here. Why?"

"Alyssa said her father was mistakenly thrown into prison because she and her family were caught between the English and those who rebelled."

Vaughn snorted violently, his blue eyes flashing disgust. "Lying little chit!"

Tray froze. "You will refrain from calling her any further names."

"What's this? Has she got you wrapped around her finger, half brother? I grant you, she's a stunning beauty." And then he grinned. "Far more beautiful than when we captured her in those filthy men's clothes, her hair muddied and feet without shoes. Don't tell me when you went to get that boy in the cell, you took pity on her? Still picking up strays!" Vaughn sneered. "Only this time, you're harboring a criminal."

Tray eyed Vaughn warily. "Tell me what you know of her and her family."

Vaughn relaxed visibly, assured that Tray's black anger was once again under control. Tray's temper was slow to be aroused, but when it was, Vaughn had no desire to invite it upon himself. "We have been hunting the Kyles, all four of them, over in Ireland for the last three years. They were part of Wolfe Tone's cause and helped smuggle stolen firearms, gunpowder and the like, hoarding them until they could come out of hiding and openly challenge us. The Kyles also raided the English manors and estates during that time."

"Did they murder anyone?"

Vaughn shrugged. "No, just stole food."

"And you say Alyssa was firing a pistol at you?"

He grinned. "It's hard to miss the color of her hair from horseback, half brother. Yes, I saw her, and I saw one of my men fall."

Tray took a deep, unsteady breath, unable to believe that Alyssa would ever kill someone. Had she been the consummate liar, making him believe that she and her entire family were victims? He rubbed his mouth, glaring at Vaughn. "And what of Sean, the young boy? Are you going to stand there and tell me that he was also firing a pistol at you?"

Vaughn laughed deeply. "No, but in our search for prisoners we found him hiding beside the carcass of a dead horse and brought him along. He was in the area of the battle and, to me, that makes him guilty."

"And Colin Kyle? Where is he?"

"In Newgate, awaiting the hangman's noose. As his daughter soon will be," he ground out.

Tray stiffened. The very thought of a hangman's rope slipping around her slender, alabaster neck sent a chill through him. No, Vaughn couldn't be allowed to take her back to London. One part of Tray wanted to strangle Alyssa by his own hand, and yet another part of him, his serrated heart, wanted to keep her with him.

"No," he decided, "Alyssa is staying here with her cousin Sean."

"Are you daft? You're hiding a criminal, a murderer! What's gotten into you?" Vaughn's mouth tightened. "This is one time you aren't going to have your way. You may be the eldest, but my jurisdiction as an English officer outweighs what you want in this case."

"She's blind, for God's sake!" Tray roared. "Blind! What threat could she be to England now? God knows, she can barely do anything for herself, much less pick up that pistol you've accused her of wielding and hurt anyone!"

Agitated, Vaughn circled the drawing room, his face livid. "She could be without legs and arms and I'd still haul her to Newgate! Get it through your thick Welsh head—she's a traitor!"

"To England," Tray reminded him. "That doesn't bother me very much."

"Don't start about Wales and your love of the Irish," Vaughn snarled savagely. "For all intents and purposes, you're practically a traitor to England yourself! You shun English parties and balls. You speak that bloody Welsh tongue and insist upon hiring Welsh and Irish servants instead of proper English ones!" He halted, his voice rolling across the room's expanse. "Don't push me on this one, Tray. There's nothing you can do to stop me from taking her to Newgate."

Tray drew himself up, his gray eyes colorless as he met and held Vaughn's glare. "Oh, yes there is," he countered softly.

"What?" Vaughn scoffed.

"I've taken Alyssa as my mistress. She's my property, and as the earl's eldest son, I have placed her under my protection. You, the courts and even Parliament itself wouldn't dare take her. Not if I know the English. No, the Trayherns' hold on the coal industry would make them all back off. They have no wish to offend us. Their homes and industry need our coal too desperately for them to interfere in this matter."

Vaughn's face turned a mottled red. "*Her?* A murderess and a hater of the English as a mistress? I would rather bed down with a snake than that murdering bitch!"

Tray crossed the distance between them in five strides and grabbed Vaughn by the lapels. He slammed his half brother into the wall, his teeth bared.

"One more word out of your mouth about her, half brother, and I'll bloody that handsome face of yours!"

Vaughn muttered a curse. "I won't let you get away with this. I'll tell Father. He won't put up with that Irish—" Vaughn felt Tray's grasp tighten, choking off his air. "Mistress or no mistress, Father won't let you keep her. She's a blot on our good name."

Tray smiled bloodlessly, his gray eyes glittering as he released Vaughn and stepped away. "Try it, Vaughn. I won't stop you. It's a well-known fact that Father cares nothing for my personal life so long as my farm and the livestock continue to fill his coffers with gold."

Vaughn jerked his coat down, brushing it angrily. "You believe her, don't you? She's turned your head."

"I intend to question her right now, Vaughn," Tray said slowly, carefully enunciating each word. "So far, I have your side of what occurred. Now I will ask for hers."

He snorted. "How very fair of you, my Welsh half brother. Go ahead, apply all those bloody rules you live by to her! But I warn you, if you end up swallowing her story instead of mine, some night soon she'll slit your throat." He took a few steps away from Tray and turned, his face taut. "Keep her, then. And when you're dead, I'll become the eldest son in the family. So draw your blind Irish mistress into your arms. Just remember, I saw her fight like a hellcat after we captured her, biting and clawing anyone she could get near."

Tray said nothing as Vaughn stalked out of the drawing room. He stood for a long moment, trying to collect his scattered feelings, then strode determinedly toward Alyssa's bedchamber.

He pushed the door wide, stepping inside. Alyssa was sitting in her favorite chair near the fireplace, her hands knotted in her lap. Her head snapped up as he entered.

"It's Tray," he said automatically. His heart wrenched in his chest when he saw the terror drain from her face. Silence built around them like brittle crystal as he approached her.

His gray eyes darkened with emotion. "I want you to tell me what happened at that battle, Alyssa. I need the truth."

Alyssa's mouth was dry and her heart pounded achingly in her breast. "M-my father and brothers needed my help when they met the English."

"Had you helped them in other skirmishes?" he asked tightly.

Alyssa shook her head. Her voice was raw and unsteady. "No, I always stayed behind to cook and mend for the men of our group. And whenever they would return from stealing food from the English, I would reload their pistols for them."

Tray knelt down in front of her, his brow furrowed. "You're accused of killing an English cavalryman. Is that true? Did you shoot him?"

Alyssa twisted the linen handkerchief savagely between her cold, damp fingers. "I—"

Tray reached out, gripping both her hands in one of his. "Don't lie to me, Alyssa," he commanded harshly. "Your life and Sean's depend upon your honesty."

She jerked her hands free, as if burned. "I was behind the barricade reloading pistols when the third cavalry charge came," she cried, gripping the arms of the chair. "They had already broken our line and they were murdering our people instead of taking them prisoner! Don't you understand? We were only defending ourselves!"

Tray rose, his face anguished. "Did you kill?"

Alyssa's face grew wretched. "One cavalry officer was coming through, cutting down children and women with his saber!" She sobbed and put her hand across her quavering lips. Huge tears streamed down her taut, colorless cheeks. "I—I saw him coming straight for me and I froze. I was so frightened," she continued in a hoarse voice. "I remember raising the pistol I had just loaded. I aimed it and then closed my eyes, firing. The next thing I knew, the man's horse fell forward, hitting me and flinging me aside. I remember being dazed, my brother Dev dragging me to my feet. A-as I got up, I saw the Englishman had been impaled upon the stake of an overturned wagon."

Tray's mouth compressed and he fought back images of the bloody scene. "You didn't shoot him then?"

She shook her head morosely. "N-no. I shot his horse in the chest. That's why he fell."

Relief surged through Tray. "Sweet God in heaven," he muttered, running his fingers through his hair. "You could have been killed."

"I didn't care, Tray!" she cried. "How would you feel if the English had taken your farm, your home? They treated us like animals! Animals! And all we had done wrong was fail to pay the high taxes that they had placed on us! Is that a crime? Is it wrong to feel angry when all you've ever loved has been taken from you?"

Tray had no easy answer for her. He rested his arm against the mantel and stared at the fire. Only the peaceful sound of wood crackling in the hearth broke the turgid silence between them. He shut his eyes tightly, unable to put aside his anguished thoughts.

"Who—who was that man?" Alyssa asked dully. "Is he an English officer finally come to take us away?"

Tray roused himself. "That's my half brother, Vaughn, an officer in the King's army. He is the one who accuses you of killing his man."

Shock coursed through her. "Brother?" she whispered, her hand flying to her aching heart. "He's your—brother?"

"Half brother," Tray answered wearily. "Vaughn and I share the same father, but little else. His mother is English, and Vaughn has been obsessed with all things English since birth."

Brothers...they were brothers! As the full impact of Tray's words hit her, Alyssa felt faint. Sweet Jesus, Vaughn was the one who had so cruelly raped her! And Vaughn had been the one who had tortured Dev's wife, Shannon, aboard the ship! Alyssa felt her gorge rise and fought down the nausea. How could she ever forget Vaughn's too-handsome face or that sinister voice? She hadn't known his name, only that he was the officer in charge aboard the ship. Murderer. Tray's brother was a murderer. Desperately, Alyssa tried to think despite an overwhelming deluge of emotions. Sean. She must protect him at all costs!

"At one time," she began rawly, "you promised me anything that I asked for."

Tray opened his eyes, staring down at her upturned face. Raw despair was clearly visible in her eyes. "Yes, I said that."

"I ask you now to grant me one request. Just one...."

Tray swallowed hard, his eyes unnaturally bright. "What is it?" he asked, his voice raspy.

Alyssa leaned forward. "Sean. Please don't let him take Sean to prison or to the coal mines. Please...it's all I ask. He's innocent, Tray, I swear it upon my soul. Wh-when the English overran us, Sean came out of hiding to protect Shannon, Dev's wife. He stopped a soldier from hurting Shannon but received a blow to his head. Another soldier picked Sean up and sent him to the ship with us." Her voice grew more pleading. "Sean never loaded pistols, ever! He never hurt anyone. He used to gather wood for me and help me wash the men's clothes. He's innocent. I swear it."

"I can't send him back to Ireland now, Alyssa. That's impossible under the circumstances," Tray said heavily, rubbing his brow.

"Keep him here, then! Be kind to him, as you are with everyone beneath your protection." Her voice grew choked with tears. "I—I couldn't bear it if he were sent to the mines to perish...."

Tray groaned inwardly, staring down at her. He wanted to reach out and hold her, to give her his protection, but he knew she would rear back as she had earlier, hating his touch. Hating all English. "He won't go to the mines," he promised in a strained tone.

Alyssa gave a little cry, hands covering her mouth as tears rolled down her cheeks. "Th-thank you, Tray." She hung her head and, after several minutes, spoke again. "I'm sorry I lied to you. You can't imagine how many times I wanted to tell you the truth... to tell you I was a prisoner on that ship and not a victim of the battle."

Tray took a chair and pulled it opposite her. His face was lined and gray as he spoke. "I've thought through everything you've told me thus far, Alyssa. If you were deliberately trying to lie to me, why would you have told me that your last name was Kyle? You must have known that sooner or later I would have found out." He stared down at his booted feet and let out a tense sigh. "I pride myself on knowing people. And unless I'm wrong as never before, you lied to protect Sean, didn't you? You didn't do it to save yourself. Well? Answer me, Alyssa."

Hearing the gentle tone of Tray's voice, Alyssa bit down hard on her lower lip to keep herself from crying out. She gripped her hands tightly together.

"Talk to me, Aly," Tray urged softly. "Tell me the truth."

She broke beneath the vibrating emotion in his voice as he called her Aly once again. "Yes, it was for Sean."

"Why? Why not for yourself, too?"

"Because I'm blind and dishonored!" she cried. "I'm of no use to anyone! Even if I could ever get back to Ireland, what man would have me?"

His eyes narrowed in sympathy with her pain. He dreaded what he had to say to her but forced himself to speak. "Now listen to me carefully. My half brother is going to try his best to have you taken to Newgate. The only way I can protect you is to take you as my mistress. You'll be protected beneath my title as the earl's son. Vaughn may contact my father and have him try to pressure me into giving you up, but I won't do that. I can't let you go back to Ireland, Alyssa, but I promise that you and Sean will be safe." Tray watched her face for a reaction. Seeing none, he continued, "I realize Wales is not Ireland. And you'll never be able to see your family again. If I know the English, after they've discovered what I've done, Shadowhawk will be closely watched."

Her heart hammered wildly as she listened to the gritty tone of his voice. A part of her wanted to reach out and touch Tray in gratitude, but still a larger part shrank back in unadulterated terror. Tray was Vaughn's brother. If Vaughn could hurt her like that, so might Tray. Did the same cruel blood run in both brothers? Her mind swam in confusion and agony. "Your mistress?"

"It's the only way I can protect you."

Memories of the rape flashed before her darkened eyes, and a well of bitterness rose up in her. "It's just as well that my family doesn't see me again if I'm to become little more than a whore. I've brought enough shame on them."

Tray's eyes narrowed to slits and he slowly rose, absorbing the hatred he heard in her wobbling voice. "Would you court the rope at Newgate instead?" he growled.

Alyssa hung her head, a sob escaping. "Death is preferable, my lord. You've given your word that Sean will be safe. That's all I care about."

In his anger and hurt, Tray reached out, gripping her arm and giving her a small shake. "Damn you!" he rasped, his hoarse voice nearly shouting. "I care what happens to both of you! Do you hear me?" Releasing her arm, he crossed the room, pausing at the drawing room door before opening it. "I don't care whether you prefer the noose to my attentions, Alyssa. Your life is worth saving. Do you think it bothers me that you're blind? Or that you were raped? Neither was your fault. How can I blame you for that? If I can accept that about you, can you not accept it yourself?"

Alyssa rose, her fists clenched at her sides, her face a mask of pain. "No! Do you hear me? I *won't* be your mistress! I won't lie with you. Ever! I hate the English! I hate what you have done to my family, my mother. Just leave me to my death. I would rather join my father and hang with him at Newgate than remain here with you!"

Her sobs followed him as he stalked out of her bedchamber and echoed through the brittle iciness of the drawing room as he made his way to the hall. Tray felt himself shattering inside over Alyssa's pleading cries. She considered death preferable to his touch. And yet, he loved her. God help him, he loved her with an overwhelming fierceness, and only Vaughn's accusations had put him into direct touch with his real feelings for Alyssa. Feelings that he had been holding at bay for her good as well as his own....

Grimly, Tray tucked all of those emotions away for a more peaceful time, when he could examine them more closely. His love for Alyssa brought an undisguised joy to his chest, making him feel almost euphoric. Yet later, he would have to force an unwilling Alyssa to lie with him in the same bed. And that prospect filled him only with bitterness.

\* \* \*

Alyssa jumped when an unexpected knock came at her bedchamber. She heard the door open and protectively clutched her dressing robe around her, fearing it was Vaughn.

"It's Tray."

Alyssa exhaled, relief evident on her pale features. "Thank God," she whispered, her hand at her throat.

Tray shut the door and came to a halt in the middle of the room. "Before the night is over, you'll be cursing me," he warned. As he noticed her exhausted form, his voice softened. "Sit down, Alyssa, I have to talk to you."

She sat without a word, her eyes trained on him as he stood before her. All day she had been aware of Tray's voice thundering through the halls, and her blood had run icy every time she heard Vaughn's returning snarl. Soon after Tray left her, Sean had come running to her bedchamber, thrown his arms around her and sobbed. Alyssa tried to soothe him, knowing the fear he must have felt upon finding Vaughn at Shadowhawk. She had stroked his short, silken hair, rocking him, trying to give him solace when she had none to give to herself.

Despite her fear of Tray, she asked in a quavering voice, "Is it over?"

Tray took off his coat, throwing it on her bed. "Over?" he asked bitterly. "No, this is just the beginning."

He sat on the edge of the bed and absorbed Alyssa's loveliness. Even now, as pale and weary as she appeared, she was stunning. That inner beauty of hers, that island of peace that seemed to emanate from within, fed him in that moment. If only they could hold each other and give sustenance to one another through the strain of the days ahead.

"What do you mean?"

Tray leaned forward, rubbing his face tiredly. "Vaughn is determined to remain here at Shadowhawk, Alyssa," he began in a low voice. "I've convinced him that I won't let you go. As my mistress, he knows he cannot simply drag you out of here to Newgate. He won't risk it. Instead, he'll try to persuade my father, Harold, to force me to release you. But until my father decides whether he'll enter this family squabble, Vaughn will be hovering over us like a hungry buzzard, hoping to catch you breaking the law." Tray glanced over at her, his face set. "Starting from this moment, you'll always be at my side, Alyssa. Either that, or with Sorche. I won't allow Vaughn to harass or frighten you."

Her heart began a slow pound, and dread flowed through her. "At your side?" she whispered meekly.

Tray winced. "In and out of bed," he elaborated grimly. "If Vaughn thinks for a moment our alliance is a sham, he'll have the grounds he wants to take you from me." He rose slowly. "And I won't allow that to happen, Alyssa. I value your life even if you don't. Come, I'm taking you to my bedchamber."

Alyssa remained in the chair, tired and emotionally wrung out. She sensed that Tray was mere inches from her, his arm extended for her to take, as she had done so often in the past. "Please . . ." she begged, "don't do this to me."

As gently as he knew how, Tray knelt down in front of her, his hands resting on the arms of the chair. "Don't cry, little one. I know you've experienced pain at the hand of another man. Do you think I want to hurt you?"

She bowed her head, a soft sob escaping from her lips. Did Tray know it had been his brother who had so cruelly hurt her and made her afraid of all men's touch? Salty tears dribbled across her lips. "N-no."

Tray lightly laid his hand upon hers. "I have a confession to make, and I want you to listen closely."

Sniffing, Alyssa accepted the linen handkerchief that he offered her. "What is it?"

"When I first brought you to Shadowhawk, little one, you were grievously injured. Sorche and I stripped you of your clothes and bathed you." He made a slight grimace as shock registered in Alyssa's eyes. "We both know that a gentleman would never take advantage of any woman like that. But Sorche was too old to carry you to the bath. Someone had to do it and I did. We wrapped you in a bath towel and then placed you in the warm water to cleanse you of all the blood and dirt. I remained with you long afterward and fell asleep in this chair near the hearth. Later, you woke me up screaming."

Alyssa blinked, her lashes thick with tears. "Screaming?"

"Yes. Screams wrenched from your very soul. I tried to talk to you, then I rubbed a cooling cloth across your brow, but you continued to sob and cry out. Finally," he admitted hoarsely, "I lay down by your side and drew you to me. I took you in my arms and began to talk soothingly to you. Within minutes, you stopped sobbing, and within half an hour, you were sleeping soundly once again, nestled in my arms."

Her lips parted, and for brittle seconds the room was silent. "H-how long did this go on? I mean—"

"Every night until you became conscious, Aly. I slept with you every night. If I tried to leave your side, you'd start to cry again." He gave a helpless shrug. "I can't explain it, nor do I forgive myself for my actions. But somewhere in your heart, you must have known I wouldn't hurt you, little one. Each night you were eager to be held. I never took advantage of you. I simply kept you safe and warm." He allowed his words to sink in, getting up and walking to the hearth. The confusion and embarrassment on her face tore at his heart. But if Alyssa were to be kept safe from Vaughn, she had to realize that he would never intentionally take advantage of her.

"D-does everyone know about this?"

"No, just Sorche. I would get up at dawn, before the servant came in to restock the fire."

"B-but if I share your bed, everyone will know. Even Sean."

"It will become common knowledge," he agreed softly.

Alyssa's lashes lifted, revealing exhausted jade eyes. "I would rather die."

Grimly, Tray walked back to her and held out his hand. "I know you would. But I want your life spared."

"Why?" The word was wrenched from her raw throat.

"Because your life is worth saving, Alyssa Kyle. Trust me on that point. Now come, it's late and we're about ready to fall over with weariness. Take my arm...."

# Chapter Nine

Alyssa's movements were mechanical as she shyly shed her dressing robe and slid into their bed. Tray extinguished the last of the candles in the bedchamber. In the muted glow from the hearth fire, he watched wretchedly as Alyssa pulled the bed covers to her chin, her face belying her fear.

As Tray carefully got into bed, he murmured, "I won't touch you, Alyssa. Just go to sleep. We'll take each day as it comes."

Alyssa lay wide-awake in the semidarkness. She heard Tray's breathing soften, occasionally breaking into a snore. Little by little, she relaxed her fingers on the pillow and drifted into sleep.

Sometime later, her nightmares flared back to livid, frightening life. Alyssa moaned, and her breath came in great, heaving gulps as she wrestled to push Vaughn off her. The glint of his blue eyes bored into hers, and she screamed as she read the evil intent in his leering features.

Tray jerked awake. Instinctively, he rolled over, as he had done that first week, and pulled Alyssa into his arms to give her a measure of solace. Her hair was tangled across her face and her eyes flew open. Suddenly, her fists began to pummel his chest.

"No!" she cried, pushing Tray away from her. The instant her hand met the hard warmth of his flesh, she shrank back like a cornered animal, huddling near the edge of the bed.

Tray sat up and turned toward Alyssa. "It's all right," he soothed, "you're safe. It's just those dreams again."

Alyssa buried her head. "They've come back! They're worse than ever!"

Tray looked at her, unsure of how best to help her. "Can you go back to sleep, Aly?"

She shook her head, her entire body now trembling with the charge of adrenaline coursing through her bloodstream. "N-no. I'm so afraid . . . it's so dark. It's always so dark. . . ."

He got out of bed, gathering up her dressing robe and gently placing it around her hunched shoulders. "Stay here. I'll go to the kitchen and make us some chocolate. Would you like that?"

Just his voice was a balm to her chaotic feelings. She lifted her head. "Oh, Tray . . . yes. . . ."

When Tray padded back to the bedchamber with the chocolate, he found Alyssa huddled before the hearth on the deerskin rug. Her face was pensive and troubled as he sat down beside her, taking care to keep a reasonable distance between them for her sake. She took the cup, her hands trembling badly. He threw some more logs on the fire, then rose to place a blanket about her shoulders. Alyssa offered him a look of thanks, and Tray took his own cup and saucer and sat near her on the rug.

"When I was a boy I used to have dreams, and Sorche would come in and bring me a cup of hot milk. She always told me milk would help me sleep again." Tray smiled faintly, looking at his emptied cup. "I believed her."

"Did it?" Her voice was raw and she took another sip of the hot liquid. The warmth of the drink soothed the irritated flesh of her throat.

Tray set his cup and saucer aside, drawing his legs up and putting his arms around them. "Fell asleep in minutes." He laughed softly.

"Why did you have bad dreams? Did something happen to you?"

He inhaled deeply and then released the breath with a sigh. "Let just say that my father never wanted me around."

"Why?"

Tray rested his chin on his knees, staring blindly at the fire. "As far as he was concerned, I killed his wife—my mother."

Alyssa twisted her head toward him. "You? Kill?"

"My mother died giving me birth, Aly. My father could never forgive me for that. In fact, I can't forgive myself."

She reached out to comfort him. The gesture shocked them both and Alyssa withdrew her fingers from his arm. "How could it be your fault?"

He stared down at his deformed and twisted foot. "Someday I might tell you the entire story, little one, but not now. You've lived through an emotional storm from the day I met you. You don't need to be told my troubles on top of everything else." Tray slowly rose and removed the blanket from her shoulders. "Come, you need to sleep some more. You still have shadows beneath those lovely eyes of yours."

Once in bed, Alyssa felt a strange sense of peace stealing through her as she lay next to Tray. This time she did not seek the very edge of the bed. Instead, she curled up much like a kitten, facing Tray, clutching the pillow to her.

"Keep your voice down!"

"Now listen here, clubfoot, I don't care what you say, I'm sending one of your servants after Father."

The familiar voices of Tray and Vaughn pulled Alyssa from the edges of sleep. *Clubfoot?* She rubbed her eyes and stretched. Darkness met her eyes as she opened them, as it always did, but the crowing of a cock in the background told her it was morning. She heard the voices moving farther away and guessed that the argument was taking place in the drawing room next door. Then her door opened, and her heart jumped in her chest. Was Vaughn sneaking up on her as he had done the first time?

"Tray?"

"Here. I didn't know you were awake," he apologized. Dressed in his normal attire of riding breeches, boots and an ivory-colored chamois shirt, he hesitated at the bed, hands on his hips.

"Do you feel rested?" he asked, watching her wake up. God, how he longed to kiss those full, pouty lips awake. Tray savagely quelled his desire and gathered up her dressing robe.

"I think Sorche was right. The milk did help."

"You slept long," Tray agreed, walking over to her side of the bed. "Come, I'll help you into your robe."

Alyssa hesitated, then reached out to find his offered hand. A blush swept across her cheeks as the intimacy of their situation dawned on her. What would Dev and Gavin think if they ever found out that she had lain in an Englishman's bed? Would Sean hate her? He was too young to understand the complexity of the problem. At the same time, she remembered Tray's honorable behavior toward her. She wondered again if he knew Vaughn was the man who had raped her. If so, how could he condone Vaughn's behavior toward her and yet treat her so differently? There was so much to mull over, to try to understand. As she shrugged into the robe, she admitted that Tray had never once hurt her.

"Thank you," Alyssa murmured shyly.

Tray found her efforts to tie the mutinous satin sash touching. "Here," he offered in a low voice, removing her hands from the offending cloth, "let me help you."

She stood there, acutely aware of his male scent, his closeness and the rush of feelings that threatened to engulf her as he ran his fingers along the circumference of her waist, untwisting the satin ribbon. He seemed to savor the simple task of tying her sash, and Alyssa swallowed convulsively, conscious of Tray as never before. Conscious of him as a man who represented protection, not pain.

Tray stood inches from her, staring down at her hungrily. My God, he thought, if she could see his face she would scream in terror. He wanted her in every way. The pleasure of helping her tie the sash built such an incredible ache within his body that he forced himself to step away from her before he could no longer control the dark, brooding emotions that seethed deep inside him.

"There," he heard himself say, his voice strained. "I'll ring for Maura so that she can bring you breakfast."

"Wait," Alyssa pleaded, "we must talk."

Sorche looked up from her needlework as Tray stalked into the green drawing room. He scowled over at her.

"Is it Vaughn again?" she asked as Tray sat down opposite her.

"I wish it were. At least with Vaughn, if I get angry, I can roar back at him."

"You've had a tiff with Alyssa?" she ventured, starting to rock slowly back and forth.

Tray angrily combed his fingers through his hair. "Tiff? God's blood, it was pure, vitriolic hatred on her part and confusion on mine. I don't understand this change. Doesn't she realize I'm making her my mistress to protect her and

Sean?'' His nostrils flared as he glared down at the dark green carpeting.

"Do you have time for an old woman's thoughts, my son?"

His shoulders fell and Tray rested his elbows on his thighs, giving her a wry look. "At this point, I would welcome any sane opinion. One day, Alyssa seems to trust me, and the next, she turns moods as swiftly as the Irish Sea during a storm. Last night she woke up screaming. We shared a cup of chocolate in front of the fire and I felt as if we were back to where we were before Vaughn came. And now she's threatening to starve herself to death because she can't stand the idea of being my mistress. Damn! She confounds me, Sorche.''

"Listen to me, Tray. She was a virgin before the Englishman raped her. A mistress beds down with her lord. Don't you think she may be frightened that you will injure her as that other man did?" She gave Tray a kindly smile.

"But I haven't touched her!" Tray rose, muttering a curse. "I haven't done a thing to make her think I'd do anything against her will. Although," he continued blackly, "I find myself drawn to her more powerfully than any woman I've ever known."

Sorche slanted a glance up at him. "More drawn to her than you were to Shelby?"

"God help me, yes!" He paced back and forth like a caged animal, hands entwined behind his back. "I won't fence with you, Sorche, I'm falling in love with Alyssa. Don't ask me how or when it happened...I couldn't tell you. But I do know that when Vaughn came to take her away, I knew with crystal clarity that I loved her." He stopped, glaring down at the hearth. "And I'll be damned if anyone, even Alyssa herself, is going to stop me from protecting her until she realizes that I love her."

A smile gleamed in Sorche's blue eyes as she bowed her head, pretending to unknot a thread. But anyone who knew of her talent with the needle knew she never made such a beginner's mistake. Tray gave her a disgruntled look and resumed his pacing.

"Have you considered marrying her, Tray? Don't forget, in her eyes, being a man's mistress is degrading and humiliating."

He threw up his hands. "Marriage? My God, she's throwing a royal temper just over the idea of being my mistress, much less my wife! How could I suggest such a thing? We've barely known each other for two months. And don't forget, I can't drag her up in front of a priest and force her to submit to marriage. At least she has no say in being my mistress."

"I see," she murmured, finally solving the problem of the knot and resuming her stitching. "But you feel Alyssa is wifely material?"

"Of course," Tray growled, pacing again. "I'm not ashamed of her. She's young, beautiful, too damned intelligent for her own good, kind, unselfish and—oh, hell . . ."

"Be her friend, Tray."

Tray shed his fierce countenance and thought about Sorche's suggestion. "So you're suggesting we keep sharing those very things we enjoy together?"

"Not only that, give Alyssa more responsibility at your side. Allow her to help you. Don't always be the one in charge. Make her feel that she is an important part of whatever you share, that you cannot make do without her. I see no reason why she couldn't ride with you at night, hunting for those poor, orphaned lambs and taking them back to the barn. Let her carry the lantern."

Tray's mouth pulled into a rare, careless smile as he leaned down to place a kiss on Sorche's hair. "Thank you," he murmured gratefully.

"And one more thing, my son. If Alyssa continues to wake up at night because of her dreams, take advantage of those precious moments. I think it might be time to impress her with how good a man you truly are."

Tray nodded, digesting Sorche's last comment. "I'll see you at dinner tonight," was all he said as he left. Sorche smiled broadly, humming an appropriate Irish song quietly beneath her breath.

Alyssa jerked awake, sitting straight up in bed, a scream on her lips. Her flannel nightgown was soaked, clinging to every curve of her young body, and her hair was disheveled. She trembled violently, trying to tear herself from the grip of the nightmare. She almost cried out for Tray, then stopped herself. Instead, she pulled her legs up to her body and rested her damp brow against her knees.

"Are you all right, little one?" came Tray's sleep-thickened voice.

"It's just the dreams again," Alyssa admitted hoarsely. She felt Tray stir, suddenly grateful for his nearness. One part of her wanted to turn and bury herself in his arms, the other part reminded her that he was the brother of the man in her nightmare.

"Would you like a cup of hot chocolate?"

Alyssa vividly recalled last night's pleasant reprieve from all the hatred and anger of her dream. "P-please?"

He reached over, gently caressing her trembling shoulder. "I'll be right back," he promised, getting out of bed.

When Tray came back, she was in the same spot, with the blanket pulled around her shoulders. He handed her a cup and placed a few logs upon the bright coals of the hearth.

The quiet of the manor surrounded them for many minutes as they sat inches apart, each lost in thought. Alyssa's hair gleamed like molten burgundy and copper in the firelight, and her features appeared peaceful.

"I owe you an apology," she began softly, holding the cup tightly between her slender fingers.

"Oh?"

Alyssa grimaced. "I behaved like a child with you earlier today. I—I didn't mean what I said." She finished the chocolate and set it aside, turning to face him. Her eyes were large and dark with confusion as she looked at him. "I—I'm just scared, Tray. Scared of—of men. You've been kind to Sean and me, but so much has happened so quickly...." Her voice trailed off. "I feel up and down, as if I can no longer control my emotions. I cry endlessly...I curse at you...."

Tray leaned forward, picking up one of her damp, cool hands. "I'm trying to put myself in your place, Aly. If I had been raped and then waited to be thrown on a cart meant for the dead, I imagine I'd be feeling a bit up and down myself." He began to rub light circles on the palm of her hand. "And you had good reason to detest me."

Alyssa felt a tingle of pleasure radiating outward from where he was caressing her palm. "What do you mean?" she asked in a whisper.

"I realize that the label of mistress is degrading to you. And for that, I apologize. I only want to protect you." Tray bowed his head, at a loss for words as his own emotions suddenly boiled to the surface. "I hope you know I would never touch you unless you gave me permission. Love between two people is a beautiful experience, not one of pain. I'd never want to cause you pain, Alyssa." His voice cracked. "Never."

Tears welled up in her eyes and Alyssa automatically reached out to Tray, her hands coming to rest against his robed chest. His body tightened with want of her, but he stilled himself, grateful that she would reach out on her own accord.

"My heart knows that," Alyssa admitted, "but my head does not. Tray, how can I become unafraid of you?"

He gently cradled her hands between his larger ones. "First, by thinking of me as your friend. Someone with whom you can share hours of enjoyment. And second, by not comparing me to Vaughn. I know he's my half brother, Alyssa, but that's where the similarity ends. Does Vaughn's presence, unlikable as he is, erase the trust you had come to feel for me until he came?"

Alyssa hung her head, a cloak of utter peace blanketing her as Tray continued to hold her hands. "I was so afraid that you would take me as I was taken before," she choked out. "And it hurt so much...."

Tray whispered her name reverently and released her hands. He gently settled his arms around her trembling shoulders to hold her, hold her until she stopped shaking like a frightened doe trapped by a hunter. "Believe me," he told her rawly, "it doesn't have to be painful. Loving is the most beautiful of all pleasures, Aly."

"Those are words, Tray. I want to believe you, but I can't."

He released her, his hands sliding down the length of her slender arms and coming to rest upon her fingers once again. "Time," he soothed, "in time, your horrible memories will fade. For now, let's learn to become friends again. Just as before, Aly, you and I taking our daily rides, visiting the foals and teaching you to play the harp. Nothing has changed with Vaughn's arrival except that you are my mistress and will share my bed." His hands tightened briefly on her fingers. "I won't demand any more from you. I want the woman who comes to me to be joyous and willing, not frightened.''

Alyssa swallowed against the lump forming in her throat. ''Just as before?'' Her voice held a note of hope.

''The same as before. The only thing that's changed is that you and Sean can never return to Ireland, Aly.''

''I know.''

''Can you accept that?''

Closing her eyes, Alyssa nodded. ''I'll never see it...''

Tray grimaced, feeling the hotness of tears in his own eyes. ''You see through your heart anyway, little one. I'm sorry you've lost your sight, but there are other far more precious things about you that make me very glad I'm your friend.''

She pulled her hands free to wipe the tears from her cheeks, managing a sliver of a smile as she lifted her face to him. ''Tray?''

''Yes?''

''Let me touch your face. I want to know what you look like. Please?''

His gray eyes grew warm with love. It took every shred of his self-control not to crush her in his arms and hold her forever. ''Just between friends?'' he asked huskily, easing the tension he saw flitting across her face.

''Yes, just between friends....''

''I'm at your disposal, my lady. I promise not to bite one of your lovely fingers should you touch my mouth.''

Alyssa's eyes grew soft with trust and she hesitantly reached out.

Tray watched, hypnotized by her hands; he saw the small, yellowed calluses on each of her palms, her short, clean nails, the slender expanse of fingers meant to play the harp, glide gracefully over the keys of a pianoforte or stroke a man's flesh into throbbing, heated life. He closed his eyes, achingly aware of her butterfly touch as her fingers lightly combed through his hair.

She laughed softly, running strands of his hair through her fingers. "Your hair feels like Rasheed's mane!"

"Is that a compliment or an insult, my lady?"

Her smile widened with wonder as she pressed her fingers across his scalp, lost in the thick silk of his softly waving hair. "A compliment, my lord. Your hair is clean and thick." She wrinkled her nose. "Many young men are so unkempt. They allow their hair to hang in dirty snarls or strands that are greasy and smelly." She leaned forward, her face lightly brushing against his cheek as she inhaled the scent of his hair.

Sitting back, Alyssa looked satisfied. If she could have seen the sheer look of hunger on his face, she would have run from him. Tray tried to control the wild explosions igniting within him that her unexpected nearness had set off. He had caught a whiff of her feminine scent combined with the jasmine soap she used every morning. *Friends,* he groaned to himself, *friends.* If he so much as made a provocative move toward Alyssa, he would destroy the crystalline trust building fragilely between them.

He gritted his teeth, forcing his hardening body to remain beneath his iron-willed command. He tried to remember Sorche's advice. If he gave Alyssa friendship, she would give him her trust. And with trust comes love.... He swallowed convulsively. "Well? From one friend to another, what is your opinion of my hair? Do I pass your inspection?"

Alyssa smiled. "You have beautiful hair, like Rasheed. I love running my hands through his silken mane."

And God, what I'd give to have you run your hands through my hair with such carefree abandon, he thought torridly. Making an effort to keep his tone light, he asked,

"Am I passable as a friend, so far? You'd better go on. I'm afraid your opinion of me will alter drastically when you meet my face."

Without a word, Alyssa lightly ran her hands over his face, causing a nerve-tingling sensation that made him draw in his breath sharply. Her expression was sober with concentration as her fingers lingered on his strong jaw. She then touched her own face as if to compare its structure to his, and then shifted her hands to his face once again.

"A square face?"

"Some would call it less kindly than that, my lady."

Alyssa smiled gently. The prickle of his skin beneath her fingertips sent tiny tingles through her. "A powerful jaw."

"Some would say stubborn."

"No, I think it's that of a man who knows his own mind," she answered several moments later. Alyssa lifted her hands, skimming his forehead, brows and eyes. She felt tiny lines at the corner of each eye, then trailed her fingers downward to feel the indented lines around his mouth. She returned to his brow.

"Do you scowl much?"

"Yes."

"I can feel the lines...."

"Lines of life, little one. I've earned every one of them."

Her lips parted as she touched his eyes. "You have thick lashes," she murmured, "like me."

"Shades my eyes from the sun. Yours, on the other hand, make your lovely green eyes look even larger and more beautiful."

Alyssa colored beneath his husky compliment. "Let's see if your eyes are set close together. You know there's an old horseman's adage that an animal or man with close-set eyes is mean, stubborn and evil? And if they are set wide, the horse or man is of a kind nature. Like Rasheed—his eyes are far apart.''

"I don't know if I like being compared to that stallion quite so much," Tray grumbled good-naturedly. He watched as Alyssa measured the distance between her eyes with her own fingers and then proceeded to measure the width of his with the same method. "Well? Am I mean, stubborn and evil?"

She laughed. "'No, my lord. You'll be glad to know that you are probably gentle-tempered, easy to get along with and intelligent."

"Do I have to live up to all those accolades, my lady?"

"Will it distress you to do so, my lord?"

Tray grinned. He was distressed right now, thinking that the bulge pressing against his robe would terrify Alyssa if she could see what kind of effect she had upon him. "I can probably meet the intelligence part, but I'm afraid I destroyed my gentle temper with you earlier today. And I never remember being easy to get along with. Could you settle for only one out of those three?"

"I must think about that, my lord." Her smile lingered as her gentle fingers grazed his nose. "Ah, another horse saying comes to mind."

Tray groaned. "Now what?"

She stroked his nose and then touched her own to compare. "You may recall what they say about roman-nosed horses? They're stubborn and mule-headed."

"And does that apply to me?"

She traced the fine, aristocratic length of his nose and his large, well-shaped nostrils. "You have a bump on your nose."

"I got that fighting one day. I took on four English boys who were calling me names because I insisted upon speaking in Welsh. Needless to say, I came out a bloodied loser.

Sorche said my nose was broken. The scolding she gave me hurt more than my nose did at that time,'' he remembered fondly.

Alyssa shared his laughter, her hands brushing across his lips. She felt his smile disappear.

"Don't stop smiling. I like your laughter," she begged. "It sounds like thunder rumbling from your chest and reminds me of the storms I love so much."

The urge to draw her fingers gently into his mouth and worship them with his tongue nearly shattered Tray. He shut his eyes, holding on to the last shred of his control as she explored his lips.

"A strong mouth," she murmured. And then she gave him a wicked, teasing look. "A mouth used to giving orders."

"And having them carried out. Don't forget that."

She smiled, liking the soft, upward curve of his lips. "If you say so, my lord."

"I suppose you're going to come up with some horse tale about my lips now. No doubt a horse with thin lips means he's a sore loser or some such thing."

Alyssa flashed him a genuine smile, her fingers lingering across his mouth. She had been kissed a few times before, sloppy kisses stolen quickly by nervous boys. The shape of Tray's mouth was bold, the lower lip full and sensual to her inspection. "No... but I never trust a man with thin lips or thick lips." She shuddered. "Thick lips remind me of a pig! I always see them on fat, rich Englishmen."

Tray burst into laughter, catching her hands and pressing a kiss to them. "My lady, it sounds as if I've passed your inspection."

She sat back, allowing her hands to rest in her lap, her features relaxed. "You have. A strong face molded by many experiences, I'd venture. You have lines of laughter at the corners of your eyes and—'' her voice lowered to a husky whisper ''—your mouth is . . . well, just right.''

''Neither a pig nor a man to be distrusted, eh?'' Tray observed wryly, lulled into the peace that enveloped them.

''No, never a pig. As for trust . . .'' She shrugged and gave him a shy look. ''I think we both have to work on that. I have to learn to get over my distrust of men, and you have to put up with me while I do.''

Tray rose, pulling the blanket off Alyssa's shoulders and helping her to her bare feet. The firelight shone through the thin flannel, outlining the shapely curves of her womanly body. He took a deep breath and led her toward the bed. ''Friends have all the time in the world,'' he reminded her.

Alyssa nodded, feeling languorously and pleasantly tired as she slid back into the bed. She curled up, the pillow nestled against her body as Tray covered her with the quilt. Closing her eyes, Alyssa was already embracing sleep when the mattress sunk with Tray's weight.

# Chapter Ten

"My lord," Stablemaster Thomas called from one end of the aisle, "Sorche has asked for you."

Tray hesitated, glancing over the back of Rasheed. They had just gotten back from their ride and he was in the middle of putting the stallion back into his stall. For the past five days, Vaughn had followed them like a hawk waiting to strike. Alyssa was holding Old Ned's reins, waiting in the center aisle. Thomas was with her, so Tray felt it safe to leave Aly in the stable.

"Very well. Come and take her horse, Thomas."

The old man hurried toward them. "Yes, my lord. Miss Alyssa?"

"I'd like to brush him down just a bit, Thomas."

Thomas risked a glance toward Lord Trayhern.

"Let her," Tray said to Thomas. "I'll be right back out and we'll finish the job on Old Ned together," he promised Alyssa, turning away.

Alyssa led Ned to his stall and unsaddled him. The ride had been exhilarating and she felt a new, powerful link with Tray since waking this morning. It was as Tray had promised—their budding relationship was back where it had been before Vaughn had shattered their lives so abruptly. How could two brothers be so impossibly different? But sweet

Mary and Joseph, her heart yearned that Tray be exactly
what he said he was—unlike Vaughn in every way. She
leaned forward, closing her eyes, resting her brow gently
against Ned's forehead. The old gray gelding stood quietly,
as if sensing her need for comfort.

As she raised her head and opened her eyes, Alyssa noticed something different. She blinked again. Was it sunlight striking her? Why did everything seem so bright? She
rubbed her eyes, keeping one hand on Ned. When Alyssa
reopened them, she gasped, her heart beginning to pound.
She could just make out the outline of her gloved hand as it
rested against Ned.

"So, there you are."

Alyssa gasped, whirling toward Vaughn's snarling voice.
She saw the vague outline of a tall, well-proportioned man
standing just outside the stall door. Alyssa gripped Ned's
mane, her lips parting in abject terror. "What do you
want?"

Vaughn smiled and let himself into the stall, making sure
it was latched. He kept Thomas busy saddling a horse for
him outside of the stable. His brows drew downward. Why
did she have to be so damned beautiful? Her features were
clean and classical; it galled him that Alyssa looked better
than most of the gently bred women of his class.

"Want?" he asked in a silken tone as he approached her.
"I should think you know what I want. I took it from you
before easily enough."

Alyssa choked back a scream and her eyes widened as he
approached. His face! God, she could see his face! It was
the same terrible visage that had leered over her like a slav-
ering animal as she lay sprawled on the deck. She backed
away, holding out her hands. "No...no...leave me alone!"

Vaughn's lips drew back in a sickening smile as he halted
a foot from where she crouched against the back of the stall.

"Never," he said softly. "I'll haunt you, you Irish whore. I'll make you wish you had died aboard that ship. Too bad that clubbing didn't finish you off. I thought it had." He reached out, idly fingering a long, silken strand of her hair.

Alyssa flinched. Her pulse fluttered erratically in her throat. She had to escape! With a cry, she lurched awkwardly past Vaughn, flying toward the door. Old Ned leaped aside as she fled by him. Just as she managed to lift the latch that would lead her to freedom, she felt Vaughn's fist wrapping cruelly around her hair.

With a savage jerk, Alyssa fell backward, landing heavily on the straw-covered floor. Vaughn started to kneel down beside her, and she screamed, trying to fight him off. Her nails raked the side of his face, drawing blood.

"Why, you little—"

Alyssa heard a snarl and saw the dark shape of another man hurtling by her. Vaughn was pulled from her as if he were a mere rag doll. She scrambled away from the two men, crawling to the safety of one corner as they fought. The Welsh gelding was frantic, his hooves brushing close to her, and Alyssa curled herself up into a tight ball in an effort to protect herself from the panicked animal. Sounds of grunts, curses and flesh striking flesh filled the air as the men rolled and flailed about on the floor. Alyssa watched in horrified fascination as the heavier, darker man wrestled Vaughn to the floor, mercilessly pinning him.

Tray's mouth tightened as he landed a blow squarely on Vaughn's jaw, and he continued to pummel his half brother until Vaughn screamed. His long, powerful fingers closed around his half brother's throat.

"I told you," he rasped, "never to touch her. Never!"

Vaughn was breathing hard, his blue eyes glazed with hatred. "You struck me!"

Tray wiped the blood from the corner of his mouth with his white shirtsleeve. "Listen to me, Vaughn. You will leave Alyssa alone or I'll kill you with my bare hands. Do you understand that? She's mine, Vaughn, mine alone. No man touches her. She's under my protection."

Blood flowed heavily from Vaughn's nose. When he tried to get up, Tray shoved him back down.

"Let me up!"

"Not until I have your promise you'll leave Alyssa alone."

"Never!"

Tray's face darkened with anger as he digested his half brother's one-word answer. "All right, have it your way," Tray snarled softly. "Get out of here, Vaughn. You hear me? When I let you up, I want you gone from Shadowhawk. Don't ever step foot onto this manor again."

Vaughn glared at him. "And if I do?"

"I'll kill you."

Vaughn lay back, staring up at his half brother in disbelief. "You're mad! You'll hang from the gallows."

Tray gave Vaughn a nerveless smile, his gray eyes glittering like ice. "It would be an even trade, half brother." Tray got to his feet, careful to keep himself between Alyssa and Vaughn. "Now get out of here. I'll see that Craddock packs your belongings and Thomas prepares the carriage."

Vaughn shakily got to his feet, holding his jaw. "Father won't let you get away with this!"

Tray flexed the bruised and bloodied knuckles of his right hand and brushed several strands of hair off his forehead. "If Father comes, he'll come without you. Whatever involves Shadowhawk is my business, not yours, Vaughn. Don't let me see your face here again."

Angrily, Vaughn brushed the straw from his tailored trousers, giving Alyssa one last, deadly look. "I hope you spawn devils between you," he snarled.

Tray waited until Vaughn had made his way out of the stable, slamming the door behind him, before he turned to Alyssa. He didn't trust his half brother not to jump him from behind. Releasing an oath, Tray turned. Alyssa sat huddled in the corner, knees drawn up to her body. Her hair lay around her face and shoulders in disarray. The lines of his mouth softened and his eyes grew dark with concern as he came and knelt in front of her, his hands coming to rest on her trembling shoulders. She looked straight into his eyes, confusion and fear in her expression.

"I'm sorry, Aly," he apologized softly. "Are you all right? Did he hurt you, little one?"

She opened her mouth, her gaze widening. "Tray?" she asked, her voice wobbling.

He frowned, his hands becoming firmer on her shoulders. She was so pale, her flesh was nearly translucent. Damn Vaughn! He had frightened her so badly that she seemed to have lost her senses. "Yes, it's me. Alyssa, are you going to faint? Do you want me to—"

With a little cry, she freed her hands from their grip around her knees and reached out, her fingertips barely grazing Tray's drawn face. This man, this giant of a man whose wide shoulders blotted out the light as he leaned over her, was Tray. The dark expression on his face clashed with the soft urgency of his voice. Poignantly, among all her cartwheeling thoughts, Alyssa remembered him saying that he was ugly. No! No, he wasn't! She hungrily absorbed all she could of him in those fleeting seconds. His hair was a bluish black, softly waving and framing his strong, square face. She looked beyond the harshness of his features to the concern emanating from his intelligent gray eyes, eyes that drew her into the burning light of their depths. She quickly slipped her exploring gaze past his aristocratic nose to his well-shaped mouth, which pulled naturally upward at the corners, as she had discovered last night. No, he was not ugly, not someone to cringe away from! When she found her voice it was filled with unparalleled joy.

"Tray, I can see . . . I can see. . . ."

He recoiled slightly, as if she had struck him. "What?"

Alyssa gave a choked laugh, crawling to her knees, tears streaming down her cheeks as she held his suddenly fearful gray gaze. "Yes! I started to see when I was here, in the stall," she cried, her words rushing like a torrent from a waterfall. "Everything started getting light—I thought the sun was shining in on me from the window. A-and then, I saw my hand as it rested against Ned."

His joy matched her own as he gripped her shoulder. "You can see?" he rasped. "You can actually see?"

She let out a little cry of happiness. "Yes. Oh, yes!"

It was true. As Tray scrutinized her intently in those breathless seconds of wonder, her eyes held a gold spark in their shining depths. "Sweet God," he breathed, "it's true! I can see new life in your eyes, Aly."

She sobbed, her hands against her mouth as she stared across the inches that separated them, her emerald eyes alight with joy. "Oh, Tray, I can see you. I can see you. . . ."

Something died inside of Tray and he swallowed hard, unable to hold her shimmering gaze. She was so beautiful, and he was far from it. If his features did not turn her away from him, then his deformity surely would. Tray choked against the sudden bitterness that welled up within him and tried to counter the agony ripping him apart with Alyssa's bubbling happiness. All that they had established, their intimacy, the hours spent in quiet companionship with each other, shattered before him. Tray tried to hide his disappointment, tried to be happy for her. His head snapped up as he felt her hesitant touch upon the corner of his mouth.

"You're bleeding," she whispered, reaching down and retrieving his white linen handkerchief. Alyssa moved forward on her knees until they rested against his large, hard-muscled thigh. Her eyes were jade with concern as she gently pressed the cloth against his mouth.

He grimaced and took the handkerchief from her, barely meeting her eyes. "It's nothing. Just a small cut. Vaughn never could do much damage to me," Tray muttered.

Alyssa remained at his side, sitting back on her heels, hands resting in her lap as he daubed at the cut. "You saved me," she whispered. "I was never so frightened. It was as if he would do it all—"

"It's over," he told her wearily, wrestling with the heaviness now weighing his heart. "He won't try it again. I can promise you that."

Her gaze worriedly swept across Tray's face. "The side of your face is swelling. I think I can stand now. Please, let me take care of you. Let me get some cool water on your cheek...."

Tray winced as she carefully touched his bruised flesh. His heart was heavy with silent anguish. When he stood up, she would know. She would realize he was clubfooted. Deformed. And then—he heaved a tortured sigh—then she would shrink away from him, and the tenderness he saw resting in her lovely emerald gaze would quickly turn to disgust. She would think him the spawn of the devil....

Tray tried to put his own pain aside for her sake. "With Vaughn leaving, it means you no longer have to sleep with me," he told her curtly, rising to his feet. "You're free to go back to your own bedchamber now, Alyssa. Come, give me your hand. It's chilly out here and you're still recovering."

Alyssa blinked once, stunned by his abruptness. She placed her hand in his, wildly aware of a new warmth tingling through her hand as he gently drew her upward to stand on her own feet. He brought her to his right side, his hand resting beneath her elbow. Tray opened the door and then closed it, leaving Old Ned in peace.

Tray silently endured Alyssa's looks as they walked toward the manor. He could feel the flick of her eyes upon him from time to time as he limped with every damn step he took. He wanted to hide his deformity somehow and felt the helpless rage of knowing he could not. At the door, he risked a glance down at Alyssa. She had bowed her head, lips pressed together, her thick auburn lashes hiding her true feelings as if she were ashamed to be seen with him. Once they were inside, he released her.

"Sorche will look in on you. I'll have Craddock send a rider for Dr. Birch. He will have to examine your eyes." He led the way down the hall and stopped to open the door to her bedchamber. He hated himself for sounding clipped and hard. This was a time for celebration. Alyssa had regained her sight. She could now see those sunsets once again and gaze upon the gulls that floated against the blue of the sky. Tray's mouth tightened as he pushed the door open. "This is your room," he stated, and turned to leave.

"Tray?"

He froze as he heard the tremble of hurt in Alyssa's soft voice. He couldn't face her; he didn't want to see the look of pity in her eyes. "What is it?" he growled impatiently.

Alyssa took a step toward him. "Your cuts. Do you want me to—"

"No. Just have Sorche look after you. I'm going to make sure Vaughn gets on that coach and leaves."

Stung by his rejection, Alyssa slowly turned away, feeling the sting of tears brimming over in her eyes. She watched as Tray walked with a broken stride down the walnut-paneled hall. Finally Alyssa turned and went into her bedchamber.

Her brief depression was lifted by the kaleidoscopic deluge of sensations her newly healed eyes beheld. She stood entranced on the thick, ivory carpet, staring like an awestruck child at her richly appointed surroundings. The walls were a pale pink in color, white ruffled feminine curtains embraced each window and a lovely dark pink quilt covered the canopied bed. Stunned, Alyssa sat down in the mahogany chair, which was covered with ivory silk. This was the chair where she had sat so many times before, warming herself by the fire and thinking. . . .

She had little time to revel in her miracle, for Maura raced into her room, skirts flying, breathless with joy. On her heels came Sorche with a broad smile. Alyssa and Sorche embraced, tears flowing freely between them. The older woman held Alyssa at arm's length, half laughing and half crying.

"You look exactly like I thought you would," Alyssa sobbed, trying in vain to wipe her cheeks dry.

Sorche grinned happily, patting her arm. "Plenty of time to look at all of us, lamb. Come, you should sit down. Can't strain those eyes too much until Dr. Birch arrives."

Alyssa clasped Sorche's gnarled fingers. "Please," she begged softly, "Tray's been hurt—"

"What?" Sorche drew her thin brows down.

Alyssa gulped back a sob. "Vaughn attacked me again. In the stable. Please, go to Tray, Sorche. He won't let me dress his wounds." Alyssa bit hard on her lower lip. "I—I think he's angry with me." She wrung the words out.

"Impossible!" Sorche exploded, picking up her skirts and waddling toward the door. "He's probably more upset over Vaughn's trickery than anything else. He cares a great deal for you—I'm sure he's just throttling his rage to keep from killing Vaughn! Never you mind, Alyssa. Tray's upset all right, but not at you. That I'm sure of. Now you just rest. Maura will see to your needs."

Sorche heard the shouting long before she reached the carriage house. She arrived in time to see Vaughn take a step inside the coach. He turned sharply toward Tray. "This isn't over yet, *half* brother. I'm going to Father. And I swear, you'll regret ever saving that Irishwoman from the death cart. I'll make you rue that day for the rest of your life."

Tray's gray eyes grew feral. "Try it, Vaughn, you spineless bastard."

Sorche gritted her teeth, yanking Tray away from where the horses pranced nervously in their traces.

"Tray, stop this! Let it go!" she said as Vaughn's coach pulled away. "There are others who need your attention far worse than that young, arrogant pup!"

"What do you mean?" he growled.

"Aren't you happy that Alyssa's eyesight is back? Mother Mary! You're pouting and sulking like an old broody hen who's had her eggs stolen out from under her!"

Tray scowled, gingerly touching his aching cheekbone. "What are you snapping about?"

Sorche came to a stop at the door to the manor, puffing madly, her round cheeks blazing with color. "Alyssa was in tears! She thinks you're angry with her. Mother Mary, Saint Joseph and Peter, you act as if she's dead or something!"

Tray's scowl deepened as he looked down at his foster mother. "Might as well be. You weren't there when she first looked at me, Sorche. And then, when I got up and she saw me limp, she couldn't even look at me."

"Bah! I ought to box your ears! You think Alyssa finds you too ugly to look at? Is that it?"

Tray felt the flush of heat in his cheeks and looked beyond Sorche, who stood like an angry banshee between him and the door. "I know women don't find me...appealing."

Sorche glared, waving her fist up at him. "Tristan Trayhern, if I was tall enough, I *would* box your ears!"

Tray grinned belatedly. Sorche never called him by his full name. She was all red, like a ripe September apple, blustering and caterwauling. "To what do I owe the honor of all this?" he teased.

"You realize you're more blind than Alyssa ever was? If you had been with me in there when I went flying to her bedchamber, you'd change your pitiful tune, Tray! There she was, sitting by the fire looking sad when she's got her sight back. And you know why, you young, impertinent whelp?"

He combed his fingers through his hair, beginning to feel some of his fear abating beneath Sorche's scolding. "I have the feeling if I don't ask why, you'll box my ears," he said dryly, the hard planes of his face easing. "Why?"

"Because," Sorche sputtered in Gaelic, "she was more worried about you than anything else! She was in tears, begging me to go after you, saying you wouldn't even allow her to tend those wounds on your thick skull."

Hope rose with fear. "She said I was thickheaded?"

"No, *I'm* saying it!"

"She was worried about me?"

Sorche shook her head. "More than you deserve, you stubborn Welshman!"

Tray's eyes lightened a bit. "Then you don't want to tend my wounds?"

"That's Alyssa's responsibility, not mine! Now get in there. Next time I see her, I want to see those tears gone and a smile on her face."

"Yes, madam," he murmured, bowing deeply and then ushering her through the door.

Maura had just left Alyssa's bedchamber when Tray stopped at the door. He knocked softly.

"Come in . . ."

Tray braced himself emotionally to face Alyssa and quietly entered the room. She stood by the window, the sunlight streaming through the crystal, highlighting her abundant burgundy tresses, now brushed and shining around her shoulders. Tray's eyes widened in appreciation as his hungry gaze swept from her beribboned hair to the simple country dress of pale lavender and lace. She held a book between her hands and was poised like a deer ready for flight.

"Sorche said I'd better come and let you tend me or she'd box my ears," he said in way of a greeting.

Alyssa's eyes softened. "Yes, please, come in. Sit here by the fire. I'll go to the water closet and get a cloth. . . ." She pulled the chair out, placing it more closely to the hearth. Her voice was breathless as she hurried out of the chamber, a flush covering her cheeks.

Tray waited until Alyssa had disappeared before limping over to the chair. He took off his dark blue wool coat, throwing it on the end of her bed. Was he going mad? Did she truly seem happy to see him? Or was she pretending because she didn't have the heart to hurt him?

Alyssa brought a porcelain bowl filled with warm water, soap and a cloth, setting it beside the chair. The anxious look on her face made him wince inwardly. She was fluttering nervously around him, her fingers trembling as she gently cleansed the cut at the corner of his mouth and the scrape on his swelling cheek. He gazed up at her, sinking into the cradle of her womanly scent and beauty.

"How are your eyes?" Damnation! He still sounded gruff and curt.

"Improving." She shyly glanced down at him, a hesitant start of a smile on her lips. "I can see the print in the book now. A while ago, it was blurred."

Tray cleared his throat. "Good." Did he have to sound so formal? God's blood, he was more nervous than she was! She patted his skin dry and then knelt in front of him. "Your hand?"

"Huh? Oh, my hand..." Tray steeled himself against her gentle touch. He should be the one kneeling in front of her. She was the one who had suffered indignity at Vaughn's hands, not he.

"Your whole hand is swollen," Alyssa whispered, distressed by his bloodied and bruised knuckles. She was secretly thrilled to be able to hold his large, well-shaped hand between her own. It was covered with thick calluses on the palm, but the nails were clean and blunt cut—a hand that could be so gentle when touching her, holding her.

"It was worth it," Tray growled, taking savage pleasure in remembering the feel of Vaughn's nose breaking beneath the force of his fist. Tray's expression was guarded as he held her unwavering gaze. "Tell me, do you think my face lives up to last night's inspection?" His stomach knotted and he tensed, waiting for her answer.

Alyssa laughed softly and finished tending to his hand. She gave him a shy smile. "You look even better than what my fingers told me."

Tray felt the cold knot in his stomach dissolve and he straightened up, a sense of utter euphoria making him feel light-headed. "You mean I don't make you run and scream?"

She frowned suddenly. "Of course not. You're not an ogre."

"Some women think I am."

Alyssa shrugged. "Just as you pride yourself on knowing people, Tray, I pride myself in being able to read a face."

"Indeed?"

"Yes, my lord. As I told you last night, eyes set close together forebode evil. Vaughn has such eyes."

A wry smile pulled at Tray's mouth as he rose from the chair. "My lady, if it wouldn't tax you too much, I'd like to continue our fascinating discussion. Perhaps if we drink a cup of chocolate before retiring, we'll both sleep well in our individual beds. Would you honor me with your presence in my bedchamber at, say, ten tonight?"

Alyssa flushed, demurely lowering her lashes. With a curtsy that would put even the most fashionable, titled ladies to shame, she agreed.

## Chapter Eleven

Tray hid the beginning of a smile as he saw Alyssa confidently walk out to meet him in front of the stable. Today, they were off to the lambing pastures, which lay nestled in the gray rocky mountains to the southeast of Shadowhawk. The morning was fresh, and sunlight lanced the gathering clouds from the north. A stimulating ocean breeze was making the horses restless, but Tray sat easily upon Rasheed, who was doing more than his share of pawing and snorting, eager to be off. The perturbed look on Sorche's face as she bustled after Alyssa made Tray swallow his smile.

Alyssa had loosely plaited her hair into one thick, long braid, which hung across the white peasant shirt she wore. As his gaze swept lazily down her young, slender body, Tray could guess why Sorche appeared so dismayed. Instead of a riding habit, Alyssa had somehow talked Sorche into allowing her to wear a pair of his buckskin breeches. Her boots hugged her lower leg, and the breeches, although far too large, clearly displayed the curved length of her thighs. Sorche looked horrified.

"Good morning, my lord." Alyssa was busily putting on kidskin gloves that matched her dark maroon wool cloak.

Tray tipped his head in respectful obeisance to Alyssa. She stood expectantly, waiting for him to say something. A spark of challenge glinted in her eyes and Tray couldn't stop the smile that now lurked at the corners of his mouth. "Good morning, my lady." Rasheed sidled and Tray pulled on the reins, quieting the stallion. He gestured to Old Ned, who stood ready beneath Thomas's hand. "As you can see, we're prepared for you."

Alyssa was so intent on having to argue with Tray over her wearing a pair of breeches that she had failed to even glance at the horse she would be riding to the high country. Her lips parted in amazement. There, on Old Ned's back, was a man's saddle, not the customary ladies' sidesaddle! Laughter gurgled up from her throat and Alyssa's gaze darted from the saddle to Tray. She reached out her hand, resting it momentarily on the hard surface of his thigh.

"You knew!" she said in an accusing tone.

Gravely, Tray nodded, merriment in his gray eyes. "Actually, when Maura came to me earlier this morning, wringing her hands and telling me that you were tailoring several pairs of my old breeches, I knew," he admitted. He looked over at Sorche, who still wore a frown on her face. "It's all right," he called to his foster mother, grinning recklessly.

Sorche crossed her stout arms across her ample bosom. "It isn't right at all," she grumbled, "wearing a man's pair of breeches!"

Alyssa ran over and hugged Sorche, then she skipped back to Old Ned and eagerly mounted. The morning was chilly despite the first long rays of the sun reaching across the ocean to warm the Welsh land, and Alyssa drew the hood of the cloak over her head. "But we're going to be working, Sorche! How could I possibly help if I were always tripping over the material of my riding habit? Would you want me to fall off that sidesaddle while holding a squirming lamb?"

"Mother Mary and Saint Joseph! Or course I wouldn't!"

"I'll be better off dressed this way, believe me, Sorche. And who else will see me? Just Tray. And he understands, don't you?"

Tray shared a secret smile with her and then directed his attention to the distressed Sorche. "Mother," he began in a conciliatory tone, "Aly was raised in a pair of trousers and a man's saddle. And you know that we'll be mounting and dismounting quite a bit, picking up orphaned lambs. I don't want Alyssa to fall when a struggling lamb gets caught in the material of her skirt and throws her off balance."

"Well," she ceded gruffly, "since you put it that way. . . . But I still say it isn't ladylike!"

Alyssa laughed, riding Ned up beside Tray, her voice silvery and pure in the coolness of the morning. "I promise that as soon as we return, I'll be back in dresses and riding sidesaddle."

"Very well, but mind you, Tray, she's a beautiful young lady and deserves to dress like one! I'm Irish, too, but you don't see me going around barefoot and in a pair of old breeches."

Alyssa had the good sense to remain silent and let Tray mollify Sorche. "And when we return, I fully expect you to have the best dressmakers from Liverpool come to Shadowhawk to sew her a wardrobe," he agreed.

Sorche's scowl left her face. "That's more like it," she muttered, and her features softened. "Both of you, be careful."

Tray nodded. "Very careful, Mother," he agreed. "We'll see you in approximately a week. Pray the weather holds."

Alyssa could barely contain the explosive excitement that threatened to engulf her as they finally set out. Even Old Ned was stepping lively. Normally anything more than a shuffling walk was an achievement; today, the Welsh cob

was smartly lifting his twenty-year-old legs. She had to admit that Tray and Rasheed were far more impressive looking. Rays of the sun set fire to the blood bay coat of the
stallion, and his proud neck arched magnificently. But what
took her breath away was Tray. This was the first time she
had had the pleasure of watching him sit astride the Arabian stallion.

Despite his size and muscularity, Tray rode with a prac-
ticed ease that bespoke a man born to the saddle, as she
herself had been. The buckskin breeches he wore hugged his
thighs and narrow hips with an awesome beauty. And he
was beautiful, Alyssa realized, in the way only males could
be. She found herself drinking him in, memorizing the
breadth of his shoulders and powerful chest. Beneath his
simple cotton shirt, dark, curling hairs showed at the base
of his throat.

Her gaze lingered on Tray's face and she found herself
smiling softly. He looked ruggedly handsome, relaxed, the
corners of his well-shaped mouth sending a tremor of heat
through her. His black hair curled slightly and she longed to
comb her fingers through the thick silk of it. When Tray
slowly turned his head to look at her, Alyssa felt an ache
beginning in her lower body, an intense feeling that left her
shaken and bewildered. Never had she experienced such
pleasure as now, beneath his tender inspection. She felt
cherished, protected and—the word *loved* sprang to her
mind.

Love? she asked herself, a slight frown tugging at her
mouth. What was love? She wasn't sure, never having experienced it. And what was this marvelous, breathless sensation vibrating through her as Tray caught and held her
gaze? Her heart beat faster, her palms felt clammy and she
experienced such a deep flush of utter joy beneath his inspection that she thought she might faint. And she had

never fainted in her life! Alyssa lowered her lashes, unable to hold Tray's hungry look. Oh, why hadn't she paid more attention to the girls who were two or three years older than herself when they talked about love?

They rode in companionable silence. Occasionally Tray would call her attention to a brown hare or a red hawk flying high above them, hunting for prey. The gentle slope of the plain began giving way to a less hospitable soil of rocks and pebbles. Wales, unlike her beloved Ireland, was wild, rocky and almost desolate in its appearance. As she looked up, Alyssa saw the craggy black mountains swathed in a white blanket of snow.

Three hours later they arrived at the lower slopes, where a huge flock, numbering well over a thousand ewes, was gathered. The wind was sharp and Alyssa drew her heavy wool cloak around her, noticing that Tray had finally donned his black one. Her attention was drawn to the sheep, their woolly whiteness stark against the green of the grass and black rocks that dotted the rolling expanse of the slope where they grazed. Several Welsh collies circled the peaceful flock, snapping quickly at any member that wanted to wander too far from the safety of the group. The head shepherd raised his hand in greeting, his bearded face breaking into a welcoming smile as they rode up. To the right of them stood a large gray-and-white stone cottage with a slate roof. A stream of black smoke wafted lazily from the chimney to be swept away by the inconstant breeze coming from the mountains far above them.

"Aly, why don't you go inside and get warmed up? Sayer and I will be in momentarily." Tray gave her a smile, noticing her nose and ears were red from the cold. "He's probably got a kettle of stew brewing, if I know him."

"It sounds wonderful," she murmured, dismounting.

Tray grinned. "I'll see you in a few minutes, little one. Get inside. If you catch so much as a sniffle I'll have not only Dr. Birch angry with me, but Sorche, as well."

After a brief meal at the cottage, they set out again at a good pace. The wind picked up, its gusts containing an icy bite. Alyssa kept the hood over her head, grateful for the warmth it provided. She had to urge Old Ned to keep pace with Tray's seemingly tireless stallion. By the time they reached the second cottage, it was late afternoon and Ned was stumbling with fatigue. Alyssa gave the Welsh cob an understanding pat as they finally drew to a halt. Everywhere she looked, they were surrounded by an ocean of bleating sheep. Lambs on wobbly legs would peek out from behind their woolly mothers to see who the new visitors arriving on horseback were. Alyssa smiled at Tray as they waited for the head shepherd to be summoned to them.

"I'm so glad you let me come along! It feels good to hear the call of the sheep. I can hardly wait to get my hands on the babies."

Tray gave her a tender look, relaxing in the saddle. "You like babies, eh?"

She flushed, catching his innuendo. "Well—of course." Then she added defiantly, "Tell me what Irishwoman doesn't love children!"

His glance was charged with meaning. "You'll make a good mother, Alyssa Kyle," he said huskily.

Alyssa swallowed, mesmerized by the intimate caress of his voice and gaze. How many times had she dreamed of having children? There was nothing in the world that she wanted more than her own babies to sing lullabies to, carry on her hip and watch grow amid the shower of her affection. Alyssa lowered her lashes, unable to stand the heated look she saw in Tray's gray eyes. What would it be like to have Tray as the father of her children? She gasped softly as the ramifications of that question struck her with full force. The head shepherd galloped up to them on a sturdy bay cob, distracting her from this troubling train of thought.

"My Lord Trayhern, I thought you'd never get here!" the man panted, pulling his cob alongside Rasheed.

"What is it, Master Reece?" Tray asked, his voice calm.

"I just came from the last cottage, my lord." The red-faced man gulped, trying to catch his breath. "Master Taffy has all his shepherds out trying to gather up the scattered flock. For the last two nights he's been besieged with packs of wild dogs that have come to hunt the new lambs. You're needed there."

"All right," Tray growled, "I'll go up there right now. In the meantime, Reece, I want you to spare me all the men you can and send them up tomorrow at first light. Send a messenger down to Sayer and tell him to get extra men from Shadowhawk. We're going to need them."

Reece bobbed his head gratefully. "Yes, my lord. Right away!" He turned, digging his heels into the cob and galloping down the slope toward the hay shed in the distance. Tray turned to Alyssa.

"I want you to stay here, Aly. It's getting dark and Ned is too tired to make the trip."

"Tray, let me get a fresh horse from one of the shepherds. I can—"

His eyes narrowed. "There isn't a horse here that can possibly keep pace with Rasheed. I need to move quickly."

Alyssa leaped off Ned, tying the reins and putting them across the cob's neck. She walked around to Tray's left side, her arms extended. "Then take me with you! You're going to need every person you have once you get up there, and I can borrow a cob when we arrive. I've lambed before. I know what has to be done. Give me a hand up!"

He gaped blankly down at her for a moment before a slow grin pulled at his mouth. "All right, my lady, but be prepared to ride the whip. If you fall off, I'll leave you behind."

She gripped his hand and Tray easily pulled her up. Alyssa settled behind him on Rasheed's broad, short back. "I'm not going to fall off," she told him tartly, wrapping her arms tightly around his waist.

Within seconds, they had left the lambing cottage behind. Alyssa gloried in the powerful, synchronous movement of the Arabian beneath them as they raced across the darkening slopes toward the craggy mountains looming before them. Clinging tightly to Tray as dusk turned to darkness, she was taken by Rasheed's incredible endurance. Riding a horse at night at any speed was dangerous, and yet the stallion, like his confident master, seemed able to pierce the veil of darkness that surrounded them. Rasheed rarely slowed to anything less than a trot to catch a second wind and then quickly moved back into another canter.

They rode into the last encampment hours later. The weak light of lanterns outlined a huge shed area and two cottages. Through tired eyes, Alyssa could see men hurrying back and forth from the lambing shed. Her arms were weak from strain and she rested her head against Tray's back as he brought the stallion down to a walk. She let her arms drop to her sides, her fingers numb. Tray seemed as tireless as his horse, still sitting straight in the saddle, as if they had merely gone for a short country ride.

"Aly?"

She roused herself, her head feeling terribly weighted. "Yes?"

"Are you all right?" There was genuine concern in Tray's deep voice.

Alyssa felt his arm come around, awkwardly encircling her and giving her a squeeze. She smiled and closed her eyes. "I'm fine."

"You seem tired."

"Why, aren't you?"

"Spitfire to the end, eh?"

She laughed with him, nuzzling her cheek against the wiry wool of his cloak. She felt bereft when he withdrew his arm. "I told you I wouldn't fall off."

A chuckle rumbled from his chest. "Only because you were afraid I'd break your slender neck if you did."

"True. I clung to you out of absolute terror, in case you chose to make good your threat, my lord."

"Why do I have the feeling you're just letting me think that?"

Alyssa slid her arms around his waist, giving him a long embrace, burying her face against his back. "Because I know you didn't mean a word of it, my lord."

His large hand covered her own. "I'm taking you over to the sleeping cottage, Aly."

"But—"

"Listen, little one, I'm proud of you. You have more stamina than I would give any woman credit for. But under the circumstances, you're so exhausted you wouldn't be of any use to me or Master Taffy. Don't forget, you're still recuperating. I love you for your courage, but you must bow to my judgment this one time and rest. You can begin helping us on the morrow."

Alyssa shut her eyes, a tightly guarded feeling uncoiling within her heart. He loved her? Tray could have easily ordered her to the cottage and provided no further explanation. Instead, he respected her enough to explain his request. And how many men had she ever known who possessed that kind of innate sensitivity? Just one. Tray. His hand upon her cold, frozen fingers felt warm and comforting. Suddenly, Alyssa had the wild urge to embrace Tray as tightly as she could. Instead, she settled for placing her hand over his and giving it a strong squeeze.

"What about you?" she asked, feeling Rasheed come to a halt.

Tray dropped the reins on the stallion's neck and twisted around, gently taking Alyssa into his arms and bringing her across his lap. His eyes narrowed as he studied her face in the dim lamplight. Her braid had come loose, and her hair was in tangled disarray around her pale face. Keeping one arm around her, Tray tucked several wayward tendrils behind her delicate ear. Her eyes were dark with fatigue, her lips slightly parted as she gazed wonderingly up at him.

"I'll be all right," he assured her quietly, his hand cradling her cheek. She looked so vulnerable and trusting, so totally relaxed within his embrace. Tray saw none of the fear that had lingered in her eyes and felt no tension in her body. She lay helpless in his arms, and without realizing what he was doing, he leaned down.

Alyssa stared up at him, mesmerized by the warm, liquid darkness in his shadowed eyes as his head came downward. Her lips parted of their own accord and she felt him grip her more tightly to him. The moist heat of his breath fell softly across her lips as he guided her chin upward...upward to meet his descending mouth.

She was totally unprepared for the charge that raged through her as his mouth slanted across her lips. The texture of his mouth was gentle against hers, tentatively tasting her, testing her response. She closed her eyes, her lashes like dark crescents against her cheeks as she shyly emulated the movement of his mouth against her own. She felt him groan...or did she hear it? An avalanche of feelings, sensations and heat all exploded inside her. He tasted strong and good, and her nostrils flared as she hungrily inhaled his sweaty male scent. Unconsciously, Alyssa lifted her hand, placing it against his chest, and felt the heavy, thudding beat of his heart beneath her palm.

"Sweet," he groaned against her wet, soft, lips, "you're so sweet and good, Aly. God..." Tray lifted his head, a fraction of an inch from hers. Alyssa's lashes slowly lifted, revealing languorous green eyes. A tender smile touched his mouth. "Come, I'll help you down," he told her in a roughened tone. "I think you'd fall if I let go of you."

Dizziness nearly felled Tray as he lowered the ewe to the muddy ground. Twenty sheep left.... He straightened up, every muscle in his body screaming for a moment's rest. Pushing his wet hair away from his eyes, he signaled Taffy and his men to join him. Drew had just returned to tell them that the fire was hot and the mutton steaks were ready to eat. Wiping his strong fingers down the length of his blackened breeches, Tray trudged toward Rasheed. All he wanted was to see Alyssa's lovely smile. She'd arrived hours earlier, going directly to the thatched hut not far away to start a fire and fix them a meal.

Alyssa met Tray at the door with a glower. Then, as she took in his exhausted appearance, her expression softened. She gave him a distraught look as he walked to the table, where the mutton was piled high on a tin plate.

"Tray, can't you stop? You're nearly falling over," she begged.

The meat smelled good and he sat down, grabbing a roasted leg. "We've only got some twenty to go, Aly, and then I'll rest."

"But—"

"We're all tired. It isn't just me."

"Taffy and his men haven't been without sleep for two days like you!"

He chewed the succulent meat, thinking that nothing had ever tasted so good. "Part of the responsibility of being a lord," he grumbled. "If I quit now, my men won't respect me, little one."

Alyssa glared at him. "You are stubborn!"

He heard the concern in her protest and looked up, his eyes bloodshot. "At least I'm not narrow between the eyes."

She exploded into a string of Gaelic. "You're impossible, Tray! Impossible!"

He rewarded her with a tolerant smile as Taffy and his men entered the cottage. "And I don't have a Roman nose, either."

Alyssa stood in front of him, tensed and scowling, then, suddenly, she broke into helpless laughter, laughter that rang like silvered bells through the old cottage. The sound was music to everyone's ears, lifting all their weary spirits.

They had no more eaten their fill of mutton when a torrential downpour of rain shattered everyone's improving mood. Tray was the first on his feet, snarling a curse beneath his breath. Taffy made the sign of the cross.

"It will take five hours, my lord, before that stream widens into a river and the mountain runoff floods those ewes off that piece of ground."

Tray looked down at his three exhausted men. Their faces were slack and muddied, eyes red-rimmed, mouths set in stubborn lines. He spoke softly in Welsh. "I need your help."

"We're with you, my lord," Taffy spoke up quickly, gesturing for the other two men to get to their feet.

"Go on ahead, Taffy. I'll be there in a moment," Tray told him. He waited until the shepherds had left and then walked over to Alyssa. Her hair was mussed and in need of a good brushing. He didn't miss the worry in the depths of her eyes as she looked up at him. He rested his hands on her small shoulders.

"It will take a while to get those sheep across, Aly. Would you unsaddle Rasheed and rub him down? There's a small shed in back of the cottage. Perhaps there's some old dried grass to feed to him."

"I'll take care of him," she promised, craving Tray's closeness.

"Thank you."

"What happens after the sheep are freed?"

"I'll have Taffy take them down this mountain and drive them back toward the main flock." Tray reached out to her and then hesitated, realizing his fingers were muddy. He wanted to caress her hair, faintly aware of its clean scent. "Stay indoors," he told her, "there's no sense in your getting wet and cold."

The rains continued for five hours. Alyssa rubbed Rasheed until the stallion groaned with pleasure, lying down in the narrow shed as soon as she completed the task. The horse had to be as tired as Tray was, Alyssa thought compassionately. Returning to the old cottage, she kept herself busy. She brought in clean straw, placing it in one corner of the dirt floor for a bed in case a shepherd needed a soft place to sleep one night. There was an ample supply of coal for heat, and after stuffing the cracks in the wall with straw, the place was suitably warm and dry. She found a small garden patch beside the cottage and was able to dig up some potatoes and turnips. It was almost as if she were at home again, foraging the land for sustenance. Inside, after she had dried off, she discovered some onions, peppercorns and a small cooking kettle.

The early afternoon sped by as Alyssa cleaned the kettle, caught fresh rain and used her newfound ingredients along

with chunks of mutton to make a passable stew. She brought in Rasheed's large, thick wool saddle blanket and laid it out before the hearth to dry. Pleased with her efforts, Alyssa found a dented tin bowl and washed her hands, neck and face. After replaiting her hair, she felt somewhat better. Taking another look out the small window, she noticed it was growing dark much earlier than she had anticipated. Was it because of the heavy curtain of rain? More clouds coming from the north? Unable to stand the suspense any longer, Alyssa donned her dry wool cloak, mounted a black cob and headed toward the waterfall.

Taffy and his shepherds stood huddled in the driving rain. Alyssa saw Tray among them and noticed that only one ewe was left on the other side of the water. Her eyes widened in shock as she realized how expansive and angry the stream had grown. The lone ewe stood in knee-deep water, cowering against the rock wall, the sound of its bleating drowned out by the roar of the cataract. Alyssa dismounted and walked toward the men.

"I want you to take them down the mountain, now," Tray was instructing a shepherd. "If that other stream rises too high, you'll never get the flock to cross. You have to leave immediately."

The Welsh shepherd nodded in agreement. "What about that last thickheaded ewe?" he asked.

Tray rubbed the back of his aching neck. His muscles felt as if they were on fire, begging for rest. "I'll get her."

"Master Taffy," Alyssa broke in, "I've made a stew for all of you—"

"They don't have time, Aly," Tray said.

Taffy gave her an apologetic smile. "Thanks anyway, my lady. If the other streams weren't rising, we'd be glad to partake of it."

"Just be careful, Master Taffy."

The old Welshman grinned at her. "We will indeed, my lady. Come on, lads!"

She stood there near Tray, acutely aware of his weariness. His broad shoulders were hunched, his face haggard and gray-looking. He slowly turned to her.

"One more."

Alyssa reached out, her fingers wrapping around his muddied wrist. "Then can you rest? Do we have to go back with the herd?"

"I'm afraid it will be too late." Tray mustered a broken smile. "And that mutton stew sounds too good to pass up. I was wondering what kind of cook you might be."

"A good one."

"Indeed?"

"If you hurry up and get that poor ewe, you'll find out."

Tray's fingers found hers and gave her hand a brisk squeeze before releasing it and beginning the treacherous trek across the swirling, rushing water. The width of the stream had increased by half since the rains had begun. Tray bowed his head against the downpour. Taffy and his men had already disappeared over the steep slope, driving the flock down the mountain. A sense of victory flowed through him; they had saved all of them. The ewes would have fat, healthy lambs within a day or two. Wearily, Tray rubbed his watering eyes, feeling the pull of the water tugging at him. The bottom was now less slippery and more adhesive, the sharp surface of the rocks providing him with some form of stability beneath his boots.

The ewe practically fell into Tray's arms when he leaned down to pick her up. She was heavy, and by the bulge of her belly he was positive that she was carrying twins. Tray looked across the raging water to where Alyssa was standing, a forlorn hooded figure, her small hands stark white against her cloak. The ewe bleated and struggled as Tray

limped into the river. Within moments, he was up to his
waist, the ewe's feet dragging through the churning water.
He tightened his faltering grip on the animal. With an unexpected lunge, the ewe wrenched him sideways. Tray felt
white-hot pain tear through his leg as his left foot twisted.

He was falling backward, holding the bleating ewe in a
death grip. Alyssa's scream rose above the roar. And
then ... icy water closed over his head, flowing into his
mouth and up his nostrils. The animal jerked convulsively
and Tray floundered toward the surface, dragging the sheep
upward to keep her from drowning, as she surely would if
he let go of her. Momentarily blinded, he swallowed huge
amounts of the muddy water. The swift current carried him
a hundred feet downstream before he was able to get his feet
under him once again and crawl toward the opposite shore,
cursing the panicked ewe he held in tow.

The instant the sheep could stand, she bounded onto dry
land, bleating pitifully and running in the direction of the
flock, which had disappeared over the horizon. Tray
groaned and rolled over on his back, gasping for air. Unre-
mitting pain shot up his left calf. He was barely aware of
Alyssa, for all her diminutive size, gripping his hands above
his head and pulling him to the safety of the bank. He heard
her sobbing his name over and over again and forced his
eyes open. She was leaning over him, hair wet and tangled,
her face frozen in terror, breathing as hard as he was.

He was weak, more weak than he had ever been in his life.
No sleep and the hard physical demands of the past two days
had finally taken their toll. Reaching out, he wrapped his
fingers around Alyssa's hand, which rested on his chest.

"I'm all right," he whispered. "Just let me rest a moment...."

"Oh, Tray, you almost drowned!" she sobbed. "I
thought you would never come back up. Damn you! Why

didn't you let go of that ewe! She was dragging you under again and again!''

''She's going to have twins,'' he gasped. ''Couldn't let her die, could I?'' He forced his lashes up, meeting her tormented green eyes.

''Bring the cob over here, Aly,'' he whispered, his voice raw. Suddenly, his injured left foot went into spasm. He damn near screamed, his body stiffening, his teeth clenching in an effort not to cry out. Oh God! Not now! Not that! God...

He heard Alyssa's voice rise in desperation, felt her shaking him. But he couldn't respond, not until the spasm eased. Sweat popped out on his glistening flesh. ''The cob,'' he gritted out. ''Get the cob, Aly. For God's sake, hurry!''

# Chapter Twelve

Tray remembered only bits and snatches of their trip back to the cottage. Alyssa managed to get him on the cob and walked beside the horse the entire way. He was in such intense pain that he could do no more than lie across the horse's neck, gripping its mane in an effort not to fall off. When they reached the cottage, Alyssa said nothing. Her eyes were huge and lips compressed into a set line as she helped him slide off the horse. Tray dared not put weight on his left foot, amazed at Alyssa's strength when she put his arm across her shoulder and tottered with him toward the little building. He managed to shove the door open with his hand.

The cottage smelled of fresh straw, and its warmth was almost overwhelming. Tray fell to his knees in the straw and slowly rolled over on his back. It was all he could do to keep from crying out as another spasm began. His great fists clenched, the knuckles whitening as he gripped the straw. Lips drawing away from his teeth, Tray sobbed for breath. He prayed and cursed the jagged, cutting pain that racked his leg.

"Tray?" Alyssa hurriedly shut the door and threw off her drenched cloak, kneeling at his side. Anxiously, she perused the tense lines of his body, looking for blood. "Where are you hurt? Tray?'' She shook him by the shoulder and he groaned. Hands trembling, she began an inspection of each of his limbs to see if he had broken a bone. His sobs tore at her and she felt his pain as if it were her own. His arms, ribs and shoulders showed no injury as she shakily pulled the shirt open off his chest, looking for bruising or the pooling of blood. Her wet hair hung in her eyes and she forced it away from her face, fighting back tears of frustration. Finally, an idea occurred to her.

"It's your leg, isn't it?" she whispered, quickly scrambling down to his feet. Of course! Why didn't she remember? Sorche had said his left leg had been injured some time ago, when Alyssa inquired about his limp. Had Tray twisted it when the ewe tried to leap from his arms? Was it broken? She glanced up at him, recalling the times when she had had to dress the wounds of men injured in battles with the English. She had never been able to shut her ears to their cries, just as she couldn't now as Tray groaned, twisting onto his side, drawing his left leg upward. His fingers reached out, gripping the boot so hard that his flesh whitened.

Reacting quickly, Alyssa took the right boot off his leg, throwing it aside. "Tray, let me help you," she begged, her fingers closing over his hand.

Tray gasped for breath, the pain becoming increasingly unbearable. Never had the spasms been so bad. He was aware of Alyssa's voice nearby. "No!" he ground out. "Don't touch it—" He tried to push her hand off his, but it was impossible. Pain surged through him, and he remembered screaming Alyssa's name before blessed darkness closed in on him, releasing him from his agony.

Alyssa sat back, momentarily stunned. She watched the color drain from Tray's hardened features, which suddenly went slack. His hand fell away from the boot he had been clutching so frantically. He had fainted. Thank God, he had escaped the pain. Quickly, she straightened him out, having no idea how much time she would have before he would awaken again. Gently, Alyssa worked the muddied boot loose, finally able to slide it off his leg. Nothing could have prepared her for the twisted, atrophied limb that lay white between her knees. A scream lurched to her throat and she stared in horrified fascination as the contorted muscles lumped and twisted before her very eyes. When her shocked gaze moved down to his ankle, her mouth grew dry.

Swallowing hard, Alyssa forced herself to look at Tray's foot. She reached her trembling hand out and barely touched the horribly arched sole, compassion coming to her eyes. "Oh, Tray," she cried softly, suddenly understanding everything. She leaned forward, cupping the knotting calf between her hands, beginning to carefully massage the angry, inflamed muscles, soothing them and quelling their protests against the ceaseless hours of work they had performed.

Tears scalded Alyssa's eyes, dropping and splashing against Tray's leg as she spread mutton fat across his lower leg and deformed foot. For the next hour she sat, rubbing the cold flesh of his leg, willing fresh blood back into the extremity and soothing away the angry spasms until her fingers were numb. Pulling herself to her feet, she heated water in the kettle on the stove and put the wool saddle blanket in it. She scalded her hands as she wrung out the blanket. Carefully, Alyssa wrapped Tray's calf and foot in the moist heat of the material, drawing out the stiffness.

Alyssa knelt down beside him, gently pushing the locks of black hair off his gray features. He was breathing deeply and evenly. As gently as she could, she removed his wet shirt and laid it out before the fire. He was covered with gooseflesh, and when she laid her hand on his naked shoulder, his skin was cold. Worriedly, Alyssa glanced over at her cloak, which she had hung in front of the fire. As soon as that dried, it would make a decent blanket to keep him warm. But until then . . . She stared down at the buckskin breeches that hugged his lower body. The damp material would chill Tray and probably serve to aggravate his left leg again. Alyssa knew what she had to do, and yet she froze, flashes of the rape looming before her tired eyes.

Biting down hard on her lower lip, Alyssa leaned forward, her fingers trembling badly as she unbuttoned his breeches. She shut her eyes tightly, pulling and tugging the wet fabric downward. Her heart was pounding in her throat as she carefully peeled the breeches off Tray's legs. Trying to ignore his blatantly male body, she got to her feet and prayed that the cloak was dry enough, but it was not. Shadowed fear hung in her eyes as Alyssa turned, giving Tray a quick glance. Shame flowed through her. Tray was injured and he didn't need her fear right now. Taking a deep, steadying breath, she walked to his side.

Kneeling down beside him, Alyssa began the painstaking process of rubbing every inch of his flesh to keep him warm and dry until the cloak was ready.

She had never seen a fully naked man in her life. Occasionally, Dev or Gavin would strip to the waist, throwing water on their chests and underarms when she was present. Even then, they would turn their backs, growling that it wasn't right for a girl to see a man's unclothed body. Alyssa swallowed, feeling the hard muscles of Tray's arms and shoulders. She stared in fascination at the wiry black hair that covered his chest, the curls silky and soft beneath her massaging touch.

As she worked her way downward, the pit of her stomach knotted and Alyssa began to feel faint. She forced herself to look upon his shaft, knowing it was like the one that had cruelly pierced her body and caused such pain. Tears squeezed from her eyes and she began shaking so badly that she got to her feet and moved away from Tray. She went over to the hearth, seeking its warmth because she was cold, cold all the way to her soul. Nausea rose suddenly, and without warning, Alyssa vomited.

Tray slowly awoke, aware that he was warm and that the room was dark, except for a flicker of light from the hearth. He felt the scratchy texture of wool around him and he raised his arm experimentally. He ached all over. Sensing movement, he let his eyes adjust and saw a darkened shape come out of the shadows across from where he lay and pad quietly toward him.

"Aly?"

"Yes, it's me," she whispered. She knelt down at his side, facing him, a pensive expression in her dark green eyes. "How do you feel?"

His mouth was gummy. "Thirsty," he muttered.

"I'll get you some water. Just lie still."

Tray frowned as she got up and walked to the other end of the cottage. He blinked, trying to remember the chain of events that was beginning to emerge from his exhausted memory. He directed his attention back to Alyssa. Was she really as pale as she appeared, or was it just the darkness? With her help he slowly sat up, the cloak falling around his waist. He ran his hand across his chest, realizing for the first time that he was naked. Alyssa sat there, patiently holding out a dented tin cup to him.

"I'm undressed."

"Your clothes were wet and muddy," she offered in a subdued voice.

Tray wrapped his fingers around the cup. "You undressed me?"

She nodded, avoiding his sharpened gaze, staring down at the floor. "I washed the mud from your clothes. They should be dry shortly." She lifted her head and stared over at the fireplace where his breeches and shirt hung. She had needed something to do to stop herself from going mad with the memories of what Vaughn had done to her; anything to keep her mind engaged, to stop from thinking... thinking...

Tray stared at her long and hard, confused. Why was she so unhappy? It was as if someone had broken her magnificent spirit. Then his eyes widened, and he felt as though a fist had been slammed into his gut. His leg! He swallowed hard, setting the cup down on the straw, his mouth tightening. This was the moment he had dreaded. Aly had seen his deformed leg. That was why she was so distraught, so... He took in a tortured breath.

"Aly?"

There was no response. She looked unbelievably fragile, her clean profile illuminated by the fire, wispy tendrils framing her drawn face. Tray experienced a deluge of shame and embarrassment for the shock, disgust and pain he had caused Alyssa.

"Aly, look at me. Please..." His voice cracked and his hand inched toward hers, their fingers almost touching. But she wouldn't want to be touched by him, Tray thought bitterly. All he wanted was to sweep her into his arms and confess how sorry he was, sorry for the way she had to discover that he was a flawed man.

She slowly raised her head, her lifting lashes revealing green eyes fraught with silent agony. She held his wavering gaze, realizing with poignancy that the glimmer of her tears was reflected in his charcoal gray eyes. A soft cry escaped her lips and she reached out, her fingers grazing his cheek.

"Tray? What is it? Are you in pain again?"

His gray eyes grew dark with agony. "Me? No, I thought...my leg," he forced out in a low voice. "I'm sorry, Aly. I know it's ugly and . . . disgusting. . . ."

She tilted her head, bewildered. "I don't understand." The tears she saw in his eyes reached to the very core of her heart, her own pain forgotten. "Is your leg hurting you again? Do you want me to rub it like I did before?"

He stared at her for a long moment, digesting her questions. Tray tried to think clearly. "You—took my boots off?"

"Yes. Your left leg was cramping, Tray. That's what was causing all your problems. You passed out from the pain."

His heart beat with a slow, dread-filled pound as he ruthlessly searched her face. Where was the disgust, the revulsion he had seen so many times before in other women's faces? "But—"

She managed a broken smile. "What's wrong with you? I treated your leg like I would a horse's sprained ligament. I took some mutton grease and began to rub the knots out." She pointed to Rasheed's blanket, which was drying again by the hearth. "And then I wrapped your leg in that to provide moist heat to the muscles. Why are you looking at me so oddly? I didn't do anything wrong, Tray. That's how you treat a cramp!"

Color flooded back to her cheeks and Tray couldn't believe what she was saying. This mere slip of a child-woman kneeling beside him, her hands primly folded in her lap, looking at him with complete bewilderment, shattered him. Tray knew that his deformity hadn't sickened her, and a fierce rush of joy surged through him. It was all he could do to stop himself from crying out with happiness. Several more minutes passed before he trusted his voice to speak to her. He reached over, gently cradling her work-worn hands between his own.

"I'm not questioning your care of me, little one. All the women who have ever seen that deformed left leg have been upset by it."

Aly managed a sheepish smile. "It surprised me, too, when I got that boot off."

Tray looked at her solemnly. "It's ugly."

She shrugged. "But the rest of you isn't."

His hands tightened around hers and he shut his eyes. "My God, Aly, do you know how rare you are?" he rasped.

"W-were you worried that if I knew you had a clubfoot, I would have nothing more to do with you?" she asked in an achingly soft voice, her eyes luminous. "After what you've done for Sean? For me? You've saved our lives. How can I be upset over such a small thing? In Ireland, there's an old saying about babies born with a clubfoot."

"There is?"

Alyssa gave him a tender look. "It's said that if a pregnant mother visits a graveyard and she accidentally twists her ankle on a grave, her child would be born with a *cam reilge* or clubfoot. Your mother must have done that, Tray. In Ireland, I've seen clubfooted girls, as well." She shrugged, giving him a warming look charged with compassion. "Do you think your clubfoot makes you less of a man, Tray? What can any man with two good feet do better than you? Taffy and his men didn't work as long or as hard as you did, and you were the one robbed of two sound feet. You ride as if you were part of the horse. You till your fields beside your men. You feed, clothe and protect those who work for you at Shadowhawk. In my eyes, you are better than any ten men put together as one."

Tray released her hands, framing her fragile face between his strong fingers. "Sweet, sweet Aly with a heart so large that she lays to rest my worst fears," he whispered, drawing her forward.

This time, Alyssa needed little encouragement to ease those last few inches and feel the pleasant, warming touch of Tray's mouth as it slid across her lips. Since undressing him hours ago, she had had time to think about many things. The lower part of any man's body could cause her pain, of that she was certain. But Tray's kiss had brought to her only wonderful, womanly feelings, not the shame and humiliation of Vaughn's violent assault. Now, as his mouth slanted hungrily across hers, Alyssa felt a flush of cleanness and purity. His kiss blotted out her fears, and a soft moan rose in her throat. He worshiped her as if she were a priceless crystal glass that would break beneath the slightest pressure. Her nostrils flared, inhaling deeply of his scent, dizziness sweeping through her as he placed small, delicate kisses at each corner of her parted lips. His tongue slid into her mouth, sending a current of liquid pleasure racing through her, making her limbs weak with need.

"Trust me, Aly," he breathed hoarsely against her lips. "Give yourself to me . . . I won't hurt you, only give you pleasure. Kiss me, feel what you give to me in return. . . ."

Unconsciously, Aly raised her arms, sliding them artlessly around his broad shoulders, her fingers tangling in the curls at the nape of his powerful neck. Shyly, she began to explore him as he had her. His mouth was strong, yielding to her, giving back to her. She felt her nipples growing hard beneath the cotton of the shirt she wore, her breasts swelling and a hot, melting sensation spreading through her lower body, leaving her trembling as Tray gently drew her to him.

"Yes, yes, sweet Aly, you're so soft, so giving," he crooned in a gritty voice. "Open your mouth, let me taste you. All of you, *Arhiannon*. . . ."

Fire uncoiled within her and she shattered beneath the caress of his tongue as he tasted her. Her nipples grew taut and she moaned, pressing herself against the hardness of his chest, wanting to somehow ease the ache within her. His hands moved up her rib cage, fingers caressing the outer curve of her breasts. A small cry tore from her lips and her knees buckled beneath her.

"It's all right, little one," he gritted against her wet, moist lips. "I won't hurt you. I only want to give you pleasure. A man can love a woman in many ways. You've suffered only pain. Let me show you that a man can give to you and not take. Let me touch you...." he begged huskily.

Her heart pounding heavily, Alyssa arched herself shamelessly into his large, waiting hands, which easily held her taut, aching breasts. Her head was thrown back, exposing the slender expanse of her throat as he unbuttoned her shirt. As Tray pulled the rough cotton material away, the fabric dragged across her already sensitive breasts.

"Trust me," he whispered, his breath caressing her soft skin. Her nipples were a delicate rose pink and Tray pulled one into the liquid heat of his mouth. He heard Alyssa cry out, her body shuddering with need. It wasn't a cry of alarm, but a beautiful animal moan, which sent a jagged bolt of heat straight to his lower body. "Honey," he rasped raggedly. "God, you taste like honey...." He gently sucked each of her nipples in turn, lost in the primal need to give her as much joy as he was experiencing, the need to worship her lovely, sensitive body.

Blood pounded through Tray as he brought Alyssa into his arms. She arched urgently to him, her fingers digging convulsively into his powerful shoulders as he teethed her responsive nipples. Her total response overwhelmed him; he could feel her shaking like a newly born lamb within his arms and realized in some part of his mind that she had given herself to him, without reservation, without the fear the rape had instilled in her. He wanted her, all of her. And he loved her with an overwhelming fierceness. The past two months had been miraculous for him. Aly had taught him to feel again, to desire and to live again. Tray cupped her small breast, placing a kiss on the hardened nipple. He felt her press her body urgently to his, mindless and begging for what she did not understand. Slowly, Tray's mind grappled successfully with his passion. He pulled her shirt closed and buried his head next to hers, inhaling the silken scent of her abundant hair.

His mind raced as he absorbed the completeness of his love for Alyssa. He wouldn't shame her further by taking her as if she were his mistress. He raised his head, seeking and finding her full lips, now swollen with the stamp of his mouth. Marriage. He would offer her marriage and then they would consummate their love for each other. As he felt her shy response to his mouth, his arms tightened around her loving body, drawing her hard against his naked chest. He gloried in the sensation of their flesh meeting, galvanizing like heated metal one to the other. The rape would make her fearful of consummating the love he held for her. But they had at least another week in the mountains for Tray to show Aly through his kisses and touches that she need not fear him as a man, that coupling was something to look forward to and not shrink from.

Gently, Tray broke the spell of their heated kiss, his eyes a turbulent gray as he stared down at her with naked intensity. He saw her nipples clearly outlined against the material of her shirt. Her cheeks were flushed and her eyes were wide with pleasure. A euphoric feeling swept through him as he combed his fingers gently through her hair, a pleasant warmth building between them in the aftermath of their exploration of each other.

"I think you wanted to be kissed," he rumbled.

Alyssa sighed, resting her hand against his magnificent chest. "Now I understand why those girls who were being

courted looked forward to stolen moments with their man,"
she whispered, her partly open lashes revealing hazy emerald eyes as she looked up at him. Just the soothing effect of
his fingers gently combing through her hair, lightly massaging her scalp, sent wonderful new sensations washing
through her.

"And did you enjoy what we shared, Aly?"

A soft sigh escaped her lips. "Yes...." Her lashes lifted
further, her eyes becoming more focused as she relaxed
within his arms, wildly aware of his strong, vibrant body
against her own. "Wh-when I had to pull those wet clothes
off you, I began getting scared, Tray."

He brushed the gathering frown from her brow. "Why,
little one?"

"Because—" She took in a deep, broken breath, her
words tumbling out with embarrassment. "I'd never seen a
man fully naked before. A-and when I saw you..." She
swallowed, lowering her lashes, unable to hold his gaze.
"All I could remember was the terrible pain of his shaft
ripping into me. And it hurt. It hurt so much...and yet, you
give me pleasure. And happiness." She braved a glance up
at Tray and found his gray eyes wet with tears. "I thought
perhaps that from the waist up, a man was able to give a
woman pleasure. But from the waist down..." She shuddered, burying her head against his chest.

A lump grew in his throat and Tray could find no words.
Instead, he held her, rocked her and occasionally pressed a
kiss to her temple. Finally, after a long time, he was able to
clear his throat and speak in an unsteady voice. "A man
who loves his woman can give her pleasure above and below the waist, little one. Trust me on that. You were a virgin until you were captured by the English. I can tell by the
way you kiss that you've had little practice in the art of being a woman." He caressed her cheek with his knuckles. "I

can't undo what's been done, Aly," he told her in a low, roughened voice, "but I can show you the opposite."

Her expression grew pained. "What do you mean?"

"Have the kisses we shared or—" he allowed his hand to slide down and gently cup her breast "—my touching your body hurt you? Have you felt any fear?"

She blushed becomingly as his hand remained against her breast. A feeling of belonging to Tray engulfed Alyssa, and she felt desired and protected. "No," she answered, her voice husky with simmering passion, "only delight and—"

His gaze caressed her upturned, flushed features. "And?"

A tremulous smile came to her lips. "You make me feel so clean inside, Tray. As if I'm not tainted. Every time you touch me, I feel the shame being carried away."

A knowing glint danced in his gray eyes. "Ever since I found you in the hold of that ship, I knew you were special, Aly," he began softly, his hand leaving her breast and coming to rest on her hair. "At first, I thought you were just a girl. When Sorche and I had to strip you out of those foul-smelling rags, I knew you were a woman, older than your lovely face revealed. We washed you each day, little one. I cleansed the blood and mud from your long, beautiful hair." He lifted a strand of her hair to his lips, kissing it. His voice became deeper, more coaxing. "When I awoke just now and you came to me willingly, I knew that I loved you."

Alyssa drew in a sharp breath, her eyes widening with hope and fear. "Y-you love me?"

"Yes."

"But I'm soiled, Tray!" She scrambled up, her shirt falling open, revealing the shadowed cleft of her young breasts as she stared at him in bewildered confusion. "I'm nothing! I'm the daughter of a man who was once a farmer and is now sitting in Newgate prison waiting to be hanged." Her voice became hauntingly soft as she stared down at her tightly clasped hands, her auburn hair framing her drawn features. "Don't love me, Tray, please."

He sat for a moment, digesting her anguished plea. "But I do love you, little one."

Huge tears formed in her eyes and rolled down her cheeks. "I—I couldn't stand the thought of being a mistress, Tray. There's already so much dishonor linked with the Kyle name. Both my brothers will be hunted down like dogs by the English. My father will be dead soon...." She raised her head, shame in her eyes. "If my brothers ever knew I was lying in your bed, they'd hate me. They'd call me a traitor. I couldn't bear that, Tray. I could never be your mistress."

He reached out, taking her cool, damp fingers into the warmth of his cradling hands. "I love you. I want you to be my wife, not my mistress. Do you think I care if you're the daughter of an Irish farmer? I love the soil and animals as much as your family does. And the only reason your father is considered a felon is because he and your courageous brothers have fought for the freedom of Ireland from England. I don't hold that against them. If I were Irish, I'd be at their side."

Tray held her shocked stare as the color drained from her face. He pressed on, gently rubbing the backs of her hands with his thumbs. "I'm not ashamed that my future wife comes to me without her virginity. There are reasons for that, Aly, that neither of us could control. To me, you are still a virgin, still pure by the very way you come to me. Your kisses are sweet and untrained. Your response to me is willing and eager, and I ache to teach you the many ways of love." He lifted her hands, watching joy replace shock in her wide, honest eyes. "Talk to me," he coaxed. "Tell me what is in your heart, Aly."

Her lips parted in awe. "My heart—my heart swells with such a fierce sweetness whenever I'm with you that I fear I will faint from the joy it holds."

A smile curved Tray's sensuous mouth. "There's another word for that, Aly. Love. That's what real love feels like."

"Oh, Tray," she sobbed, throwing herself into his waiting arms. She hugged him as tightly as she could, burying her head against his neck. The strength of his arms coming about her slender body gave her respite from the fear lurking deep within her. "I'm so frightened."

He ran his hand down the delicate line of her strong, beautifully formed back. "I know you are."

She clung to him, her eyes tightly shut. "I don't even know if I can give you children now," she cried softly.

"Shh, little one, let's take this one day at a time. I need you, not children." He ran his hands down her narrow, almost boyish hips, a snaking fear crawling through him. Shelby had been built similarly, and she had died because the baby had been unable to pass through her small hips. And the baby, when finally pulled out of her by Dr. Birch, had a clubfoot. That thought haunted Tray. He had killed his own mother with his deformed foot, and he had killed Shelby and his son with his rotten seed. He held Alyssa close, praying to God that he would not kill her as he had Shelby. He couldn't stand another loss. Not a second time. Not Aly. "Sean is like a son to me already. I need no other children. I need you...your sweetness, your kindness and your love. Just your love...."

Alyssa gripped Tray with all her strength, tears falling against his cheek. "But I love children so much...and I want to feel your life within me, Tray. Your children. Sean loves you like the father he lost, and I'm grateful that you love him." She eased back, encased within his arms, searching his gray eyes. Gently, she caressed his thick black hair with trembling fingers. "I love you, Tristan. Your name may mean sorrow in Welsh, but you have showered me only with happiness. You've brought joy to my heart and laughter to my lips when I've experienced neither in so many years. If this is love, then I can never want for more. If God wills it, I will have your children. Children fashioned out of our love."

He gently gathered Alyssa back into his arms, simply holding her, feeling the beat of her heart.

"Sometimes," Tray began, "I think you're a vision I've had all my life come true. And sometimes, when I'm with you, I think my heart's going to break with joy."

A tremulous smile of understanding touched her lips. "I know, I feel it here," she admitted, touching her heart with her hand.

Tray smiled wryly. "You like those feelings, little one?"

"Very much."

"And have you ever experienced them before?"

"Perhaps once," she admitted, frowning.

He smoothed her brow with his hand. "What do you mean?"

"Well, my mare gave birth to my foal, Cassie. I sat there beside this dark little baby, helping the mare dry her off, and I felt then a little bit like I do right now, as if my heart would break." Alyssa gazed up at him gravely. "Does that count, too?"

Tray swallowed a smile. "In a way it does, Aly. Sometimes a special animal or place or—" he raised her hand to his lips, kissing it gently "—person makes you feel that way."

She laughed softly, closing her eyes. "Oh, I wish it could last forever!"

"It can, Aly," he promised her quietly. "It can last for-ever, believe me."

Wonder glowed in her eyes. "You've taught me so much, Tray."

"No less than you've taught me," he replied, his eyes bright.

"Look at us," she sniffed, dashing the tears from her eyes, "we even cry together."

"That's the kind of thing you share with another, Aly, when you feel as we do."

"I want to do something other than cry, Tray. I've shed enough tears these last few months to last my lifetime. I want to smile and laugh."

"And so you shall," he promised. "You've come out of the darkness and now the sunshine awaits you."

Alyssa gave him a humorous look and pointed toward the window. "It's still raining!"

"It'll be clear and bright tomorrow."

## Chapter Thirteen

The week passed quickly, the weather turning unexpectedly warm and the sunshine drying up the mud in the pastures used for the flocks. Every day, Alyssa discovered, was more achingly beautiful than the last. She rode in Tray's arms atop Rasheed between the three flocks, content to share kisses that scorched her body with a new longing and left her hungering for more. Their laughter was infectious, and their feeding and caring for the baby lambs together only welded them more closely to each other.

Master Taffy had asked them to go up to a place where more wild dogs had scattered the flock. Alyssa mounted her small black Welsh cob and they spent another two hours riding together toward that lonely, desolate area. They met two weary shepherds with several lambs resting across their saddles on the way up to the hut.

"Lord Trayhern, we found two more ewes up there by that waterfall. Too close to lambing to move."

Tray nodded, sitting relaxed on Rasheed, his hand resting on the blood bay's rump. "All right, tell Master Taffy we'll find them. If they've birthed, we'll bring them down this evening."

"One might, but the other looks like her teats aren't waxed up yet. Might mean you leavin' her behind. She looks like she's holdin' twins and probably won't birth till the morrow.''

Tray nodded, pursing his lips. "We'll see what can be done, Drew. You've done a good job."

As they neared the waterfall an hour later, Alyssa spotted the ewes. "Oh, Tray, look!" She spurred her cob into a gallop. There, standing on very unsure legs, was a black lamb with his exhausted mother. The other ewe was huge but hadn't birthed yet.

Alyssa dismounted in one fluid motion and walked quickly up to the little black lamb. Her eyes saddened as she knelt down near the bleating baby. His front right leg hung brokenly as he lifted it off the ground, wobbling unsteadily on the other three. "Oh, you poor youngling," she crooned, reaching out and drawing him into the cradle of her arms. Examining the broken leg, Alyssa bit down on her lip as Tray approached. He hunkered down beside her, a scowl on his brow.

"He's a runt," Tray growled. "Got everything going against him, Aly—he's black, stunted in growth, and it looks like his mother probably rolled over on him after he was born and broke his leg." He slowly got to his feet and unsheathed the knife he carried at the back of his belt. Alyssa stared horrified at Tray as the blade glinted dully in the sunlight.

"What are you going to do?"

"Cut his throat. He'll die, Aly," Tray told her gruffly, kneeling down next to her. "His mother won't feed him because he's injured."

Tears stung her eyes and she shielded the black lamb. "Let me try! Sometimes they won't reject them."

He gave her a patient look. "It won't work."

"Let me try!" With that, she picked up the lamb and carried it over to the mother. The moment she put the baby down by the mother's nose the ewe lowered her head, gave a bawling bleat and rammed the baby. The black lamb tumbled end over end, and Alyssa gave a short cry, coming to the struggling baby's rescue, sweeping him back up into her arms. She turned to Tray, her face distraught.

"Let me kill him, Aly. He won't live. Not with a broken leg," Tray pleaded quietly, coming over to her.

She was crying, tears streaming down her flushed cheeks as she gave him a mutinous look. "No!"

"Do you think I *want* to kill him?" he asked impatiently.

Alyssa hugged the lamb carefully to her breast. "From the way you're behaving, yes! You won't even give him a chance! You won't even try to think of another way to help him!"

Tray combed his fingers through his hair. "God's blood! There is no way to help him. My men don't have time to play nursemaid to him, Aly. Sure, he could be milked by hand, but he's got a broken leg! No one can do anything about that. Even if he did survive, he'd get eaten by a wild dog because he couldn't keep up with the rest of the flock." Tray lowered his voice, her sad expression tearing at his heart. "Please, little one, try to understand. Let me put him out of his misery. He's crippled and of no use to anyone. Don't you see? You're just prolonging his agony by trying to keep him alive."

With a cry, Alyssa turned away from him and walked a few feet. She whirled around, her face etched with anguish. "I once had a lamb on the farm that had a broken leg," she cried, "and I wrapped it up. My father told me the same thing, that it would die eventually. But I fed it and kept its leg supported and it lived, Tray. It lived! Please, let me try to wrap its leg . . . let me try to save it. . . ."

"Damn it, it's a cripple, Alyssa!" he thundered, walking toward her with the knife.

"Well, so are you!"

He halted, as if struck, all the color draining from his face as he stared at her.

"You're crippled," she sobbed, "and no one slit your throat. Sorche loved you and cared for you even though your father didn't want you. She as much as wrapped your leg and tended you, Tray." Tears blurred Alyssa's vision and she choked on several sobs. "Crippled doesn't mean useless, don't you see that?" she went on rawly. "You aren't useless. And neither is this lamb, as long as you let it be tended like you were. I have the time, Tray. I know the baby will take work, but I want to do that. I don't believe he'll die or be worthless just because he's crippled."

Tray lowered the knife, his mouth tightening to stem his emotions. He sheathed the weapon and slowly walked up to her. "Stop crying." He started to slide his hands around the lamb and she shrank back from him, her eyes large and shadowed. "Let me have him. How can you mount your horse?"

She opened her arms, allowing Tray to take the lamb. His hands were so large that they almost swallowed up the black runt as he gently handled him. Her lashes were matted with spent tears as she lifted her eyes to meet his tortured gray ones. "I love you," she said tremulously, and then turned away to mount the cob.

Tray's face was dark and unreadable as he carefully placed the runt back into her arms. "Go down to the cottage and get a fire started."

Alyssa picked up the reins, feeling suddenly drained. "What about you?" she asked tonelessly.

Tray looked at the other ewe. "I'll bring the runt's mother along. Between the two of us, we ought to be able to hold her still while he gets a meal or two. That other ewe will probably birth tomorrow morning and I see no reason to leave her out here as prey for wild dogs. We've got the time to wait on her. We're not needed that badly down below.'' He put his hand on her thigh, giving her a small squeeze of reassurance. "We'll stay here tonight. You go on. I'll be there as soon as I can.''

Alyssa knew she had hurt Tray badly. The next two hours were sheer agony for her as they wrestled the ewe to immobility so that the runt could suckle. Afterward Alyssa bound his leg so that it could heal. She avoided Tray's charcoal gray eyes, her stomach twisting each time she accidentally met his gaze. Fighting back tears, Alyssa made the runt a bed of straw and placed him in a box near the hearth to keep him warm until his next feeding. She busied herself with rebuilding the fire and placing a kettle of mutton stew over the coals. Tray disappeared for about an hour after that and the pain in Alyssa's heart increased. She wanted to apologize to Tray, but he gave her no quarter to do so. As night fell, he finally came back to the cottage. After feeding the runt again, she ladled out a bowl of stew and handed it to Tray. He took it, saying nothing and going over to the straw that had served him as a bed a week earlier.

Miserably, Alyssa forced herself to nibble at bits of the stew, the silence growing more and more strained between them. The night was inky, broken only by the light of the embers of glowing coals in the fireplace. Her heart was beating like a bird that had been captured, and Alyssa pushed herself upward, running her damp hands down the length of her thighs. She turned, pinned by Tray's unreadable gray eyes. Mouth dry, Alyssa forced herself to go to him as he lay on his side in the straw. Kneeling before him with her head bowed, the sheets of her auburn hair hiding her features, she began to speak in a low, strained voice.

"I had no right to call you a cripple, Tray, and I'm sorry." Her hands fluttered helplessly to emphasize her words. "I, of all people, have no right to say something like that. I'm not whole myself. I'm less a woman than—"

"No!" he snarled, gripping her by the arms, giving her a little shake. His eyes were nearly colorless as he stared at her, and when he spoke, his voice was deep and trembling. "You had every right! Every right, Alyssa. It's you. I'm forgetting that you don't see my deformity. In your wonderful world, cripples exist alongside whole men. You act as if there's nothing wrong with me and so, when I tried to take that lamb's life, you rebelled."

Tears scalded her eyes and Alyssa stared numbly up into his troubled features. "Oh, Tray, I didn't mean to hurt you. I saw the pain in your eyes when I screamed at you. I only wanted you to trust me enough to work with the lamb. All he needs is a little love and attention. That's all...." She pressed her hands against her heart, fearing it would break.

He blinked back his own tears, his hands sliding upward to cup her face. "That's all?" he whispered rawly. "Do you know how much you willingly give me, Sean, that lamb and everyone else? No, I don't suppose you do." He groaned, shutting his eyes tightly and pulling her roughly to him, crushing her in his arms. "God, Aly, I'm sorry. I'm not angry at you," he rasped. "I'm angry with myself! What right do I have to pass judgment on anyone or anything? Especially another injured human being or animal? My God, I've become so hardened because of my deformity." He drew in a tortured breath, his eyes red-rimmed as he stared off into the darkness, holding her tightly in his arms. "In your unselfishness to save the lamb, you reminded me to take stock of myself. I've lived in a shell for so long and been so alone."

Her fingers moved upward, pressing gently against his cheek, touching his tears. "We're both crippled," she whispered, "you physically, me emotionally. Don't you see, Tray? There is no one who is perfect or whole. Your weakness is readily seen, mine is not, until you try to love me and then . . . then all that fear comes screaming back at me, and I know I cannot please you as a woman should her man."

"No," Tray said raggedly, kissing her eyes, nose and finally her lips, softening them, taking away her pain. "That's not true, Aly. Yes, we're all crippled, little one. But if I can force myself to do the work of a man with two good feet, then you can overcome your fear and be all of the woman I see in you."

Blindly, Alyssa moved forward, her arms sliding up his chest. "Take away my fear, Tray . . . please, I ache so much. I love you, and I'm so afraid I can never make you happy. Help me, Tray. I know you won't hurt me, beloved. Oh, please . . ." she whispered against his lips, pressing hungry kisses against his mouth. "Prove to me that I'm not as crippled as I feel now. . . ."

A groan tore from deep within him, a powerful shudder working its way up through his body as he tried to resist her plea. God, they were not married yet. If he did love her thoroughly, would this day be a black mark against them? What if he hurt her? If he couldn't please her? Tray's hands trembled as he pulled her away from him, trying to avoid the warm, seeking lips that threatened to dissolve his control. "Aly, Aly . . . what if I do hurt you? I'm a man, like any other—"

"No, you won't hurt me. I know you won't. I saw how gently you handled that lamb." She drew back, her hands linked behind his neck, her eyes misted with tears. "Handle me with such love, Tray, and you cannot possibly hurt me." Leaning forward, Alyssa placed her lips inexpertly against his mouth, trying to crumble his tremulous barriers with each touch of her body against his.

Her childlike trust matched with her courage and vulnerability destroyed Tray's every hesitation. Gently, he drew her down, down into his arms, her hair lying like a dark wine halo about her beautiful features. "All right," he whispered hoarsely, "I'll love you, Aly." His fingers trembled as he caressed her cheek, and he drowned within her wide emerald eyes, lost in the explosive heat kindled between them. "But, sweet God in heaven, if I hurt you, I'll never forgive myself. I'll only have made you that much more fearful of—"

She placed her fingers against his lips. "I trust you."

He gripped her hand, kissing it hard and then pressing it against his stubbled cheek, drawing in a deep, shuddering breath. "I'm not an expert lover, Aly. I've had a few women in my life. I've made mistakes, but I'll try not to make the same mistakes with you. You, of all women, don't deserve my fumbling attempts to—"

Alyssa's fingers brushed against his mouth. "But I love you, as you love me. We'll guide each other with our love, Tray." Her lips parted in unconscious provocation, full and begging him to worship them.

His fingers trembled as he lightly touched her hair. Reaching up, Alyssa pulled him down upon her, the weight of his body satisfying against hers as he cupped her chin, drawing her lips to his own. The instant their mouths touched, a storm of longing exploded violently to life between them. Each time his lips nipped and teased her earlobe, the slender cords of her neck or her collarbone, she reacted out of pure desire. Tray placed moist kisses between her taut breasts as he eased the shirt from her body, pushing it aside. A cry of pleasure came from deep in her throat as his mouth closed lovingly over the first, erect nipple. Pulses of pleasure spiraled within her, sending a pulling, fiery feeling to the very core of her womanhood. His sure hand slid down her rib cage and he patiently freed the buttons on her baggy, ill-fitting breeches.

"Lovely," he breathed softly against her lips, "you're so lovely, sweet Aly. Such beautiful, small breasts, pink-tipped with inexperience, like honey to suckle...." His lips closed over one, drawing it deep within his heated mouth, and she cried out in exquisite pleasure, arching against his hard male body, her fingers digging convulsively into his back. She was mindless, feeling, reacting, her heart beating in rapid unison with his own. The breeches slid off her narrow hips and she felt her nerves leap as his palm lightly brushed her auburn triangle. A gasp escaped her lips, and her breathing came in little sobs as he gently eased his calloused hand between her beautifully curved thighs. She was damp and more than ready for him but he made no move to touch her. Not yet...

Tray felt her begin to tense as his hand eased her thighs apart, and he leaned down, gently teething her nipple, assured that she reacted strongly and positively to his worship. Without realizing it, Alyssa arched to him, her swollen core grazing the heel of his hand. His breath choked off as he felt her tremble from the contact. Did it remind her of the rape, of the brutal invasion of her lovely, small body? A mewing cry slipped from her parted lips, and Tray felt her move against his hand again. Relief flowed through him and he released his withheld breath.

"Good, good, sweet Aly...yes, that's it, feel the pleasure I can give you. Rub against me, little one...all you want," he whispered against her wet, soft lips.

Tremors shot through her and she trembled violently, clenching and unclenching her fingers against Tray's back. She moved against him, her body straining, a fine sheen of

perspiration covering her. And then, she felt his further exploration of her, and a cry tore from her lips. Pleasure
stroked her like molten fire, and she lost all control, mind-
lessly floating, pushing, needing, until an explosion, violent and sudden, shattered her. She stiffened against Tray,
clinging tightly as he brought her to a quaking, all-
consuming climax. How long she lay panting in his arms,
her head thrown back, tendrils of hair damp and clinging to
her face, she did not know. For a moment, Alyssa felt Tray
leave her, but she was too weakened, too oblivious in her
euphoria, to make a verbal protest.

When he came back to lie at her side, she felt the dry
warmth of his naked flesh. She barely had the strength to
open her eyes, and when she did, she drowned in the gray
depths of his tender gaze. Tray swept the dampened tendrils from her temples, leaning down, kissing her with great
gentleness.

"Did you enjoy it, little one?"

Alyssa closed her eyes, barely nodding her head. "It
was—wonderful...."

"That's just the beginning of our night together, Aly," he
promised thickly, claiming her nipple between his lips. Immediately, the peak hardened in the heat of his mouth and
he felt her arching against him. "Good," he praised, allowing her to feel the hard curve of his maleness as she
pressed against him. Almost instantly, she shrank back, but
he placed his hand against her hip, slowly bringing her back
up against him.

"It can't hurt you, Aly," he told her, his gaze probing her
suddenly frightened eyes.

She swallowed painfully. "But, it's so hard...."

He gave her a patient smile, taking up her hand. "Just as
I touched you moments ago and gave you so much plea-

sure, I want you to touch me. Remember, this is me, little one. I'm not the one who hurt you. Trust me.''

To her surprise, Tray guided her fingers across his hard, warm length. She felt him shudder as she tentatively stroked him, his swift intake of breath making her eyes fly open.

''Did I hurt you?''

Tray tried to speak and couldn't for several seconds. ''No, beloved, you make me feel good when you do that. Just as I made you feel good.''

He allowed her to explore him, lying on his back so that she could examine him visually and physically as she chose. Her fingers were delicate as she ran her hands across his nipples. He clenched his teeth, willing his body to rein its desire. Slowly, ever so slowly, her hands gained confidence. The shyness was still there, but he saw the fascination in her eyes, as well. Tray smiled to himself. His Alyssa was as hot-blooded as a spirited Arabian. After a while, he reached out, sliding his hand between her thighs, watching her face suffuse with drowsy pleasure as he stroked her swelling, moist core. Tray gently eased her back as she began to tremble with very real need of him.

She breathed in short, sharp breaths, that familiar fire uncoiling from her lower body. She was totally unaware that he had removed his stroking, caressing hand until she felt a filling sensation, as if she were gradually welcoming Tray into her confines. Her eyes barely opened and she realized dazedly that he covered her body with his own, keeping most of his weight off her. He lay very still, watching her closely, perspiration beading his drawn, taut features.

He leaned down, caressing her lips, his breath moist against her face. ''Now we're one, Aly, as it should be. You and I. No pain, perhaps some pressure, but no agony.''

He placed his hand beneath her back, curving her torso slightly upward to gain access to a flushed nipple. He smiled to himself as she automatically pressed upward against him, feeling her tremble as she slowly got used to him being embedded within her liquid core, which held him tightly in its loving grasp.

"Do you like that?" he whispered, running his tongue around her earlobe. He gently moved his hips and heard a sigh come from her lips. "Yes, you like it," he growled thickly, sliding his hands down her rib cage and settling them against her hips. Her lashes fluttered closed as he carefully began to move forward, a little more each time, his penetration going deeper and deeper until finally her body had accepted all of him.

She lay beneath him, begging his body to love her. He brought her into rhythm with himself, calculating his movements to give her maximum pleasure. Moments wove into a timeless world bright with shocks of pleasure, and Tray felt Alyssa become boneless in his hands. It was then that he knew Alyssa was beyond the fear, having placed herself in total trust to him. Gripping her hips, he stroked more deeply, watching as a flush of pleasure colored her features. Her fingers clasped his arms and fire rushed through him as she arched upward, her legs encircling him.

Liquid heat molded and fused, and both were overwhelmed with the suddenly frantic need to give to each other. Sweat gleamed across his body as Tray fought to control himself. Teeth clenched, he raised her hips, feeling her stiffen. A breathless cry tore from her lips, a glorious cry heralding the completeness of their union. It was only then that he relinquished his iron control and hungrily surged into her, taking her, needing her, until the moment when he released himself deeply into her loving, sharing body.

## Chapter Fourteen

"My lord?" Craddock came to the door.

Tray looked up from his desk. He and Alyssa had been back at Shadowhawk for six weeks, and tomorrow they were to wed. "Yes?"

"The gift has just arrived for Miss Alyssa." The butler's stout Welsh face broke into a wide grin.

"Where's Alyssa right now?"

"Out in the stable feeding Inky, my lord."

A slight smile brightened Tray's face as he came around the desk. "Excellent. Have the gift brought to the stable door. I'll bring Alyssa out and we'll see if she's pleased with it."

"Yes, my lord!"

Stablemaster Thomas grinned, telling Alyssa another Welsh tale while he supported the black lamb she nursed from a glove containing milk. Tray rested his arms on top of the small door, absorbing Alyssa's quiet beauty. Typical of Alyssa on any given day, she wore one of the many cotton dresses that had been made for her. The pale blue dress was tied with a dark blue sash and, as always, a lace collar adorned her slender throat.

Her thick mane of auburn hair had been tamed into a single braid that hung like a richly colored wine rope across her shoulder and down between her breasts. Tomorrow, he thought warmly, tomorrow you'll be my wife, Aly. God, I love you so much. . . .

"Tray!" Alyssa twisted around and greeted him with a blinding smile. "How long have you been standing there?"

He returned her smile and roused himself. "Just a few minutes."

"Inky will be done in just a moment. To what do we owe the honor of seeing you come out of your study at this time of day?" she teased.

"I was wondering if the future mistress of Shadowhawk would like to accept a wedding gift from her husband-to-be?"

Her eyes widened. "A gift? Oh, Tray!" She handed Thomas the glove, begging him to finish feeding Inky. Wiping her hands on a nearby cloth, she got to her feet and rushed over to the door, which Tray opened for her. "But I didn't expect anything," Alyssa told him breathlessly, leaning up on tiptoe to kiss him.

Tray returned her chaste peck and slipped his arm around her waist, leading her down the aisle. "Didn't you know it is proper for the groom to give his young bride gifts?"

She shook her head. "No. I don't know much about Welsh customs." And then she added with a mischievous smile, "Yet."

He smiled down at her, drinking in her unabashed enthusiasm. Tray drew her to a halt. "All right, my lovely bride, close your eyes now. I shall lead you out into the stable yard and I'll tell you when to open them."

She smiled, obeying him. "Oh, Tray! I'm so excited. Hurry! Hurry!" She gripped his hand eagerly.

Laughing, Tray carefully guided her out onto the cobblestoned yard. "You may open them now, sweet Aly," he whispered near her ear.

Nothing could have prepared Alyssa for the gift as her eyes flew open. There, standing in front of her, was an exquisite Arabian mare held by two grooms in green livery. The animal's dappled gray skin shone in the sun, her mane, tail and legs coal black. Alyssa gasped, her hands going to her mouth in disbelief. She felt Tray's hands settle on her shoulders, drawing her against him.

"Ohhh . . . she's beautiful!"

"And she's yours," he whispered, smiling. "Her name is Ghazieh and she is of the Seglawi Jedran strain, one of the most elegant and beautiful of all Arabian breeding." He placed his arms around Alyssa, resting his chin against the crown of her head. "Do you like her, little one? I know your love of horses and I wanted to purchase one that would do justice to your own beauty."

Alyssa gave a cry and turned, throwing her arms around his thickly corded neck. "She's lovely, Tray! Thank you! Thank you!"

Ghazieh stamped and snorted, her fine ears moving nervously, her thin nostrils flared. Alyssa released Tray and quietly talked to the mare as she approached. Tray smiled, crossing his arms as he watched the two females become acquainted. The joy in Alyssa's face wove a blanket of warmth around him. Even the Earl of Culver's grooms were smiling. The mare stood more than fourteen hands, tall for her breed, and was the most exquisite example of Arabians in England. He had contacted Culver immediately after getting back from lambing. Her high price seemed a small sum in comparison to how rich Tray felt having Alyssa's love. And typical of any animal on Shadowhawk, Ghazieh immediately fell under Alyssa's spell as she was gently caressed and stroked by her new owner.

"She's so lovely!" Alyssa said over and over again, running her knowledgeable hands down the mare's straight legs, marveling at her nearly perfect conformation.

"Well, are you going to spend the rest of the day doting on Ghazieh or are you going to join Rasheed and me for our daily ride?" he taunted, grinning.

Alyssa straightened up, meeting his smile. She gave a deep curtsy. "We'd be honored to ride at your side, my lord. If you'll give me a moment, I'll return in proper riding clothes and meet you shortly."

Tray nodded. "Hurry, love of my heart," he said softly.

"Heaven. Sheer heaven, Tray!" Alyssa laughed, reining in the elegant gray mare. Having donned a forest green riding habit and white silk blouse, Alyssa had allowed her hair to remain loose and rode without the customary hat perched on her head. She met Tray's smiling gray eyes, her heart blossoming with love as they slowed to a walk at each other's side. The sun was actually warm for early May, and birds flitted through the azure sky with nesting material in their beaks. It was a time for birth, Alyssa thought, touching her own stomach, trying to imagine what it would be like to carry Tray's child.

"You are heaven, my lady," Tray corrected, looking darkly handsome in his canary yellow breeches, black boots and a white peasant shirt that he always wore opened at his throat. His ebony hair was slightly curled, highlighted with blue from the sun's rays.

Alyssa leaned over, patting Ghazieh affectionately. Her expression became pensive. "Are you nervous about tomorrow, Tray?"

He gazed over at her. "No," he answered softly. "Are you?"

She picked worriedly at Ghazieh's silken black mane. "You've gone through this before. I haven't." Dismounting, Alyssa knew she must tell him the truth about everything. Her conscience would not allow her to do otherwise. She tied Ghazieh's reins to a wrought-iron circle hanging from the stable wall. "There are things I must tell you, Tray. Things that may, perhaps, change your mind about marrying me."

She avoided his look of concern as he dismounted and came to her side, his hand resting on her slumped shoulder. "Tell me," he ordered heavily. "Whatever it is, we'll deal with it—together."

Alyssa glanced up at him, seeing gentleness in every feature of his craggy face. Swallowing hard, she whispered, "My father was aiding Tone in the rebellion. And I was caught up in a skirmish near Wexford. But I was there to protect the children of the men who would go up against the English. After the third charge, the rebellion was broken. The English were murdering our children and raping our women. And I'll never regret picking up that pistol and shooting that horse in the chest."

Her voice trembled as she scanned his set face. "After we were taken onto ship, as prisoners, your half brother, Vaughn, took my father up on deck and tortured him, trying to force him to tell where the rest of the weapons were hidden. My father wouldn't answer, no matter what Vaughn did to him. When torturing Father proved fruitless, Vaughn ordered my sister-in-law, Shannon, dragged from our cell." Alyssa choked, fighting back the tears. "Vaughn tied her to a mast and began flogging her with a whip. Each time my father refused to answer a question, he struck Shannon. I heard her screams and my father begging Vaughn to spare Shannon." Her voice cracked. "He laughed! Your half brother laughed! He murdered my brother's wife!"

"Aly..." Tray begged, walking toward her.

"No!" she cried, holding out her hand toward him, her green eyes piercing. "My father was told that if he didn't give the whereabouts of the weapons, I would be raped before his very eyes. Do you know who pulled me from my cell by my hair, up those wooden stairs and across Shannon's freshly spilled blood on the deck?" Her voice rose in near hysteria. "Vaughn did that! He had me splayed out in front of my father, and he tore the clothes from my body!"

Alyssa saw Tray moving toward her and fled, running as hard as her riding habit and boots would allow. Her sobs were raw, choking sounds as she tore through the stable door and slammed it shut behind her. Perhaps she'd just sealed her fate and Tray would never marry her, but she could not have become his wife without having the truth out in the open between them. Unable to stop weeping, Alyssa buried her face in her hands and walked to the stall that housed the injured lamb, Inky. The little black runt bleated and limped into her arms, nuzzling and butting against her. Alyssa gently gathered the lamb to her breast, sobbing.

She didn't hear Tray's approach. It wasn't until he knelt down beside her and drew her into his arms, holding her and the lamb, that she became aware of his presence. Tray held her so tightly she thought he might crush her as he kissed her hair, temple and wet cheek.

"Why didn't you tell me?" he asked hoarsely. "Why, Aly? Why?"

She choked and hiccuped, trying to halt her tears. "I thought Vaughn had already told you what he did to me."

"Oh, sweet God, sweet God, no...my half brother keeps his bloody deeds to himself."

Confused, Alyssa raised her head. She saw Tray's ravaged face glistening with tears. "Y-you *didn't* know...."

His hands shook with barely controlled anger as he cupped her face. "Vaughn said nothing! I knew nothing of this until just now, Aly."

Her eyes grew dark. "I couldn't understand how you could forgive and tolerate Vaughn for what he had done to me...."

"My God," he rasped, "if I had known that, Aly, I would *never* have allowed him near you." His lips drew away from his teeth. "I'd have killed the bastard on sight." He bowed his head. "My God, what he did to you...my own half brother. I can never forgive myself, never...."

Alyssa clutched Inky protectively, content to be held by Tray. The lamb bleated and began to butt vigorously against her. It was feeding time again. Tray leaned down, kissing her cheek. "How about if I get the milk bag and we'll feed him?"

Alyssa's heart swelled with fierce love for him. "Then...it's all right? You still want me?"

"Of course I do. Nothing has changed." Tray handed her the glove containing the milk, bothered by Alyssa's still troubled expression. As he knelt next to her, his arm around her waist, he whispered, "What else bothers you, Aly, about our getting married?"

She lifted her chin, her eyes jade. "I wish I could tell Dev and Gavin. To explain. What if they hear I've wedded an Englishman?"

"No doubt they'd be upset."

"I don't know why I'm so nervous. I may never see my brothers again, but I would want them to know that I'm marrying you out of love."

He smiled warmly, reaching out and clasping her hand. "Not because I'm Welsh?"

She returned the smile. "I love the man and the country he was born in."

"And I love you, my sweet Irish colleen. And tomorrow at noon," he promised her thickly, "you shall become my wife, and the mistress of Shadowhawk."

The small wedding chapel was filled to capacity with friends and servants. A glittering spectacle of more than a hundred candles only added to the breathtaking beauty of the bride. Farmers who tilled the soil of Shadowhawk stood with their wives beside the liveried servants who burst with pride as Alyssa walked down the aisle to where Tray stood with the priest. Sorche dabbed her eyes again and again, huge tears rolling down her cheeks when she saw a look of tenderness and pride come to Tray's face as he saw his bride for the first time. Indeed, all of them were awestruck as Alyssa was escorted into church on the arm of Stablemaster Thomas.

The ivory silk of the simple dress had pearls sewn into the lace of the bodice, the throat and long tube sleeves, enhancing Alyssa's natural beauty. Sorche had had the seamstress take great pains with the dress, the delicate veil and heavily brocaded train. Her flesh was peach-colored with a rose flush, making her emerald eyes look even larger than usual. And now, with her hair down, a single strand of pearls encircling her head and soft wisps of bangs brushing her brows, the wine-colored tresses flowing down across her small breasts, she looked like a princess come to life. Their princess.

Tray swallowed hard, his gray eyes bright as he reached out to claim his bride's slender hand. He hung on to each word of the ceremony and mass, sending each phrase he repeated from his heart to hers. Alyssa's voice was quiet but sure as she said the vows that would bind until death. When Tray slipped on a delicate gold wedding band encrusted with tiny emeralds, the color of her eyes, Alyssa felt her chest constrict with so much love for Tray that she almost cried. And as he leaned down to kiss his wife, she tasted the salt of his tears on his lips.

Afterward, the manor rang with music, dancing and feasting. The local Welsh and English gentry had been invited. Those who had dealt with Tray over the years and knew of his fairness and the tragedy of his first marriage had come with offers of congratulations. They had only to dance with the shy but beautiful bride to know she would breathe new life into the manor. And one look at Lord Trayhern was enough to realize how much he loved his young wife, who smiled radiantly and laughed often. Yes, Shadowhawk would once again be happy....

"Sorche, I don't know what's wrong with me." Alyssa sat up in bed, her hair in mild disarray around her pale features.

"You've been sick every day since the wedding," Sorche admitted, helping her with the dressing robe. "Come on, lamb, join me in the drawing room for a cup of hot tea. That will help settle that stomach of yours."

Later, Alyssa sat near the fire while Sorche sewed. She held the cup with both hands, staring down at the tea. Ordinarily, the fragrant odor would smell good to her, but now it didn't. She gave Sorche a bewildered look.

"Tray is beginning to worry about me."

Sorche snorted. "He would! I swear, if you sneeze the wrong way, he's ready to hustle you off to bed and call Dr. Birch!"

A slight smile came to Alyssa's lips. "I think he's afraid of losing me, the way he lost Shelby," she said softly.

"I know, I know. He can't help it, lamb. I've never seen him so in love."

"We're very happy," she added wistfully, forcing herself to sip the honeyed tea.

"Except for these morning bouts of sickness, you are. Five days in a row. Perhaps we should let Tray call Dr. Birch out to examine you."

Alyssa grimaced. "The nausea goes away at noon, Sorche. The rest of the day I feel fine!"

Sorche gave her an odd, probing look. Alyssa was so pale! "Tell me, lamb, are there any other signs?"

"Signs?"

"Yes, you know…headaches or some such? Think now."

"Just—my breasts. They feel swollen and tender to touch."

Sorche compressed her thin lips, taking a stab at the stitchery in her hands. "And you've been feeling emotionally up and down of late?"

"Why, yes. How did you know?" She set the cup down on her lap, hope in her voice. "Oh, Sorche, do you know what it is? Is there an herb you have in the kitchen that will cure me of this awful sickness?"

Grimly, Sorche put down her needle and thread, looking directly at Alyssa. "I need you to answer one question for me."

Alyssa tilted her head, perplexed. "You know you can ask me anything."

"Did you lie with Tray before you got married?" Sorche asked bluntly.

Blushing a fiery red, Alyssa held the old woman's gaze. "Y-yes. Once. About six weeks ago. Up at one of the huts when we were lambing."

Sorche's eyes narrowed. "Not before that? Think, girl. Did you lie with him about three months ago?"

"Why—no! That would have been three weeks after I had arrived here. I couldn't possibly... Sorche, what are you looking like that for? I know it was wrong to lie with Tray, but—"

"That's not it, lamb," she whispered in an aching tone. "I really do think we should get Dr. Birch out here. I've a feeling you're pregnant, and it's not with Tray's child, either."

Alyssa's eyes widened. "What?"

"You've got all the signs," Sorche pointed out, her eyebrows drawing into a scowl. "And it takes three months for signs of a pregnancy to show up that way. Three months," she repeated heavily, "and that's about the time you were raped aboard that ship."

Alyssa's cup and saucer clattered to the carpet. "My God, no! No!" Alyssa stared down at the fragmented china cup and saucer, barely noticing as Sorche came over and began guiding her back toward the bedchamber.

"I'm going to fetch Tray to get the doctor."

"Sorche, don't tell him!" Alyssa gripped the woman's arm, her face suddenly contorted with fear. "Don't tell Tray anything, please . . . not until after Dr. Birch examines me."

"Lamb, you might as well prepare yourself. Tray will have to know the truth eventually. Come, come. Back to bed with you."

It wasn't ten minutes after Sorche left her that Tray burst into their bedchamber. His face was ravaged as he shut the door behind him and walked over to the bed. Alyssa raised her head, her heart constricting. "Tray—"

He held out his hand. "I've sent a servant to get the doctor," he rasped. He walked across the room, staring out the window. "Is it true?" he asked finally.

Miserably, Alyssa fought back the tears. "I don't know."

His mouth thinned, and his tone became little more than a growl. "If you're pregnant with Vaughn's child—" His voice broke and his shoulders tensed.

"I can't be! I don't feel that, Tray!" she cried softly. "I do feel different, but I—I *know* it's not Vaughn's! Don't ask me how I know that," she begged. "I only feel it here, in my heart. Please…don't torture yourself. Wait until Dr. Birch gets here."

Tray felt his stomach twist into a hard knot. Vaughn, the filthy bastard, would have the last laugh. And if it was Vaughn's child? How would Alyssa feel about carrying it? Would she try to miscarry it, or worse, kill herself because of the shame? He rubbed his face. Everything he ever loved became tainted. And he loved Alyssa more than anyone in his entire life. What would it do to her? Would she hate him because it was his half brother's child whom she carried? Could she safely deliver a baby? Oh God, what if she died in birth because the baby was too large to pass from her small body? He looked longingly at Alyssa. She sat up in bed, a modest pink flannel nightgown on, looking more like a child than a woman carrying a baby in her body. What would Birch say? God, he'd go out of his mind until he found out.

"I'll be in my study. When Birch gets done with you, tell him I want to see him," he said tiredly, leaving.

Tray's insides were clenched as Dr. Birch knocked and entered his study. The doctor's face was grave as he came and sat down.

"She is pregnant, my lord."

"There's no doubt?" he asked in a weary voice.

"No doubt."

Tray hid his face between his hands, drawing in a great, ragged breath. "She told you everything?"

"Yes, she did. I've examined her, my lord. And quite frankly, I don't know whether she's three months or a month and a half along. In all honesty, it could be your child or Vaughn's." He watched as the lord raised his head, hope flickering in his red-rimmed eyes. "It takes a woman nine months to birth. If the baby is born in December of this year, it will be Vaughn's. But if it's born in February of next year, it will be your child. Anyway, in a few more months, I'll have a better idea of how far along she really is. At first, it's difficult to tell, my lord."

"But Sorche said women don't begin their sickness until the third month."

Birch shrugged, giving him a kindly smile. "Some women start it from the moment they conceive, my lord. Others in the first month or second. It's true, most women get the sickness in the third through sixth month."

Hope entwined with fear. "Then—then Aly could be pregnant with my child?"

"It's very possible. Remember, I was the one who treated her after the rape." He shook his head. "She's healed quickly from that, I must admit. But I find it difficult to believe she could have conceived under those circumstances. It's possible, but improbable."

Tray clenched his teeth, worry shadowing his eyes. "If it is my baby she carries, will she have trouble delivering it?"

Birch recalled all too readily Shelby's death in childbirth. "I know what you're thinking, my lord. And I can't easily answer that question for you."

"God, she's build exactly like Shelby," he uttered in a low groan.

"Not really. Lady Alyssa is far more active than Shelby was." A slight smile crossed Birch's mouth. "According to your wife, she's been riding horses like a man since she was old enough to walk. Society may frown upon that, but what it has done is widen her hip area, made her more flexible, if you will. I think she may have a long labor, but knowing her spunk and spirit, I'd say she'll deliver a healthy baby."

A slight glimmer of hope flared in Tray's eyes. "And you say in two months you'll know when Aly will birth?"

Birch got to his feet. "I should know, my lord. For right now, I'd try to comfort her. She's very fearful that the baby might be Vaughn's. We'll all have to wait, I'm afraid."

Tray found Alyssa standing at the french doors in their bedchamber after he had bid the doctor farewell. Her profile was silhouetted against the crystal, her hands laid flat against the doors. He walked quietly to her side, words useless as she slowly turned her head, her eyes fraught with fear and confusion. Her face was so pale, making her jade eyes look like deep pools of grief as he studied her in the uncomfortable silence.

"Dr. Birch spoke to you?" she asked in a low, tortured tone.

"Yes." Tray held her gaze. If only he could know what she was thinking and feeling. "Aly, I—"

She turned away, staring out the window. "I won't stop you from annulling our marriage, Tray. I don't blame you." She hung her head, fighting back tears. "I—I can barely stand the idea that it might be Vaughn's baby and not yours...." Her fingers dug into the wood of the door frame. "I won't blame you for whatever you must do."

He gripped her shoulders, turning her toward him. "What are you talking about? What annulment?"

Bravely, she met his dark, anguished eyes. "How can you accept my carrying a child that might not be yours? A child conceived out of anger and hatred?"

His fingers tightened on her flesh. "Now listen to me," he said hoarsely, "whatever happens, it does not lessen my love for you, Aly. I want no annulment! I love you."

Her eyes became luminous. "You mean that, Tray? After I've shamed you? I'm the daughter of a felon. And now

I may be carrying Vaughn's child and not yours! How can you still love me?'' She choked back a sob, watching his features soften. ''By the laws of our church, I won't try to miscarry the child. That would be murder.''

He groaned, whispering her name, pulling her against him. Alyssa melted against his hard body and he held her in a crushing embrace, his face buried in her long, silken hair. ''No matter what the outcome, Aly, I love you,'' he said thickly. ''And if you do carry Vaughn's child and not mine, I do not blame you for that, either. You were taken by force, beloved.'' He kissed her hair and then gently cradled her face in his large hand as he lifted her chin upward. His gray eyes were curiously bright as he gazed down upon her. ''You're my life, Aly,'' he whispered brokenly. ''We'll weather this together. Whatever you do, don't shut me out. Together we can give each other strength.''

She nodded, unable to speak for a long moment. ''Oh, Tray, what if it is Vaughn's child? Could I find it within my heart to love the baby? I feel as if God is punishing me. What have I done so wrong that I must carry Vaughn's baby and not yours?''

''Hush, little one, it will be all right,'' he soothed, caressing her hair with a trembling hand. ''Dr. Birch will be able to tell us in two months or so if it is ours or Vaughn's. And then your fears may be put to rest.''

Miserably, Alyssa leaned her head on his chest, her voice broken. ''I hate him, Tray. I hate Vaughn for all he's done to me and now to you. Sorche told me how much he teased and made fun of you while you were growing up. He's got a black heart! He spreads nothing but pain and suffering wherever he goes.''

Tray kissed her cheek tenderly, cradling her protectively in his arms. ''God would never punish you, Aly. You've done nothing wrong except help fight for the freedom that Ireland deserves.''

She sniffed, angrily swallowing the tears she refused to let fall. ''If I didn't know better, I would say God is an Englishman!''

Tray chuckled and gave her a squeeze. ''I doubt that He is, beloved. It just seems like it, sometimes. Now, do you feel up to some tea with me in the drawing room?''

An incredible sense of warmth spread through her as she looked up into Tray's face. He loved her, unequivocally and without reservation. ''Yes, I'd like that.''

# Chapter Fifteen

Vaughn lounged lazily on the settee, having changed from his hacking clothes into a well-tailored set of dark blue trousers, a matching coat and a pale blue silk shirt. He took a sip of rich red sherry before finally bringing himself to open his father's most recent letter from Briarwood. Harold had last written to advise him to keep away from Shadowhawk, after Tray had warned their father that he risked losing his younger son. Taking a deep breath, Vaughn quickly read the first lines.

His eyes narrowed. Alyssa Kyle pregnant? He felt a cold blade go through him as he glanced at the letter's date—a mere ten days after Tray's wedding. She was carrying *his* child! His hand tightened around the slender stem of the goblet, his mouth thinning as he pondered the ramifications, the ways that she might use the child against him. He wanted no half-Irish brat going around claiming him as his father. Harold would be humiliated if he ever talked to one of his compatriots who had been aboard that ship when he raped the Kyle girl. Then, the truth would be known.

Small beads of sweat dotted his furrowed brow. Yes, Alyssa could easily use the brat to dishonor him in the eyes of his family. She had reason enough to come after him. Not to mention what Tray might do.... God's blood! He had totally discounted Tray. Sweat glistened on his tense face as his mind raced. His half brother would come hunting him in earnest. He had no wish to meet Tray in a fight to the death. Did Tray believe that he had been the one to rape her? Tray must have or he wouldn't have sent that letter to Harold.

Vaughn abruptly stood, strode with urgency through the halls of his well-appointed London house and escaped to the well-manicured garden in back. He had to think! Think! Alyssa would bear the brat in December. That was five months away. He halted at a hedge, staring blackly into space. Was Tray going to annul the marriage? There had been no word on that. The idiot would be stupid enough to stay married to her, Vaughn thought savagely.

Alyssa would have to meet her death. Slowly, a plan evolved in Vaughn's mind, and a smile began to blossom at the corners of his mouth. Yes, why not? Why not, indeed? Alyssa always rode horses, according to Stablemaster Thomas. Why not ambush her on Shadowhawk property? He would ride to Liverpool, hire some men and then patiently wait until the proper moment. They could have sport with her before they slashed her throat, just as Paige's throat had been slit by those Irish brigands. A just and fitting revenge, Vaughn thought, congratulating himself. He would be rid of Alyssa and the evidence she carried in her body, and he would be free of any retribution that she might have tried through blackmail in the future. Suddenly, the sunny day turned brighter and more beautiful as Vaughn slowly turned and walked back to the house, a smile lingering on his mouth.

"No you don't, you're riding with me." Tray leaned down, placing an arm around Alyssa, easily drawing her up in front of him on the saddle. Rasheed stood still, neck magnificently arched, while Tray made her comfortable across his lap.

Alyssa laughed, throwing her arms around Tray's neck. "You, sir, are a highwayman."

Stablemaster Thomas smiled and made a quick bow. "Enjoy your ride," he called.

"I practically have to abduct my own wife," Tray muttered, moving Rasheed into a gentle walk, "she's so busy with the manor."

Alyssa closed her eyes, content to be held in his arms. The sun was bright, and a light breeze occasionally caught strands of her unbound hair. She wore a simple pink cotton dress that brought out the heightened color of her cheeks and lips. "I see you in bed each night, my lord. And do I not pay total attention to you then?"

Tray leaned down, brushing his mouth against her welcoming lips. She tasted of tartness and honey. "That you do," he agreed. "You've been drinking the lemon water," he added, kissing her once more.

She hugged him fiercely, her eyes sparkling. "Dr. Birch says no alcohol, and you monitor every scrap of food that goes in my mouth. I've been reduced to drinking hot tea and cool lemon water."

He grinned. "And you're growing more beautiful by the day because of it, my lady."

Alyssa rested her head against Tray's broad shoulder while her hand skimmed his wonderfully virile chest. "I think Dr. Birch is right, Tray. The baby I carry is yours, not Vaughn's."

His gray eyes darkened. That thought had haunted them for nearly two months now. Next week, when Dr. Birch came out to examine Alyssa, their questions finally would be put to rest. One way or another. "I hope you're right, little one."

"Sorche has been a midwife, Tray. And she pointed out that although my breasts are tender and I'm nauseated, my clothes still fit me, and there isn't a woman who doesn't complain of her waist growing at three months." She patted her tummy. "And look at me! I haven't gained an inch! There is no roundness to my stomach, no weight gain. Do I look as if I'm five months along?" she demanded.

Tray shook his head, feeling some of his fear melting beneath her teasing. "No, you don't look pregnant. But your breasts are slightly fuller."

"Well," she added petulantly, leaning up to kiss his cheek, "I don't believe I will begin putting on weight until late August. And that would be after the third month of my pregnancy." She wrapped her hands around his neck, nibbling on his earlobe. "With your child," she whispered.

He grinned, dodging her lips, tiny shivers of pleasure racing through him. "Wench," he accused, pulling her away. "Keep that up and I'll ride to that grove of beech in the distance and take you."

Alyssa's eyes sparkled. "Tray?"

"Hmm?"

"If this is our baby," she began in a softened voice, "what name would you choose?"

He frowned. "Welsh or Irish?"

She laughed, hugging him. "I love you so much! You always think of me, don't you?"

He met her smiling emerald eyes. The wind blew a lock of his black hair onto his forehead and she reached up, taming it back into place. "You're always first in my heart, little one. Now, as for names, I can think of two Welsh ones. I'll let you think of two Irish ones."

Alyssa settled contentedly back into his arms, closing her eyes. "All right. If it's a boy, our boy, what name would you like for him?"

"Griffith. It means fierce chief in Welsh."

"Griffith." Alyssa tested the word and looked up at Tray. "Could we call him Griff? Then I could pronounce it properly."

He laughed. "Griff is a good name, too."

"And if our baby is a girl?" she prodded him lightly.

"Meredith. In Welsh that means guardian from the sea. And she would be raised by the sea."

"Meredith sounds so...staunch. What if we shortened it to Merry? I'd like that—Merry sounds so happy. Like bright sunshine."

Tray agreed, praying inwardly that the baby Alyssa carried was theirs. "Yes," he murmured, "I'd like Merry better than Meredith."

Alyssa sat up, her hands on his broad shoulders. "Oh, Tray, I just know this is our baby. I feel it here, in my heart."

Tray's face became tender as he regarded his young wife. "I feel it's our baby, too, Aly. And in another week, we'll know."


"That's her! It's Alyssa!" the dark-haired man spoke in a fervent undertone to the larger man beside him.

"For once a lead paid off," the other growled, his blue eyes narrowing as he watched the two people on horseback move farther and farther away.

"I can't believe it. We've finally found her...finally...."

Dev slowly stood up to his full six feet two inches of height, his well-chiseled features pensive as he watched the horse grow smaller and smaller in the distance. He turned his attention to his younger brother, Gavin. "Yes, at least we've always known where Father was. And now, Alyssa."

"What about Sean?"

"I couldn't get any information down in Colwyn Bay. What about you? What have the farmers around this area said?"

Gavin sat down, his lanky body poorly clothed, his knee-high boots scuffed and muddied like Dev's. His hazel eyes crinkled as he studied Dev. "Nothing. Everyone's excited about that English Lord Trayhern having married Alyssa."

Dev snorted violently, his blue eyes flashing fire. "Marriage! The bastard forced her! Alyssa would no more marry an Englishman than I would wed an Englishwoman. No, she was forced or coerced into it."

He hunkered down, absently picking up a blade of grass and chewing on it. His face was broad and well proportioned, his hair short and the same wine color as Alyssa's. His face boasted wide and intelligent eyes, an aristocratic nose and well-shaped mouth. Alyssa had always teased him about how handsome he was, and how it was no wonder Shannon had fallen madly in love with him. His gaze darkened when he thought of Shannon. She was dead; they had established that much. Alyssa had been taken off the ship and forced to become the mistress of Lord Trayhern. And Sean? No one seemed to know if their cousin was in a Welsh coal mine, dead or alive. He released a deep, painful sigh, throwing the blade of grass down.

"What are we going to do, Dev?" Gavin asked, breaking into his brother's thoughts. "We can't rescue Father. No one makes it out of Newgate. He'll hang soon and there's nothing we can do."

"No, but we can rescue Alyssa and take her back to Ireland with us, where she belongs."

"And then?"

Dev rested his long, large-knuckled fingers on his hips. "Then we'll begin where we left off. We'll gather the rest of those arms and try to enlist aid from Napoleon. One way or another, we're going to win freedom for Ireland.''

Gavin got to his feet, dusting off the twigs from his breeches. Although much shorter than Dev, and his hair carrot-colored, he possessed the Kyle hallmarks of wide, well-set eyes, freckles and a square face. Making sure both pistols were fitted snugly in the leather belt at his waist, Gavin began to walk back to the tree where their horses were tied.

"The locals said Alyssa rides every day with Lord Tray- hern."

Dev strode to his side, picking up the reins to his black gelding. "We'll see if that's true. We'll watch them for the next few days. Once we know what time she rides and where, we'll be able to rescue her."

Gavin mounted his rawboned bay gelding. "What about Lord Trayhern?"

Dev glanced sharply at his brother. "I'll kill him. After what he's done to Alyssa, the dog deserves no mercy. No Englishman is going to take our sister and force her into his bed," he growled.

Worriedly, Gavin held his glare. "If you kill an English lord—"

"That's one more aristocrat who can't come over to Ire- land and levy taxes against our people! Come, we've got to familiarize ourselves with this estate and find something to eat."

"Are you nervous?"

Tray glanced over at Alyssa. "A little." They rode on in companionable silence, their legs occasionally brushing against one another. The July winds were warm, the sun low on the horizon to the east of them. The day had finally come. In less than an hour Dr. Birch would be at Shadowhawk to examine Alyssa. He drank in her beauty as she rode Ghazieh beside him. The past week they had grown even closer to each other, and Tray began to share Alyssa's belief that the child she carried was theirs. He gripped the reins a bit more tightly, feeling Rasheed dance nervously beneath him. He frowned. It was unlike the stallion to be so fretful and jumpy. Perhaps, Tray thought, the stallion sensed his anxiety over Birch's visit.

The sun's long rays slanted across the golden sand of the beach where they rode, and small waves lapped at their horses' hooves. Alyssa inhaled the tangy salt air, turning her face to the sun, a feeling of happiness blanketing her. "I will be all right, Tray. I just know it," she told him softly, reopening her eyes and smiling up at him. He looked so handsome, his hair unruly, face darkly tanned by the sun that he loved to work beneath, his hands large and yet so gentle when they touched her. Tray reached out, caressing her cheek.

"I believe you, little one. But no matter what Dr. Birch finds, I'll still love you. Just remember that. I'd move heaven and hell to keep you as my wife."

Rasheed snorted violently, jumping sideways, nearly knocking the gray mare down. Tray cursed and was about to reprimand the frantic stallion when he heard hoofbeats coming up rapidly behind them. Alyssa had clung to Ghazieh and was just finding her balance again when Tray turned his horse around. He cursed richly.

"Aly! Ride!" he barked.

Shaken, Alyssa froze for a second. She turned and saw two riders dressed in dark clothes riding on the whip toward them, pistols drawn. Tray cursed again. His eyes were narrowed, terror written in their depths.

"Go!" he roared. "They're brigands!" He took his whip, slashing it down upon the mare's rump.

Alyssa clung to the saddle as the Arabian mare charged through the heavy sand at a gallop. Brigands! She grappled with the runaway horse, trying to control her. Tray? Where was he? Alyssa twisted, catching sight of him standing his ground between her and the fast-approaching men dressed in black. Her throat closed in terror as she jerked the mare to a halt, turning her around. She wouldn't let Tray fight them by himself! Alyssa dug her heels into the horse's sweaty flank, the wind tearing at her face as she screamed out Tray's name, her cry drowned out by the pounding surf.

Alyssa's throat went dry as she saw the hood fall back on the nearest brigand. Her eyes widened in disbelief. Dev! It was Dev! And he was raising his pistol, aiming it directly at Tray.

"My God! No! *No!*" Her scream tore above the sound of the waves, echoing off the rugged black cliffs above them as the pistol was fired. Horror knifed through her as Tray tumbled backward, falling off Rasheed. The stallion leapt away, eyes white and rolling.

"Alyssa!" Dev yelled, pulling his gelding to a halt. He grabbed at the bridle of the gray mare. "You're saved!" he gasped. "Come on! We've got a boat—"

"No! Dev, you shot Tray!" she screamed, gripping at the reins. She tried to dismount.

Dev cursed. "Damn it, Alyssa, we have to go, now! They'll be sending soldiers after us!" He leaned over, pulling her off the mare and into his arms. He spurred his gelding.

"*No!*" Alyssa cried. She struggled and fought to no avail. Her brother's arm around her was too powerful to combat. They galloped past where Tray lay on the sand, a huge bloodstain spreading out across his chest. Alyssa's eyes widened and a sob tore through her. "You don't under-

stand, Dev!" she screamed. "You killed him! You killed
Tray! Let me go! Please...oh, God...no!"

Gavin hung to the rear, continually looking over his
shoulder as they rode hard around the curve of the beach.
The sand beneath gave way to slick pebbles, yet Dev rode
like a madman, spurring his foaming horse on at break-
neck speed. Gavin heard Alyssa's cries, perplexed. What was
wrong with her? She should have been happy to see them!
Grimly, Gavin tossed all his questions aside, whipping his
lagging gelding. If they didn't get off English soil soon,
they'd all end up hanging at the end of a yardarm.

They rode for nearly an hour until they reached a shel-
tered cove where a small sailboat bobbed in the water. Dev
released Alyssa and quickly dismounted. Gavin took the
saddles, blankets and bridles from the lathered horses, running to the boat. The tack would be necessary once they
landed in Ireland, where they could borrow some horses
from a local farmer. He frowned, hearing Alyssa screaming hoarsely at Dev as they came up behind him.

"You killed my husband! What did you think you were
doing, Dev! Oh God, you killed Tray...you killed him!"

Dev jerked her along by her arm. "Husband?" he
snarled. "An English dog? You've been too long in England, sister. Now get aboard!" Damn her! Dev was
breathing hard, his body soaked in sweat from the hard ride.
He took the tack from Gavin, tossing it aboard. "Cast off,"
he yelled.

Gavin untied the rope, pushed the small boat off into
deeper water and then lightly hopped aboard. Alyssa's eyes
were wide with shock, her disheveled hair framing her taut,
frightened face. He scrambled by her as she lay in a heap in
the center of the boat, going to release the sail while Dev
took the tiller. "We're taking you home, Lys," Gavin
gasped. "Home. Back to Ireland, where you belong."

Morosely, Alyssa hung her head, shock flowing through her. She shut her eyes and all she could see was Tray tumbling from Rasheed's back and the dark stain spreading across the white of his shirt as he lay unmoving on the sand. Covering her face, she sobbed. He was dead. Dead! Oh, sweet Mother, why? Why?

"Look!" Gavin warned, pointing toward shore.

Alyssa's head snapped up, and she saw a man standing on the bank. A gasp was torn from her. She would never forget that blond hair and mustache. It was Vaughn, sitting astride a black horse with five men surrounding him. Dev lunged forward, shoving Alyssa down flat against the deck. "Stay down!" he snarled.

Shots rang out, the balls striking around the ship. Alyssa's mind was spinning. Vaughn wasn't allowed on Shadowhawk soil...why was he here now? She huddled against the splintered wooden flooring, shutting her eyes tightly as another volley of musket and pistol balls pinged into the water and against the boat.

"Fix that sail!" Dev shouted at Gavin. "If we don't pick up more wind, we'll be drifting back to shore—to that welcoming committee!"

Gavin, keeping low, adjusted the sail, allowing its patched canvas to catch the sea breeze. Suddenly, the small boat took off, aiming steadily out toward the Irish Sea. Each minute carried them farther and farther away from the shore and out of range of English fire.

Farther and farther from Tray, Alyssa thought, unable to stop the tears that spilled down her cheeks.

"Why are you crying?" Dev growled. "We rescued you! Did you want to spend more time in that bastard's bed?"

She choked back the tears. "Oh, Dev, he was my husband. My husband! I loved him. A-and you killed him!"

He winced, his face darkening. "He's English!"

She buried her face in her hands. "Tray was Welsh, Dev. Welsh! He hated the English as much as we do!" she wailed.

Dev bowed his head, anger soaring through him, woven with guilt. His hand tightened on the tiller as they began to ride the growing waves into the open sea. He tried to shut his ears to her sobs, his stomach knotting. Alyssa loved that man? He didn't care if he was Welsh. The bastard lived in England and that was enough.

# Chapter Sixteen

"Why's she so sick?"

Dev continued to hold Alyssa, one hand on her shoulder, the other on the tiller. "I don't know."

But he did know. Dev recalled with agonizing clarity how sick he had become upon learning of Shannon's death. His hand tightened on Alyssa's shoulder as the small boat pitched and wallowed between the eight-foot waves. That morning, she had done nothing but vomit until only clear liquid had come up, and he forced her to drink a little water and held her in his arms. Dev couldn't bear to meet her dark, grief-stricken eyes. He had killed her husband, the man whom she loved so deeply. He shifted his thoughts again to Vaughn Trayhern and his hand tightened on the rudder, his own stomach beginning to feel queasy. Dev was torn between what he had done to Alyssa and the fact that Shannon had been brutally tortured to death.

The coast of Ireland was barely visible in the distance. Their lives were all scattered, like their hearts. Dev took a deep, ragged breath. If their father were here, he'd know what to do... he'd have the right words to make them feel better. But there was no use in thinking about that, either. Their father would be hanged in a month. A helpless rage burned inside him. So much misery...and all because of the English. The damned, accursed English!

Alyssa stirred, slowly opening her eyes. She felt Dev's hand on her shoulder.

"We're almost home, Lys. Feel like getting up? You can see Ireland in the distance."

She roused herself, feeling incredibly weak. Blankets provided her with needed warmth besides giving her a shield against the seawater that continually sprayed into the boat. She followed Dev's finger as he pointed toward her homeland. She should have felt elated, but she could feel nothing. Settling back, she leaned against her brother, closing her eyes.

"How soon before landfall?"

"By dark."

"And then?"

Dev scowled. Her voice seemed so far away, as if she no longer cared about anything. It frightened him. "There's a local farmer who will loan us two of his Irish cobs when we land. He'll hide the sailboat and cover it in the cove."

"And we'll be on the run again?"

"We have no choice, Lys." Dev's fingers tightened briefly on her shoulder. He ached to take away the pain he heard in her voice and saw in her face. "We're wanted, you know that."

"Dev, I don't want to fight anymore. I'm so tired...."

He felt his heart twist in his chest. "I know you're tired, Lys. And I'm doing all I can to make it easy on you. But those English bastards back there on the coast of Wales will put a bounty on your head. They'll think you killed Tray. I'm sorry, Lys, but we're going to have to go deep into the forest to hide. At least for a month or so."

Alyssa bowed her head. "Just like before."

"Yes. We'll live off the land. It's summer now. Food's plentiful. Plenty of animals to trap, berries to pick. We shouldn't have to steal much from the surrounding areas. Not until winter."

She shivered. The sun was peeking out between the rifts of clouds, but still she was icy cold. Trembling, Alyssa wrapped the blankets more tightly around her. She felt Dev lean down and awkwardly put his arm around her in an embrace.

"Dev?" Her voice was unsteady.

"What is it, Lys?"

"I'm pregnant." She took in a ragged breath, clutching at his arm. "With Tray's child."

Dev froze, his eyes momentarily widening as he realized the implications of her words. "When?"

"February of next year," she whispered faintly. Alyssa had awakened knowing that the child she carried within her body was Tray's. She could not prove it, she simply knew it. August was a month away. By then, her waist would begin to thicken and she would know... know that on that beautiful night at the lambing hut, Tray had given her a child created out of the purity of their love for each other.

Dev pressed a kiss to her damp hair and slowly released her from his embrace. "All right. Once we get to land, I'll do what I can to find some farmer who's for our cause to take you in."

"Then they'd be killed by the English if they were found to be hiding me, Dev. I can't abide any more slaughter. I— I just can't face it anymore."

Dev turned over options and half-formed plans in his mind. Since she was pregnant, Alyssa would not be able to ride the whip. He couldn't risk her being chased by soldiers and taking a fall from a horse. No, she must be kept safe and carry the child to full term. He had killed her husband

and he would not see her child taken from her. At least Lys had the baby, Dev thought. Shannon had not yet conceived. He had only memories of her sweetness and goodness to comfort him.

"Rest, Lys. I'll think of something, I promise."

"I'm sorry, Dev. I didn't mean to make things so hard on you."

Dev ruffled her hair. "Silly goose, quit mumbling. Come on, we've got a bit of that rabbit left. You've got to eat for your baby, Lys. I know you're not hungry, but I'll bet she is."

"He."

Dev's blue eyes warmed as he met her green ones. "He?"

"It's a boy."

He hooted, a grin breaking his tensed features. "Oh, and how do you know that? Did some fairy come and whisper it in your ear?"

The corners of her mouth stretched into a broken smile as she placed her hand across her stomach. "It was no fairy, Devlin Kyle. I just know."

He chortled and brushed her pale cheek. "And I suppose you've got a name for him, too."

She nodded, closing her eyes again. "Griff. We decided to call him Griff."


Vaughn jerked open the door to Tray's bedchamber. He glowered at Sean, who sat on the edge of the bed with a cloth in his hand.

"Get out," he snarled to the boy.

Vaughn waited until the child had skittered around him, running out the opened door. His eyes narrowed as he walked to the foot of the bed. Tray slowly raised his lashes.

"Leave . . ." Tray gasped softly.

"When I choose, half brother. But first, I want you to know what I'm going to do."

Pain throbbed without remission through Tray's heavily bandaged chest, and his gray eyes were ringed with exhaustion as he studied Vaughn. In the past five days, he had continually passed in and out of consciousness.

"Do what?" he demanded with an effort.

A smile drew Vaughn's lips upward. "I've already been to Liverpool, giving the authorities a description of Alyssa. By the time I land in Wexford, her name will be all over England and Ireland. What's the matter, Tray? She's a felon's daughter who tried to kill an earl's son." He placed his hands on his hips, watching Tray's skin turn ashen. "I've been given orders to hunt her down. There's a five hundred pound reward for her head." His voice lowered to a snarl. "I'll hunt her down like the animal she is, and I'll see to it that she swings from the hangman's noose at Newgate. There's not a thing you can do about it, half brother." Vaughn raised his gloves. "And don't worry, I'll never set foot on your accursed Shadowhawk again. Not as long as you live."

Tray's heart pounded heavily in his chest as he watched Vaughn saunter out of the bedchamber. He was going after Alyssa! He had framed her, making the authorities think that she had shot him. Sweat glistened over the taut planes of his face as he weakly raised his arm to pull the bell cord beside the bed. By the time Sorche arrived, Tray was gasping for breath, his dark gray eyes wide with pain.

"Tray? What's wrong?" she asked, coming to his side and leaning down.

"Vaughn . . . he's going to hunt Alyssa down and . . . kill her . . . got to get help . . . get up . . ."

"No!" She gently held him down on the bed, noticing a pink stain growing across the wound in his chest. "Rest, Tray. Let me get the doctor. Please, don't struggle."

He clenched his teeth, shutting his eyes tightly, tears squeezing out from beneath his lashes. "Aly... got to help her... can't let Vaughn..." He lapsed into unconsciousness.

"What's wrong?"

Sorche looked up to see Dr. Birch hurrying into the room. "Thank the saints, Doctor. Tray's gone delirious. He's feverish and talking out of his head."

Birch frowned and placed his hand on Tray's sweaty brow. "He has a fever," he agreed, noticing the seeping wound. Mouth pursed, Birch glanced over at the anxious Sorche. "He's overtaxed himself too soon. Quick, fetch me my bag. We must keep his fever down or, more than likely, he'll die."

"Oh, no... why was he so upset? I don't understand it. He was resting so peacefully, Doctor."

Shrugging, Birch pulled up several more covers to keep his patient warm. "Fever does odd things to people, Sorche. Have one of the maids bring a bowl of cold water. We must bathe him frequently."

Brilliant sunlight filled the room, its rays snaking across the bed. Tray's brow slowly wrinkled as he became aware of the warmth of the sun on him and the sounds of birds chirping outside the french doors. He was weak, more weak than he could ever recall being. He tried to lift his arm from beneath the blankets and forced his eyes open. As his blurred vision cleared, so did the cobwebs that inhabited his memory. Tray recalled everything with crystal clarity, and the ache in the region of his heart far outstripped the agony of his chest wound when he tried to move. He felt pitifully incapacitated.

"Ah, you're awake."

Tray recognized Birch's voice and slowly turned his head in that direction. "I'm thirsty," he whispered rawly.

Birch smiled pleasantly and sat on the bed after pouring him a cup of water. Lifting his patient's head, he allowed him to drink his fill. "Not too fast, my lord. You've been unconscious off and on for nearly three weeks."

Tray lay back, savoring the cool liquid. "Three—weeks?"

Retrieving another cup of water, Birch came back to his bedside. "Indeed. Your wound became infected and we didn't know whether you would live or die, quite frankly. And you've a lingering case of pneumonia. Every time you coughed, your wound began bleeding." Birch gave him one of his rare smiles as he fed Tray the second cup of water. "Like Sorche said, you're as strong as a bull. That and many prayers pulled you through. Now all you have to do is remain quiet and allow that wound to heal properly and regain your strength. You've lost nearly two stone."

Tray blinked. "Three weeks. Alyssa? What about her?"

Birch set the cup aside, his face growing sober once again. "We've heard nothing, my lord. I'm sorry."

"But—Vaughn. He said he was going after her. To kill her. Didn't anyone try to stop him?"

"What?"

Tray sank back into the pillow, angered by his weakness. "Doctor, my half brother stood here and told me he was going to hunt down my wife. Not only that, he had fabricated a lie to the Liverpool officials saying that she shot me." He opened his gray eyes. "Nothing could be further from the truth. The brigands that attacked us shot me. Alyssa is innocent."

"Dear God, we thought you were delirious, my lord. We never took what you said seriously." Birch looked apologetic. "I'm sorry."

He wanted to cry. He wanted to scream. Tray swallowed back the lump in his throat, shutting his eyes. "Get Sorche, Doctor. Right away."

The bedchamber soon filled with people. Tray lay propped up in the bed, his flesh sallow and sunken as he looked at them. Sean's welcoming smile was Tray's only comfort. Every other face present spoke of strain and worry as they looked on at him in silence.

"Sorche, get me quill and parchment. I intend to write a short letter, which I want my attorney to deliver to the magistrate in Liverpool. Vaughn must be stopped."

"Very well, my son."

"Thomas?"

"Yes, my lord?"

"Send your best rider on our fleetest horse south to Briarwood. Have him tell my father what has occurred. Tell Harold that if he doesn't get to Vaughn as soon as possible and force him back to Wales, I'll hunt Vaughn down myself. Tell him that if Vaughn so much as touches Alyssa, I'll find him and kill him."

Thomas bowed. "Right away, my lord."

"And have Rasheed and Ghazieh shod. I want supplies gathered and prepared for the journey to Ireland."

"But, Tray," Sorche protested, "you can't go anywhere yet! You've nearly died!"

"She's right, my lord," Dr. Birch seconded. "To ride horseback would greatly aggravate your healing wound. You could have a relapse."

Tray tiredly closed his eyes. "These are preparations, good doctor. I'll be little use to anyone in my present condition for quite a while. What I can do is prepare for the time when I'll leave."

"A wise decision, my lord."

He opened his eyes, his gaze settling on Sean. "All of you," Tray said, his voice growing weak, "may go. Sean, I want you to remain."

They bowed and quietly left the bedchamber, shutting the door behind them. Sean walked over, sitting carefully on the edge of the bed, watching Tray.

"Would you like some more water?" Sean asked shyly.

Tray felt his strength dissipating. He reached over, grasping Sean's hand. "Please."

Tray's hands were shaking so badly that Sean had to hold the cup for him.

"Thank you," he whispered.

Sean blinked, watching Tray. "Are you hungry?"

Tray shook his head. "Just very tired right now."

"Dr. Birch said you should eat, Tray. He says you've lost too much weight."

He managed a poor semblance of a smile for Sean's benefit. "Perhaps later. Come, sit by me. I need to talk to you."

Obeying him, Sean crawled up on the bed, facing Tray.

"I need to know where Alyssa might be in Ireland," Tray began with an effort, fighting off the grogginess that was stalking him. "Can you remember any places specifically where your family used to hide?"

Sean shrugged. "We moved so much, Tray. The English were always after us. We'd sometimes stay with squatters, becoming like them so the soldiers couldn't find us."

The squatters. They were the poor who had been ousted from their farms and lived in tattered, ill-formed groups anywhere that they could build their one-room, window-ess thatched huts. They survived by cultivating potato patches and little more. "Where? Can you give me any idea of where Colin Kyle took all of you?"

"Mostly in southern Ireland. We've been as far north as Galway Bay on the western side and as far south as Bantry Bay."

"Did Colin have a favorite haunt? Somewhere he considered safer than any other place?"

Sean searched his memory. "Colin always liked the mountains. He said there was less chance of the English soldiers taking the time to scour the hillsides or heavy groves."

"Which mountains?"

"There's Knockmealdown and the Slieve Bloom mountains."

Tray was not familiar with either location. That didn't matter, though. Right now he had to try to piece together where Alyssa might be. And his instincts told him that the brigands had been her brothers. Otherwise, they would have attacked both him and Alyssa and left them for dead on the beach. His gray eyes narrowed on Sean's face. "What about Devlin Kyle? Did he have a place he favored over all others? Think, lad. Think hard."

Sean chewed on his lower lip, his mind racing. "D-do you think that Dev and Gavin took Lys?"

Tray nodded. "I think so."

Sean bowed his head, ashamed. "They almost killed you. I know they wouldn't have tried it if they had known you loved Lys."

"I'm not angry with them, son. All I want to do is find Aly before Vaughn gets to her. That's why I need your help. Did Dev favor those mountain areas, too?"

"Whenever the English were pressing Dev, he'd always disappear into the Blackstairs Mountains. There's an old mud hut up on the eastern side of Mount Leinster that he used.''

''And where is the range located?''

''They're near the Slanely lowlands in County Wexford. The slopes rise up and out of the Barrow Valley.''

''And the closest town?''

''New Ross.''

''If Dev did take Aly, what do you think he'd do?''

A pained expression came to Sean's small forehead. ''I— I don't know....''

Tray closed his eyes, weariness encroaching upon him. ''Tell me what kind of man Devlin is, Sean. Perhaps I can piece together what he might do.''

''Dev is like Colin Kyle. He's got a temper.''

''Is he cruel?''

Sean shook his head. ''No.''

''What was his relationship to Aly?''

''He loved her.''

And so do I, Tray thought in anguish. ''Was Dev protective of her? Did he allow Aly to go on raids against the English?''

''Never. He always saw to it that the women and children were safe before the men left camp to attack the soldiers. Dev seemed to keep that in mind when a lot of the other men didn't.''

''What do you mean?''

''Well, Dev always made a point of providing escape for the families in case anything happened.''

''What kind of escape plan, Sean?'' Tray held his breath.

''Dev made sure enough cobs were available so that the women and children could ride for the mountains if they had to hide.''

The mountains. Tray patted Sean's hand. ''You've been a great help, son. Thank you.''

# Chapter Seventeen

Gavin brought in another armload of peat, piling it near the east wall. He glanced at his sister, who turned a freshly killed rabbit on the spit above the glowing embers of the fire. His gaze narrowed as he studied Alyssa. The green fabric of her dress stretched tightly across her breasts, which were swollen with milk. He wondered how she managed to work the hours she did each day with her belly as large as it had become. Her hair hung limply around her thin face and Gavin felt a spasm of anxiety. So many women lost their babies because they couldn't get enough to eat.

He brushed his sleeves free of the peat and straightened up. "Dev ought to be here anytime now," he said, coming over to Alyssa. "Here, why don't you lie down? I'll finish cooking the rabbit."

Alyssa gave her brother a nod, slowly getting to her feet. Her fingers massaged her lower spine, trying to ease her protesting muscles. Her belly was large and the shift in weight had made her miserable in the last months of her pregnancy. Alyssa sat down on a small stool that Gavin had made for her.

"You look thin, Lys." Gavin frowned. "You aren't eating enough."

Alyssa shrugged tiredly. The winter had been hard on everyone and food was scarcer than usual. Even Gavin, who was an expert at killing small animals, seemed unable to snare them with his usual efficiency. She stared at the rabbit that was being roasted, her stomach growling. For the first six days of February, they had subsisted on a few potatoes and turnips. Her mouth watered at the thought of eating a portion of the rabbit.

"I'm getting enough food," she assured him softly, sending him an affectionate glance through the dim grayness of the hut. Outside, a fine drizzle was continuing, leaving the mountain muddy and impassable. "It's just that as I draw nearer to having the baby, I don't have much of an appetite, Gavin."

"Humph. Ask me, you ought to be eating for two! Look at you, Lys. You're skinny."

She smiled. "Only in some places. What I'd give to have my waist back." Her breasts, once small, were now full and tender. She had noticed in the last week that a clear, colorless liquid would occasionally drip from her nipples, staining the fabric of her chemise and dress. Soon, Alyssa thought, glancing down at her belly, soon you'll come. . . .

They were interrupted when Dev rode up. His dark burgundy hair was plastered against his skull, and his clothes clung to his large frame as he entered the hut, pushing aside the curtain.

"Well? What did you find out in New Ross?" Gavin asked.

Dev wiped the water from his glistening features, hunkering down by the fire. He cast a glance up at Alyssa. "The English are paying local farmers for information about us."

Alyssa frowned, her hands automatically moving to her baby. She knew it would be impossible for her to run again if the English decided to begin combing the mountains for them. She bit down on her lip, watching Dev's hard features.

"Is there anything we can do?" she asked.

Dev shed his cloak, spreading it out to dry. Black breeches clung to his lower body and his white peasant shirt outlined his chest. Alyssa felt an ache move through her. The clothes he wore reminded her sharply of Tray.

"The farmers in Barrow Valley have seen both Gavin and me on occasion," he muttered. "They know we disappear into the scrub brush of the Blackstairs Mountains. It's possible, because of the scarcity of food this year, that one of them could give them that information."

Gavin looked over at his brother. "Lys can't be moved."

"I know that."

"Did you find out anything else?"

Dev rubbed his face harshly, chilled by the long ride in the cold rain. His voice was dangerously soft as he spoke, holding Alyssa's gaze. "Yes. Captain Vaughn Trayhern is leading a special group of English cavalry to find us."

Alyssa gasped, her eyes widening. "No!" Oh God, all her terror and worry that Vaughn would come after her was materializing.

Dev nodded tiredly. "He's staying at the manor of Lord Caldwell. Apparently Trayhern started his sweep from Drogheda and is slowly heading south. Word is that he's staying in this area until the weather clears."

Gavin sucked air in between his teeth. "We can't let him find Lys. She's going to have that baby any day now."

"Don't you think I know that?" Dev suddenly stood, anger in his blue eyes as he paced the length of the small hut. His head spun with options and plans. There was little food available on the mountain, and Alyssa was incapable of hunting at this point. He ran his fingers through his damp hair, his eyes glittering with frustration.

"Lys, as soon as we can stockpile enough food for you, Gavin and I will leave."

"But—"

"Hear me out. Trayhern means to find you, and right now, we're practically sitting beneath his nose. You can't travel in your present condition. You probably won't be able to do anything for at least a month after the baby is born. I want Trayhern. I'm going to kill the bastard. Gavin and I will lead him away from the mountains. We'll make him and his unit follow us to the west, toward Lough Derg. We can lose them in the lake marshes, circle back and then come back here to pick you up."

Gavin stared at him. "You're going to leave Lys alone up here? She's going to have a baby. She might need help, Dev."

"Damn it, don't you think I'm aware of all that? Do you think I like the idea of her alone in this hut, having the baby? I know she needs help, but we can't afford to have a midwife up here. And what if the woman talked? If Trayhern knows Lys is up here, he'll come for her."

"I'll be all right," Alyssa told Gavin. "Dev's right." She compressed her lips, already feeling a sharp pang of loneliness. And fear. Women having their first child frequently had complications and needed help. She would have none. They couldn't risk Vaughn finding them now.

Gavin cursed roundly. "But what if Lys has trouble, Dev?"

Alyssa saw the utter anguish in Dev's eyes. "There's been more than one woman who's birthed alone, Gavin," she said. She wished she could reassure them both that she would survive the ordeal.

Gavin grumbled under his breath. "When do you want to leave, Dev?"

Dev came back and knelt by the fire. "Tomorrow morning we'll start getting in a supply of food for Lys. Maybe in a week." His voice lowered. "And then, if we get the chance, I'll kill Vaughn Trayhern. If not, we'll at least lead him and his men away from here."

The morning was cool and the sun was shining once again. Vaughn's mood was sour as he guided his black thoroughbred gelding to the front. The other ten soldiers in their freshly cleaned red uniforms were moving in two orderly columns as he rode by them. The road was drying up, although rutted badly from the wheels of farmers' wagons. Stone fences wound like gray ribbons on either side of the road that led up through Barrow Valley. To their right were the brush and oak-laden Blackstairs Mountains. Vaughn glared up at the tranquil scenery. Perhaps Lord Caldwell had been right, searching the Barrow Valley would be a wise choice. He would politely question the farmers while his men routed out the squatters, seeking information on the Kyles. This had been the region of the rebellion, which meant little voluntary assistance from the residents.

"Captain Trayhern!" the sergeant cried.

Too late, Vaughn twisted toward the man's voice. Pistol shots broke the calm of the morning and Vaughn felt a white-hot sting as a ball grazed his upper arm. He jerked his horse around, shouting orders for his men to form a battle line and drawing his own pistol. Two riders dressed in black cloaks appeared on the other side of the stream to his left, galloping wildly up across a sloping hill and quickly disappearing.

Angered, Vaughn glanced down at his left arm. Blood! The bastards had tried to ambush them!

"After them!" he thundered, sinking his heels into the horse. He guided the gelding down through the brush, the branches swatting and stinging at his lower legs as they raced by. At the stream, Vaughn leaned forward, giving the gelding his head. The black easily cleared the water, his hooves sinking deeply into the mud and grass on the other side. Several more soldiers followed on his heels and Vaughn whipped his horse unmercifully. The animal clawed its way up the slope. Just as Vaughn crested the hill, another shot rang out. The gelding grunted, its knees buckling beneath him.

Vaughn threw up his hands as the gelding crashed to the earth. He was thrown over the horse's head and landed heavily on the lush grass, rolling away from the flailing, deadly hooves. The column circled back to Vaughn as he slowly got to his feet. His eyes were black with rage as he saw the two riders fleeing over another hill to the west. Cursing soundly, Vaughn walked over and picked up his pistol. He then mounted behind the sergeant and ordered pursuit.

Alyssa heard the shots, their echo reeling through the valley and up the slopes of the mountain. She stood outside the hut, wondering if Dev had killed Vaughn. Or if Vaughn had discovered them before the ambush and both her brothers were now prisoners. The agony of not knowing only increased her sense of desolation. She had to keep busy, to keep her mind off the future.

Sunlight filtered through the bare branches of the oak next to the hut, sending warming streamers all around her. Alyssa pulled her well-worn black wool cloak more tightly around her shoulders. The Barrow Valley was beautiful in the morning light, the hills a verdant green from the recent rain. Here and there, woolly white dots denoted sheep grazing. Again, poignant memories of lambing season rose in her mind. And Tray... She shut her eyes tightly, feeling the sting of tears against her lids.

A cramping pain began low and worked its way up across her belly. Alyssa gasped, her hand going to her abdomen.

The pain, coming and going at first, was like nothing she had ever encountered. She slowly made her way back inside. As her labor intensified, she wouldn't be able to leave the hut. She had to ensure that enough water was available.

Walking into the hut, Alyssa pulled her pallet, now stuffed with straw, close enough to the peat fire so that she could throw extra fuel on it when necessary. The nights were cold; winds whipped across the mountain, draining the hut of warmth unless the fire was kept going. Thick smoke hung in the air toward the ceiling, slowly finding escape at the edges of the curtain draped over the dwelling's entrance. Her eyes darkened as another achy pain began. Alyssa had to lie down, finding no position comfortable.

The melodic call of birds seemed to welcome the sun back to the land. From time to time, Alyssa would leave the hut and gaze at the valley below her. Were Dev and Gavin safe? She looked overhead at the azure sky, fondly recalling how desolate Shadowhawk had appeared, set high on the rocky cliffs overlooking the Irish Sea. A small thread of hope found its way into her heart as she watched several birds float on the invisible wings of the breeze. Each time she experienced a labor contraction, she was that much closer to holding Tray's child in her arms. Alyssa took a deep, unsteady breath. If only Tray were here. If only...

Wearily, Tray stared up at the dark, almost forbidding Blackstairs Mountains that rose above them. He had scoured every inch of the other two mountain chains, searching for Alyssa. This was his last hope. Had Dev brought Aly here? He squeezed his calves to Rasheed's barrel and the stallion began the climb up the lower slopes covered with thick brush and budding purple heather. The last of the sun's rays shot up above the range's highest peak, Mount Leinster.

Tray missed little as they climbed a more steeply wooded slope, gazing methodically from right to left. Sean had said there was a small mud hut hidden deep on the slopes of a high peak, near a stream. He had found several likely candidates in the other mountain chains. Sometimes he found squatters living in them, sometimes they had been empty. He leaned over, giving Rasheed a well-deserved pat on the neck. The stallion responded by snorting and flicking his ears.

By dusk, the shadows were deep and gray. Tray had come to realize that much could hide in the waning light. There were no huts in sight; he would have to camp out beneath the spreading arms of the many oak trees. It wouldn't be the first time he had slept out in the open and probably wouldn't be the last. At least it wasn't going to rain tonight. At first light he would again begin to circle the eighteen-hundred-foot mountain in search of that hut.

Alyssa tensed, lying on her side and gripping her belly. Sweat gleamed off the taut planes of her face as she let out a low groan. Ordinarily, darkness didn't frighten her. But now, unreasonably, she was scared. Only the dull red glow of the peat fire broke the inky blackness of the hut's interior.

The labor contractions were closer together now, and she knew that her time was drawing near. Already, her chemise was damp with milk leaking from her nipples. At least she would have milk for her baby. Alyssa recalled that some women were dry because they were so close to starvation. It was a wonder they had even carried their babies to term.

She lay there, waiting for the next pain, trying to relax, trying not to tense, because then it hurt even more. Breathing deeply seemed to alleviate some of the pain. With her arms wrapped around her swollen body, she lay exhausted, ceasing to think.

By the time the morning sun showed through the tattered cloth over the doorway, Alyssa was in constant agony. She rolled her head from side to side as the pain bore down on her almost incessantly. It hurt to touch her belly, and yet all she wanted to do was hold herself against the undulating throes. Sweat rolled down her pale, drawn face, her hair long ago dampened and snarled by her movements. She was scared, more scared than she had ever been. Earlier, toward dawn, there had been a rush of warm fluid between her legs. She tried to rise and change the cloth beneath her but could not.

She had no concept of time, only of stitching, gut-wrenching pain moving unendingly across her abdomen. Her body was completely bathed in sweat, and whimpers of pain tore from her tightly clasped lips. The pressure in her lower body was increasing minute by minute. Alyssa kept pushing, hoping to help expel the child from her body, but nothing happened.

By dusk, she could not move from her position on her side. To move was agony. To lie still was to feel the knife-cutting pain shearing her apart. Drained and dehydrated, she lay there, her eyes glazed, staring blindly into the encroaching darkness. For the first time, Alyssa wondered if she were going to die. Somewhere in her numbed mind, she knew a long labor was dangerous. The longer the labor, the greater the potential for her to die. She tried to lick her chapped lips, thirst clawing up her throat. She had long ago consumed the rainwater she had collected in the small tin cups, but she was too helpless to walk to the stream and drink. Or even to feed the dying fire.

## Chapter Eighteen

Tray awoke with a start. The gray dawn lurked on the horizon as he stiffly threw off the wool blanket. What had awakened him? Rasheed stood nearby, his nostrils flared, drinking in the surrounding still, early morning air, his ears pricked forward. Pushing a lock of hair off his brow, Tray noticed that the gray mare, staked farther up the hill, was also listening to something with equal intensity.

He slowly got to his feet and began to pack his saddle bag. Rasheed nickered softly. Tray looked up from folding his blankets. The stallion heard something. People? Animals? A new sense of urgency filled Tray and he hurriedly saddled his stallion. Whatever the horses were hearing was in the direction of the mountaintop. His heart began beating more rapidly as he swung into the saddle.

The ground became firmer as they climbed up toward the ridge that formed the back of the small cluster of mountains. Sean's directions pounded insistently through Tray's head as he angled his stallion up a steeper climb. The hut, Sean had said, faced east, toward the rising sun. He was on the eastern slope. But there was so much brush and heather between the mighty oaks, ash and occasional beech trees that a mud hut could blend into the shadows and be hidden.

Tray was grateful when he came upon a gurgling stream with sweet, succulent grass on both banks. His stallion was breathing hard from the climb, flanks heaving. Tray placed his hand on the horse's shoulder, giving him a pat. Suddenly a weakened scream tore through the dense oak. Rasheed jerked his head up, whinnying. Tray's heart slammed into his throat. To the left! He stood up in his stirrups, craning to catch a glimpse of anything in the direction of the scream. His eyes narrowed. There! A mud hut sitting at the edge of a small clearing of oak.

"Come on!" he called to his stallion, leaning forward. The horse needed no encouragement, lifting his legs and easily clearing the stream. Mud and rock flew from beneath the stallion's hooves as he scrambled madly up the slope toward the hut that sat no more than a quarter of a mile away.

Alyssa groaned, the sound coming out low and deep from within her. The last pain had nearly made her faint. Her body was bathed in sweat and her thrashing movements had pushed the straw from inside the pallet, so that a thin blanket was now the only barrier between her and the dirt floor. It was chilly in the hut, although strong beams of sunlight edged the curtain in front of the doorway. She panted, feeling the blackness begin to claim her again. She was dying. She could feel the weakness stalking her limbs and her will to live trickling away with each savage labor convulsion. Eyes glazed with pain and exhaustion, Alyssa remained on her side, her arms wrapped around her swollen belly. Desolation entwined with grief as she realized with icy finality that she was too small for the babe to pass through her.

Shivering, she sobbed for breath as she felt another knifing contraction begin. Her body jerked convulsively, her spine bowing, and she threw back her head, a hoarse scream tearing from her raw throat. Blackness danced before her widened eyes. Oh, please, she begged, let me faint. I can't take any more pain. Let me faint again... God, have mercy on me... I can't... Her vision blurred and she felt the blessed blackness beginning to close in on her again. Her body went limp and she felt her arms dropping to her side, her head lolling back. Yes, merciful unconsciousness. Sweat dribbled from her brow into her eyes. It didn't matter.

Just as the numbing feeling was sweeping up from her chest to engulf her into the welcoming blackness, Alyssa became aware of another noise. Horses. Horses? Her brow wrinkled as she tried to catalog the various movements outside the hut.

Sunlight spilled blindingly into the hut as someone jerked the curtain aside. Alyssa stared uncomprehendingly at the huge form of a man's body lighted from behind by the brilliance of the sun. Darkness rimmed her vision as she stared at him through dazed eyes. Tray? Tray was here? She recognized his frame, his broad, powerful shoulders. Tray had come for her. Alyssa fought off the faintness pulling at her. She heard him utter her name in a low cry. She heard Tray calling her. She was dying.

As she closed her eyes, a wobbly smile crossed her chapped and cracked lips. His arms went around her and she felt herself being gently lifted upward. As her dirt-smudged cheek met the wrinkled cotton of the shirt that spanned his deep chest, Alyssa sobbed his name, too weak to fight off the stalking darkness. Her lashes fell against her cheeks and she capitulated to the unconsciousness, knowing at last that Tray would be there. Love did conquer all. It had conquered death. He was holding her as she slipped over the edge into oblivion.

* * *

Jagged, tearing pain brought her awake. She began to roll her head from side to side, whimpering.

"Easy, Aly. Try to relax. It's going to be all right, little one."

Her brow wrinkled and she forced her lashes upward. Brightness seemed to vibrate from everywhere within the hut. Pain tore away the last shreds of her faintness. Blinking, Alyssa turned her head as she felt someone's hand on the blanket across her shoulder. Her pupils dilated as she stared up into the face of the man she had loved without reserve. A cry tore from her lips and her eyes widened in shock.

"Tray?" she whispered.

He was kneeling at her side, his face taut. His fingers trembled as they touched her glistening brow. "Yes, beloved. I'm here."

Bewilderment entwined with hope surged through her. "B-but, you're dead . . . you're dead. . . ."

"No, Aly. I almost died. I've been searching for you since September, when I landed in Ireland." His smile was tender as he leaned over, pressing a kiss to her forehead. "And I've found you."

Tears crowded into her eyes. The touch of his hand was real upon her flesh. Alyssa could feel his rough skin as he stroked her brow. He hadn't died. Tray was alive. Alive! She sobbed, the effort creating even more agony in her body. "Oh, God . . . Tray . . ."

"I know, I know, beloved," he soothed, taking a cloth and pressing it against her cheek. "How long have you been in labor?" There was fear behind his words. Judging by the waxen color of her thin features, Tray was afraid of her answer. Bits of straw were tangled in her once beautiful hair, now hanging in damp ropes around her contorted face.

"Days. Oh God, days... The baby, Tray... he's yours, not Vaughn's."

"Shh, don't talk, Aly. I know he's our baby. Just try to rest between the contractions. I'll help you."

"I'm dying, Tray, I'm so thirsty...."

His eyes grew dark, her sobs tearing at his heart. "Don't say that! You aren't going to die." He lifted her shoulders, placing a tin cup to her lips. She drank in gulps, water dribbling from the corners of her mouth. He refilled the cup four times before her thirst was slaked and he carefully laid her back down on the clean pallet.

Weakly, Alyssa's fingers sought and found his strong, powerful hand. "I'm too small... too small...."

He gripped her fragile hand in his. "No! You aren't going to die, Aly. Not when I've just found you. Hang on! Listen to me. You're going to have our baby and then I'm taking you home. Do you hear me?"

Tears trickled down her cheeks and she sobbed harder. Home. Shadowhawk. Tray. She felt him rubbing her hand between his own, giving her the warmth she so desperately needed. If only... if only she could go home with Tray. His voice felt like a balm across her shattered senses.

"Listen to me, Aly. I've got hot water and clean towels with me. This is just like any other animal giving birth. I can help you, little one. Have you been able to get up into a kneeling position?"

She garnered strength from his fervent, low voice and the pressure of his large, warm hand on her own damp fingers. "N-no. Too... weak..."

Grimly, Tray released her hand. He had built up the peat fire and placed a lantern inside the chilled hut. Sunshine flooded through the opened doorway. "I'm going to take the blankets off you, Aly. And then I'm going to pull you up. Up to your knees. You're ready to birth. You need to push, like any ewe would when she's ready to deliver her lamb. Can you do that for me if I hold you? Can you push?''

Alyssa nodded. She had been too weak to get to her knees without help. And she knew that most women birthed in that position. Opening her eyes, she allowed Tray to take her into his arms. As he brought her up, a tearing pain lacerated her. Biting down hard on her lip until she tasted blood, Alyssa rested against Tray, who helped her to settle to her knees. The downward pressure of the baby made her start panting.

"Aly, remember the animals. They take deep breaths and then push," he said hoarsely, his lips near her ear. He tightened his arm beneath her breasts. She had absolutely no strength left with which to support herself. "Come, little one, take a deep breath. That's it, one more...one more..."

Blackness rimmed her vision, the agony constant now. And yet, just the steady drone of Tray's voice, his strength and belief in her, kept Alyssa clinging to a thread of hope. Sweat ran in small rivulets down her face and through the tangled strands of hair clinging to her brow and cheeks. She leaned heavily against him. With each breath and each push, the pressure between her legs became greater and greater.

"Good, good, Aly. He's coming. I can feel his head. Come, beloved, deliver him into my hands. I won't let him fall. I'll catch him and hold you. Push...push hard, Aly. Do this for us. Because I love you. God, how I love you...."

Every muscle in her body strained; Alyssa clenched her teeth, her body taut as she gave one final push. Hot, ripping fire tore up through her and a scream clawed at her throat, but she kept pushing, pushing. Finally, blackness overtook her, and the last thing she heard was Tray's voice soothing her, making her believe that she would live, telling her that their baby was born.

Tray gently deposited the baby on the pallet as he repositioned Alyssa so that she was lying down again. His eyes were wide with fear and welling emotion as he drew the blanket across Alyssa. He reached down, picking up the slick baby with trembling hands.

From his years of experience delivering foal and lambs, he quickly wiped the mucus from the baby's face. The child was listless, his color far from normal. Tray brought the baby's face to his own and blew small puffs of air into his nostrils, as he had done many times before with weakened lambs who had endured long, hard labor. Gradually, the infant responded, the bluish cast fading from his flesh. His heart thudded with elation as the child lifted his tiny arm and gave a weak cry. A smile broke Tray's tense, sweaty features and his gaze moved downward. The boy was perfect. Perfect. His tiny feet were perfect. Tears blurred Tray's vision as he laid down his black-haired son and cleaned him off, then tenderly wrapped him in a blanket.

Alyssa's lashes fluttered and she slowly raised her arm. The pressure was gone. She felt movement near her head. Tray's arm slid beneath her damp neck, gently drawing her into the haven of his embrace. She forced her eyes open as he placed the baby against her.

"A son, Aly," he breathed. "You've given me a healthy, perfect son."

Tears ran down her face as she stared lovingly into that small, wrinkled face topped with thick black hair. "Oh, Tray..." she cried softly, gathering the baby to her.

"He's beautiful, Aly. Beautiful." Tray held her carefully, afraid that he might crush her in his happiness. He pulled her chemise off her shoulder and unbuttoned it, exposing her left breast. "I think he's ready for his first meal."

A new warmth flooded her as she brought their child to her milk-swollen breast. They both watched in silent awe as

the rosebud-shaped mouth eagerly latched onto her dusky
nipple, suckling noisily. Tray laughed softly, his fingers
touching his son's plump cheek. A drop of milk welled from
his baby's mouth and he took his finger and caught the
drop, tasting it. He gazed down at Alyssa. "Sweet, like his
mother," he whispered, cradling her head against his chest.
"God, how I love you, Aly."

She nuzzled into the safety of his embrace, contentment
washing across her. "That's all that kept me going," she
admitted rawly, closing her eyes. "All these months. Horrible months without you, Tray."

"I know, I know, *Arhiannon*. But it's all over now.
You're going to live, and so will our son. Rest. I just want
you to rest. I'll take care of Griff while you sleep. And when
you wake, I'll be here at your side."

She felt Tray's hand against her arm, helping her support their son as he fed hungrily at her breast. Exhaustion
flowed through her bruised, battered body. Her strength
gave way, but Tray continued to hold Griff so that he could
feed. Without a word, she gave in to the demands of her
body, moving into a deep, healing sleep in the arms of the
man who loved her so fiercely.

Tray held his son, watching him sleep. Awe lingered in his
gray eyes as he memorized each detail of the child. And then
his gaze moved to his wife. She slept deeply, covered with
several wool blankets. Her skin was almost translucent, with
dark shadows beneath her thick, auburn lashes. He had
made a clean pallet, covering it with blankets from the pack.
Tucking Griff beside her as she slept, he had lovingly washed
Alyssa's limbs with warm water. Then, he patiently picked
out the straw from her hair and pulled a brush through her
damp tresses. Through all his ministrations, he had held at
bay emotional revulsion to the squalor of her life in the hut.

His fingers trembled as he divested her of the soiled chemise and dressed her in a clean one. He did not know how she had survived this long.

He rocked Griff absently. The child had drunk voraciously from both her breasts before burping contentedly and falling asleep as Tray held him. The fire he had made earlier outside the hut held two small kettles suspended over the peat coals. He had cut up dried venison and thrown in potatoes and turnips for a stew for Alyssa. He was frightened at how weak she was.

Tray looked up, noticing that she stirred. He rose and went to her side with Griff cradled in his arm.

Alyssa took a deep breath, her entire lower body feeling excruciatingly tender. Most of the pain was gone, only cramping sensations reminding her that she had delivered a baby. Her lashes rose and she saw Tray at her side, holding their son. A soft smile touched her lips and she weakly raised her hand, touching the blanket surrounding Griff.

"How long have I slept?" she asked.

"Probably five hours. How do you feel?"

She hungrily drank in Tray's face, thinking he looked thinner than she recalled. "Better."

"Feel up to eating?"

The idea of food appealed to her. "Yes."

"Here, hold our son. I've made a kettle of good stew for you."

Alyssa drew Griff down into her arms, her eyes tender with love as she looked at their baby. "He's so beautiful," she whispered.

Tray smiled and nodded. "Beautiful like his mother."

Within minutes, Tray had her propped up, using his saddle as a backrest against the wall. Alyssa was still too weak to hold Griff in her arms for very long, so Tray held him in one arm and spoon-fed her the succulent stew from a bowl at his side. Afterward, he brought her a cup of cold water and settled down beside her.

Alyssa leaned her head back against the saddle, content. Already she could feel the food renewing her strength. Griff awoke and Tray smiled.

"He's hungry, too."

She reached up to unbutton her chemise, noticing she no longer wore her old one. Lifting her head, she met Tray's tender gray eyes.

"My chemise . . ."

"I washed it in the stream. It's drying right now."

"But how? I mean . . ."

"When I came to look for you, Aly, I packed with the idea that I'd find you. Ghazieh has been relegated to a pack animal and she carries extra blankets, food and decent clothing for you."

Tears glimmered in her eyes. Just the roughened contact of his calloused hand easing the chemise off her right shoulder made her ache with love for Tray. "I thought you had died when Dev shot you," she whispered brokenly, holding his gaze. "You were lying on the sand, bleeding heavily."

"Shh, it's all over, Aly," he soothed, nestling Griff into her awaiting arms. He caressed her newly brushed hair. "Vaughn found me a few minutes after the attack and took me back to Shadowhawk. Dr. Birch was already waiting there to examine you, and that saved my life. If Birch hadn't been there, he said I would have bled to death."

Alyssa blinked back her tears, watching as Griff suckled just as noisily as before. She lifted her chin, her eyes jade with anguish. "Dev didn't know, Tray. He didn't know that we loved each other. I tried to tell him as they carried me off to the sailing ship. I was in shock. Dev thought I had been forced to marry you."

Tray grazed her cheek, which was now beginning to show some color. "I thought it might have been your brothers who had come to get you. I'm not angry at them, Aly. I understand why they did it. I won't press charges against Dev." His voice lowered. "All I want is to get you off this mountain and into cleaner living conditions. You can't be moved yet, but as soon as we can, I'm taking you down to the valley to better accommodations." He looked around at the disheveled hut. "This is worse than what a pig lives in."

Alyssa winced and hung her head, her arms tightening around Griff. "We've lived like this since I was six, Tray. And more farmers are being thrown off their land every day, forced to become squatters."

His face was grim as he looked down at her. Obeying the impulse of his heart, he cupped her chin, guiding it up so that he could worship her full, parted lips. "I love you no matter where you came from, *Arhiannon*," he whispered against her. "Your heart is mine, your soul . . . you're mine, forever." He gently pressed more surely against her lips, feeling her warm, total response. A groan shuddered through him as he parted her lips, tasting the moist depths of her. She was so alive, so completely his in every way. Tray forced himself to break contact gradually, afraid that he might hurt her.

"And I love you," she trembled, her eyes large and flecked with the gold of life in their depths once again.

He caressed her cheek, pushing strands of hair behind her delicately formed ear. "That kept me alive, Aly. I remember getting struck and slamming to the ground. And then I heard your screams. I fought the darkness but I couldn't move. Every breath I took was an effort." His eyes darkened and held hers. "Fourteen years ago my half sister, Paige, was struck down by brigands on that very beach. I remembered finding her, bloodied and raped. Hearing your cries before I lost consciousness, I wondered if God was punishing me again for not riding with her on that day.''

Alyssa shuddered, closing her eyes, grateful for his palm against her cheek. "I'm sorry, Tray."

He leaned over, kissing her cheek, a tender gray flame burning in his eyes as he watched his son drink hungrily from her breast. "For the next three weeks, I didn't remember very much." His brow furrowed. "Vaughn came into the room a week after I had been wounded. That's when he told me he was going to hunt you down."

She moved Griff to her other breast, touching his downy black hair. "Why, Tray?" she asked tremulously. "Why does Vaughn want to kill me? I don't understand it."

He grimaced. "I don't know why, aside from the fact that he hates the Irish. He blames them for what happened to Paige." He rubbed his face wearily.

"Vaughn's in this area, Tray," she told him quietly, holding his shocked gaze.

"Are you sure?"

"Yes. Two, maybe three days ago, Dev and Gavin made themselves targets to Vaughn's soldiers. I heard pistol shots, but I couldn't see anything." Anguish rose in her voice. "Dev wants to kill Vaughn. He's bent on it. He was going to try to ambush him. Whether he did or not, I don't know."

"I saw no soldiers in Barrow Valley when I came through yesterday."

She chewed on her lower lip. "Dev and Gavin were going to try to lure the column to Lough Derg. Dev said he'd be back here in a month if they were successful."

Tray scratched his stubbled jaw. "There's more to this, Aly."

"What?"

"Vaughn went to the authorities in Liverpool and said you were the one who tried to murder me."

"I know. Dev brought a poster from Wexford with my likeness on it."

"Before I came to Ireland, I rode to Liverpool and straightened it out with the authorities." Tray's eyes hardened. "They sent out a messenger to find Vaughn and stop him. Right now, Vaughn is up on charges. The moment he gets back to any English post here in Ireland, he's under arrest."

Griff's small mouth parted and he relaxed into sleep. Alyssa gently transferred him to Tray's arms, pulling up her chemise and rebuttoning it. "What made Vaughn think he could get away with a lie like that? You were alive. Didn't he think that you'd dispatch a letter to clear me?"

Tray wrapped the blanket around his son, holding him carefully in his arms. "When Vaughn left, I had just contracted pneumonia. No one gave me any hope of surviving."

Alyssa jerked her head up. "With that wound to your chest you could have died."

Grimly, Tray agreed. "That's what Vaughn was counting on. But Dr. Birch pulled me through, along with many prayers from everyone."

Her eyes grew anguished and Alyssa reached out, her hand resting on his arm. "You've suffered so much...."

"We all have, little one," he whispered, holding her hand gently.

"And it's not over yet."

"No, it isn't. If that messenger doesn't find Vaughn, he'll still hunt for you."

"Or Dev will catch up to him and kill him."

Tray frowned. "Your brothers are in enough trouble, Aly. They don't need the murder of an English officer on their hands, too."

She managed a sad smile. "There's nothing you can do to save them, Tray, even if you wanted to."

"If I could get to them, I might be able to get them smuggled into France. At least I can stake them to a new life that way."

A sob rose in her throat as she stared at him. "You'd do that after what Dev's done to you?"

Tray turned, meeting her heartbreakingly vulnerable eyes. "I'm tired of the bloodshed, Aly," he began wearily. "You're my wife. I love you. I don't care if you're Irish any more than you care that I'm an English subject. There isn't much of your family left. I owe your brothers for keeping you safe until I could find you. Your life is worth everything to me." He pressed a kiss to her hand. "And I want you happy. I don't want you worrying if your brothers will someday be caught and hanged. I can give them money and references if they'll go to France. I have contacts there. Or they can sail to America. I just want them safe so that you no longer have to worry, little one."

Tears spilled down her cheeks as she stared at him. "And Vaughn? What of him? Will he ever leave us alone?"

"I wish he would, Aly. I don't want to kill him, but I won't allow him to ever come near you or Shadowhawk again. He ignored the direct order from my father to quit this insane vengeance against you. And for Vaughn to disobey my father is unheard of. I don't know what's going on inside that head of his."

"Vaughn's as rabid as Dev is at this point, Tray."

"I know. Hate is a powerful companion to anyone who has lost as much as Dev has. Vaughn not only raped you, he murdered Shannon in front of your father." He combed his fingers through his hair. "Right now, all I want is to get you and Griff to a place of safety."

"Dev's coming back here Tray. He doesn't know you're alive...."

"He'll know soon enough." He traded a warm glance with Alyssa. "Hopefully, this time he won't try to shoot me."

"He wouldn't. Believe me, he'd sooner shoot himself. He knows I love you as much as he loved Shannon. Dev may have killed, Tray. But he never murdered. Not like Vaughn."

"Well, let's pray that Dev and Gavin make it back here."

# Chapter Nineteen

"Damn that Trayhern," Gavin growled, sitting wearily on his horse. He gazed at his brother and wondered if he looked as exhausted as Dev looked.

"It isn't working," Dev agreed. They stood just within a line of trees, allowing their horses to rest. For as far as they could see from their vantage point on a hill overlooking Callan, sunlight spilled across the verdant hills and farmland. But gut instinct told Dev that Vaughn Trayhern was close by, on their trail.

"We underestimated the bastard."

Dev's eyes narrowed. "He's tacked us at every turn. I thought we could lose him at Lough Derg."

Gavin dismounted, loosening the cinch on his saddle. His square face was pensive as he went and sat against an oak tree. "We're getting too close to the Blackstairs."

"I know," Dev growled, dismounting. He never ceased his vigilance, sweeping the country to the west of them, where they both knew Captain Trayhern was coming from. There wasn't a day that went by during the flight that they didn't catch sight of the redcoat column. Wearily, Dev sat next to his brother, resting his brow against his arms. "I have a plan."

"What?"

"One of us has to lead Trayhern back north. The other will go fetch Lys and the baby. She'll be out of food soon, and with a new baby, she won't survive, Gavin. One of us has to go back and help her."

"Where will you take her?"

Dev raised his head. "I said one of us. You don't have to be the fox for the hounds."

Gavin gave him a half smile, his hazel eyes wrinkling. 'I'm volunteering. Besides, I'm not much with a new babe."

"And I am?" Dev snorted.

"You go. I'll swing around to the south and get that devil to chase me. Where will you take Lys?"

"North, to Cloghan. The Brady farm is there and I know they'll put Lys up. Then we can begin gathering the United Irish again for another go at the English."

Gavin nodded, his face sober as he stared out at the lush beauty that spread beneath them. "We need to get Trayhern. You know he isn't going to stop hunting us."

Dev tipped his head back, closing his eyes. They had gotten little sleep over the past two weeks. The column of ten English cavalry soldiers, by various methods, had struck fear in the hearts of the Irish they had met with. There were few Catholics who didn't know of the Kyle family and wouldn't zealously protect them. But the Protestants were another story altogether. Dev's mouth thinned. In Barrow Valley there were a few Protestants among the heavy Catholic population. If they recognized him, they would willingly turn him in to the authorities at New Ross.

"You sure you want to be the fox?"

Gavin nodded. "Why not? If I get a clear shot at the bastard, I'd like nothing better than to see him take a permanent tumble from his horse."

Dev slowly stood, stretching his tall, well-muscled body "Just be careful, Gavin."

"Don't worry, I will. And when you see Lys, give her a kiss for me, will you?"

Moving to his horse, Dev recinched his saddle. "Lys will probably scream at me because I left you behind."

"Kiss her anyway. She'll blow hot for a moment and then forgive both of us," Gavin said with a laugh, rising.

"Meet us in two weeks at the Brady farm."

Gavin mounted his horse, giving Dev an ear-to-ear grin "Nothing will stop me."

Alyssa jerked awake. Tray's arms tightened around her.

"What's wrong, Aly?" he mumbled, barely opening his eyes.

She sat up, her hair spilling around her damp face. Sun light streamed in beneath the curtain of the hut. Instinc tively, she looked to her right. Griff was sleeping deeply in the blankets, surrounded by fresh straw. Shakily, she pushed the hair off her face and closed her eyes. "A dream," she whispered in a strained voice.

Tray roused himself and sat up. It was time to get up anyway, judging from the slant of the sun beneath the cur tain. He slipped his arm around Alyssa, drawing her into the fold of his embrace. She came willingly, resting her head on his deep chest.

"You're trembling." He began to stroke the length of her back. She hadn't slept well recently, often waking up, dis turbed for no reason. He pressed a kiss to her hair, inhaling the scent of her. "Your brothers again, little one?" he asked huskily.

Sweet Mother, but she felt good against his naked body The flannel of her nightgown provided only a thin barrier between them, and Tray had tasted his hunger daily for Aly

He waited, realizing just how stiff and sore she was from birthing Griff. There would be time for that after they got back to Shadowhawk.

Alyssa closed her eyes, seeking his warmth and strength. "Y-yes. I heard Gavin screaming." She took a long, shuddering breath, her hand tightening on Tray's arm. "It was awful. Awful."

"Shh, Aly. You're worried about them—that's to be expected."

"One more week. Oh God, Tray, one more week and they'll be back here. There isn't a minute that doesn't go by that I wonder if Vaughn hasn't captured them. Tortured them...."

Tray kissed her temple, cradling her jaw within the palm of his calloused hand. "Today I'm going down to the Riley farm to get a wagon," he told her in a soothing voice. "I'll take you and our son off this mountain early this evening. I think you can stand to ride a horse down to where the wagon will be, don't you?"

A few days before, Tray had ridden down the mountain to find a farmer with a room to rent. Alyssa fought back the terror that had invaded her. Today they would leave the hut for Riley's farm at the neck of Barrow Valley. Tray would leave a note for Dev and Gavin, telling them where she could be located. Nodding her head, Alyssa nuzzled beneath Tray's jaw. "Yes, I'll do it."

"I know it will be uncomfortable, little one, but I want you out of here. This is no place for you or our son."

"I know...."

His gray eyes grew warm as he tipped her face upward, drinking in her wan features. "Dev will find us. I've already alerted the English at New Ross to be on the lookout for Vaughn. He's as good as lost his commission once they get to him." He leaned over, brushing his mouth against her parted lips. She was so soft, willing and sweet as he tenderly explored her with his tongue, outlining her lips. A groan shuddered through him and he offered her a wry smile as he drew away.

"You make me hungry," she whispered, gazing up at him.

"Hungry? I'm starved for you, little one." He kissed the tip of her nose. "Soon," he promised her throatily. "Soon we'll share ourselves with each other."

Alyssa delighted in the wiry hair beneath her hand as her fingers grazed the solid mass of muscle across his chest. For the past week she had found herself aching to be one with Tray. Each time he looked at her, her stomach curled and she felt that strange, uncoiling sensation in her lower body. And at night, when he held her so close to him, she wanted to press her body to his.

Griff stirred and Tray smiled down at her. "Stay put," he told her, rising.

There wasn't an ounce of fat on Tray's body, Alyssa thought, reveling in his masculinity. She watched, her green eyes tender with love as Tray walked over and picked up his son. Griff appeared lost in his father's darkly bronzed arms as Tray brought him over to her.

"I think our son is hungry, too," he said, smiling as he gave her the baby.

Alyssa took Griff, settling him comfortably at her breast as soon as she had pulled down the shoulder of the flannel nightgown. She lifted her head to meet Tray's smile. She had never seen him so relaxed or so happy. What they shared was rare, she realized. After dressing, Tray fed the fire outside the hut and put on one kettle for the morning tea. Since he had arrived, Alyssa had rapidly started to gain back lost weight. Leaning down, she cuddled Griff and kissed his wrinkled little brow, the soft black curls of his hair brushing against her cheek.

\* \* \*

"I'll be back by late this afternoon," Tray promised, swinging a leg up on the stallion.

Alyssa nodded, holding Griff comfortably in her arms. The kiss Tray had just branded upon her lips made her ache with love for him. She was dressed in a warm, heavy cotton gown of crimson that brought out the flushed quality of her cheeks as she stared up at him. "Be careful," she called.

Tray nodded. "I will, little one. Remember, take the pistol with you wherever you go."

The warning sent an icy shiver through Alyssa. She gave a jerky nod of her head and raised her hand in farewell. Tray gave her a warm, intimate smile and turned his stallion around, heading in the direction of Barrow Valley.

The morning was spent at the stream, where Alyssa sat on her knees, the sleeves of her dress rolled up above her elbows as she gingerly washed several sets of clothes. Griff lay beneath the shade of an oak that spread its mighty limbs out across the stream, protecting him from the March sun. The birds in the meadow were vibrant in song, and more than once, Alyssa would sit up, her chapped and reddened hands resting on her thighs as she listened to their symphony.

Ghazieh's whicker broke into Alyssa's reverie. She scrambled to her feet, looking in the direction of the gray mare. Her heart leapt to her throat as she saw a dark, shadowy figure making his way through the heather and brush toward her.

Turning, she ran the few feet to the pistol, which lay beside Griff. Standing in front of her baby, Alyssa grasped the pistol with both hands, shakily training the barrel on the approaching rider. Perspiration made her tense features glisten as the rider drew near. And then, when the man broke through the clearing, relief flowed through her. Dev! It was Dev! Her eyes darkened. Where was Gavin? Oh,

Mother Mary, had something happened to her brother? Alyssa put the pistol down and lifted her skirts, running awkwardly across the meadow to meet her brother.

Dev dismounted and gave her a welcoming smile, his features gray and dirt-stained. He opened his arms and she flew to him.

"Lys," Dev groaned, taking her full weight. "How are you?" he rasped, giving her a careful hug.

She dashed her tears away. "Fine, fine. Dev, where's Gavin? What happened?"

Dev placed his arm around her shoulder and they walked toward the stream. "He's trying to lead Trayhern away from here. We couldn't shake him, Lys. I came back to take you north, where you'll be safe." His face was lined with exhaustion as he studied her. "The baby. You must have had the baby?"

"Yes. A boy. He's beautiful, Dev. And Tray. Tray's here!" She turned, her eyes wide with excitement as she gripped her brother's arm.

Dev stopped, staring at her as if she were a madwoman. "Tray? Your husband? How?"

With a little laugh, Alyssa again threw her arms around him. "Oh, Dev, he lived! Tray survived your gunshot wound. He's been in Ireland for months trying to find me. And he did! He helped me deliver our son."

"Praise all the saints," Dev muttered, shaking his head. And then his blue eyes turned shadowed. "Where is he?"

"Down in Barrow Valley. He's bringing a wagon to the foot of the mountains to take Griff and me to a farmhouse. He'll be back late this afternoon."

Dev craned his neck, seeing an infant wrapped in flannel blankets beneath the oak. A grin cracked the planes of his face. "And will he kill me, or try to turn me in?"

Happily, Alyssa walked at his side. "He bears you no malice, Dev. Tray is Welsh, not English. He understands why you did what you did." She gave him a beseeching look. "All we want is peace. For both families, Dev. He wants to give you money and safe passage to France. Or to America."

Exhaustion and relief overtook Dev. He dropped the reins to his horse, allowing the animal to suck noisily from the stream, and followed Alyssa to where the baby lay. Tray was alive. He hadn't killed him after all. One look at Lys and his heart wrenched in his chest. He had never seen her so happy. Tears came to his eyes as she picked up the black-haired baby and gently deposited him into his arms. They stood there several seconds, emotions clearly written on their faces as they looked down at the child.

"He's beautiful, Lys," Dev said with some effort, clearing his throat. "And big." He looked up at her. "Did you have a hard time?"

"I thought I was going to die, Dev. If Tray hadn't come, I don't think either Griff or I would be alive today," she admitted softly.

Dev blinked back tears, lightly touching the boy's hair. "I'm sorry, Lys. We should have been here for you."

She pressed her brow to Dev's shoulder. "Under the circumstances, Dev, I understood. If Vaughn Trayhern had found me—"

"The bastard would have slit your belly open."

A chill swept through her. "Don't talk of it, Dev. Here, let me take Griff. Come up to the hut. I have a stew warming on the fire, and you need rest. And a change of clothes."

Dev wrinkled his nose. "A bath would be more like it. We've been hounded by Trayhern for almost three weeks without rest."

Alyssa gripped his arm, tugging at him. "Then come. Let me get some food in you and then you can take a dip in the stream. Tray has some extra clothes that I know will fit you. You're both the same height and nearly the same weight."

The whinny of horses jerked Dev out of his deep, badly needed sleep. His hand moved to the pistol that he kept by his head, and he was on his feet in one lithe movement, looking out of the door of the hut. He saw Alyssa wave and walk down the gentle knoll toward the meadow. There, in the distance, was her husband. Shoving the pistol in the leather belt at his waist, Dev rubbed his face and went to join his sister. How would Trayhern react to his being here? Dev felt a moment of distrust; even though Lys had begged him to remember Tray was Welsh and not English, he had misgivings.

Tray's face grew tense as he pulled the stallion to a stop and dismounted. Alyssa came to him, rapidly explaining. He recognized Dev's face as he drew near, remembering the hatred etched there as Alyssa's brother had raced toward him, both pistols raised. His gray eyes narrowed as the tall, broad-shouldered Irishman halted a foot away from him.

"Tray, I want you to meet Dev, my brother," Alyssa said breathlessly, her gaze moving from one man to the other.

Tray studied Dev. He was a soldier in stature and bearing. Years of fighting were etched on the man's face, and Tray found himself thankful that he was a farmer, not a soldier. He thrust out his hand toward the Irishman.

"At least you aren't pointing a pistol at me this time. That's a great improvement," he growled.

Dev's eyes glimmered and a slow grin came across his well-shaped mouth as he firmly gripped Tray's hand. "And there will be further improvement. Your love of Alyssa is all that matters to us. I'm sorry for almost killing you."

Tray released his hand, a smile creasing his face. He saw Alyssa give each of them a look of relief as she rested beneath his arm. "Apology accepted, Dev. From here on in, we're family." Tray smiled down at Alyssa. "Our son is proof that all of us can get along, if given a chance." His smile faded as he studied Dev in silence. "More than anything, I want peace between us. Bloodshed only means more bloodshed."

Dev threw his hands upon his hips, nodding his head. "I can speak for my brother, Gavin, and myself—we're at peace with you. It's your brother, Vaughn, who's after us. He cares only that the Kyles swing at Newgate."

Tray glumly agreed. "Where is your brother?" he asked.

Dev began to lay out their plan to Tray. Alyssa held an awakening Griff and sat with them as they discussed their options.

Dev gave his sister a warm look as she nursed the hungry infant. A sharp ache centered in his heart. If Shannon were alive, they could have had children, as well. And then his gaze moved back to Tray. It was his half brother who had murdered Shannon. Dev tried to ferret out that same murderous streak in Tray, but to no avail. Each minute spent with Tray reassured Dev that Alyssa had indeed been blessed. Tray was the epitome of steadiness, and the love they shared was as fierce and binding as the love he and Shannon had once shared. In spite of all the hatred between their families, a child of love had been born. Hope rose in Dev and for the first time he felt lighter. Happier.

"Once we get Alyssa to the farm, I think it best you find Gavin."

Dev roused himself from his thoughts, focusing on Tray's words. "Yes."

Tray got up and went into the hut. When he came out, he handed a leather pouch to Dev.

"Gold coins. There's enough money in there for passage to France or America. Anywhere that will be safe for you. Even when Vaughn is caught and brought to justice, you'll still be hunted here in Ireland."

Dev weighed the heavy purse, listening to the clink of the coins in his hand. "The French were going to help us overthrow the English here in Ireland. Did you know that?"

Tray sat back down, his arm going around Alyssa. "No."

"I don't know what Gavin will do, but I intend to go to France and join Napoleon's army. Once he gets done crushing the English in Europe, maybe he will send his fleet here to help the Irish overthrow them."

Alyssa saw hatred flare in Dev's blue eyes. She was grateful for Tray's hand absently drawing patterns on her upper arm as she finished nursing Griff. "Take a ship from Cobh and sail directly to France, Dev."

"We will, don't worry." He tucked the pouch inside his white peasant shirt and looked over at Tray. "Thank you."

"I'm doing it for Alyssa. I have no wish to see her worried and unhappy any longer." Tray gave her a warm look. "I'll help you all I can. I'll send a letter of introduction with you to my friend in Paris as soon as we get back to Shadowhawk. Go to him and he'll be able to help you."

Rasheed's bugling cry across the hillside broke into their conversation. Tray was on his feet instantly. Dev came to his side, a scowl on his face.

"Horsemen," Tray growled, pointing to five men in red uniforms on the hill far below them.

"English soldiers," Dev breathed through clenched teeth. He turned to Tray. "The same ones who have followed us to hell and back. It's your half brother leading them."

Would Vaughn listen to reason if he rode out and met him? Tray's gray eyes narrowed as he watched the straggly column begin to make the ascent toward the top of the mountain. "How did they find us here?"

Dev shook his head. "I don't know. Gavin was supposed to lead them north."

Alyssa paled. "You don't think Vaughn captured Gavin, do you?"

Tray pursed his lips. "He probably split the column. He had ten men, didn't he, Dev?"

"Yes. That would make sense. He could have sent five after Gavin and the other half after me." Then he swore violently. "I should have thought of that! I left a trail anyone could follow back here to the Blackstairs."

Gripping the baby to her breast, Alyssa came and stood between the two men, her heart beating hard. "What are we going to do, Tray?"

His icy gray eyes thawed momentarily when he turned and looked down at her. "First, you get to the safety of the hut. There's a pistol in there. You can't ride and we couldn't outrun them with you along." He gripped her arm, propelling her toward the hut. "Dev, I'm going to intercept them. If it is Vaughn, I'm going to try to talk some sense into him. I'm not going to tell him you're with us, but stay out of sight, just the same." He glanced over at the grim-faced Irishman. "Take the gray Arab mare. She's small, but she can outrun any horse over a long distance. Head north to Cloghan and meet Gavin at the Brady farm. Then get out of Ireland at your first opportunity."

Dev picked up his saddle and threw it over the gray mare's back. He didn't like the idea of leaving Tray with the soldiers, but he said nothing. Looping the reins across the animal's neck, Dev gave his sister a fierce hug, kissed Griff on the head and then gripped Tray's hand. "Thanks. For everything."

Tray released his hand. "Let us hear from you once you get to safety."

Dev mounted with easy grace, swinging the gray around. "Lys will tell you we're not letter writers." And then he grinned down at his sister. His voice lowered. "But we'll write. God be with you."

Alyssa choked back the tears welling in her eyes. So much was happening so quickly. She watched as Dev disappeared over the other side of the hill at a gallop. Tray had already mounted Rasheed. The stallion moved nervously, sensing his rider's tension. Tray's face was dark and unreadable. Alyssa held Griff protectively, looking up at him.

"Be careful..."

"I will, *Arhiannon*. Just stay in the hut. If you have to use the pistol, then use it."

Again, a cold chill swept her and Alyssa nodded jerkily. Within moments, she stood alone next to the hut. Memories of Vaughn's cavalry unit charging their position washed over her. She remembered the savage pleasure on his face as he had charged forward, sword drawn, galloping through the defeated Irish. Turning, she hurried into the hut, putting Griff in a corner and placing several blankets protectively around him. Hands trembling, Alyssa picked up the pistol and stood guard in the doorway. Waiting.

"Halt!" Vaughn thundered out, holding up his hand. He saw a man on horseback rapidly approaching them, winding in and around the thick brush. As the stranger drew near, Vaughn's eyes widened in disbelief. No! It couldn't be Tray! Damn him! When he had left Shadowhawk, Tray was near death—even the doctor had thought it was only a matter of hours before Tray expired.

Vaughn's gloved fist tightened around the reins. Other questions came to mind. He had lied to the authorities about

Alyssa's killing Tray. Had Tray told them the truth? Knowing Tray, he had. Sweat popped out on Vaughn's wrinkled brow. His military career was as good as over, then. Another plan formed in his mind, one that would rid him once and for all of Tray and leave him the eldest, heir to the Trayhern fortune. By killing Tray and Alyssa, the truth could never be proved and he could salvage his career.

Vaughn jerked one of his pistols from his belt. "There he is!" he shouted to his men. "One of the Kyles! Form an attack line! I want him dead! Dead!" He watched as his men drew abreast of one another, the horses well rested and eager to engage. His face screwed up in fury as he glared over at his men. "Do you hear me? That's Devlin Kyle. I want him dead. Charge!"

Pistol shots shattered the afternoon silence. Tray jerked Rasheed to a skidding halt. Balls popped and slammed into the trunks of trees nearby, the bark splintering in all directions. Tray cursed, close enough to see that Vaughn indeed led the charge. The hill was steep and Tray had a few seconds to watch the horses scrambling and sliding up the muddy expanse before he turned away. Vaughn intended to kill him! He had been close enough to recognize him. That meant Alyssa was in grave danger, and so was their son. Tray leaned forward, clapping his heels to the stallion. He had to lead them away from the hut!

Vaughn caught sight of a hut up on the last hill. A woman stood in the doorway. His blue eyes glittered. "Sergeant!" he barked. "Continue to pursue. The Kyle woman is up on that hill. I'll be there."

"Yes, sir!"

Vaughn grinned, spurring his black gelding up the slope. Alyssa Kyle. Finally, he would have his revenge on her. Whose child did she have? His or Tray's? It didn't matter.

By the end of the afternoon his half brother would be dead, a victim of mistaken identity. Alyssa Kyle would be dead, too, and so would the brat. The horse grunted and snorted heavily as he made it over the last crest, galloping hard across the flowering meadow toward the stream. With effort, the gelding leapt over the stream, landing and scrambling toward the mud hut not more than a quarter of a mile away.

Alyssa's face went white and her heart pounded wildly as she watched the progress of the English soldier. She held the pistol out in front of her, finger on the trigger. Terror ripped through her when she recognized Vaughn's blond features. Her hands shook badly as she saw him skid the horse to a stop, mud and pebbles flying in all directions. He dismounted with lazy ease, his blue gaze never leaving her face.

"Now," Vaughn snarled, dropping the reins to the horse and halting a few paces from where Alyssa stood, "I have you, Irish bitch. Where's that brat of yours?"

"Stay where you are, Vaughn! I swear, I'll kill you!"

He eyed the pistol and slowly pinned her with his malevolent gaze. She was trembling so badly that the barrel of the pistol wavered. A slow smile crawled on his mouth. "When did you have the brat? Answer me!"

"Three weeks ago. He's mine and Tray's. Do you hear me? Ours. Not yours."

Vaughn lifted his head, a pistol hanging in his right hand. "The brat's in there?"

Alyssa took a step back, her eyes large with anguish. "Leave us alone, Vaughn! Why are you chasing Tray? He's done nothing! Nothing!"

"Oh, yes he has. He's alive, that's the problem." His mouth tightened as he glared at her. "Typical of the Welsh, my half brother came back from hell's gate. Now, put down that pistol."

"N-no."

Vaughn studied her. And he hated her even more because she looked so damned beautiful and defiant, standing there before him. "I'm going to take you one last time," he breathed.

Tears sprang to Alyssa's eyes, the pistol getting heavier by the second. "You'll never touch me again. Never!"

"You won't shoot me, Alyssa," he said softly, taking a step forward. "I saw you at that skirmish. You couldn't shoot a man then. You shot the horse instead."

"Don't!" The barrel of the pistol steadied.

His smile widened and he advanced another step. "You wouldn't shoot me. I'm a man. Not an animal."

Her face contorted and she took a step back, her eyes wild with confusion. "Take another step and I'll kill you!" she cried.

"All right, have it your way, bitch." Just as Vaughn raised his weapon in a lightning-quick motion, he heard the bark of another pistol. White-hot pain ripped through his left knee and a scream tore from his throat. He toppled backward, the pistol flying out of his hand. Vaughn fell and writhed on the ground, holding the injured, bloody leg.

Alyssa whirled to the right. Dev stood there, pistols in hand, his face devoid of any emotion. With a cry, she fled to him, sobbing.

Dev held her briefly, never once allowing his gaze to leave the English officer groaning and rolling on the ground. "Come on," he rasped, guiding Alyssa back to the hut. "Tray's being pursued by the other soldiers. I have to help him." He gently released Alyssa, striding over to Vaughn.

Vaughn groaned as he rolled onto his back. He opened his eyes to see the barrel of a pistol staring at him. His eyes widened in terror. The Irishman leaned over and jerked him up by his hair, pressing the pistol to his temple.

"Now you're going to die," Kyle snarled softly, "first, for murdering my wife, Shannon. And second, for raping my sister. I'm sending you to hell, where you came from...."

"No!" Alyssa flew to Dev's side, jerking his arm aside. "No more killing!" she sobbed. "No more, Dev. Please, for God's sake."

He glowered at her, breathing hard. "He murdered Shannon, Lys. He's going to pay."

Alyssa stood between them, her face taut and flushed with tears. "Tray was right—no more killing, Dev. Let the English ruin Vaughn. That's a far worse death for him. Don't you see? He won't be able to stand living in disgrace. Please..."

More pistol shots echoed from below and Dev snapped his head up. Tray would never be able to handle four soldiers by himself. Cursing, he glared over at her.

"If he so much as moves while I'm gone, shoot him!"

Shakily wiping the tears from one cheek, Alyssa nodded. "Be careful, Dev. God, be careful...."

Tray whipped his stallion between the high bushes, narrowly missing the trunk of an oak. The earth was muddy and dangerous on the steep hill they now plunged down to avoid their pursuers. A fallen oak three times the girth of a man loomed before them. Tray threw the reins high on Rasheed's neck, bracing himself for impact. Instead, the stallion gathered his haunches beneath him, uncoiling like a spring at the last second. Grunting heavily, the animal lifted his front legs, carrying him and his master cleanly over the unexpected obstacle. Tray praised the horse, urging him into a gallop as they intersected a meadow before beginning their perilous descent down the next slope. More shots rang out behind him and he leaned forward, his face nearly touching his horse's whipping mane.

Tray risked a glance backward. The four soldiers were struggling with the oak in their path. None of their horses had the courage or the strength to leap the obstacle. Swinging Rasheed into a grove of trees, Tray circled back, remaining well hidden by the brush and shadows. He was breathing hard as he pulled the horse to a halt. The animal was breathing even harder, foam flecking his neck and hindquarters.

"Stand," Tray ordered the stallion. Obediently, the horse followed his command. Tray pulled out both pistols, getting ready for the cavalrymen to cross in front of him. The pounding of hoofbeats came toward him, and Tray lifted the pistols, aiming them at the approaching soldiers. He'd never fired a pistol from Rasheed and swiftly wondered if the horse would bolt. There was a great likelihood of it. Tray gripped the stallion tightly with his thighs and calves, drawing a bead on the English now within range of his pistols.

Two sharp reports echoed through the meadow. And two horses suddenly dropped like felled oxen, throwing their respective riders clear. Tray shoved the pistols back into his belt. He had no time to put powder or ball into them now. Tray heard the two remaining soldiers shout to each other and he turned his horse around. His eyes widened as he recognized the gray Arab mare coming on the hill above them. Dev!

Tray urged his horse into a gallop through the grove, the last of the English soldiers following him. They hadn't seen Dev, who now was well within pistol-shot range. Within moments, two more shots were fired. Tray chanced a look across his shoulder. Relief slackened his tense features as he saw that Dev had killed the horses and not their riders. Reining Rasheed to a halt, Tray waved to Dev, who remained on the hill. The Irishman slowly raised his hand and turned the gray mare, disappearing quickly into the trees, heading toward the top of the mountain.

Wiping the sweat from his face, Tray aimed Rasheed back up to the hut. Vaughn was nowhere to be seen and fear spread through him like a winter chill. He knew Rasheed was exhausted, but the overwhelming need to make sure Aly and his son were safe forced him to ask the animal to gallop.

Alyssa gasped as she heard horses approaching. Vaughn lay in agony, still clutching his shattered left knee. She stood with the pistol in hand at the doorway to the hut. To her relief, she saw it was Dev and Tray. She allowed the pistol to fall to her side.

Dev remained in the saddle after Tray had dismounted, his entire attention focused on Vaughn. A warmth spread through his chest as he saw his sister fly to the arms of the man who loved her so much. Maybe something good would come of all this, after all, he thought.

"Help me!" Vaughn yelled hoarsely. "He shot me!"

Tray turned, looking down at his half brother. "What happened, Aly?" he asked huskily.

"Vaughn was going to shoot me. If Dev hadn't been here, I'd be dead."

"After he raped you again," Dev added grimly.

"They're lying, Tray! I swear—"

"You've sworn an oath to the devil himself," Tray snarled, glaring down at Vaughn. "And you've the devil to pay, once I get you to New Ross. You're up on charges, Vaughn. Your career is at an end."

Dev grinned, keeping an eye on the meadow in case one of the horseless cavalrymen came up on foot. "You know, I think Lys is right, brother-in-law."

Tray lifted his head. "Right about what?"

"I was going to kill him. I had put a pistol to his head and was going to put him out of his misery. But the more I think about it, the more I think Lys is right." Dev held Vaughn's black glare. "Not only will you be a disgrace to the Crown, but you'll be crippled for life, Trayhern."

Vaughn gulped back nausea, pain shearing up through his shattered knee and leg. There was little blood now, only excruciating agony. "I'll get you, Kyle. If it's the last thing I ever do, I'll kill you," he hissed between clenched teeth.

Dev's laugh was deep. "Then you'll have to follow me to France, English dog. Come hobbling over on the cane that you'll have to use from this day forward." Dev's face burned with hatred. "Your half brother may have been crippled from birth, but you're the deformed one in the Trayhern family. You murder innocent children and women for sport, calling it right in the name of the Crown. Well, not a day will go by that I won't smile and remember I put the ball into your leg that brought you to your knees."

Alyssa squeezed her eyes shut, hot tears rolling down her cheeks. Tray held her tightly within his embrace.

"You'd better go, Dev. Those soldiers won't be long in climbing up here."

Dev nodded, exhaustion shadowing his features. "I like this mare. Mind if I keep her?"

Alyssa looked at Tray. Ghazieh had been her wedding present. She saw the beginning of a smile on Tray's mouth as he looked down at her. Alyssa gave a nod of her head.

"She's yours. A gift from us to you for saving our lives."

Reining the mare around, Dev smiled at his sister. "May the wind always be at your back, Lys." And then he focused his attention on Tray, a glimmer of respect in the depths of his azure eyes. "May the hinges of our friendship never grow rusty, Tray."

"They won't," Tray promised.

An ache rose in Alyssa's throat as she watched her brother ride away. Away to an unknown future. Would she ever see Dev or Gavin again? But what mattered was that they would be safe in France. She turned, burying her head beneath Tray's solid jaw, needing his strength. As she felt his arms tighten protectively around her, she thought of home, of Shadowhawk. There was happiness in that Welsh manor, and Alyssa yearned to return to the land that had given her new life.

# Chapter Twenty

'Aly?" Tray's voice carried to the stone balustrade outside their bedchamber.

"Here," she called softly. The mid-April evening was unusually warm, the apricot sunset a mere ribbon on the horizon now. Alyssa turned, a welcoming light in her eyes as Tray strode through the opened french windows and across the stone terrace to where she stood. He looked darkly handsome, attired in a pale blue shirt that brought out the grayness in his eyes. Had it been three days since they arrived back at Shadowhawk? She walked into his open arms.

"Ah," he murmured, fitting her along his length, "this is what I needed. Wanted." Tray pressed a kiss to her hair. She looked exquisitely fragile, the white dressing robe in sharp contrast to the luxuriant length of her auburn hair, which tumbled in careless abandon about her shoulders and breasts. He inhaled her jasmine scent, starved for the touch and feel of her.

"Did you kiss Griff good-night?" she asked, closing her eyes and allowing him to take her full weight.

Tray chuckled. "The little beggar started to cry every time I walked away."

Laughter rose in her. "How many kisses did he steal from you this time before he gave you his permission to leave?"

"Five."

Alyssa raised her head, a glint in her emerald eyes. "Now you begin to understand how he has wrapped me around his little baby finger." And then she smiled wistfully. "Just as his father did," she admitted, reaching up on her slippered toes to place a kiss on his shaven cheek.

Tray joined in her laughter, rocking her gently to and fro while they enjoyed the splendor of darkness overtaking the dusk. "No, little one, it was you who snagged me. From the moment I saw you on the deck of that hellish ship, I was yours."

"That seems so long ago, Tray. Last March. A little over a year has gone by...."

"The most important year of our lives," he agreed, nuzzling her slender neck with moist kisses. His hunger for Alyssa had soared over the last week. He could barely hold himself in check for her sake. Dr. Birch had arrived at Shadowhawk yesterday and examined Griff and her. The Englishman grinned broadly as he dandled Griff on his knee, exclaiming how healthy the boy was. And Alyssa was fully healed, thank God. She moved her arms upward, sliding them about his neck. He groaned, feeling the hardness of her nipples against his chest despite the clothing between them.

"I feel sorry for Vaughn," she admitted. Tray had taken his brother to the English post at New Ross for medical treatment after seeing that she and Griff were safe at the farm in Barrow Valley. It had been Tray who had turned his half brother in to the authorities. Alyssa sighed, resting her cheek against Tray's powerful chest. Tray had traveled to New Ross several times because of Vaughn. On his last trip Alyssa had seen the strain around Tray's eyes and mouth

Vaughn was being shipped back to London for trial. Eventually, he would be dishonorably discharged from the King's army.

Tray shook his head. "Don't." The word came out as a guttural growl. "No one brought the shame on his head but himself."

"I'm glad it's over, Tray. I'm not like my brothers. I don't want to fight any longer. I never thought I'd find myself protecting Vaughn as I did when Dev was going to kill him. I've seen too much blood spilled. Too many families broken apart by the fighting."

He soothed her with Welsh words of love, stroking the length of her long, delicately curved back. "Vaughn has to live his own life the way he sees fit. Dev and Gavin are safe. If they want to join the French army against the English, that's their decision. As for us, we'll stay here at Shadowhawk, raise lambs, fine Welsh cobs and—" he tipped her head up, his mouth slanting across her lips "—beautiful half-Welsh and half-Irish babies who will be as courageous and beautiful as their mother."

Alyssa smiled beneath the brush of his masculine lips. "And as gentle and strong as their father."

His gray eyes glittered as he studied her in the shadowed darkness, the light from their bedchamber spilling out onto the terrace. His hands followed the lush curve of her breasts, recently drained of their milk by their hungry son. He felt her tremble as he moved his thumbs in lazy circles around the pebbled hardness of her nipples. "I want you, Aly. Now," he rasped thickly, drowning in the tenderness shining from her eyes. Her lips, still wet from his recent kiss, parted in answer and he scooped her into his arms, carrying her to their bed.

He gently deposited her on the quilted bed and then shut the french doors. As he walked back to their bed, he divested himself of his clothes and boots. Standing naked before her, Tray saw the adoration in her face as her gaze me his. This woman, who sat like a small, fragile child on th huge expanse of his bed, made him feel whole. He no longe shrank inwardly as her hands lovingly massaged his de formed foot or the tightly corded muscles of his calf. Hi deformity didn't exist in Aly's world. He sat next to her an combed his fingers lovingly through her silken tresses. A overwhelming emotion flowed up through his chest.

"I love you," he breathed, framing her face, drawing he forward to meet his descending mouth. He felt her softnes yielding to him, giving back as richly as he gave to her. A shudder wound through him as her small tongue traced th outline of his strong mouth, her touch reminding him of delicate butterfly. His hands gripped her upper arms and h dragged her to him, crushing her against his naked body reveling in the wonderful curves and ripeness of her form.

"Love me, Tray," she whispered tremulously. "Please, need you so badly. I ache for you...."

A tender flame burned in his eyes as he lightly kissed he feathered lashes, the tip of her nose and, finally, thos wonderful, full lips. "You're sweet meadow honey, *Ar hiannon*. You're life...my life...forever," he murmured pulling the sash free and drawing the folds of her robe aside

Firelight bathed her alabaster body and Tray felt hi breath stolen by her exquisite beauty. Woman. She was a woman in a way that made him tremble with excitement an awe as he ran his fingers around the curved lushness of he breasts. Her nipples were hard and stained a dark pink begging to be further seduced. Gently, he laid her back o the bed, drawing one into his mouth. Sweet Mother of God but she tasted good to him. Alyssa arched unconsciously t him, her fingers digging deeply into his heavily muscle shoulders. He heard a small whimper of need rise in he throat and he teethed each nipple in turn as she thrashed more demandingly against him.

He lifted his head, kissing her lips. "Now I see why that son of ours is so reluctant to leave your breast," he murmured, smiling.

"And if he finds you've stolen his milk, my lord, *you* will put up with that burgeoning temper of his."

Laughing softly, Tray drew the robe the rest of the way off her body, leaving her naked before him. He ran his hand down the length of her, watching as her flesh tensed wherever he teased her. "I don't have a temper, so he must have inherited that from you, my lady."

"And I suppose you want to blame his stubbornness on me, also?"

A grin lurked at the corners of Tray's mouth as he rose up on his knees beside her, his large hands following the contours of her body. "He's not stubborn. He simply knows what he wants."

She laughed with him, purring beneath his knowing touch. Her lower body felt as if it were aflame, throbbing, needing, longing for Tray. The smile died on her lips and she lifted her hands, setting them on his well-muscled arms. "And I know what I want, beloved. You . . . just you. . . ."

"Then you shall have me, *Arhiannon*." He eased his hand between her dampened, taut thighs. She was ready to receive him, and as he settled his knee between her legs, Tray saw love burning in her eyes as never before. He felt humbled as he drew her upward, hands on her slender hips. Her eyes closed as he gently probed her, not wanting to hurt her after such a long period of abstinence. A fire arced through him as he melted within her moist, welcoming depths. His blood pounded heavily, and Tray froze, afraid that he might abandon all his good intentions and simply plunge into her swollen confines.

A keening cry broke from Alyssa's throat and she arched to receive all of him, her hands tightly gripping his arms. "I need you, need you…" she pleaded brokenly. And then she felt his power, his shaft filling her. All of her. A new sweetness invaded her aching body as they froze in ecstasy for those golden seconds afterward, each savoring the other. The moment Tray drew her nipple into the moist depths of his mouth, a cry was wrenched from her. But it was a cry of joy, of celebration. She felt his hesitation and knew he didn't want to cause her pain. But there was no pain, only hunger to fulfill each other. She moved her hips against him and she heard a low growl reverberate through him. She wrapped her legs around him, moving suggestively again, feeling him shudder. His lips drew back from his clenched teeth, sweat standing out on his tense features.

"Sweet God, Aly," he rasped, "I—can't control myself if you—"

She twisted against him, and almost instantaneously, his fists gripped the bedding on either side of her head as he plunged forward into her. This was what she wanted, what she hungered for. Here was the man who took her, lifted her on a shower of golden love until she was breathless with desire. Each stroking plunge as he held her hips tightly to him increased the pleasure. Each thrust. Each grinding movement claimed her as never before and she gave herself willingly to his male instincts and guidance, flooded with unparalleled joy.

Tray heard a gasp tear from her, felt her tense, and he knew that he had given her the ultimate gift that could be shared between man and woman. He brought her hard against him, continuing the pressure, watching as her face and body melted and then glowed with rosy fulfillment. It was only then that he surrendered to the screaming, thirsting needs of his own fires, bathing her with his life, his love.

Breathing heavily, Tray rolled off her, gently bringing Alyssa to his side. Small rivulets of sweat bathed his face as he lay there, content as never before. He could feel her heart pounding like a small bird in her breast as she pressed herself to him. The musky smell of her body was like an aphrodisiac, making him want her all over again. He softly ran his hand down the curve of her back.

"You're a slice of heaven, *Arhiannon,*" he whispered thickly.

Alyssa nuzzled close, kissing away the drops of sweat from his cheek, tasting him, loving him. "If there is such a thing as heaven on earth, then you are mine," she agreed faintly, her hair spilling across his darkly curled chest hair as she laid her head on him.

Later, Tray opened his eyes, feeling pleasantly tired. Alyssa stirred and he instinctively tightened his embrace. "We must have slept," he mumbled. It was dark outside the french doors, and only the flickering embers from the hearth lighted the chamber.

"We've both been tired for a long time, beloved. Now we'll have time to recuperate." Her brothers had been just as exhausted as they were when they had briefly joined her at Riley's farm. Alyssa thanked God for those last few days spent with Dev and Gavin before, under the cover of night, they slipped away. Away to a new life in France.

Tray snorted softly, running his fingers through her rich hair, watching the play of copper and gold in the firelight. "Lambing season is next week. Or had you forgotten so soon, little one?"

Alyssa groaned and slowly sat up, facing him. Her face held an ethereal, almost translucent quality. "I won't be able to go with you, this time," she began, regret in her voice. "And I want to. I love the lambs. And the orphans."

"I know. Perhaps next year, Aly." A tender look came to his eyes as he reached out, settling his hand across her belly. "Unless you'll be delivering a lamb of your own next March."

She reached down, her hair cascading across his chest, and she kissed him long and slowly. "I want a little girl this time," she whispered. She delighted in his strength as his mouth claimed hers more aggressively. As his hands caressed her breasts, Alyssa trembled with rekindled longing.

"I suppose if you have another son, I'll get blamed for it," he growled, smiling up into her eyes.

She settled herself on top of him, delighted with the hardness of his body. "Griff is going to have your gray eyes, black hair and build. I want a little girl with hair the color of mine and green eyes."

He lovingly grazed her flushed cheek. "And what a little girl she will be, *Arhiannon*. Beautiful like her mother. Kind. Giving." Tray sighed, wrapping his arms around Alyssa as she laid her head on his shoulder. "More than what they look like, Aly, I hope we pass on our love of the earth, the animals and kindness to people."

Alyssa rubbed her cheek against his. "Love can conquer anything, Tray. Look what your love for me has done. If you could turn me from a frightened and angry girl into a woman who has grown to know love and crave peace, then our children can be taught to cherish those same values."

"Love conquered us both, little one," Tray agreed softly, drinking in her shimmering gaze. "And we'll share that love for as long as we both live. Forever."

\* \* \* \* \*

# my VALENTINE 1992

Celebrate the most romantic day of the year with
MY VALENTINE 1992—a sexy new collection of four
romantic stories written by our famous Temptation
authors:

> GINA WILKINS
> KRISTINE ROLOFSON
> JOANN ROSS
> VICKI LEWIS THOMPSON

My Valentine 1992—an exquisite escape into a romantic
and sensuous world.

---

 *Harlequin Books*®

VAL-92-R

## presents
## MARCH MADNESS!

Come March, we're lining up four wonderful stories by four dazzling newcomers—and we guarantee you won't be disappointed!
From the stark beauty of Medieval Wales to marauding *bandidos* in
Chihuahua, Mexico, return to the days of enchantment and high
adventure with characters who will touch your heart.


LOOK FOR
  **STEAL THE STARS** (HH #115) by *Miranda Jarrett*
  **THE BANDIT'S BRIDE** (HH #116) by *Ana Seymour*
  **ARABESQUE** (HH #117) by *Kit Gardner*
  **A WARRIOR'S HEART** (HH #118) by *Margaret Moore*


So rev up for spring with a bit of March Madness . . . only from
Harlequin Historicals!

MM92